Perian: The Seer's Rebirth

J. C. Leppard

Perian: The Seer's Rebirth

©J. C. Leppard 2024

Published by Magic Sphere Books

Website: jcleppard.com

ISBN: 978-1-7636321-6-5 - paperback

ISBN: 978-1-7636321-9-6 - ebook

Cover art by Peter Crocker

Typesetting by Rack and Rune Publishing

rackandrune.com

Perian:
The Seer's Rebirth

J. C. Leppard

For Hugo

PART I

1

Perian slid down the bars of his cage, exhausted. His throat was sore and his last song had been more a croak than a melody. Word had spread that there was a caged minstrel at the top of the garden steps who had been instructed to sing whatever the festival guests requested, and he thought just about every one of them had approached him at least once in the last three days. They thought it amusing. Many returned in the evening, glistening with too much wine and breathless with desire. They wanted something romantic, a blessing to the fulfilment of their burning lust. Others required his most lurid ditties. They would gnash their teeth and grasp at each other's clothing. He learnt to skip most of the lines.

There were also those guests who appreciated his voice and just enjoyed listening to him sing. They would sit beside the caged bird opposite him on the outer spiral of the courtyard's mosaic, smiling happily. Sometimes they tried to engage him in conversation, ask why he was in a cage. But he was not permitted to talk to anyone, so he shook his head. What could he say? That he had strayed into a forbidden part of Jasperen Palace, sung a few lines to the Shanahan's youngest daughter and been arrested with the promise of fifty lashes? He had sung to make her laugh, nothing untoward, but he couldn't convince the palace guards.

The Shanahan's sorcerer, Radia, had saved him. He'd thought Perian a fellow sorcerer, especially once he had seen the morning star tattooed on his left forearm. Even now Perian broke out in a sweat whenever he recalled Radia forcing him to remove his leather wristlet. Satisfied, Radia hadn't asked about the other arm, which hid a tattoo of his family crest, one that Radia wouldn't like. Despite Radia's insistence that he could feel Perian's power, Perian thought his father's sorcerer had made a mistake when he'd needled a morning star into his arm. Perian had very little magic. Certainly not enough to qualify as a sorcerer. He could enhance his voice, which really wasn't necessary most of the time, and kill a small animal such as a biben if it was close and standing still. He could muster a little more force if he was angry enough, but little else.

The sun had begun to sink below the horizon in a fanfare of colour. The lake revelled in ripples of orange and purple and the bushes melted into dark shadows. With a sigh of relief and a sense of peace, Perian let his eyes stretch beyond the wide sandstone stairway into the palace garden with its undulating lawns and curved flowerbeds.

The guests had gravitated to the dining room, hidden from his view by a conservatory of large-leafed plants and extravagant blooms. This was a moment of calm before the servants lit the garden lights and the music from the dance hall began to fill the air. The birds further down the stairs – exotic birds with horrible voices, one either side of each landing – screeched and complained. The bright orange tanga, with whom he shared the courtyard, was quiet as usual. Perian sometimes talked or sang to it, but nothing lifted its hunched melancholy. He felt some empathy with the bird.

He had hoped the Shanahan's extravagant celebrations to mark the anniversary of his grandfather's conquest of Rashinder would be a lucrative venture he could rely on in the future, but not now. He wasn't sure what he would do once he was released. Back to the taverns, he thought, since he had no coin with which to travel.

Too soon, the lamplighters arrived in a line. They swiftly descended the stairs and spread into the garden. Some continued down to the lake; others peeled off down various neat, leaf-free pathways, leaving a trail of lights behind them. Perian found the quiet regularity and formality of lamplighting beautiful and soothing.

In their wake came Radia. He was a tall, dark-haired man with a pointy face. This evening he wore a sweeping robe of deep blue. On the middle finger of his right hand he always wore a large sapphire ring that Perian assumed he used to enhance his power when necessary. The sorcerer was probably in his early thirties, ten years older than Perian. Small dark eyes over a hooked nose peered at Perian through the bars. Radia had come each night after dinner, to ask questions and pass the time. Tonight he brought a lump of bread. It had traces of pumpkin on it where Radia had spilt his soup. Perian didn't care; he was starving.

'Is Perian your real name?' Radia asked.

Perian shoved the bread into his mouth to plug an irritated response before it burst out uncontrolled. He frowned at Radia. Trying to respond to the sorcerer's questions without actually answering them was extremely tiring. 'Why are you so interested in me?' he asked when he could talk again.

Radia raised his eyebrows. 'Because you are a mystery, Perian.'

'You think me a spy?'

'Possibly. Or an assassin. Though having observed you these past few days, I would say you aren't very good at either, if that is your game.' He tilted his head slightly. 'I can feel magic in you, yet you demonstrate little power. You even failed to break through the simple wards I placed on the locks.' He tapped the cage's decorative lock with his index finger.

Perian blushed in the growing darkness. If Radia had seen his other tattoo, he wouldn't bother asking such questions. Perian would still be in a cell. And how did Radia know he had tried to get out?

'Don't look so startled. I hid in that bush.' Radia pointed at a bush shaped like a cockerel and spotted with pink rosettes. 'Another demonstration of your ineptitude as a spy or assassin.' He stood and stared down at Perian. 'You have two more days to endure. Please don't try to escape now. I will not be able to stop your punishment a second time.'

Perian watched him walk away until he disappeared into the palace, leaving a trail of spicy perfume with the swirl of his robe. He couldn't answer the man's question concerning sorcery. He had once asked his mother why he bore a sorcerer's mark, but she hadn't known.

He turned toward a sudden familiar shift in atmosphere where the wispy form of a young woman had materialised near his cage. He flushed hot and his pulse quickened with pleasure at her unexpected appearance.

'Where have you been, Cerister?' Perian asked. 'I can't tell you how boring it is in here singing all day.'

The spirit flicked her blond hair back over her shoulder and squatted by his side. 'What did you expect us to do, entertain you?'

'That would have been nice. Where are the others?'

'They've gone to look at something beyond the outer wall. Jolint said she could feel something building.'

'What kind of thing?' He was vulnerable and helpless locked up. Being in a cage wouldn't help him if a pack of wolves decided to picnic on the palace pets. He was too big, too close to the bars.

'An attack, she said, but I think that highly unlikely.' Cerister passed her insubstantial finger absently back and forth through one of the bars.

Men! That is far worse than a pack of wolves. Perian shot up without thinking, banged his head on the scrolled peak of his cage, then fell back into a squat. 'An attack? Surely not. What does Elian think?'

Before Cerister could answer, two more shadowy forms appeared beside her.

'The palace is under attack!' cried a slender woman with bright red hair.

The other ethereal form, a man Perian's age, pushed in front of her. 'Get down, Perian! They'll be over the wall any minute, with too few guards to fight them off. You need to hide.'

Perian's mind emptied of thought. His body froze. He stared down the steps, hoping this was a horrid joke or that Elian was mistaken.

Cerister stopped playing with the cage bars and stood up. She leant over Perian so half her body was inside the cage. 'Didn't you hear him? Curl up and cover your head! We'll protect you as best we can.'

'Since when has a disembodied spirit been able to stop a material force?' Panicked, Perian grabbed his food trough and banged it against the bars in the hope of rescue, or at least to warn those within the palace, but the sound was lost to dancing and merriment. 'What's happening now? Can't one of you have a look?' He was becoming hysterical; he needed to calm down. He rattled the cage to vent his frustration and then bent to fiddle nervously with the lock.

A tingle he normally found thrilling passed over his head and down his cheek: the touch of Cerister's hand. 'Shush,' she urged. 'Stay calm and put your head down. They may not see you.'

'I need Radia to release me. He must be warned!'

'I'll go,' said Jolint, red hair flying as she vanished.

By now Perian didn't need Elian to return with his report. He could see dark figures swarming over the lawn, silhouetted against the lakeside and pathway lamps. Screams rose from around the water and from rustling bushes. Lovers. Clandestine meetings. Guests began running this way and that, shouting and pleading.

Elian reappeared suddenly, shaking his head. 'They're savages. Curl up, Perian. They may miss you – they won't be expecting to find a human in one of these cages.'

Behind him was Jolint. 'He turned when I shouted in his ear – the sorcerer,' she said before she was fully visible. 'But he's having a very nice time, so I doubt he took any notice.' She glanced down the steps toward the noise and slaughter, a frown crinkling her smooth forehead.

Perian could hear muted footfalls on the lower steps. The attackers had moved with remarkable speed. The three phantoms swarmed about him, urging him to make himself small.

'Get off me, I can't see!' Perian hissed. But he could see. He recognised the purple bands about the invaders' heads as they stepped into the palace's light, their vests of a deeper purple, the sygrilien wings painted on their naked arms. He knew each man would have a smaller version of the bird's wings tattooed on the inside of his wrist: the symbol of Tarse, Darna's god.

The land-locked Darna were taking their long-desired kingdom near the sea, and they just had to do it while he was in Rashinder and stuck in a cage.

He couldn't believe his luck. The Darna must be running out of slaves and exotic goods. But why Rashinder? There were other coastal kingdoms that would have been easier to conquer. Rashinder was a richer catch, though, and clearly easier to capture than he would ever have imagined. Of course, it wasn't over yet …

Terrified birds shrieked further down the steps, sending a violent shudder through his body. He curled over his knees and hoped his friends could obscure his presence, if not hide him completely. He thought briefly of exposing the tattoo on his right arm, but he doubted that any warrior would bother to look before skewering him with their blade.

The music from the palace stopped abruptly. Rashinder guards finally began shouting. Against all their warnings, guests spilt onto the courtyard, preventing the servants from closing the doors. Swords drawn, the dark figures accelerated past his cage. They hacked their way through the guests as if they were so many overgrown weeds blocking their path. Perian covered his ears and pressed his eyes against his knees to block out the slaughter. He wanted to scream with helplessness; at his inability to escape or assist.

A salty breeze blew in from the harbour, gathering the smell of blood, death and human effluent as it passed over the courtyard. Groans and weeping rumbled across the tiles and down the steps. These were people he had sung his songs to; he had watched their flirting and their happiness. He had come to know them by sight. He pressed his face harder into his knees and prayed without conviction that this was merely a nightmare.

A wave of dissipating magic washed over him from the direction of the palace hall. *Radia!* He blinked his eyes back into focus and squinted across the courtyard at the conservatory, but before he could work out what was happening in the hall, a fight broke out next to his cage.

He pressed himself hard against the furthest bars. A guard he recognised, Floren, sliced a red gash along a Darna's arm, right through his painted sygrilien wing. The Darna warrior jumped backward and lashed out at the guard's legs. Floren tripped on the step and the Darna swooped in. Knocking Floren's sword from his hand, he pushed him face down against Perian's cage and swiftly plunged his sword through the guard's back.

Perian raised his food trough for protection and squeezed further against the bars opposite. His spirit friends blinked and flinched about him as though they were physical.

Floren's life faded rapidly in a wheezy exhalation. His sightless eyes bulged at Perian, and bloody drool dripped a silvery thread from the side of his mouth, just missing Perian's foot.

Perian stared at the end of the Darna's long sword protruding from Floren's chest. It had gone straight through Jolint's spirit body and scratched the food trough.

With one foot on Floren's back, the Darna warrior pulled his weapon free. Floren slid from the cage, leaving Perian exposed, and for a terrifying moment he locked eyes with the warrior.

The man turned and ran through the courtyard. Perian sank to the floor. He could scarcely breathe. He checked his right wristlet; it was intact. He was merely a weaponless prisoner. No threat to the warrior.

The force of the encounter had unhooked Perian's cage from the stone, and it wavered precariously. He waited quietly until the steps were empty and the fighting had moved on. When he was sure there was no one near, he stood slowly and pushed against the bars. They gave easily at his touch. His muscles were weak from his confinement and he wobbled rather than ran, his knees complaining, to hide behind the cockerel bush.

'They're rounding people up in the hall,' Jolint whispered near his ear. He wondered why she bothered to lower her voice, since no one else had ever shown any sign that they could hear or see her.

'What of the Shanahan and his lady? Radia?'

'They're alive. The invaders hold one of the princes with a knife tight against his neck. The sorcerer can do nothing. It's over.'

'That was quick!' The speed with which the Darna had overtaken the heart of the most powerful empire this side of the Central Ranges was astounding.

'Like herding compliant sheep into a pen,' said Cerister, with a depth of disgust that surprised Perian. She wasn't the most empathetic of the three, but her snarl seemed extreme, even for her.

'The Shanahan is a scholar, Cerister, not a warrior,' said Elian. 'One of his younger brothers should have been Shanahan. Either one of them would have done.'

Jolint turned her back to the sounds of battle still taking place on the other side of the palace and folded her arms across her chest. 'So they could suck the kingdom dry more openly, you mean? Being a scholar is no excuse for complacency and neglect.'

Perian shook off the creeping fog of despair that had begun to fold about him. The Rashinder Empire had shone so bright: wealthy, magnificent, peaceful. Or so he had thought. Whatever it was that Jolint was hinting at, they wouldn't be able to suck anything dry now. Darna's Zamir had Rashinder's beautiful gem in his foul maw.

He tried to listen, to figure out where the battle was thickest and where the invaders were in the courtyard so he had a clear picture of the scene before leaving his bush, but it was hard to concentrate or hear anything beyond his friends' debate.

'Can you stop this useless discussion? I'm trying to concentrate on how to get out of this mess alive,' he spluttered. Cerister opened her mouth to reply, but changed her mind at a look from Perian. 'It's obvious that this defeat was enabled by someone within the Shanahan's own household. Someone he trusted.'

The courtyard had emptied except for a handful of Darna at the far end, rounding up those not dead or dying on the mosaic paving. Stooping low, Perian slipped around the bush and ran toward the conservatory, dodging the bodies that dotted his pathway. Shadows and blood merged in the angled light from the building, the smell of death and fear smothering all but the strongest perfumes.

Perian slipped and fell to his knees on the trailing skirts of a woman with a gaping neck wound. He fought back a cry and forced himself to control the bile that burned in his throat, the quaking of his limbs. Breathing deeply, he wiped the blood from his hands on a clean patch of her bodice and continued his grim race toward the cover of foliage near the glass walls. The stain of this day would never scrub out.

His friends followed him in an eerie cloud. 'What are you doing?' hissed Jolint. 'You should be going the other way!'

'Stop bothering me. I want to see what's going on for myself.'

She swirled up beside him with a look of disbelief. 'How are you going to do that?'

'Shut up,' Perian snapped. He couldn't answer her; he just knew that he had to see for himself, compelled to confirm the source of this disaster.

A Darna warrior not far from the entrance turned as though he had heard Perian's comment. He peered into the darkness, but seeing nothing, struck out at a captive. Perian used the distraction to slip through the doorway of the conservatory and dove amongst the stunted trees and large-leafed climbing plants. He pressed himself against the central vine-shaped pillar. Glancing up to where it spiralled outward to support the glass roof, he took a shuddering breath. A moment of respite.

Slowly, he worked his way toward the inner doors of the large hall. In a room at the far end, Perian could just make out the central dining table, where servants had been clearing away the aftermath of a great feast. Their bodies and those of nobles alike had been pushed up against a dividing wall. Along the opposite wall stood a row of trembling, white-faced nobles, servants and musicians, their instruments and chairs in disarray behind them. Darna warriors watched them closely from either end of the line.

But it was those in the centre of the hall that held Perian's interest. As Jolint had said, a Darna warrior clasped the young prince tightly, holding a long knife at his throat. The warrior and prince stood at a short distance from Shanahan Leren and Shanessa Beitris, so the couple could see their son clearly. Radia stood next to the Shanahan, his hands open and displayed against the folds of his tunic. The Shanessa's hand was at her mouth, and another woman stood close at her side, keeping her upright. The Shanahan himself stood grim and erect, watching the tall, muscular figure that paced and gesticulated before him: Zamir Maltha of Darna.

Perian's father.

Perian stared in shock, even though he had known who he would find at the centre of the drama. Nineteen years had passed since he had last been in his father's presence. He had been four years old. He remembered the look on his father's face, his mother's screams as she banged on the door. The Zamir looked no older now than he had then; he had a strong, square face and angled green eyes. His thick black hair hung long and loose about his shoulders, his carefully clipped black beard stark against his pale skin. Perian had inherited his Faran mother's tanned complexion.

'Where's Grison?' he whispered. 'The shaman?'

'To the left, not far from the Zamir,' said Elian.

Perian moved a branch out of the way so he could see properly. The sight of his father frightened him, but the shaman filled him with terror. He hadn't remembered Grison clearly until now: a short, thin man with pale red hair and claw-like hands. He could still feel them ripping the clothes from his small body and hear the harsh, excited voice ordering the guards to hold him down. He remembered the twisted smile, the laughter as Grison fiddled with the tools required to tattoo Perian's arms and chest. He remembered waking, bundled in his mother's arms as she ran through the forest toward the marshlands that would be their new home. Only she wasn't his mother – she was his mother's slave, Esper. They had lived in a stilted house Esper built herself upon the watery landscape of the marshlands. There, she had loved and protected him until he was a man and able to care for himself.

Elian was shouting at him. 'Concentrate! Leave the past behind!'

Perian shook his head to free himself from the memories. He looked down at his long, slender hands to remind himself that they were the hands of a man, not a terrified child.

'Get up.'

The gruff voice made him jump. He whirled about, lost his balance and fell back into the tall flowering stems, then rolled to his feet – just as a Darna warrior lunged at him, curved sword still dripping the blood of a recent victim.

2

Clasping his hands together tightly, Perian hit the man between the shoulders, following up with a hard kick in the small of the back. The warrior stumbled forward and crashed headfirst into the conservatory wall. The sound of shattering glass vibrated through the air.

Cerister came up close to Perian as he stared at the startled faces of those inside. 'Well, that's got their attention. You didn't mention that this was a suicide attempt.'

He heard rushing feet from within and saw movement in his peripheral vision. With no other option, he ran for the doorway that led out to the garden, hoping he was faster than the enemy.

He wasn't. A heavy-breathing monster brought him down in a tackle. The air left his crushed lungs and his cheekbone cracked loudly on the tiled floor. Rough hands pulled him up by his arms. Dazed, he staggered and fought to remain upright, but before he could find his balance someone hit him in the face and knocked him to the ground again. Pain surged through his jaw, shockwaves running over his skull and down his neck. Someone pulled on his shirt, and he thought he heard the worn fabric tear. He hoped not. He really didn't want them to know who he was.

The monster lifted his hand to hit him again, but a Darna with a bleeding ear stopped him.

'Better not. They'll want him for the slave market. You don't want to damage him. He'll bring a good price.'

Perian's breath returned with a gasp, his heart pounding faster than was good for him.

The one with the bloody ear gestured to the hall. 'Check him for weapons. Then we'll put him with the rest.'

The monster groped him all over with a leer. Jolint made a clicking noise with her tongue, which wasn't very useful.

'You'd better get used to that,' said the monster. 'With those looks you'll be a plaything for some wealthy master or mistress.' He laughed loudly, displaying the gaps in his yellow teeth.

The man with the bleeding ear pushed at Perian to make him walk into the hall. Perian's head spun. His legs felt distant, as though they belonged to someone else. He doubted that he'd be recognised immediately, but once they took his clothes, all would be revealed. He wondered morbidly if they would complete the task Esper had interrupted so many years ago.

In the hall, the Zamir had returned to berating Shanahan Leren. Perian glanced about for a gap, some means of escape, but Darna warriors blocked every doorway. He caught Radia's eye and jolted with the contact. He wanted to cry. He suddenly longed for his cage and mourned the tanga opposite, whom he belatedly realised must be dead.

A hefty thump on the back sent him sprawling again. He heaved himself up, encouraged by a kick in the thigh.

'We have to do something!' Jolint demanded.

'We'll have to chance it,' came Cerister's calm voice. 'The shaman has seen him. He knows.'

Elian's wispy form suddenly hovered next to Radia. To Perian's surprise, Radia's expression changed as if he could hear Perian's friends, though probably not see them. Perian wondered what Elian was saying – then noticed the Zamir's words had faded to nothing.

His father was staring at him.

Maltha's eyes grew large and round. He paled and flushed at the same time. The shaman was at the Zamir's side; how he had moved so fast, Perian couldn't say.

Grison rushed at Perian, and before Perian could block him the man grabbed at his shirt. He knocked Grison's hands aside and hit the shaman across the face with the length of his arm. Grison fell sideways onto one knee, one arm swinging through the air. Magic crackled about Perian. His body stiffened and the room filled with colour – then he crumpled to the floor. Looking shocked, the Darna with the bleeding ear shakily pulled him up, forcing him to stand.

'It can't be.'

The voice snapped Perian back to his senses. The Zamir strode toward him, pushing Grison aside. In a panic, Perian grasped at the shreds of his shirt to cover himself, his blood pounding through his body so hard he thought he would faint. The skin across his chest burned hot where the shaman had tattooed the wings of a great white bird with a blue neck: a sygrilien. The symbol that marked him for sacrifice and ensured he would live in fear of discovery his entire life.

'This is a sign,' shouted the shaman in the same high-pitched voice he'd used when he needled the ink into Perian's skin. 'Tarse has brought him back to us. His wish is clear! This is indeed an auspicious outcome!' The joy on his face was sickening.

The Zamir stepped closer, enclosing Perian with his heat and heavy perfume overlaid by the smell of sweat. He stroked Perian's face with a gentleness Perian had not expected and certainly didn't trust. 'You are her image,' he said softly.

The encounter was brief. Perian became aware of his friends

gathering close behind him. A force he wasn't expecting emanated from their combining, and the hall vanished in an explosion of whiteness.

All about him white light blazed so brightly that he was amazed he could bear to look at it. Warmth and a peace he had never before known enclosed him as he floated into nothingness, leaving all fear behind.

The speed at which Perian was sucked back into his body resembled falling from a great height. He felt heavy and crushed. His head was twisted awkwardly against the floor, making it difficult to breathe. Every heaving inhalation filled him with an ache so severe he would have screamed aloud if he had been able, but his muscles would not obey him, and he lay limp and helpless. The ensuing stillness was terrifying, the thin silence shocking.

As though the room had finally released a long-held breath, chaos broke out all around him. People running. Radia shouting orders, others repeating them. The deep angry tones of the Shanahan boomed over Radia's voice as though they were arguing. Perian couldn't understand what had happened: why was he on the floor, why couldn't he move? Why did no one come to help him? Feet thundered about him, but no one stopped. Did they think he was dead? He tried to shout, but nothing came out. The stink of magic was nauseating.

'Perian? Perian!'

Elian. He was so close to Perian's face that Perian could see through him. Tears of frustration leaked from his eyes onto the floorboards. He'd be buried alive with all the bodies, or thrown onto a pyre. Or perhaps they'd just put him out for the sygrilien after all

– their long-lost sacrifice to Tarse, the Sky God —

'Radia's coming,' said Elian above the din. 'Hold on, he'll be here in a moment.'

All his fear and panic must have shown in his eyes, because suddenly Elian's hand tingled over Perian's cheek and through his shoulder.

'Help's coming.'

'Is he all right?' came Cerister's voice from somewhere above him.

'Of course not,' Elian snapped.

Strong hands jammed into Perian's armpits and a Rashinder guard hauled him over his shoulder as though he were a damp towel. Perian whimpered his relief and gratitude into the man's back.

Upside down, with his head bouncing off the guard's back, he could make little sense of his surroundings. Only the lingering aromas of meat and mouthwatering dainties told him that they were passing through the dining room. His eyelids began to droop. He forced them open again, desperately trying to stay alert. He concentrated on his rescuer's movement as he dodged fallen chairs and displaced furniture, racing toward a doorway along one wall that Perian glimpsed each time the guard twisted slightly to look back.

Radia, just ahead, was close behind the last of the guests disappearing into the wall when whoever was holding the door open slammed it in his face and slid the lock shut from the inside. Radia banged on the panelling with his fist and shouted to be let in, but no response came from within. They had gone.

Radia spun about, his narrow features pinched and his eyes wide and hard. He looked past the shocked faces of the guards who had followed him to the hall beyond, and gestured to the three men as he ran through the main door into the dimly lit corridor. They hugged the wall so as not to alert a group of Darna warriors checking rooms further down. Perian's shoulder brushed against the panelling and the sideways angle of the guard gave him an alarming view of Darna warriors now gathering behind them. Radia pushed open the first door they came to, and they slipped into a lounge full of lush chairs and sofas. The lamps had been lit for guests who wanted to get away from the main entertainments, and long velvet curtains covered the windows for privacy. Not surprisingly, the room was empty.

Shouting and the pounding of feet followed their small group into the room. Perian's head spun with a sense of defeat as he watched the warriors swarm through the door, until the stale air of an unused passageway drifted up his nose. He knew even before he heard the section of wall slide back that Radia had opened another hidden doorway.

Radia threw himself into the opening, followed by the closest guard. A knife whistled past Perian's head and lifted his hair as his rescuer stepped into the darkness behind them. The guard at their rear shrieked and fell against the panel opening, a long knife protruding from his back. Perian's rescuer stopped and swung about at the sound, squashing Perian against the tunnel wall.

Radia pushed the body quickly from the threshold, slammed the door shut and threw the lock. 'He's dead,' he said into the sudden darkness, and squeezed past them.

A wall torch burst into flames at a sweep of Radia's hand and he led them rapidly through the corridor's twists and turns. Shouting and screaming seeped through the walls, replacing the receding sound of Darna warriors banging uselessly on the panelling behind them. After a while, the small group pushed through another doorway that creaked and groaned at Radia's touch. Perian felt a rush of cold damp air, sharp with the tang of bitter mould, then the stark chill of a tunnel. The men's feet crunched over the gravelly ground, but he counted only three pairs of footfalls; no one followed.

Perian drifted on the edge of consciousness, their uncomfortable, stumbling flight seeming endless and unreal. He sagged helpless over the muscled shoulder of the Rashinder guard and gave himself over to the rocking motion, back and forth, reminding him of something he was too tired and confused to remember. It came on its own, though. A memory of rolling with the motion of a cramped wagon. The wagon smelt of warm blankets and familiar bodies – of love, fear and endless monotony.

'Get up, Perian.' It was Elian. He gave Perian a shove. 'Come stretch your legs while you can. Gisela has gone into town. We could go for a swim.'

He found that he was both observer and participant, as one is sometimes in a dream. This did not surprise him, but Elian's solid presence shocked him.

They clambered from the wagon and he followed Elian to the edge of the stream. Jolint and Cerister were already there, splashing and laughing —

The Rashinder guard tripped, and Perian emerged briefly from his dreaming with a jolt. Fresh, reviving night air cooled his exposed cheek, but was not stimulating enough to keep him from drifting back into that uncertain space between sleep and awareness.

'What do you see, Perian? What is your vision showing you?' It was Gisela, the tribe's leader, her patience fractured and thin. He saw so much – how could he tell her all of it, or even get it into any sort of order?

Then there was nothing, only fear and exhaustion – Gisela had gone.

The whinny of horses brought him back into awareness. The guard's breath came short and tight beneath him and his legs trembled slightly as he bent low and scurried along the outer palace wall toward a group of tethered mounts. He threw Perian over the back of the nearest steed. As soon as he had mounted, they followed Radia and the other guard into the dark night. The ground raced beneath Perian's head, leaving behind the sound of shouting and rushing feet as he drifted back into the world within the wagon.

'Let's return to the wagon, Perian. Jolint has saved us some food and ale.' Elian put his arms around him and he sank into the loving warmth of his twin brother. He allowed Elian to guide him toward the wagon that was their home, where Cerister and Jolint awaited them. Cerister stroked his head as he lay in Elian's arms and trembled from his ordeal. She smelt of cloves and the honeysuckle that peeked over one ear.

'What happened?' Jolint asked. She knelt by his legs and leant forward.

'She wants him to die and be born again as a Darna prince,' Elian responded for him. Tears hovered on his eyelids, then splashed onto Perian's head.

A shockwave sped through Perian's body with Elian's words. He surfaced briefly, then returned.

Cerister laughed. 'That's nonsense. What did she really say?'

Perian grasped her hand and held it close to his chest in which his heart fluttered like a trapped butterfly. 'It is as Elian says. She said we lost twelve more of our people to slave traders just a few days ago. She said we are persecuted beyond what the tribes can bear. It is my destiny and my duty, she said, to put a stop to the persecution of the Faran tribes and set them free, and I will do this when I become the Zamir of Darna.'

'No,' Jolint shouted. 'It is too much. It is not fair you should do this alone.'

'He won't,' said Cerister. Her voice was calm and hard with determination. 'We will go with him. If Perian can choose his next birth, then so can we. We will remain together and see this mission through together.'

He surfaced briefly into the cool rush of air that whipped about his hair, the sweat of the horse that heated his cheek, until the pounding of hooves drew him back into his strange imaginings.

Elian's face tilted over him, his breath sour with ale and fear. Cerister stroked his face. Her touch sent a thrill through his body and her frown unravelled into a knowing smile. She gave him a little shove with her knee and squeezed his hand.

Whatever Cerister was about to say was lost when someone dragged him from his horse and placed him on the hard ground. His head dropped heavily onto prickly twigs and dry leaves. His body thrummed with shock, every nerve lit up like stars on a clear night. He coughed and choked on cracked clods, dry as a summer drought. The hands that had dragged him from the horse pulled him to a sitting position and poured rain down his throat, filling the fissures on his tongue and smoothing its surface. He choked again. Every part of him hurt with every breath, with every coughing spasm. The water went up his nose, dribbled coldly down his chin and neck. A hand patted his back as he gasped for air.

'You took your time,' said a voice he recognised.

Perian cracked his eyelids open a little and saw Jolint staring down at him. He knew he was fully awake; he could see through her again. A groan of frustration, loss and sadness rose from his depths.

He opened his eyes a little more. They had looked so real. He had been able to touch them. They had felt so solid, and it was hard to believe that it had been a dream born of delirium.

Elian and Cerister huddled beside Jolint, their faces almost merging. Vignettes from his fantastical dreaming drifted to the surface, but quickly sank when Radia placed his hand on Perian's shoulder and brought with it the memory of the palace, his father, the shaman. He closed his eyes again. The air smelt of the forest; it was day now, and birdsong filled the air, not the groans of the dying and terrified. He was safe.

He wriggled his fingers and tested his legs. Life had returned to his body. His relief was immense and debilitating at the same time. He wanted to sing his joy to the sky, but didn't have the energy.

'Welcome back,' came Radia's grim voice. 'How do you feel?'

'How do I look?' Perian croaked.

'Dreadful.'

'Then there's your answer.' He shifted to ease a cramp forming in his leg and wriggled his fingers again. 'Where are we and how did I get here?'

'First,' Radia said, 'I will know who you are. Both the Zamir and his shaman knew you. In fact, the Zamir appears to have some feelings for you. So, Perian, itinerant minstrel, it's time you told me the whole story. Who are you and what is your relationship to those two?'

Perian hesitated. He had planned for this moment, practised until his response was perfect and natural. But as with most things, in his experience, the real event was never the same as the imagined scenario. Radia had seen him with his father. A lie or the truth? If he told the truth, Radia would think he was an informant, his father's man on the inside, or possibly use him in some way. Lying might be worse. Radia would know to look beneath the wristlet on his right arm.

He took a deep breath.

'Zamir Maltha is my father.' Perian was amazed he didn't choke on the words; he had held them in secret for so long. He braced himself for an assault, either verbal or physical. The Darna were hated by everyone.

'A Darna prince!'

Radia spat the words out. His voice pierced the bristling air, leaving an icy silence in its wake. Creaking branches ticked off the seconds and the wind shuffled dry leaves against each other in a surreal replication of the changing mood.

A sword scraped the sides of its scabbard. Perian felt sick.

Slowly, he began to remove the leather binding about his right forearm with stiff and shaky fingers. One of the guards took a step toward them, but Radia held up his hand to keep him back. His eyes flicked down to stare at the rich blue symbol tattooed on Perian's forearm. When he looked up, Perian caught his eyes for a moment, but they gave Perian no clue as to the sorcerer's feelings.

'The outline of the sun above a wave,' Radia said finally. 'If I am not mistaken, this represents both the rising and the setting sun over the ocean; the beginning and the end, the giver and taker of life. I knew you held a secret, Perian, but I never expected this.'

Perian covered the mark with his left hand. A shiver rumbled through his body as he thought back. 'I'm surprised he recognised me,' he said, keeping his voice low and even. 'But Esper always said that I looked just like my mother. I don't remember her. I was four when Esper rescued me. She was my mother's slave. She took me to the marshlands, where we lived until I turned eighteen.'

'Rescued from what?'

Perian winced at the sharpness of Radia's voice. He pulled his knees up to his chest, forcing his own voice into a neutral tone. 'From my father, and Grison.' Perian could see the next question forming on Radia's face. 'They didn't like me.'

Jolint floated to Radia's side with a look of extreme irritation on her face. *What's your problem?* she mouthed. *Tell him the rest!*

Perian glared at her. Couldn't she see that knowledge of his sacrificial tattoo could be used against him – used to manipulate him?

Amazingly, Radia let it go. It occurred to Perian that his sorcerer's mark had tempered Radia's reaction; there was a sense of fellowship between those who could wield magic. 'My curiosity can wait,' Radia said. 'I'm a patient man. We need to keep moving and find somewhere to stop for the night. If they've followed us, they can't be far behind.'

He took some dried meat from a Darna saddle pack and waved it beneath Perian's nose, making Perian's empty stomach growl. The effort of sitting forward and crossing his legs forced another groan from his lips like a whistling bellows. He bent his painful fingers about the rigid flesh of a small animal – a biben, by the smell. They were delicate, timid creatures, much like small antelopes, black with yellow eyes and small twisted horns, and shorter than a medium-sized dog. They smelt like stagnant water, but tasted delicious.

Elian thrust a concerned face through the strip of biben Perian held. 'Are you all right?'

Perian's arms and legs ached, as did his head. His skin burned and he looked quickly at his arm again to satisfy himself that he hadn't been flayed. Even his eyelids hurt. He waved a hand to shift Elian aside and broke off a piece of the dried meat with his teeth.

'I told you,' he said, chewing carefully, 'I feel dreadful. What did you do? I thought I'd exploded.'

Cerister appeared at Elian's side, a look of derision upon her face, her chin high and her arms folded across her chest. 'He's fine,' she said. 'No one eats like that when they're sick.' She glanced at Perian again, then began to turn away. 'We'll tell you what we did when you're in a more grateful frame of mind.'

They moved away to hover about Radia, who appeared not to notice, and it occurred to Perian that if there was any truth in his dreams, his friends had not been able to choose their rebirths as Cerister had thought.

3

Cerister was right; he didn't feel ill as such, just a little jittery. After an hour or so in the saddle with the wind blowing through his hair and buffing up his cheeks, he felt fit and strong again, the ghastly sense of helplessness no longer foremost in his mind. He could almost have been back to normal except for the continued images showing another life with his three spirit friends.

The little things made it all so real. How they huddled together in the wagon at night, how Elian talked in his sleep and Jolint and Cerister had calloused hands from training with swords. How Gisela used Elian, a shapeshifter, to spy on the tribe so she could 'dispel discontent before it escalated', and how she used Perian to see her way ahead and keep her people safe through his visions. In this other life he had been a seer of some skill, but with little control of his ability.

And then there was the dark figure from his childhood nightmares, more physical and present than any night visitation, who had flashed into his mind and nearly unhorsed him with the shock. The figure had not haunted his dreams for many years, yet his presence still held the same power to terrorise him.

Perian remembered Elian telling him stories when he was little of the nomadic Farans and their life in wagons, but the images he was seeing were too real, too personal to be stories dredged up by his disturbed and disoriented mind. There had been no stories of dying. He began to wonder if perhaps he had done as Gisela had asked and died to save their people. He would have liked to discuss it with Elian and the two women, but they had vanished. They were always together, the four of them, and his friends' occasional absence always left Perian feeling lonely and vulnerable – even more so now that he had, he thought, glimpsed their shared past.

The road they travelled was sodden from a brief, heavy burst of rain. Pale sunlight washed over the fields through thinning clouds and flickered on dripping trees and hedgerows. When they came to an unmarked fork in the road, Radia turned his horse toward the southward road on his right.

'Surely we should go east?' said Turnell, the guard who had rescued Perian. 'That's where our people will be.'

'Yes, but not yet.'

Turnell turned his horse about and lifted in his seat to look back the way they had come. 'Do you think they're following us?'

Radia followed Turnell's gaze and wrinkled his long nose. 'Somewhere, yes. How far behind they are, I cannot say. That they have not come upon us by now suggests we left more chaos behind than I thought, and if the shaman is with them, they would have had to wait for his recovery. That gives us a good head start. But we must be sure. I don't want to risk leading them to the others.'

'Why would they bother to waste a patrol on just four men?' asked Moson, the other Rashinder guard.

Radia tilted his head toward Perian. 'The shaman wants him. Rather badly, I believe.'

'What's so special about Perian? Surely they have other princes.'

'Perhaps.'

Turnell shook his head and made a clucking noise with his tongue. He turned his horse and led the way south.

They stayed on the road a short while longer, then turned into a field of ripening corn. The heavy cobs knocked against their legs as they rode between the rows, and Perian picked a few to roast over their evening fire should they dare to have one. The thin veil of cloud had blown away, and the blistering sun bore down on their uncovered heads. Its glare hurt Perian's eyes.

Beyond the field of golden cobs, a lush green carpet flowed ahead of them all the way to the horizon. Little nesting birds darted here and there to distract them as they galloped through fields of grazing cattle and goats. Shirian horses, bred for battle, ran alongside them for a while. Their ride would have been thrilling had they been certain there was no one in pursuit.

When they finally stopped to make camp within Mount Carpen's forest, Turnell again suggested that it might be time to turn east toward the lower slopes of Porffer's Peak. 'Pick up the troops at Underidge if they haven't already been sent for.'

Radia stared at Turnell for some time without answering. 'Another day, then we'll turn,' he said at last, before drifting back into deep contemplation.

When it was obvious that he wasn't going to share his thoughts, Perian left the camp to climb halfway up a tall tree and squint back over the fields. He could see nothing out of the ordinary – no movement of men, no flash of purple, no glint of weaponry in the sunlight. His branch swayed a little under his weight and with the gusty wind caught in the foliage. He found its movement oddly comforting. He was in no hurry to return to the ground and the emotional tensions of his travelling companions.

His mind drifted lazily back to their conversation earlier in the day, when they had stopped to rest the horses by a stream. His friends had hovered near the water just behind Radia and he had asked them again what had happened to him in the palace. They were slow to answer, and Radia, who assumed Perian was speaking to him, answered for them.

'You burst into flames. I've never seen anything like it.' He shook his head slightly, then glanced up at the guards, who sat side by side on a log next to Perian. They shrugged in response. 'It shocked us all, including that shaman. He's an unpleasant character.'

'I know that,' Perian replied impatiently. He tugged at his waistcoat with one hand, automatically sliding a finger over the wing tattoo on his chest through the gap between the buttons.

'I suppose you would.' Radia sighed. 'Then a great wind – at least I think it was a wind – rose from the fire and blew the shaman, the Zamir and his warriors across the room. They weren't dead, just dazed, but it was enough.' He raised his eyebrows and gave Perian a questioning look. 'One of your *voices* had warned me, so I was able to recover quickly and rally the men still remaining in the hall. They gathered up the Shanahan and his family and have hopefully taken them off to safety. Shanahan Leren was difficult at first – he wanted to kill the Zamir and stay to fight – but when I pointed out that his army had been defeated and the palace taken, he reluctantly complied. Though, perhaps we should have killed the Zamir.' He gazed at the ground with a look of regret.

Perian studied his hands and legs for burn marks, but there were none. How could he have burst into flames? How could he have created the wind Radia talked of? He looked at Elian, who smiled and shrugged. He remembered the three of them gathering behind him, and the pressure in the middle of his back; it surprised him that his friends could do such a thing, but then his wagon dreams came back to him. Jolint and Cerister had been powerful in the way of magic.

'What was I doing?' he asked at last.

'Lying face down on the floor. I thought you were dead until your voices assured me that you weren't,' Radia said. 'Turnell put you over his shoulder and we left through the dining room. The palace is riddled with secret corridors for easy escape and the occasional spying. Everyone who could stand had gone through, but someone slammed the door in my face.' He shook his head. 'Do you really remember nothing of this?'

'No. I was barely conscious. It wasn't me who caused the wind. I was just the instrument, apparently.' Perian glared at his three friends over Radia's shoulder.

Radia frowned. 'I don't believe that, Perian. There has to be something within you that would enable such an event. Your voices merely used what power you already possess.' He turned his attention to the guards. 'Do either of you know who pulled the guards from their duties along the wall and outside the garden entrance?'

Turnell and Moson stared at him as though he had addressed them in a foreign language.

'No,' said Turnell. 'I didn't know they had been pulled away. I assumed they'd been overtaken.' He turned to Moson. 'Did you know?'

Moson glanced at Turnell, then back at Radia. 'I could see there weren't no one at the garden entrance. That was plain for all to see. I thought nothing of it, though. As to orders, I don't know. Captain Mark was on duty. I suppose he gave the order.'

Radia bit his lower lip. 'We have a traitor – one who has most likely escaped with Shanahan Leren, which would account for our being shut out.'

Perian's attention snapped back to the present with sudden movement below his branch. But not for long. Soon, his thoughts returned again to his increasingly real other life with Elian, Jolint and Cerister. Either he had gone mad, or their magic – the event of his incineration – had awoken the memory of a previous life. If it were the latter, why had his friends not mentioned this life to him, other than in terms of stories told to a child, nor spoken of the mission that had been entrusted to him? He put his hand on his chest, the answer clear. He was marked for sacrifice and exiled. He would never be Zamir.

A terrible wave of sadness washed over him; a sense of loss and debilitating heartache. He had failed them. Failed his tribe and Gisela. He had failed his three friends, their lives lost for nothing. That they were with him in spirit was a precious miracle; that they did not blame him was extraordinary. He would never feel Elian's touch again or see himself reflected in his brother's face. He would never feel the warmth of Jolint as she snuggled beside him or hold Cerister so close that their hearts beat against one another's and their bodies grew hot with the stirring of desire.

He put his hands to his face and breathed deeply into his palms until he was calm once again. Then he rubbed at his eyes to erase the images and stop himself from lingering on what could never be, and may never have been. He pictured his life within the Darna royal household, with its wealth and luxury, but also its restrictions, expectations and responsibility. When he compared that with his current life as an itinerate minstrel, he found he was thankful that fate had chosen another path for him.

Below, Turnell was whispering to Moson about the Underidge troops. Underidge was close to Shadow Valley, the sunless pass through the Erolon Ranges east of Darna. His father's men would surely have marched that way. That was why the Shanahan stationed troops there. Yet no one had mentioned fighting on the borders of Rashinder, and Turnell clearly thought the Rashinder troops might still be there. Why? Was it because they had had no word to the contrary? How was it that a large Darna army had marched across the Empire unnoticed and unreported? Esper had taught him the ways of the Darna so that he would know his enemy: they would have sacrificed villagers along the way, burned cottages and taken slaves, and news like that would surely have spread faster than the plague.

He slid down the tree, jumping the last few feet.

Moson laughed, his small eyes turning to slits above the folds of his bunched cheeks. 'Did you see anything?' He raised a questioning eyebrow.

'Nothing,' Perian replied. He walked to stand beside Radia, who sat uncomfortably on a rock, his forearms resting on his thighs. 'Where do you think they came from, Radia? The Darna warriors?'

Radia looked up at him, the horrors of Jasperen's invasion written in the lines of his gaunt and worried face. 'I don't know. I've been running all the possibilities through my head, but only one is likely, and even that seems too elaborate to me.'

'Which is?'

'That they crossed into the Kingdom of Nor, with or without the blessing of King Arnden, then hugged the border all the way to the ocean. From there, the main body of Maltha's troops approached Jasperen's harbour by ship. There are many deserted coves along the way, and if they hired passenger ships and sailed one boatload at a time, it's possible that they might not have been noticed.'

Perian thought this unlikely but had no better solution. 'Some may have come through Rashinder,' he suggested. 'Many people go to Jasperen for the yearly celebrations. Without their uniforms and with their hoods up to cover the slant of their eyes, they would blend in well enough with the movement of people going north, and the swell of numbers in the city and its surrounds.' Perian absently watched Moson polishing the blade of a long Darna knife. 'A well-thought-out plan, executed with precision. I'm impressed.'

Radia clenched his hands together and cocked his head to the side to look at Perian. 'It didn't go completely to plan, though. You were there. If you hadn't been, Leren and his family would not have escaped and would probably be stretched out on suitable stones by now. Your father will have to find them if he wants to control the people.'

The next morning, dawn broke on a clear sky. Perian had taken last watch and he was bored almost beyond endurance. He had struggled to keep sleep at bay, so the relief he felt at the growing hint of pink beyond the trees was immense. He stamped his feet and rubbed the chill from his hands. Radia stirred with his increased activity, and he perched on the log next to Perian, dragging his blanket with him. Turnell grunted from under his own blanket, pulling it up against the growing light and turning over to continue his sleep. Moson stood, brushing dead leaves from his clothes —

Without warning, an arrow whistled through their camp and lodged in Moson's chest.

He grasped at it, his eyes wider than Perian had ever seen them, and sank to his knees. Turnell was up and clutching his sword before Perian could grasp what had happened. Radia knocked Perian backward off their log and crouched beside him, sword and dagger instantly in his hands.

They watched and waited. Cerister and Elian darted about the edges of the clearing, disappearing through the trees and bushes.

'Eleven of them,' came Cerister's voice. Jolint joined them and pointed out where they were.

The Darna warriors broke cover in a rush. Radia waved his arm and a group of three men dropped to the ground in a blistering wave of blue sorcery that sparkled through his ring; Turnell turned about at a sound behind him, and both of his knives hit their mark, two warriors going down before they even reached the edges of the camp.

Perian scrambled to his feet and ran toward his blanket where he had left the sword Radia had given him. A boot slammed into his side before he could get there, and he fell against Moson's body, which still knelt, torso curled over his knees and held in place by the protruding arrow. The dead man fell sideways with Perian's weight, revealing the hilt of his knife. Perian muttered a silent *thank you* to Moson and whatever god was listening, and pulled it free. He twisted about and slashed at his assailant's ankles. The man screamed and his sword swung wide as his legs crumpled awkwardly beneath him.

Perian rolled to his feet and crashed into a hefty warrior twice his width. He dodged to the side and dropped to one knee, away from the warrior's blade. Spinning about, he jabbed his knife into the man's thigh. The warrior roared, sweeping his sword wide. It would have taken Perian's head off had he not overbalanced at that moment.

He recovered quickly and ran toward his bedding. The warrior's shadow fell over him in an instant. Panic thrummed through his body, yet his hand remained strangely steady as it grasped his sword. With no time to think, he clutched the hilt in both hands and turned, wildly swinging the blade.

His strike severed the man's sword arm.

For the briefest of moments, the two men stared in shock at the bleeding stump. Perian glanced up, catching the warrior's eyes, and the hatred he saw there spurred him into action. He stepped deftly through the spurting blood and plunged his knife toward the man's chest.

It skidded across his hardened leather armour. The Darna growled through clenched teeth, muttering something that sounded like *'taking him alive, but not now'*, and swung his bloody stump about as though to beat Perian with it. He grasped Perian's throat with his left hand and pushed him hard against a tree.

Perian's lungs expelled precious air with the impact and strong fingers tightened to cut off his ability to replace it. His feet scarcely touched the ground, even though he was a head taller than the warrior. The light rapidly began to dim around him. He felt himself fading, his mind going numb.

'Get a move on, Perian!' Elian shouted into his ear.

Startled, Perian's eyes flew open, and he found himself staring down at the brute's swollen red face. Anger and disgust rallied his strength. He remembered his sword still squeezed tightly in his fist and, with a quick movement, rammed it deep into the man's neck.

The warrior fell backward like a toppled statue, dragging Perian with him. He rolled to the side and across the dirt, distancing himself from the man's last struggling moments. Still gasping for breath, he stood, quickly ready to defend himself against the next attack. But it was over.

Radia was bent forward, breathing heavily. Turnell was testing the bushes nearby with his sword. The Darna warriors lay in bloody pools. The overwhelming smell of blood and sweat was suffocating. Perian made himself do a quick count of bodies to stop himself from being sick: five in the bushes, five on the ground and one still alive but incapacitated. That was the eleven Cerister had spoken of. Then he vomited into the bushes anyway.

He glanced sideways at the man lying beside Moson. Someone had put an end to his misery.

Turnell bent over Moson's body, rummaging about in his pockets. He pulled out a pouch and dropped it in his bag without saying what it was. 'We should bury them.'

'Moson,' said Perian, wiping his mouth with his sleeve. 'Just Moson.'

Perian's blood-drenched clothing and hair dried quickly to stiffness in the sun. He and Turnell had scratched a shallow grave for Moson amidst the trees, and Turnell spat on the mound before covering it with stones. 'To ward off the body-takers and shapeshifters,' he said in response to Perian's look of surprise.

Perian shrugged and started to walk back the way they had come.

'Where are you going?' asked Elian.

He flapped his shirt and waved an arm. 'To the stream to wash off this stinking mess.'

The horses had already drifted down to the water, which meandered around and bubbled noisily over rocks and pebbles smoothed by its constant flow. Perian took off his boots and waded into the stream, where he rolled about and patted the blood from his clothing, splashed his face and rubbed his hair. The spirits stood at the edge of the stream and watched, talking amongst themselves and being careful not to get their ethereal feet wet.

When he judged the water about him to be clear enough, and he felt cleansed of the miasma of sudden death, he heaved himself out of the stream and found a large rock to drip over. He closed his eyes and turned his face to the sun, letting its warmth dry him and ease the tension from his muscles. The birds had returned, and he found the constant rush and tinkle of running water soothing – a peaceful moment after the ghastly business of battle and burial.

'I would like to think that no more followed,' said Radia, when Perian returned to the others, 'but we cannot be sure. We must keep moving.'

4

They left the Darna horses at a posthouse and continued south, stopping only briefly in one of the larger villages to eat and buy supplies and new clothing. As the sun touched the hilltops on its descending path, they set up camp in the vast wooded area that opened out onto land owned by Lord Fimian. Radia had met Fimian many times and was certain of his loyalty to the Shanahan. Turnell had caught two biben en route and was preparing a fire. Radia scouted about the area to see if they had been followed. Perian watched his progress from a branch, but had little confidence in his ability to spot any approaching enemy after his last effort.

He noticed Jolint hovering at Radia's shoulder. He could tell she was speaking to him by the smile on his face, though Radia remained quiet. Perian had never had to share his friends with anyone before. Unexpectedly, he was gripped by a sense of betrayal and resentment, but the unwelcome emotion receded as quickly as it had emerged. None of them would leave him; they had been together forever. Their worlds revolved around each other and he couldn't imagine his life without them. Jolint was enjoying herself, and he found, with relief, that he was pleased for her.

Perian was still watching them when Elian appeared beside him, decoratively framed by the bright yellow flowers of the catrall tree in which he sat. Now was his chance to share with Elian the disturbing images that had haunted his waking hours ever since they had used him as a conduit for their magic.

'Those stories you used to tell me when I was little, the ones about life as a Faran nomad living in a wagon,' he began. 'Were they from your own experience or made up?'

Elian looked surprised. He stared at Perian for a moment without speaking. Then one of his most wicked smiles crept across his face. 'You've remembered, at last! I thought you were giving us a few strange looks with a hint of nostalgia.'

Elian's response made him feel stupid and cross. 'How can it be nostalgia when I'm not sure whether I'm deluded or not?'

Elian put his hand through Perian's shoulder and rested it over his hand. 'I'm sorry, Perian. You had full awareness of your previous life, the life we had together, when you were very little, before Esper took you away. But the trauma of that event seemed to block it from your mind, and we have waited for you to remember, thinking it would make the whole thing easier for you to accept. We would have had to tell you soon, though, with or without your recall.'

There it was. He was right. It was truth and not delirium. His eyes grew hot with unexpected tears. 'You should have told me earlier.'

'Tell me what you have seen,' Elian said calmly.

Perian woke to the sound of movement and Turnell's toe in his shoulder. His head felt thick and sleepy. He sat up and tentatively lifted a heavy, crusted eyelid. The barest hint of dawn shone between the trees. Even the birds twittered uncertainly, not sure if it was yet day or still night.

They rode through lush pastures and forests of ancient trees. Blood-sucking insects fought over the smallest patch of exposed skin, and Perian scratched his arms and neck to scabs. Heavy rains had soaked their blankets through the night and low clouds drizzled on them most of the morning. By midday, though, the sun broke through to dry their clothes and beat mercilessly upon their heads. Perian wished he had thought to buy a hat.

'What a horrible climate,' he said to no one in particular.

Turnell laughed. 'Good for the crops, though.'

Just as the day reached its peak, the city of Asper came into view – Lord Fimian's seat of power, as Radia put it. Radia stopped his horse on a hill covered with tufted, red-tipped grass, not far from the city walls. Men and women laboured about the base of the outer wall, repairing its stonework. Marble spires glowed fresh within. Some were covered with wooden scaffolding and bustling with activity. The image of a white benga – a mythical beast with a human head on a white horse's body – rippled on a green background as Lord Fimian's banner flapped in the wind. Perian found the beast grotesque and tried not to look at it.

'Looks like they're expecting trouble,' he commented as he stared at the people repairing the walls.

'This is a different city to the one I visited not five years ago,' Radia said. 'That was a city in disrepair, and Fimian was heavily in debt. It would appear that he has come into money.'

'Perhaps he's discovered something of value in those mountains other than crops,' suggested Turnell.

'Yes, but what exactly?'

Perian urged his horse forward. 'Let's find out. The taverns call, and my belly is empty.'

'Fimian can feed us,' came Radia's voice as he followed. Perian gave him a quizzical look. 'He is loyal to the Shanahan,' Radia answered. 'I want to know what he has heard and what he intends to do about it.'

They rode through the simple iron gates of the outer wall, challenged only by the wary looks of nearby labourers. Building and repair works disrupted the smooth movement of traffic along the thoroughfare, making their progress slow and tedious. Men and women ran up and down ladders and across precarious wooden scaffolding. Dust got up Perian's nose and made him sneeze until he could scarcely catch his breath.

Traders still displayed their goods along the roadside, and people crossed back and forth or lingered about the wares in tighter groups than was probably normal. Perian was surprised to see traders from all over the Empire and surrounding kingdoms. Some were from even further afield, wearing long robes and feathered caps. The closer to the castle they rode, the richer and more exotic were the goods. This was a wealthy and prosperous town, no longer in debt.

Not surprisingly, considering their shabby appearance, no one stopped them until they approached the castle gates. A young woman wearing a hard leather breastplate and a helmet of decorative metal strips with four tusks at its crown called them to a halt.

'I am Radia Serema, the Shanahan's sorcerer,' Radia said with a superior air. 'Inform His Lordship that I am here to see him.'

She stared at him suspiciously. Sunlight flashed off her helmet and set shadows dancing before Perian's eyes.

'Do as I ask,' Radia snapped. 'I have a message of importance for Lord Fimian.'

Without taking her eyes off them, she nodded to someone hidden in the shadows. The three waited calmly, their horses shifting uneasily beneath them as irritated pedestrians squeezed past and a hail of curses flew from a queue of wagons behind. Eventually, after a length of time that was inappropriate for someone of Radia's standing, an officer appeared. He approached the group at a leisurely speed and, some twenty paces away, turned his horse as though to bar their entry.

Radia's shoulders relaxed and he rode slowly toward the officer, his right fist on his heart. 'William, how nice to see you.'

The officer put his hand to his sword, but his stern features melted into a smile of pleasure once he recognised Radia.

'Much has changed,' Radia was saying as Perian and Turnell joined them.

'Yes,' said William. He beamed proudly at the populace encompassed by the sweep of Radia's arm. 'Our fortunes have changed at last. It was very generous of the Shanahan to waive all our debts, large as they must have been.'

'I wasn't aware that Lord Fimian owed Leren any money.'

William laughed and led them toward the castle. 'He probably didn't bother his sorcerer with such trivial things as debt. 'Twas his brother's man always dealt with such matters.'

Jolint's comment about sucking the Empire dry suddenly made sense, but Perian thought it unlikely that the Shanahan would have waived any debts incurred by this lord. He was looking about, vaguely wondering at the real source of such sudden wealth, when Radia's voice caught his attention again.

'I must see Lord Fimian as soon as possible. I gather you have received no news of Jasperen, then?'

The urgency in his voice caused William to pull in his horse. 'No. What news?'

'Not here. When I speak to Lord Fimian.'

They followed William into a large room he referred to as the Receiving Room. Even though they had scraped the mud from their boots at the entrance, they still left a smudgy trail on the red patterned carpet that covered the floor beneath seats set out in an oval. Two larger, heavily ornate chairs had been placed at one end of the room. Ruby eyes shone from bengas carved into the arms and emeralds glistened in the rolling hills along the back supports. Finely woven cushions ensured seated comfort.

Radia and Perian took seats within the oval. Perian nodded at the two chairs once William had gone. 'Thrones, do you think?'

Radia stared at the chairs. His face had turned the colour of the white marble fireplace, and a slight flush emerged high on each cheek as he swivelled back and forth to survey the entire room.

'Turnell, Perian, you will stay very close to me. If I say to do something, do it immediately and without question.' He didn't look at them as he spoke, and his normally active hands lay still upon his knees.

'Do you suspect something?' Perian asked, suddenly alarmed.

'It is hard to believe that they do not know about Jasperen, although it is possible. Our journey has been fast; there was no time to send a messenger bird.'

Perian watched Radia's eyes travel about the room again, tracing the opulence of their surroundings. Rich tapestries and intricate candelabras graced the walls; the chairs on which they sat were finely carved; the room still smelt of freshly turned wood and new plaster. This was a rapid turnaround for a castle that had been falling into disrepair only five years ago.

Turnell stood stony-faced at Radia's side. 'You may not recall, Radia, but I came as part of your guard on your last journey. There's something amiss here.'

Perian didn't have time to ponder Turnell's words, or ask him to clarify his thoughts; the door flew open and a portly gentleman rushed in, clutching at a hastily thrown-on robe. His bulging red cheeks puffed into a smile and he extended a podgy hand toward Radia, who stood stiffly at his entrance.

'Radia, what a pleasant surprise.' The man squeezed Radia's hand and asked to be introduced to his companions before sweeping into a seat he dragged closer to them. 'To what do I owe the pleasure of your visit? The Shanahan is well, I hope, and his family.'

Radia looked toward the door where William stood. His pent-up emotion broke into his speech, despite his obvious misgivings about the loyalty of his host. 'Jasperen has fallen. Taken by the Darna.'

Lord Fimian's smile fell from his face, although his high colour remained. 'What are you telling me, Radia? How can that be?'

Radia leant forward over his knees. His posture was intimate, as though he had suddenly forgotten his doubts. 'They came on the night of the festival. Swept through the palace before we knew what had hit us. We three managed to escape, but we were followed and ambushed.'

'And Leren? What has happened to my old friend and his family?'

'I cannot be sure. It all happened so quickly, and I was not at his side when they were taken,' Radia lied.

Lord Fimian's features changed rapidly with the apparent passage of conflicting emotions. Perian studied him carefully, hoping to be able to interpret how this news had truly affected him. If they had walked into a trap, he wanted some advance warning. But if Fimian lied, as he thought Radia suspected, then he was very convincing.

A slight breeze touched Perian's right cheek as though someone had quietly entered the room. Lord Fimian's eyes flickered past him for barely a millisecond before Perian bounced to his feet with the distinctive feel of magic behind him. He caught the briefest glimpse of red silk —

When Perian regained consciousness, he was lying on a mattress of bedstraw. His head throbbed. A single wall lamp spread a dull light across the room and filled the air with the smell of cheap oil and herbs. Turnell sat on the bed near his legs.

'Where is Radia?' Perian wheezed. 'What happened?'

'You tell me,' Turnell said. 'You fainted. Radia is with Lord Fimian. Dining, I believe.'

Perian sat up quickly. The hammer in his head took on a new, determined pace and he nearly fainted again. He tentatively rubbed his temples and rallied his scrambled memory. Someone hidden within the curtains had struck him down with magic. Radia would have sensed it, even if Turnell could not.

'They'll poison him. We have to get away.'

'No, not yet they won't, so calm down.'

Turnell stood and Perian bounced slightly, setting off the hammer again. Turnell held Perian's boots out and gestured for him to get up and put them on.

'We're safe for the moment,' he continued. 'Lord Fimian will be trying to find out where the Shanahan is hiding.'

'Did Radia tell them that he escaped?'

'No. But they're hoping he might reveal where the Shanahan would go if he *did* escape. Lord Fimian knows, though, about the attack. And he knows that Shanahan Leren has gone.'

Turnell dragged two seats to a table and seated himself in one so that he could see the door. The room was small and without decoration – servant quarters. Ones that hadn't been used for some time, judging by the damp smell of the mattress and the layer of dust Perian could see on the table. But at least it wasn't a cell.

He didn't have the strength or wit to ask any more questions. He slid carefully from the bed and struggled into his boots, then joined Turnell. He put his head into his clasped hands on the tabletop, and like Turnell, waited for someone – hopefully Radia – to come through the door.

A familiar tingle ran through the back of his head. 'Are you all right?' Cerister asked.

He waved her away with his elbow without lifting his head. 'Don't do that.'

'Head hurts, does it? I'm not surprised.'

Perian wanted to strangle her. 'Go away. Where are the others?'

'With Radia.'

'Radia!' Perian lifted his head sharply to look at her. The room went red, then black, then spun about. He waited until his stomach had settled and he could be sure he wasn't going to vomit before he asked, 'What are they doing?'

'Being overly nice to him. They're in Fimian's map room with a few officers and your attacker, one Clementina Senorista. Fimian's sorcerer.' She clipped the words, exaggerating the final 'ta' of the sorcerer's name, and turned as though to leave. Imitating the sorcerer, Cerister looked over a raised shoulder, she licked her lips slowly and seductively, with a look of such blatant lust that Perian's breath caught and he felt the heat of a deep blush infuse his face. Cerister laughed loudly at the success of her performance and winked at him. 'She's a nasty piece of work, and very powerful. You need to leave as soon as possible, before they turn their minds to something a little messier than seduction. All of you.'

Perian massaged his eyes until he saw black spots. Once they had cleared, he took a deep breath and pushed the pain of his headache to one side as best he could. Cerister had moved around to hover behind Turnell. 'Do we need to rescue him now?' Perian asked.

Turnell's eyes widened with alarm. 'Are you talking to me, or to one of those spirits of yours?'

Perian spluttered with impatience. 'Cerister. I'm talking to Cerister.'

'Not yet.' She vanished.

Perian let out a long sigh. 'I'm sorry, Turnell. It must be frustrating for you, Radia and I talking to the air most of the time.'

'It's spooky, that's what it is. I'm going to retire once this is over and claim a special pension for excessive trauma. Is she still here?'

Perian shook his head. When he had finished telling Turnell what Cerister had said, Turnell stood to listen at the door, then began pacing up and down the room. Perian watched him in silence for a while, then looked down at the table's highly polished surface, which had been revealed by the movement of his hand in the dust. He could see bits of his own haggard reflection and stared at his nose to stop the painful movement of his eyeballs.

'Please sit down, Turnell, and conserve your energy. It may be needed quite soon.'

'There's a guard at the door,' Turnell said, but sat with a noisy scrape of his chair.

Suddenly Elian appeared, making Perian jump. 'The pretence is over. You'll have to get him.'

Perian stood and clutched at the table to steady himself. 'Where's the map room? Can you take us there?'

'Yes. Hurry!' Elian disappeared through the door.

Turnell didn't need an explanation of what had been said. He was already on his feet. 'Get the guard in here on some pretext and I'll deal with 'im.'

Perian knocked on the door, wondering why he was doing such a thing, and pulled on the handle. A skinny guard with a large sword that looked too big for him blocked the doorway. He glared at Perian as he took a step backward.

'I need some more water,' Perian said, taking another step back so he stood beyond the edge of the door.

The guard grunted and followed Perian into the room, gesturing with his hands to indicate that Perian should move away from the exit. 'I'm no servant. Get back to bed. I'll order some when I can.'

Too late, he noticed Turnell's shadow. Turnell hit him hard on his shoulder, knocking him into the doorframe, then brought up his knee to hit the man in the face as he fell forward. Turnell relieved him of his sword, then hit him again until he lay unconscious.

Elian was waiting anxiously for them in the hallway. 'They're just down the corridor.'

Hugging the wall, the two men followed Elian down a series of conveniently empty hallways. What Elian had referred to as 'just down the corridor' turned out to be in another section of the castle, but finally he came to a stop where the corridor turned. Perian peered around the corner. A guard stood erect in front of a doorway about halfway down. Shouting punctured the tense silence.

He was turning to warn Turnell when a wave of magic stopped him. Another wave, and the guard turned toward the door, hesitating only a moment before rushing in.

5

Turnell dashed ahead, throwing his weight at the partially open door and into the guard who stood behind it. Perian, close behind, pulled the knife from his boot and threw it at a guard further inside the room. The guard dodged to one side and the knife skittered across the floor, but he tripped with the sudden movement and dropped his sword in an attempt to save himself. Perian scooped up the weapon without losing pace and swivelled back to find Turnell standing over the man's unconscious body. He spun about to see what was happening in the centre of the room.

Lord Fimian and two officers lay crumpled at the base of one wall, maps and papers scattered about their feet. The maps on the central table had burst into flames and burned quickly to ash with the rush of air from the doorway. The three spirits were hovering around Radia, who knelt on the floor near the table. Along the opposite wall, Lord Fimian's sorcerer frantically swiped at flames that threatened to engulf her long red sleeve; her circlet sat at a comical angle on her blond hair. With a twisted snarl, she flicked a sparkling light at the intruders. It caught Perian in the chest and knocked both him and Turnell back through the door.

Her strike was not a powerful one, yet lightning flashed about Perian and danced upon his breast. An acid finger traced the outline of the sygrilien wings tattooed over his heart. He screamed with the pain of it and curled forward, clutching his chest. Elian shouted at him, but Perian couldn't understand what he said.

The sorcerer glanced over at Perian again, and in that moment of distraction, Radia attacked. A blue line flowed smoothly from his outstretched hand, enhanced by his sapphire ring, and pinned the sorcerer to the wall until she was unconscious.

The guard by the door had recovered and was engaged with Turnell. The sound of feet thundered along the corridor.

'To me,' Radia shouted at Turnell and Perian. He turned away from them and blew the windows out with a great force of magic. The blast sucked blackened paper through the opening and scattered embers across the floor. Dying fires revived, and tiny sparks flared and spread over the rug. 'To me!' he repeated, louder.

Elian's stricken face looked up at Perian from the space between his knees and his face. 'Get up, Perian. Follow Radia through the window!'

'What?' More pain ate into his chest. He clutched it tighter. 'Are we on the ground floor?' he squeezed through clenched teeth.

'It'll be fine. Just do it!'

Perian didn't get time to answer. Turnell dealt his opponent a final blow and scooped Perian up by his arm, dragging him toward Radia and the shattered windows.

'Go!' Radia shouted. He put his head out through the opening, then looked back. 'Trust me. Jump.'

Turnell leapt from the ledge, still holding Perian tightly. Radia followed.

It wasn't the ground floor, nowhere near it. Perian's lungs stopped their movement and his stomach squeezed itself into an approximation of a pebble, but, somehow, he managed not to scream. As the ground came closer, the air around him thickened and his descent slowed until he and Turnell landed on their feet.

'Now run,' said Radia, 'before every guard in the castle is upon us!'

Jolint circled about Radia's head. 'There's a break in the wall behind the stables, where they've been doing repairs.'

Radia nodded and followed her voice; Elian drifted a few yards ahead, while Cerister hovered about Perian, muttering words of encouragement. Perian ran just behind Turnell, bent forward and holding his chest tightly. Every jolting footfall caused a new surge of agony. He had forgotten about his headache.

As Jolint had said, the wall had a large gap at ground level, and Perian could hear the sound of drunken laughter and music on the other side. Lord Fimian's men probably kept it open for clandestine visits to the night district.

They squeezed through into a street alight with oil lamps and outdoor diners. No one bothered to look up at their appearance through the hole. The windows of the tavern opposite glowed dully and the distorted figures of waiters moved to and fro within, while young men and women twirled and danced to the songs of a small troupe of musicians on the street. Any other time, Perian would have loved nothing more than to join in the merriment.

Turnell grasped Perian's arm and struggled through the crowds behind Radia. They turned down a side street to another tavern further along, where Radia slipped through a covered entry to the stables. He dug into his purse and presented the stable boy with two gold coins, and as they waited impatiently for him to saddle three horses, Perian collapsed onto the cobbles. Something tugged at his chest tattoo. He pressed his hands over it in an attempt to stop the sensation. Elian flitted about him in a kind of frenzy and Perian wished, hazily, that he would go away; Elian's frantic movement was beginning to frighten him more than the threat of Lord Fimian's guards or the possibility of a heart attack.

When the horses were ready, Radia gave the boy another gold coin and led them through a back entrance. Already they could hear the guards disturbing the festivities in the main street. The three men ran with their mounts through a series of darkened back streets until Perian could smell the fresh, clean air of open fields wafting over the outer wall.

As they approached a side gate, Turnell pushed Perian into his saddle. They rode slowly toward it. A sleepy night guard appeared at the doorway of the guardroom and Radia exchanged a few pleasantries with her, apologising for disturbing her. She rubbed her eyes and laughed at something Radia said, then waved them through with a smile. Perian felt sorry for her. She'd probably be cleaning out sewer channels for the rest of the year.

They nervously trotted through the makeshift dwellings that radiated from the outer wall until they came to the last of the roadside cottages; then, although it was nearly impossible to distinguish ruts and potholes from shadow, they pushed their steeds to a careful gallop. Amazingly, there were no tumbles. The dark impression of fields and pasture sped past either side in a blur until Radia suddenly turned his horse into a crop field, and soon they were riding through the trees toward the deep forest lit by the moon that had finally broken free of the distant mountains.

Perian clung desperately to the pommel of his saddle, letting his horse follow the others. There was another tug at his tattoo, and he nearly slid sideways; he could hear Jolint chattering to Radia, and eventually the sorcerer slowed down and pulled his horse to a halt. They remained in their saddles for a moment, listening for the telltale sounds of following hoof-beats, and Cerister and Elian drifted back the way they had come to see if Lord Fimian's guards were gaining on them.

Nothing. For the moment they had lost their pursuers. Perian folded over his saddle, clinging to the horse's mane with sweat-drenched hands, drifting in a spiral of pain.

Radia dismounted and looped his horse's reins loosely over a branch. He approached Perian and pulled him to the ground, where Perian curled up on the twigs and tufted grass and waited for Radia to kick him, although he couldn't say why. Elian and Cerister stood anxiously either side of him. He wanted them all to leave him alone. He wanted the pain to stop.

'You must do something,' said Jolint.

Radia bent over Perian and stared at him, his expression pinched and stern. His face had turned to silver in the light of the moon, the beams bouncing off his hooked nose, giving the impression that he wore a mask. His dark pupils were overly large.

'Show me,' he said testily, and nodded at Turnell.

Turnell grasped Perian's shoulders and knelt on them while holding his hands back. Perian struggled and groaned with pain and frustration at his helplessness as Radia undid the buttons of his vest and yanked his shirt up around his neck. Perian cursed as another searing tug pulled at his tattoo.

'What's this?' The shock on Radia's face was unmistakeable. He stared at the tattoo. 'You were marked for sacrifice! Oh, now the pieces come together. No wonder the Zamir and the shaman were so pleased to see you.' He sat back on his haunches, his hand resting on Perian's heaving belly. 'The question is, why does it suddenly cause you so much pain, and why is it moving in this way?'

Perian tilted his head forward to see over the mass of his shirt. The outline glowed a deep red and pulsated rhythmically, a continuous wave. 'What's it doing?' No wonder it hurt so much. No skin, tattooed or not, should move like that.

Jolint appeared between them. 'It's the shaman's magic. The sorcerer has activated it. It calls to the Great Sygrilien.'

Radia lifted his eyes a fraction to focus on the space where he believed Jolint's face to be.

'He put it there so he could activate it at the appropriate time,' she continued. Tears ran down her cheeks and her delicate hands rested on Radia's chest, a gesture completely lost on the sorcerer.

Radia jolted backward as Elian's voice overlapped Jolint's. 'You must stop the process. The Great Sygrilien already stirs and responds to the call.'

'You never told me that,' Perian wheezed. He didn't really know what the Great Sygrilien was, apart from another name for the bloodthirsty Darna Sky God, Tarse, who demanded constant sacrifices. It certainly wasn't any ordinary sygrilien that could be discouraged with a stick despite its size. He had thought the Darna religion a fiction, merely a way of controlling the people, with the added benefit of being an outlet for nasty, sadistic priests. And now Elian was telling him that it was not only 'something', but 'something' that was tugging on his tattoo?

He dropped his head back, not sure whether to cry or shout at Turnell to get off him. Another pull, harder than before, wrenched a muffled scream from him. Turnell clamped his hand over Perian's mouth, and Perian panted between his fingers as the pain subsided. He was beginning to think that the thing might be pulling itself along some invisible cord that Grison had coiled within his chest. *What if it's invisible? It might devour my heart before anyone can stop it!*

At a sign from Radia, Turnell moved and, before Perian could register what was happening, jammed a lichen-covered stick between his teeth. Turnell knelt harder on his shoulders, until the pain there was worse than the pain in his chest. He was cursing Turnell through the stick when his chest exploded and caught fire – or at least, that was how it felt. The acrid smell of burning flesh and something else he could not identify crawled up his nose. He coughed, his nose running. Tears flooded down the sides of his face and into his ears.

This time he really was going to die.

'That should do it,' came Radia's tired voice.

'Well done, Radia,' said Elian. 'That was an impressive bit of sorcery. Look at how it changes!'

Radia's fingers were like ice on Perian's hot skin as he traced the lines of the tattoo. 'Is it still painful, Perian?' His voice was softer, the anger gone.

Perian shook his head. His lungs filled with blessed air, and he closed his eyes with a sigh of relief. Turnell grunted and stood up. Perian removed the stick from his mouth and spat out bits of bark and lichen before looking down to see what Radia had done.

The tattoo had turned black. He thought that was probably a good thing. At least, he hoped it was.

Radia stood slowly and retrieved his horse. 'I suppose we have yet to see whether this thing follows or not.'

Turnell had already mounted. 'What thing?' he asked over his shoulder.

'A thing we really don't want to meet, Turnell.'

Just a few hours before dawn they had to stop so Radia could sleep for a while, before he fell from his horse, he said. Perian wasn't surprised. Using too much magic could sap a sorcerer's energy, even one as robust and powerful as Radia.

Still jittery and unsettled, Perian said he would keep watch. He leant on the trunk of an old oak, listening. Elian sat silently beside him. Perian's feet crunched on twigs and dried leaves as he shifted his footing, releasing the pungent aroma of damp soil. He stared into the darkness and stretched his hearing into the night, seeking similar sounds that might forewarn of an attack, but beyond the small noises of chirruping crickets and foraging animals, all he could hear was the rush of water.

He stepped away from the tree to get a clearer view of the stars and some idea of where they were. The glow of the descending moon shone above the canopy to his right; the rays of dawn would soon appear on his left. If he was right, the Erolon Ranges were straight ahead, and the rush of water was the dividing line between Lord Fimian's lands and old Lord Zier's ulla forests. If they could get over the water before being set upon, they would be safe. Fimian's men wouldn't dare step into the ulla forest for fear of Lord Zier's notorious Ulla Patrol – hardened warriors, deranged by constant contact with the hallucinogenic sap of the ulla tree, the source of Lord Zier's wealth. Zier's ulla collectors harvested the bright yellow discharge that constantly oozed from the trees, dried and crushed it to a powder, and sold it to the smokehouses of every town in Rashinder and beyond. Or so Perian had heard.

When birds high in the canopy began their welcome to the day, Perian woke the others. Radia walked down to the river and squatted at the edge of a small, swirling inlet to splash his face and bring colour back into his cheeks. 'Do either of you know where we are?' He had to shout to be heard above the tumbling of water in its rush to escape the mountain.

Perian pointed over the river to an embankment of shale and rocks that led to the forest beyond. 'I believe that's Zier's lands, and his ulla forest.'

Turnell spat in the water. 'And his Ulla Patrol.'

Perian shrugged. 'A difficult choice, I agree, but better to chance the Ulla Patrol than Fimian's men, who most certainly have torture and death on their minds.'

Elian stirred from his contemplations at the foot of the oak tree. 'I'll go back and see where they are. Jolint thought they were about half an hour behind us.'

'What!' Perian swung about, only to find Elian already gone. 'Why didn't anyone say they were so close?'

Cerister hovered over a small whirlpool in the river, following its circling motion with her toe, and clucked. 'Do try not to panic, Perian. I'll see if I can find you somewhere to cross.'

Perian sank onto his haunches and rubbed his face. Now he was cross as well as panicky. Turnell squatted heavily beside him with a look of confusion, just as Elian and Jolint reappeared together.

'They're on the move. You'd better get to the other side quickly,' said Elian.

Perian and Radia grasped the reins of their horses; Turnell was a little slower, not having heard the warning. Cerister waved at them from further along the track that hugged the river. How close Fimian's men were, Elian didn't say, but they ran anyway, the sound of the river covering the clatter of hooves and tack. Not far up, the river spread wide and shallow. They led their horses through freezing, ankle-high water that left Perian's toes numb. On the other side they turned onto a narrow path between the rocks to a plateau, where they stopped briefly to look back.

Jolint reappeared before he realised she had gone. 'Twenty horsemen. They'll break through the trees any minute. They have messenger birds with them. They sent one back to Fimian while I watched.'

'Doesn't matter,' Radia mumbled. 'It's probably just to tell him that they've lost us.' He mounted his horse and turned toward the distant haze of Lord Zier's special forest. 'Let's get going. We need to find Leren, and we have a long way to go.'

Perian had one foot in his stirrup when Cerister turned about, one eyebrow lifting. Her eyes moved back and forth as though searching for something.

'What is it?' asked Jolint. 'Did you see something else?' She moved to Cerister's side and looked in the same direction.

Cerister turned to her, but didn't respond immediately. 'No, it's nothing.' She smiled and shrugged. 'Nothing else.'

Perian wasn't convinced. She was withholding something. He hoped she would tell them later if it was as important as her expression indicated, but for now, he slid into his saddle and raced ahead to catch up with the other two men.

Even at a distance, Perian could feel the strangeness of the forest. The intoxicating substance held within the boles of the ulla trees leaked into the air with the expanding heat of the day. Elian walked at Perian's side, though his feet did not touch the ground.

Turnell rode up beside Radia. 'Are you thinking of trying Zier's hospitality?' he asked with a hint of sarcasm that Radia didn't notice.

'It's a thought. He's a little uncouth, but hospitable. We'd at least get a lavish meal and a decent bed for the night.' Radia turned to look at Turnell with a bitter smile. 'I doubt that he's in debt to Leren!'

Perian watched as a wide-winged messenger bird flew overhead. He urged his horse forward to join them and pointed to the sky. 'Perhaps not such a good idea.'

Radia reined in his horse and studied the bird as it disappeared over the treetops. He said nothing for a while.

'I think I'm beginning to understand how it was so easy for your father to reach Jasperen without detection, Perian, and where Lord Fimian's sudden wealth has come from. These are Rashinder's westernmost lands; they border with Darna. Fimian's eldest son, Orenel, was at the festival, yet Fimian didn't mention him once.' Radia rubbed his eyes and blinked in the light. 'At least, I hope this was the route, and the other lords haven't seen fit to rebel against their Shanahan. If they have, Leren's position is very precarious.' He squeezed his horse's sides and walked on. 'We'll ride on into the forest and turn east as soon as we can. The sooner I am at Leren's side, the happier I will be.'

'What if he's already been overtaken?' asked Perian.

'That is what we must find out. But I am confident of the loyalty of the eastern lords. He is safe for the moment.'

Perian stifled a response. Radia had been confident of Lord Fimian's loyalty, and Lord Zier's. But Perian had no better plan and nowhere else to go, so he would stay with Radia.

Finally, they reached the shade of the tall ulla trees. Perian wiped the sweat from his face with his sleeve. His head spun with the acrid fumes emanating from their trunks, and his lungs ached. He stretched out and touched a bulbous bit of bark as he passed. Finding the trunk moist, he wiped the viscous deposit on his trousers. Sprays of small leaves jutted from fat, knobbly branches high above him, reminding Perian more of giant root vegetables than of a tree. The clinging stench stirred in a gentle breeze that swept along the pathways and swirled about the trunks. The only sounds Perian could hear in this strangely quiet forest were the plodding footsteps of the horses, the crunch of leather, the soft jingle of metal and the splash of a nearby stream. There was no birdsong, no normal forest noises of rustling undergrowth.

Radia coughed softly, breaking the silence. 'At least we'll hear any approaching patrol …'

'If the maps we have at the palace are accurate, it'll be hours before we break free of these cursed trees.' Turnell's hair clung to his head and his sodden clothing to his body.

They stopped at a watercourse to let the horses drink while they ate what was left of their cheese and bread. Perian's stomach complained at the sparseness of the meal. There was no game to kill for supper, but at least he had seen fish in the stream; they could fish later if it was safe to light a fire.

'You could always eat it raw,' came Elian's response to Perian's unspoken thoughts. Perian ignored him and lay down beneath the wavering shade of a tree, his head on his rolled blanket.

Elian looked back suddenly, and Jolint and Cerister did the same. 'What's wrong?' Perian asked. 'Is someone coming?' He lifted his head to look in the same direction.

'Nothing.' Elian smiled. 'It's been a long day.'

Perian lay back and closed his eyes. He couldn't quite see how it could have been 'a long day' for them. It wasn't as if they had had to fear for their lives too.

6

When Perian opened his eyes again, he was in complete darkness. He sat up with a jolt. *How could I have slept into the night?* Then his foot slipped into empty space and he fell forward, hitting his head on a hanging root. His breath rasped against his throat and his stomach jammed up into his lungs as he grabbed the root tightly and sat very still until his eyes slowly adjusted to the near absence of light.

A hint of moonlight, struggling to penetrate thick cloud, revealed the ghostly outline of a massive tree. Blood rushed noisily and irregularly in his ears, and he commanded his pounding heart to slow, his breath to even out. With the calming of his body, he was able to release his mind from the fright that had scrambled his thinking. He stretched all his senses, listening and watching. He found himself squatting in the fork of a thick branch, but how he got here, he did not know. Slowly twisting to touch the main trunk with his palm, he inched backward so he could feel its support against his body and took a moment to let the thunder in his chest subside.

He was imprisoned by thick aerial roots, the only way out being up. He pushed on one, then another, but all were deeply embedded in the ground below and each as solid as a slender trunk. Beyond his prison, he could just make out the shape of other trees set widely apart. They were different: compact and smaller, with no hanging roots, and they were leafless – or dead. He thought the latter, since the air was warm. In fact, the tree he sat on was also barren. There was a feel of death about the place; a soullessness.

A long way down, massive roots spread wide around the tree's base. He studied their crisscrossing pattern until his eyes were drawn to a dark tangle where the intertwined roots had been broken, creating a small opening. The wood about the breach was charred. It stank with the residue of old but powerful magic. His skin prickled at the sight and smell of it and left him in no doubt that something horrible had happened beneath the tree.

He forced his attention away for fear of disturbing anything that might still linger there. His heart had begun to thump again, and he sat back to feel the trunk against his spine and stop his growing panic.

A gust of wind blew freely through the naked boughs, carrying a voice he remembered but could not place. It called his name, he thought, and he listened more closely, but then the tree began to shake and he clutched at the hanging roots for support —

'Wake up!' came the voice.

His eyes flew open. Radia's face, superimposed by Elian's, appeared in front of him, bright in the midday sun. The light made his eyes water.

All three spirits drifted closer to Perian and Radia asked if he was all right; he had become agitated and whimpered in his sleep. Perian sat up and affirmed that he was fine, although his hands shook.

'What did you see?' asked Cerister. Her voice was tight and troubled.

A knot slowly tightened inside him. Cerister also knew this had been no ordinary nightmare. There was a quality about it that felt vaguely familiar.

Radia joined Turnell to sit on a nearby rock and listened intently as Perian described his dream. With the telling, Perian tried to convince himself that he was only experiencing a nightmare influenced by the ulla trees, nothing more sinister, but his friends were too interested, and he found their looks of concern disturbing.

'What does it mean?' he asked them.

They looked at one another, then, with a glance at Radia, Elian indicated to Perian that he should follow them as they drifted further along the row of trees. Perian stood and raised his eyebrows at the others, then followed his spirit friends to huddle behind the bole of an exceptionally large ulla.

'You must come to us, Perian,' Elian said in reply to his question. 'No more time can be wasted. We cannot wait.' He spoke softly, with a seriousness that was unlike him.

Perian stared at Elian. How could they ask such a thing of him? 'What are you talking about? How do you propose I do that? I don't want to die. Not again. Not yet!'

Jolint moved forward and put an ethereal hand on his arm. 'No, Perian, you mustn't die. We don't want that. But Elian is right: you must come to us now. The troubles of Rashinder can wait.'

'I don't understand. What's wrong? What does this dream mean? How can I go to you?' He pulled away from Jolint and ran a hand through his thick black hair. He was exhausted, and his narration had left him drained. He felt hollow and strange. And now they wanted him to think about dying!

Cerister's eyes grew wide. She took a step toward him and opened her mouth as though to speak, but Elian pushed in front of her.

'We're not asking you to die, Perian. Why would we want that?'

To Perian's amazement, Elian actually looked puzzled, but he was too tired to moderate his words. 'It's obvious, isn't it? You're dead. Disembodied spirits. How can I go to you without dying?'

Elian looked shocked, hurt – on the verge of tears, even. Perian hadn't meant to hurt him. It belatedly occurred to him that his friends might not have even realised they were dead, but that didn't seem possible. There was something else going on that they hadn't told him, and suddenly he was confused and annoyed.

Cerister and Jolint gathered about Elian, protectively, he thought. They looked so vulnerable of a sudden, like frightened children. Perian's irritation evaporated and he put his hand out toward them, but they had begun to fade.

'I'm sorry,' he said. 'I …'

But they had gone.

Perian and his companions continued through the ulla forest for another day before they came to pasture and crop fields. Thankfully they had managed to avoid the Ulla Patrol and had been attacked by nothing bigger than the occasional biting fly. In the distance they could just make out the town of Mest with the towering spires of Lord Zier's castle at its centre; Radia led them east to avoid it, and they began their journey to find the Shanahan and those who had managed to escape from the palace.

Perian's friends had not reappeared, but they had begun to inhabit his dreams. Frustratingly, he remembered little when he awoke. He felt refreshed and peaceful, but his days were empty without them. A faint shadow periodically passed over him, its content uncertain: sometimes fear and sometimes guilt. But he could not fully account for this sensation, though it occurred to him more than once that perhaps he didn't want to.

Away from the ulla forest and its mind-altering atmosphere, Perian's thoughts became clearer, and he was glad to breathe the clean air that swept down from the Erolon Ranges. They passed back into the Shanahan's lands and rode into the natural forests of black-trunked pesimine and yellow-flowered catrall trees, with their thick canopies and healthy undergrowth, where birds sang, the leaf litter rustled with the movement of small animals, and herds of antelope, deer and biben roamed. That night they lit a fire and feasted on antelope.

Perian took first watch. He sat on the raised root of a pesimine tree, his back resting awkwardly against the stem of a large creeping plant that clung to the tree's black bole. An array of frogs croaked along the edge of a thin stream, and in the distance he could hear the *peep peep* of the black mergan, a large night bird with a hooked beak and very long claws. Stars winked behind the movement of high branches as they danced in the westerly wind.

Perian glanced enviously at Radia and Turnell, cocooned in their blankets close to what remained of the fire. He was struggling to keep sleep at bay when Elian suddenly appeared at his side. Perian was still offended that he had stayed away so long, so he ignored him for a while, but Elian didn't speak. He knelt beside Perian and waited patiently.

'Where are the others?' Perian eventually asked. He was neither good at sulking for long nor as good at remaining silent as Elian.

'I'm here,' was all Elian said.

Perian turned to face him. Elian looked pale, even for a ghost. 'What's wrong?'

Elian smiled, but there was no light in his eyes. He moved closer to Perian until his knees overlapped Perian's feet. 'You must leave them, Perian, and come to us. I'll be your guide. We need to go south, through Shadow Valley and toward Morlust's Forest.'

Perian stared at him for a moment, trying to discern his purpose.

'I can't. We must go with Radia and find the Shanahan. They will be preparing to retake Jasperen. I can never be Zamir as was intended, but by helping to free Jasperen and pushing the Darna back over the border, I can make sure their obsessive persecution of the Farans will again be restricted to the smaller Empire of Darna. It is the only way I can see that will enable us to salvage at least part of our old mission. We must try, for Gisela's sake and the future of our tribe. Once Rashinder is back in Shanahan Leren's hands, we can think again on how best to proceed. We need to be there to see what opportunities may present themselves.'

'No, Perian. You can best help by coming with me.'

'In what way would that be best? How can I help free Rashinder if I'm not there?'

Elian looked deep into Perian's eyes, his gaze piercing him with its intensity and sadness. 'We'll die if you don't come.'

The words cut into Perian's heart. Suddenly he was afraid. 'But you're already dead!' he blurted without thinking.

Elian did not reply. He ran his fingers over some small stones on the ground. Perian knew that if he had been alive, he would have tossed them up and caught them, and he found it frustrating to watch. He couldn't imagine what Elian was talking about. His request made no sense. They had been together forever, bound by love and loyalty. Elian was a part of him. All three of them were his family. He could not deny their request, but it would help if Elian would explain why he needed Perian to come.

'You must come now, Perian, to release us before you are once again incapacitated by visions, and before you are too far away,' he said at last, in response to Perian's unspoken thought. 'I'll come back in the morning.'

He faded, slowly, as though he lacked the energy to vanish faster.

Perian stared for a while at the mossy rock Elian had partially obscured with his ethereal presence, turning over in his head what Elian had said about the return of his visions, until Radia shuffled up beside him, still wrapped in his blanket.

'Did I hear Elian?'

'Yes. He's gone. He wants me to go south – through Shadow Valley, to Morlust's Forest.'

Radia frowned and pulled his blanket closer. 'Did he say why? Will you go?'

Perian nodded. He didn't really need to think long on what he would do. 'I must. Strange as it may be to say this, Elian looked ill, and the other two didn't come.'

Radia hesitated. He looked toward a nearby bush, scrunching his lower lip over the top one. 'Perhaps their spirits have been trapped all this time, and now they need to move on. I can only assume that it is their graves you will find at the end of your journey.'

From the hint of sadness Perian saw in Radia's eyes, he guessed that he was thinking of Jolint.

'Do you think they need some kind of ritual to release them? I know of no such thing.'

But Elian would tell him what he needed to do. It occurred to him that the others might be too weak to return, if Elian's appearance was anything to go by. And if Perian performed this ritual, they would be gone forever. He'd never see them again.

The thought of a lifetime without them near crushed him, yet he could not deny them such a request.

He turned to look at Radia. 'I will go. When whatever I need to do for them is completed, I will rejoin you.'

'Make sure you do, Perian. When this is all over and we have

Jasperen back, I have a fancy to take you on as an apprentice – tease out that power you hold within you and put it to use.'

Perian laughed. He found that the idea pleased him. But Radia wouldn't need to tease anything from him. It was already starting to emerge. He had tried to ignore it, even deny it, but he knew deep down that his nightmare in the ulla forest had been a vision, not a dream. Elian had said they had put a temporary block on his seer's power so he could live a normal life for a while. He was grateful. Even though he had seen only brief snatches of his previous life, he knew Elian was right: soon he would be taken over by visions, his freedom and certainty gone, as it had been then. Only this time, without Elian, he would have no one to support and guide him.

Radia patted him on the back. 'Go, get some sleep. It's my turn to watch anyway.'

When Perian woke the next morning, he was lying on his side with a stone pressing into his shoulder. He groaned and shifted, opening his eyes slowly. He could see Turnell's empty blanket crumpled on the ground not far away, overlaid by the green fabric of Elian's trousers, and then Elian himself, bending down to peer into Perian's sleepy face. 'Will you come?'

Perian groaned as he sat up, rubbing his shoulder where the stone had made an impression. 'Of course I will.'

Elian beamed and straightened. 'The others are packing up and loading their horses. It's time to go.'

Perian scrambled to his feet and quickly saddled his horse. They rode on through the forest together until the sun was at its zenith and Elian indicated that it was time for Perian to leave the others and begin his journey south. They stopped to rest and eat what remained of the antelope, then Perian said his farewells.

Radia hugged him tightly. 'Safe journey,' he said, and handed Perian the herbs he had collected along the way. 'If you attach the bundle to your saddle, the sun will have dried them by the time you reach your destination. Burn them and wave the smoke over their burial mounds. It will release their spirits and ease their journey.'

Perian took the bundle and hung it from his saddle as suggested, ignoring Elian's look of alarm. 'How will I find you?' he asked Radia.

'Go to Ollamore, a village hidden within the folds of the mountain. You can reach it via a tunnel located along the steppes of Porffer's Peak, near the border with Wellorn, Ishra's kingdom. I will find you. Or, if we have already left for Jasperen, you should be able to follow easily enough. Wait five days.'

'Good luck with that pension,' Perian said as he clasped Turnell's hand. Radia raised his eyebrows and, with a snort, urged his horse into movement.

The first day of his journey was lonely despite Elian's presence. Elian was uncharacteristically quiet and left Perian to initiate what little conversation they had. When they came to the mouth of the Shadow Valley early on the second day, Elian floated ahead and pulled Perian along at an increasingly urgent pace. The valley passed between the Erolon Ranges and the Central Ranges, and the high, curved cliffs on either side created a tunnel, effectively blocking out the sun for most of the day. In the slender gap where rain and light penetrated, a strip of grass and scrubby bushes grew in a line along the middle of the valley. Clumps of spiky, thick-leafed plants dotted the dusty slopes where little else would grow, and the hollow entrances of caves and rocky outcrops spotted the cliffs above, where flocks of birds nested on little ledges and in small pits. The cheery click of insects dominated the valley's lower level, while a mind-numbing cacophony of birdcalls filled its upper region.

Around midday, Elian was saying that they would soon be free of the valley when a bird appeared high in the sky. Its presence caused the birds along the slopes to stop their chattering and the sudden cessation of their calls left Perian feeling slightly dizzy.

Elian put his hand through Perian's arm. 'Quick! Find somewhere to hide!'

'What?'

'Hide! I think it's an almonos.'

Perian squinted upward. The small white dot he had scarcely noticed was rapidly growing into a large white bird as it spiralled downward and began to circle above their heads. He looked frantically about at the wide, open space.

'Where? There is nowhere —'

Elian darted to Perian's side and looked up. 'Stand very still, then. It may go for something smaller.'

Perian dismounted and unsheathed his sword. Shrieking suddenly broke out amongst the nesting birds on the cliff. Small flocks darted this way and that in a frantic attempt to distract and intimidate the predatory intruder, but the white bird paid them no attention, continuing its languid downward spiral. It circled above Perian, coming so close that he could see it clearly.

It was the biggest almonos he had ever seen. Its scaly black-and-yellow-striped legs were pulled up into its white underbelly, enormous shiny talons curled within. With its neck thrust forward, two of its four pendulous eyes extended about its hooked beak to survey the ground below; the other two were withdrawn for ease of flight. It screeched as it passed uncomfortably close to Perian, nearly bursting his eardrums. His stallion pulled on his tight grip.

The bird circled once more, higher this time, and finally flew off beyond the cliff.

The pressure in the air lifted with the bird's departure and Perian took a deep breath. Elian whispered into his buzzing ear, 'It might come back. You'd better hurry!'

Perian didn't need any encouragement; he urged his horse on faster, nervously scanning the sky, and less than an hour later, they rounded a bend and the valley expanded before him into a carpet of lush grasses that spread into the opening as though to greet him. Beyond, a sparkling lake stretched to the horizon. The long grass about his horse's legs bent fluidly to the touch of the wind, replicating the disturbed surface of the water.

He dismounted at the lake's edge and looked over the expanse of spangled light. If Elian had not said that it was a lake, he would have thought he had taken a wrong turn and come to the ocean. On his right, not far away, stood the outer trees of Morlust's Forest. He could see by their height and wide girth that this was an old forest, and even at a distance its ancient interior curled faintly about him.

'You must set your horse free,' said Elian. 'We have to go into the forest, which holds a magic of its own. He won't survive the journey and will only draw attention to your presence. Hide his tack by the rocks over there.' He pointed to a rocky pile near the water's edge.

A burial mound, Perian thought as he walked closer, *or perhaps someone else's horse.* He looked up beyond the mound to gaze at the lake and the landscape about him. There was something familiar about it, but he couldn't recall having been here before, nor anywhere else that had the same configuration of high, ragged mountains and endless water with such an old forest nestled on its shore.

The burial mound at his feet sent tingles through his body, drawing him in as though the occupant were reaching out to grasp him with the quiet echoing of his name. The sensation frightened him. He took a step back, and at that moment a sharp pain seized his chest and his body shivered with a sudden chill sweat. He dropped his horse's tack beside the rocks and turned his attention to the agitated movement of Elian at his side.

'You won't need that,' Elian said sharply as Perian grasped the bundle of herbs that Radia had given him.

He attached it to his pack anyway.

7

Perian's skin prickled as he walked between the trees on the outer edge of the forest. At first the forest shone beneath a cathedral canopy, and small rainbow-coloured auras burst from leaf dew in a concert of light. But as he went deeper to where the oldest trees existed, the air changed. The forest became deeply shaded, humid and hot. Perian was beginning to see what Elian had meant about the magic here; it clung thickly to the trunks. His body felt heavy, and sweat moistened his skin as he trudged on, each step more difficult than the one before, his mind numb with the effort. All the while, Elian glanced about nervously, adding to Perian's foggy discomfort.

He came upon the epicentre of power unexpectedly. If he hadn't been concentrating so hard on each footfall, he would have been more alert to the significant increase in magic. Before he could stop himself, he had stepped into a bare ring that surrounded the largest tree he had ever seen: the massive tree of his nightmare. His heart nearly stopped at the same time as his feet.

The tree looked even bigger and more imposing from below. Its roots spread in a tangled mess over the ground, reaching out to the closest of the surrounding trees, and its thick aerial roots drilled down into the soil, obscuring much of the main trunk. But, unlike the barren tree in his vision, it was still lush and vibrant, with no hint of leaf loss. A glow as soft as moonlight thinly veiled by cloud shone from its trunk and boughs, pulsing with magic in a way that the other trees did not. Perian was captivated by its beauty, yet it terrified him.

'Quickly,' Elian whispered. The urgency in his voice and expression only increased Perian's nervousness.

'Where are you, Elian? Are you buried below the roots?' He reached uncertainly for the herbs attached to his pack.

'No. Leave them. Follow me.'

Elian moved between the hanging roots and beckoned. Perian shook his head. His legs were shaking so badly that he wasn't sure he could move.

'Come. You must!' insisted Elian. His panic was palpable. It twined with Perian's own fear and the persistent pulse of the tree, dancing about Perian in conflicting waves. A rock was lodged in his chest and his eyeballs hurt from a need to cry. But he had come so far; how could he not do as they wished, even though it was breaking his heart?

Gathering what little courage he had, Perian forced his legs into movement and followed Elian between the tight aerial roots, pulling his pack after him. Once through, he found himself standing on the tree's knotted woody base. Strands of magic pulsated about his feet, surging up through his body, making his stomach heave and his head spin.

Elian pointed to a gap between two roots that crossed over each other. Perian recognised them. It was where he had seen the burnt-out hole in his vision.

'You must come in here, Perian. Be brave. You're safe. I would never risk your life.'

He'd already been brave, and now Elian wanted him to slide down a hole too. He wanted to scream.

'Surely you don't want to me to bury myself alive beneath this tree? I can't do it. And even if I could, the hole isn't big enough, and I can feel protective wards forming a barrier under there. I do not have the sorcery to break them.'

'You do, Perian. Trust me. Put your pack down and follow me.'

Perian put his pack down, but he still had no idea how Elian expected him to find the courage or the strength to do as he asked. His sense of failure became overwhelming. He wanted to bang his head against the tree's great trunk to rid himself of the paralysing fear that gripped his mind and body.

Elian stopped his agitated movement and spread himself about Perian, enclosing him so that two became one. 'Relax. Give yourself to me, Perian.'

Elian felt almost alive, and for a moment Perian thought he could feel the pulse of Elian's heart against his own as he had in his moments of recall. Elian had done this sometimes when Perian was a child, enclosing him, making him laugh with the thrill of it. He would run across the marshes with a sense of life beyond his own ability to see and feel. But he had never felt as though that life truly stirred in him.

'Trust me,' Elian coaxed.

His encompassing presence eased Perian's mind and took his will. He stepped to the gap and felt the protective wards melt away beneath his feet, heard the creaking of the roots as they parted. He looked down in muted amazement as he slipped fluidly into darkness. A part of him wanted to shout his terror, but another sighed with the peace brought on by a total lack of external stimulation. *Is this just another nightmare?* He couldn't tell.

His body slipped through the tight channel into a spacious chamber filled with a soft glow. Supported by Elian's gentle energy, he floated slowly downward until his feet touched the ground, where his legs crumpled beneath him. Kneeling, he bent forward and dropped his head onto his folded legs for some time, breathing deeply and gathering his wits.

When the sweat on his skin began to chill, he sat up slowly and looked about. Elian had gone, but he was not alone; the chamber was round and domed, carved out of the rock on which the tree had grown, and three stone pallets stuck out from its walls, with three bodies lying on them beneath blankets of dried fern fronds.

Radia had been right. Elian had brought him to their burial chamber. It felt strange and disappointing, in a way, to see the physical remains of his friends, so vibrant in spirit, so solid and still in death.

Perian called out softly to Elian. Surely he wouldn't just leave without saying goodbye – not after all this time? But there was no reply. There was no sound at all. A wave of desolation overwhelmed him. An emptiness opened within him, one that he thought would never fill. How could he be complete without his brother? What was the point of anything without his spirit friends?

Long moments went by before he was able to gather himself and think clearly again. He looked about for the source of the chamber's light, but there was no lamp or torch that he could see. No doubt it was part of the magic that still lingered here. He hoped it would last until he could get out.

Forcing his chilled joints into movement, he stood. He thought some of the fern fronds shifted slightly, making him jump, but then he chided himself for being so nervy.

Beneath the ferns he could see the still-bright colours of his friends' clothing. He approached the pallet on his left, knelt beside it and moved the dried fronds aside. He already knew what he would find: Cerister's face, as white as the stone on which she lay. Her blond hair flowed over her shoulders, and in his mind's eye he saw her toss it back as she so often had in life. Her clothes were those she had worn in her ethereal state, only brighter, and she wore tanned leather boots that Perian had never noticed before.

All three, he noticed, looked as though they had died just moments before, the life still lingering in their limbs. No doubt it was the magic he could feel in the chamber that kept them so … *Fresh* came to mind, but that sounded obscene. *Preserved* was almost as bad.

He stopped juggling with words and ran two fingers slowly about Cerister's mouth. He would have kissed her if it hadn't suddenly felt a little indecent. Instead, he ran his fingers over her cheeks and brushed back a few stray strands of hair. He kissed her gently on the forehead, then covered her face again with the ferns.

I should have brought the herbs after all, he thought. *What does Elian expect me to do now that I'm here, if not release them?*

In a sudden panic, he looked up. The hole he had slipped through was near the top of the dome, just off to one side. Out of reach. Had Elian brought him here to die and be entombed with them?

'Surely not.' His voice echoed disrespectfully about the tomb.

'Surely not,' laughed a croaky voice he could not mistake.

He spun around to find Elian staring at his hands. The fern fronds had fallen from his pale but certainly not lifeless face. On the next pallet, Jolint groaned and blew at the fronds that covered her features. They didn't fall, but moved gently with her breath. *Breath!*

Perian was terrified and elated all at once. He watched their tentative movements blankly, hardly able to register the overwhelming joy and love slowly rising in his shocked mind and body. In all their years together, it had never occurred to him that his friends might yet live, that they were merely asleep: in hibernation, their spirits wandering free.

But his happiness was cut short. The magic that had been drifting about the cavern like strands of colour in water began to coalesce around him. Silver tendrils emerged from the mass, and all his attention switched rapidly from the miracle unfolding before him to what was happening within his own body. The tendrils ran up his spine, pierced his heart, entered his seeing eye, tearing apart the barrier that had contained his seer's power.

Perian closed his eyes and slid to the ground in a great blast of inner sight – a spray of visions, brief snippets, scenes he could make no sense of …

He would never be free again.

The visions kept coming in a flow he could scarcely manage: the parts of his previous life that he had not remembered and possible futures mingling together. Rain on the oiled cover of their wagon; Elian changing into a wolf so they could snuggle up to his furry body to keep warm; sunny days when the four of them wandered about the small periphery of their wagon to pick bluebells or watch Garin make a fire to cook their meals; leaning on Elian in a haze of visions; Cerister's hand in his while Gisela berated them for some misdemeanour or pushed him to share what he saw; Garin snatching moments during her absence to teach him how to use a sword. Scenes of battle and blood in a terrain he had never seen. Snatches of Jasperen Palace and a view of the great boulevard that led to the palace gates from a window above.

His breath came erratically and he put a shaky hand to his chest in an attempt to slow his physical reaction. At that point, the voice of a dark figure from his childhood nightmares boomed into his head.

'There you are, my poppet. At last our time is almost upon us, when we will fulfil your destiny together.'

Perian's visions scattered so only the figure's hideous laughter remained. The sudden rigidity of his body threatened to snap his tendons until the laughter faded and he fell flat to the ground, his mind thankfully empty.

'Now that you're back, we could do with some assistance over here,' Jolint called.

Her voice was strained and tight, but it was enough to pull Perian slowly from his stupor. He opened his eyes and blearily looked up. Stiff and frozen after years of lying on the stone shelf, Jolint hadn't moved.

'I wouldn't normally ask you, your hands being so calloused and your massage skills so inadequate,' Jolint continued, 'but since you are the only one standing, or should I say, kneeling, at present —'

Perian grunted, and, rising unsteadily, shuffled toward her. Blurry images began to return and flashed over his inner eye, interfering with his sight. He wished they would stop. He stretched out his hands to feel for the stone shelf, then ran his fingers up to Jolint's face, poking her in the eye. She yelped, but he found her shoulders and gripped one arm firmly, squeezing and rubbing until she groaned and gasped with the warmth returning to her skin. He did the other arm and then, slipping his hands beneath her, rubbed her back. He could hardly believe that he could touch her, feel her solid beneath his hands.

Ecstatic. He was ecstatic. Yet the word was wholly inadequate. He was experiencing something far beyond words. He wanted to hold her, squeeze her, rub his face in the curve of her neck and feel her soft red hair against his cheek. Just feel her alive in his arms. She was his sister. Not by blood as Elian was, but in every other way.

But Elian wasn't his brother by blood anymore either. He pushed himself to his feet to erase the thought.

'You can do your own legs now while I help Elian,' he said, groping his way to Elian, who, with a sigh of gratitude, surrendered his arm to Perian.

When he was finished, Perian sat back on his haunches, watching Elian struggle to sit up. 'That'll teach you both to sleep in,' he said, a little crossly.

Why was he so cross? Because, technically, he and Elian were no longer brothers, and his life was yet again consumed by visions he could not control. But most of all, they had not told him that they lived.

'I thought you were dead. You never said that you were just in hibernation!'

'It never came up,' Elian said, then added, 'I see the visions have started.'

'Sadly, yes. What do you mean "never came up"?'

Elian shrugged and eased his legs over the edge of the pallet with a quick intake of breath.

Perian felt there was little point in pursuing the subject. He looked over at Cerister. Elian followed his gaze and shook his head.

'She wanted to stay with us for as long as possible, so I healed her as best I could, and then Gisela had her put into suspension with us. We all knew that once the wards were breached she wouldn't be able to stay any longer.'

Perian's heart twisted in a wave of agonising sadness. He remembered the smell of her, her laughter and teasing scorn, the touch of her silken hair across his arm in the confined space of their wagon. He stifled a sob, then wondered why he was suddenly so shocked and bereft when only a short while ago he had thought them all dead for years.

It seemed unfair that Cerister had not survived as well. 'Why? Was she ill?'

Elian put up his hand against the questions. 'There's no time for explanations now. We have to get out of here as soon as possible. The next time the wood mage pays us a visit he'll know we've gone by the absence of our shield.'

Perian pointed at the roof, although he could not see exactly where the hole was through the images flickering in his vision. 'I think there may be a problem with that, unless one of you has learnt how to levitate.' He put one hand to his head and rubbed his eyes with the other. He just wanted the visions to stop before he threw up, or fainted.

'There's another way out,' said Elian. He held out an arm so that Perian could assist him to stand, urging him toward Cerister's shelf. He moved the fronds away from her face and stroked her cheek tenderly with the backs of his fingers.

'Goodbye, Cerister. We'll all be together again one day.'

Elian bent down, kissed her on the cheek and placed his hand upon her head. Then, wiping his eyes and nose on his sleeve, he reached behind her body for something on the wall. Jolint shuffled to his side and together they carefully pulled Cerister's shelf outward to reveal a small opening. Elian bent to look within, then unfurled his fingers, releasing a few mage lights. They were dull compared to his usual display as Perian remembered it, and he thought this must indicate just how weak Elian was from his long hibernation. Perian was amazed that he could produce light at all after such a time.

Elian scrambled through first, blocking the soft glow.

'You next, Perian,' said Jolint. 'Elian will guide you through. I can see by your eyes that the visions still flood your sight. I'll follow behind.'

Perian banged his shin on Cerister's pallet and his head on the roof of the entry. He assumed that the swirling worms reaching for him in the gloom were Elian's fingers and followed them. The narrowness of the passage soon expanded into a tunnel where they were able to stand, though the walls were still rather close at the sides.

The tunnel filled with their raspy breathing and their shuffling feet echoed strangely. Water seeped down the walls, and more than once Perian put his hand inadvertently on a slimy mound. Roots dangled down from above, spilling droplets of water down their necks, making their hair wet and slapping them in the face. It smelt of rock and soil and roots.

Eventually the ground began to rise and Elian said he had to rest before tackling their ascent. By now, Perian's vision had begun to clear, leaving him wondering whether he preferred the bright colours of his visions to the bleak darkness that surrounded them.

'Where are we going?' he asked, his voice ringing along the tunnel.

'Up into the Erolon Ranges,' whispered Jolint.

'But that'll take forever!'

'Almost,' said Elian. 'A little further up on this side of the ranges, away from the forest, there's a hut where we can rest. At least, I hope it's still there.'

'What if it's occupied?'

'Then we'll have to think of something else.' Elian stood, leaning heavily on the wall. 'Let's keep going. The ascent is steep, but it's not long. Or at least that's what Gisela told us.' He didn't sound very convinced, and Perian doubted that Gisela had ever made the journey herself.

A wisp of dark, woody magic travelled down the tunnel from behind them, followed by a loud crack that made their ears pop.

The sound spurred them on and they moved upward with greater speed. It was amazing what a little fear could do for one's energy levels, Perian thought.

They scrambled upward for what seemed longer than Elian, or Gisela, had indicated, before the tunnel levelled off and Elian stopped again to lean against the wall. He held up his hand to stop the others from talking and listened for signs of pursuit, but all was quiet.

'He hasn't found the opening yet,' he gasped. His breath came hard and steamed from the drop in temperature. Perian's legs shook beneath him with the effort of climbing, and he wondered again how the other two had managed to come so far without collapsing.

A cool breeze touched Perian's cheek from ahead. Elian felt it too and smiled at him. He pushed himself away from the wall and continued on, and soon the breeze became a forceful gust. Then they were out in the open: stars shone brightly above them in a dark, clear sky, and the freezing wind whipped about Perian's clothing and tousled his hair. Jolint pulled her cloak about her, as did Elian; Perian didn't have a cloak, so he rubbed his arms and stamped his feet in the hope of stimulating a little heat. His cheeks and ears were numb. They weren't dressed for such temperatures. They would die of exposure if they didn't find shelter soon.

'We should stay inside the tunnel entrance out of this wind for now.' His teeth chattered so much he could scarcely get the words out. 'When the moon comes up we'll at least be able to see our way.'

Elian nodded. 'We can listen for the wood mage from here. Or at least feel his presence if he has the sense to be quiet.'

Perian spun his head about. 'A wood mage?' He vaguely remembered Elian mentioning something like that before but had been too busy fending off his visions to take much notice. 'Don't tell me – Gisela didn't bother to get his permission to use the vault beneath the old tree.'

'There wasn't time,' said Jolint from within the folds of her cloak. She sat down heavily against the entrance wall. 'And he wouldn't have agreed anyway.'

'He lost a few trees when the battle entered the forest periphery,' Elian added.

'What battle?' Perian couldn't remember a battle.

Jolint cocked her head at him, giving it a slight shake. 'A terrible one. Cerister and I had never been in anything like it. Dissenters and troublemakers trying to take over the tribe, Gisela said. All our own people. All Farans. We didn't know who was with us or who was against until they actually attacked us personally. Until then we'd only ever gone with her when there was a difficult dispute; as support, I believe. We'd never had to do anything. Never had to kill anyone – kill our own.' Her shoulders slumped at the memory, and she stared at the ground. 'Then Cerister went down. Gisela was so intent on bringing the rebels to account that she walked straight over Cerister without realising who it was and ordered me to follow her. I didn't, of course. I stayed with Cerister.'

She was talking about rebellion from within their own tribe, or the amalgamation that their tribe had become. But she offered no further explanation, and both she and Elian fell into the deep sleep of the exhausted before Perian could ask any more questions.

He stared down the tunnel, forcing himself to listen and remain alert. Wood mages were powerful, angry beings, and none of them were in a fit condition to face this one should he decide on revenge.

8

A blast reverberated through the darkness just as the moon lit up the entrance of the tunnel. Perian's eyes flew open and his friends sat bolt upright.

'Quick,' croaked Elian. 'He's found the way in.'

He scrambled to his knees and used the wall to help him stand; Perian pulled Jolint up by her arm, and they staggered into the bright light of a waxing gibbous moon. Tall pines dotted a landscape of rock and stark shadows. Cold-loving ferns jutted from rock crevices to form decorative skirts about their bases, and the flowerheads of alpine plants bobbed colourless in the wind. Elian pointed to a group of stunted trees to his right and staggered off in that direction, cursing as he slid helplessly on the loose rocks that covered the upward slope until they reached the trees.

Elian stopped to catch his breath and look about. 'Jolint. Do you agree? This is the way?'

A faint burst of woody magic tickled their backs. Jolint turned to look back and squeezed her shoulders together, then walked up and touched the rough bark of a peripheral tree. 'Yes. There's Gisela's mark.'

Perian peered over her shoulder and ran a finger over the shape gouged into the bole – a waxing gibbous moon. The impression still held a sense of its carver, a familiar trace, and the face of an old friend emerged before him: Garin, Gisela's personal guard, the man who had spent time with them and taught them to ride, to fish and to fight. He was flooded by the warmth of memory and hoped Garin had survived.

'How could she have known?' Perian asked as Elian pushed past them.

'You told her, I imagine.'

'How could I? I didn't foresee the shaman marking me for sacrifice, so how could I have known we'd pass this way on a night of the waxing moon?'

Jolint pushed him aside and followed Elian. 'One of those irritating side paths you occasionally came up with when she pushed you to it.'

He remembered it now. Gisela had pushed him, hard, forcing him to travel down so many possible futures that he had thrown up beside her caravan. They would always have come this way after releasing Elian and Jolint. It amazed him that he had been so precise about when.

The hut stood within an area cleared of trees. Healthy vegetables and herbs grew in ordered plots, and to the left of the building, almost as big as the hut, stood a lean-to stable, beyond which they could see a piebald stallion quietly grazing in the dewy grass of early morning.

Elian fell against the tree where Garin's last mark had been placed and let his head fall upon his chest. Jolint slid to the ground beside him.

Elian held out his hand. It shook violently. 'I can't go any further. I need to sleep.'

'You've been sleeping for the past twenty-plus years!' joked Perian. But his attempt to lift their spirits fell flat. He knew they couldn't go on, and wondered for the hundredth time how they had come as far as they had.

'We need time to adjust,' said Jolint. 'Our bodies have been dormant for too long. I don't have the strength to keep us both going any longer.'

Perian stared down at her curled amidst the roots. Her power always had amazed him.

Above her head was Garin's last carving. Perian ran a finger over its curves. Next to the moon Garin had carved two linked ovals, the symbol for good luck and long life. Perian hoped it was true, and he quietly breathed the wish into the wind to carry back to its carver —

'What are you three doing?' came a deep, cracked voice behind them.

Perian turned, his hand on the hilt of the knife he had slipped into his belt, and saw a crossbow pointed at his head before his eyes found the man who held it. None of them had heard his approach. An old man, bent with age, but still strong by his build. He had a shaven head and a long straggly beard, and wore a knee-length tunic bound at the waist by a leather cord. Small grey eyes stared at them unblinking, yet not unkindly, Perian thought. He removed his hand from his knife.

'Forgive our intrusion. We mean you no harm,' he said. 'My name is Perian, and this is Elian and Jolint. We have travelled a long way on foot. My friends are exhausted and in need of rest and food.'

The man didn't move or respond.

'We can pay if you would allow us to rest here for a while and share a meal.'

With two fingers, Perian carefully removed his knife from its sheath. He placed it on the ground and stepped back a few paces.

The old man stared at them for a moment longer before lowering his crossbow. He picked up the knife and walked past them.

'Come,' he said. 'Porridge is cooking and I have ale. Your friends can sleep on the floor.'

They watched him disappear through his doorway. Perian pulled Jolint to her feet and put his arm about her waist, Elian grasped his shoulder, and the ungainly trio staggered into the warmth and comparative gloom of the hut.

It was more spacious than it had appeared from the outside, going back further than could be seen from the front. Once his eyes had adjusted, Perian noted that the man had placed his weapon near the door. A small table sat in the centre of the room with bench seating either side, and to his right, in a corner, was the old man's straw bed. At the furthest end a fire danced beneath a blackened pot. Mingled with the smell of hot porridge was the aroma of dried herbs and dogs. Where were the dogs?

The man had already placed four mugs on the table with a jug of ale. He filled another jug from a bucket. 'The water's clean, straight from the spring. You look in need of that first, if I'm not mistaken.'

Perian eased Jolint onto one of the benches and poured water for her and Elian. Elian fell on his mug as a man dying of thirst, but a few gulps later his pallor changed dramatically. Perian grabbed his arm and pulled him outside, where he retched loudly beside the wall.

'Is it poisoned?' Perian whispered urgently into Elian's ear.

Elian shook his head and wiped his mouth on a large leaf. 'It's delicious. But you try drinking after so many years asleep.'

When they returned, Jolint was sipping her water carefully. Steam rose from bowls of porridge. Perian's stomach flipped over with joy. The old man watched them from a chair he had placed at one end of the table, where he held his spoon with bent fingers and sucked noisily as he ate. Perian forced himself to eat slowly and watched the others as they took a few small mouthfuls.

Perian was scooping up the last of his porridge when the dogs appeared in the doorway – a large black one followed by a smaller one with shaggy grey hair. They walked up to Elian; the black dog put its head on his knee, and a small sigh issued from Elian's lips as he scratched its ear and let his hand rest on its head. Perian knew that if Elian had the energy, he would have liked to run with the dogs.

The old man nodded at the black dog. 'Them's the reason I knew you meant no harm. Otten there wagged his tail when he saw you.'

Well done, Otten. No animal was afraid of Elian.

Elian and Jolint slept through the day, despite having eaten very little. Perian slept for a while too, then helped the old man, whose name was Morven, gather wood. He collected kindling from the forest and chopped up the logs Morven had begun to collect and store alongside the cottage. When the wood chopping was finished, he helped the old man weed his small vegetable plots and gather herbs for their evening meal. It felt good to be out and doing such simple, homely tasks after the trauma of near capture and escape. It reminded him of Esper and their life together on the marshes during his growing years: gathering water weeds, making eel soup. They were happy days full of laughter and only a few minor disasters.

He watched Morven rummage about in the soil, planting seedlings for the summer months to come. He was a nice man, quiet as solitary people often are.

Later, the two of them sat on the porch, talking and sipping ale, relaxing in the lowering sun on a wooden couch carved from the trunk of a single tree. Morven had lived in the cottage for many years, he said, having come across it while hunting. He was originally from Nor, but had left to escape the restrictions and cruelty of the king's men.

'Your friends are Farans, if I'm not mistaken. Not seen one of them in near twenty years. Not pure Farans, anyways. Didn't know there were any left on this side of the ranges.' Morven's pale grey eyes drifted aside as he searched his memory. 'Caravans of Farans were a common sight in Nor once, before King Arnden. They'd come through in spring and summer mostly. Some would hire out to farmers during the sowing and harvesting. But when things got hard in Nor, they weren't so welcome, especially after the witch and her army went through. Hearsay, of course, but what I heard was they left a trail of fear and unrest behind them. Word of their journey travelled throughout the country. An oppressed and poor people like the Norians – now, they don't need no extra trouble.'

'What happened to them – the witch and her army?' Perian held his breath.

'Heard they wandered into the barrens of Soluwi. What happened to them then I don't know.' He looked at Perian from beneath his bushy eyebrows. 'You, Perian, where're you from?'

'Rashinder,' Perian said, rather quickly.

Morven nodded thoughtfully, turning his mug about between his hands. 'Nice place, the Empire. Mostly.' He got up and went into the cottage, and the smell of biben stew burst through the doorway, followed by his voice. 'Fallen to the Darna, I heard. Is that right?'

The news was travelling fast. Neighbouring kingdoms would be fortifying their border defences and strengthening their armies. He heard Jolint answer Morven, and Elian came to the door.

'Feeling better?' asked Perian.

Elian yawned. 'I don't know. I'm too tired to work it out. My muscles ache. It's going to take a bit of work to get fit again.' He stepped out and sat next to Perian. 'Did I hear him mention Farans?'

Perian nodded. 'He was surprised to see "pure" Farans. It would seem we haven't been forgotten, though. You'll have to keep that cloak of yours handy, especially when we travel through Rashinder. If this old hermit knows Jasperen has fallen, so will the rest of Rashinder, and someone may want to gain favour with their new Darna lords.'

'That's jumping ahead a bit, isn't it?'

'Not unless you want to find out the hard way.' Perian stood. 'Let's eat.'

Elian grasped his arm before he could leave. 'Garin hid a trunk beneath the hut. Or at least, it was meant to be a hut.'

'Morven's extended it. Once he decided to stay and no one came to claim it, he built on, he said. Do you know exactly where Garin left the trunk?'

'No. He just said that we'd find a hidden door in the cupboard.'

'That'll be the food cupboard. We can have a quick look when Morven goes out next.'

But when they stepped inside, Jolint was already sorting through an old Faran trunk. She threw a coarsely woven shirt at Elian.

'Here's a change of clothes. You've been wearing those for far too long. Oh, don't look so surprised! I asked Morven if he'd come across a trunk when he added his extension.' She flashed a winning smile at them. 'The cupboard Garin spoke of was at the far end.'

Perian peered over Elian's shoulder as he sorted through an amazing array of items that Garin, or someone, had thought they might need. A rosy flash caught his eye.

'Oh, look. There's my lucky rosen bracelet!' He stretched out his hand to pick it up, but Elian grabbed his wrist.

'No! No, you mustn't touch it.'

Perian was surprised at the fear and shock in Elian's voice. 'But it's mine. I want it.' He tried to pull his arm free, but Elian's grip remained remarkably firm.

'Yes, it is yours. But it shouldn't be here. It was buried with you.'

Jolint came back to the trunk and stared at the bracelet. 'Come away, both of you. There's something very wrong here.' She turned a worried face to Elian. 'Who would do such a thing? Come away, Perian. It's a trap. Who knows what else may lie within?'

'She's right. We need to stop and think about this,' said Elian, and he stood and pulled Perian away.

Perian suddenly understood their reaction, and the danger inherent in touching the bracelet. He allowed himself to be drawn back. His breath quickened at the thought of what would have happened had he unthinkingly grasped the stone: one touch and he would have been thrown into a seer's trance, caught in the web of his own death.

Someone had been trying to sabotage their mission.

'Come and eat,' said Morven behind them. The smell of stew filled the small room as he ladled it into wooden bowls, and even though he had lost his appetite, Perian's stomach growled.

'Is there something wrong?' asked Morven. He slid onto one of the benches and laid a hand on his spoon, waiting for the others to join him.

Jolint took a seat opposite him. 'We found something that shouldn't have been there.' She plunged her spoon into her bowl as though to pierce the bottom.

Perian bent his head to blow into his bowl impatiently; steam rose into his face and he put his spoon on the table, resigned to waiting for it to cool a little. He looked over at Morven, wondering whether they could trust him. Had Morven opened the trunk and interfered with it in some way?

Jolint looked around at Perian. 'It was locked,' she said quickly.

Morven glanced up at Perian and nodded. 'I kept it, in case the owner came back. Then forgot about it until you three arrived. I could see it was Faran. Pity. I could have done with some of those clothes over the years.'

Elian turned to Jolint. 'Why don't you check it while your meal is cooling? Once we've changed our clothes, I'm sure there will be something left for Morven. He's slender like you and me.'

Jolint nodded and left the table. First, she passed her hand over the exterior of the trunk, then carefully opened the lid again, running her hand over the contents. Perian could see her projecting her senses throughout the interior, looking for anything with power. Finally, she sat back on her haunches and shook her head. 'Nothing,' she said over her shoulder.

She picked up Perian's bracelet and returned to the table, opening her hand so they could see. Perian stared at it: a circular band of rosen – the magical roseate stone. He had found it washed up on the shores of Azure Lake.

With a start, he remembered that that was the lake he had looked over before entering the forest. It occurred to him that the pile of rocks where he had dropped the horse's saddle was probably his own burial mound. But he wouldn't ask about it. The thought made him feel strange. He didn't want to know.

When he had shown the crystal to Gisela, she had used sorcery to fashion it into a bracelet and moulded it tightly about his wrist. Whoever had taken it must have cut his hand off to get it. No wonder Elian and Jolint were so shocked! Perian pushed the thought aside. Better not to think about such things. But the bracelet's presence in the trunk was certainly no mistake.

Jolint wrapped the bracelet in a handkerchief and put it in her pocket.

When Perian woke the next morning, Elian and Jolint were already outside, going through the sequence of exercises needed to strengthen their bodies and prepare them for any encounter with the enemy. They had changed into the common attire that had been left for them – rough cotton shirts and loose trousers. Their movements were awkward and lacking precision, but this would change quickly with practice.

Perian pushed himself up from his straw bed on the floor, his limbs stiff and cold. He brushed the straw from his clothes and shook it from the cloak he had retrieved from the trunk the night before to use as a blanket, then went to the fire to prod the thickening porridge with the wooden spoon Morven had left in a bowl.

The old man blocked the light from the doorway, then shuffled up beside Perian, carrying a small bucket of milk. Perian smiled at his new clothes: trousers and tunic of rough cotton, no patches or holes.

'Is there nothing in the box to fit yourself?' Morven asked.

'I am broader and taller than my friends. The clothing in that trunk is for Farans, not me.'

'And you are?'

Perian let out a hollow laugh and glanced wistfully through the window at his friends. 'A mixture.' He suddenly felt cumbersome, his muscles thick and tight. His body was stronger than a Faran's now, but he missed the ease of a quick, slender physique. He left Morven to tend the porridge and joined the others outside to do a few stretches.

'We should leave as soon as we've eaten,' said Elian. He came and stood beside Perian as he stepped forward into a lunge. 'But first, we need to discuss where we're going.'

Perian straightened and headed over to a group of old trees that bordered the cottage garden. Shading his eyes from the rising sun, he squatted at the base of a tree and studied the others as they sat on the ground beside him. He still expected to see through them. It was a shock of wonder and delight to see them solid, alive. This was the fulfilment of his greatest wish. Jolint laughed, and Elian smiled and placed his hand on Perian's arm. Perian shook his head and smiled back.

'While you are a sorcerer, Elian, and I can squeeze out a bit of magic in an emergency, we are not strong in the way that Jolint is and Cerister was. This is why I think we should find Radia and see what his plans are for retaking Jasperen. We can decide what to do then.'

'That was our thinking,' said Jolint. Her eyes gleamed as she spoke, and it occurred to Perian that she was more than a little pleased by the idea.

'East it is, then.'

Perian placed his hands on his knees and pushed himself up. He looked over the trees toward the growing light, focusing on the distant mountains and pushing aside the visions that threatened to blind him. Soon enough he would have to embrace the seer within, but not yet. He could put off another life of never-ending visions for a little while at least.

9

Perian and his companions came to the edge of the Erolon Ranges two days after leaving the cottage and Morven. From the cliff edge Perian could see over Shadow Valley, dull and colourless with the approach of evening. The top of the high cliff opposite caught the light of the lowering sun: a bright line Perian found difficult to look at against the darkening sky. He returned to where the others sat and watched Jolint divide up their sparse meal – a little cheese left over from the food Morven had given them, and some dried meat. They had eaten all the bread.

'We're a little close to the valley,' Elian said, seating himself near to the fire. 'But safe, I think. The almonos has no doubt given up.'

Elian's voice was soft, his words measured. He glanced at Perian as he nibbled on his cheese. *Safe for you,* Perian thought. He'd forgotten about the almonos until then.

He knew what they wanted, what Elian's meaningful look meant. Perian stared at their faces, full of anticipation, as he filled his mouth with dried meat and chewed slowly.

'It's time,' Jolint urged.

Perian continued to chew. They wanted him to make contact with Gisela, to tell her that they were safe and let her know what had happened. They also wanted to find out what had happened to their tribe. Had they survived? Were they safe?

These were questions that Perian also needed answers to, but he had put it off. In truth, he was afraid. Not so much of the answers he might get, but of the consequences for himself. To contact Gisela he would have to open the doorway fully, and once it was open, he would not be able to close it again and put his visions aside. And for what? To make the same mistake he'd made before, when he'd missed that crucial sign of Grison's extraordinary actions: wings tattooed across his chest?

Twilight had already enclosed them in its mystical chill, silencing the cheerful call of birds and dulling the scents of the surrounding flowers, and now, within its gloom, a dark mantle of guilt wrapped itself about Perian. A distance of his own making formed between himself and his companions. His head and shoulders slowly drooped under the weight of his misery and his growing sense of isolation.

'Your faith in my abilities is mistaken,' he said when he could stand the silence no longer. He could not keep the bitterness and disappointment from his voice. 'We cannot rely on my precognition. I may take us in the wrong direction, as I did last time.'

He put the remnants of his dried meat down on his blanket and squeezed his knees tightly to his chest, staring at the ground. Elian got up and slid his warm arms about Perian, his face pressed against Perian's cheek. The gap between them evaporated. He felt safe in Elian's embrace, but Elian's love could not dispel his sense of failure.

'She pushed you too hard,' Elian whispered against his cheek. 'We all knew that. She knew it herself. We all wondered what might have been missed in the array of possibilities you brought forth that day.' He tightened his grip on Perian and stared into his face, so close that Perian could not keep him in focus – or was it the tears that moistened his eyes?

'Fate changes on a whim,' Jolint added. 'You can't be held responsible for what does not present itself. You're the best chance we have, Perian.'

'It is possible I didn't want to see it – to see what Grison would do to me.'

Elian shifted and took Perian's face between his hands. 'You were exhausted, Perian. Stop torturing yourself. As Jolint says, the future is all in flux. You know this better than any of us. No one expects perfection, just a guide so we may make the most favourable choices.' Elian settled onto his haunches with Perian's face still between his palms. 'But I sense an unwillingness to open the way. It will come soon, my brother, whether you speak with Gisela or not. You know that. And I will be at your side. We two together, as it was before.'

A surge of anger and disappointment swept unexpectedly through Perian. 'It can never be the same.' He clenched his jaw to stop himself from shouting. 'We are different now – no longer one.' But at the look of hurt on Elian's face, he immediately regretted the words.

Elian withdrew his hands and searched Perian's face. 'We'll see. We may no longer look the same, but in spirit … Well, we'll see.'

They sat in awkward silence for a while, trying not to look at each other. If Perian were to do what they wanted, he knew he should do it soon.

He stood and walked to a small tree that bent over the abyss to stamp about, shift his mood and dislodge his resistance. He turned to let his eyes sink into the dark mass of forest. He thought of all the years Elian and Jolint had spent hidden beneath the roots of the old tree, of their tireless companionship during his growing years and their unwavering faith in his abilities – their unfailing love for him. He remembered his joy at finding them alive. That he could touch them and feel their warmth was more than he had hoped for in this life. As Elian had said, his visions would come, no matter what, and soon. Whether he reached out to Gisela or not, he could not hold them back for much longer.

He drew deeply on the crisp air and concentrated on the gusting wind as it touched his cheeks, wound about his fingers spread at his sides and pushed its way beneath his cloak, letting it blow the tension from his mind and muscles. Then he turned to face his friends again. They had been watching him and looked away quickly, as though caught in some misdemeanour. It made him laugh, and suddenly his mood had changed completely. Striding toward them, he knelt between the two and held them both close. Elian was right: they could be as they were before, even if he did feel like a great monster in their midst.

Perian refolded his blanket and placed it carefully on the ground to sit on, crossed his legs and stretched his back sideways and forward, before rolling his shoulders to find a point of balance and comfort. Then he put his hands in his lap and nodded to Elian. Jolint stood close to them, so she could hear what was being said while watching for any trouble. Elian sat facing Perian. He didn't smile. He grasped Perian's hands and held them to his lips.

'I'm sorry,' he said.

Perian knew that he meant it, but he saw no sympathy in Elian's large, round, violet eyes, for which he was thankful. Replacing his hands in his lap, Perian closed his eyes to begin his journey inward, concentrating on his breathing until he felt at peace and all thought rolled aside. Then he turned his attention to his mystic eye, located just behind the centre of his forehead. He relaxed his concentration and allowed his awareness to expand into emptiness.

Two small Faran boys filled that emptiness. They laughed and splashed in the shallows of a large lake, the water clinging to them and caressing the smoothness of their naked bodies before slowly sliding away. Elian scooped up a handful of water and flung it at Perian. It stung his eyes, and for a moment he stood motionless, the lake gurgling about his legs. Then he ran after his brother, hooting and shouting dire threats.

The scene changed rapidly: the two boys were descending large stone steps, their hands clasped together. Their small bodies looked so vulnerable, Perian thought as he watched. So beautiful.

Darkness surrounded him with a suddenness that took his breath away. He felt his body jump, and a small cry issued from his mouth. From a long way off, Elian's hand touched his knee; it anchored him, and his fear dissipated. Images darted about the periphery of the darkness, pushing for release, but they needed to wait until he had completed his communication.

He thought of Gisela and called her name, sending it out into the space beyond the physical. A spark of light pinged back at him, but there was no other response. He waited a moment, then tried again. Another spark answered his call, but Gisela's voice did not fill his mind as it should. Elian's finger pressed on his knee.

'She's alive,' Perian said. The sound of his own voice echoed strangely about him. 'But it is as if my call hits a wall and bounces back as light.'

Elian did not answer, and Perian began to panic in the loneliness of his trance. Elian squeezed his knee gently again to reassure him of his presence.

'She has protected herself with wards, Perian,' he said. 'Wait a moment and try again.'

Perian could feel Elian's tension and sense Jolint turning to look at them. He waited, then tried a third time with the same result.

Elian sighed. 'Leave it for the moment. Come back. We'll try again another time. She'll know you made the attempt, no matter how heavily she's guarded herself.'

Perian was only vaguely aware of his head nodding in response. He knew he would not be able to return, not yet.

As he relaxed his hold on the empty space he had created, the peripheral visions flooded in like a storm tide. Wave after wave of images crashed over each other, obscuring any sequence or sense. Beads of sweat burst through the pores of his skin; his stomach churned and his body began to slowly vibrate. Elian's hand continued to press upon his knee. His trance held him captive. He would have to wait for the images to outrace themselves before he could return to his physical body …

Perian's eyes opened to a starlit sky. He lay cushioned on his blanket, warm beneath his cloak. He turned his eyes to the figure that sat cross-legged beside him, one hand still on his knee. Elian's eyes were closed, but Perian could tell he wasn't asleep.

'How long?' he rasped. The words caught in his throat and he sat up quickly, gasping for breath. When the spasm had passed, Jolint placed their waterskin between his hands and he drank deeply of the cool spring water.

'Dawn isn't far off,' said Elian, his voice husky from lack of sleep.

Perian handed him the waterskin and watched as he drank. His head still echoed with voices and pain throbbed at his temples. Too long, too uncontrolled. He hoped it was just a backlog of visions that had waited for release.

'How do you feel?' asked Jolint. She knelt down beside him, next to Elian.

'Empty. Weak.'

'What do you remember?' asked Elian. He moved closer and took Perian's hand, rubbing a thumb across his palm. The gentle massage was soothing and relaxing.

'Nothing. I remember nothing. A horrible jumble that made no sense.' He looked from one to the other. 'Did I say anything useful?'

Elian snorted. 'No. You said nothing, except at the beginning when you couldn't get through to Gisela. We should wait a day or two before trying again.' He forced a smile onto his worried face. 'This is a start. It will be all right. Hopefully your mind will be a little clearer next time.'

Perian hoped so too. He looked back briefly at the images that had passed through his mind, but they began to spin about again, so he left them alone. If there was anything of relevance there, it would come again at a more appropriate time. He stood and wrapped his cloak about him; then, leaning against a tree, he stared out at the inky outlines around them to keep watch while the others slept for a few hours.

Just before setting off, Elian pulled Perian's old stick from his pack – the one he had always carried with him when they were allowed out of the wagon or taken on occasional walks into their surroundings, to use as a guide when his visions overtook him suddenly.

'You may feel a little more comfortable with this,' he said with mock formality.

Perian stared at it, wondering how he had not seen it poking out from Elian's pack. 'Is this my reward for trying to contact Gisela?'

Elian gave a little shake of his head, but didn't answer.

Perian grabbed the stick before Elian changed his mind and was relieved to find that someone had cleansed it so that nothing of his past remained. He ran his hand along the black wood, hollowed out to contain a long-bladed knife, then over the upper part of the stick, where the knife hilt fitted into an opening decorated with silver filigree depicting a clinging vine with leaves and drooping flowers. Garin had given it to him when he'd grown afraid of leaving the wagon without holding Elian's hand.

He had all but forgotten the terrible dread that had marred their periods of freedom, the fear of being blinded by his visions and the ensuing scramble to get him back into the wagon. He tried to look pleased, though in truth the sight of the stick depressed him. But when he buckled the plain belt on, he found, to his surprise, that it did give him a sense of comfort.

They crossed the mouth of Shadow Valley and travelled along the lower slopes of the Central Ranges toward Rashinder's wheat belt. They encountered only the odd shepherd or hunter and passed isolated huts and farmhouses, stopping twice to work for a decent meal and a night on straw beneath a roof. Their journey was spotted by Perian's need to stop and allow his visions to pass.

At one small village they bought horses, and when necessary, Perian was able to ride double with Jolint or Elian. Gisela had said that the Darna were obsessed with Faran slaves, so Elian and Jolint cut their hair and bound their heads with the brightly coloured material that was common in Rashinder; it wasn't much of a disguise, but it was enough. They kept mostly to themselves. No one looked carefully, but it occurred to Perian that they might need to use a little masking sorcery once they entered larger villages if there were Darna about.

They were still many days from the steppes of Porffer's Peak when they stopped on a hill that overlooked the fortified town of Crenonfelt.

Perian dismounted and knelt to pluck at the grass. 'The area Radia spoke of is three or four days beyond Crenonfelt. It is still early. We could wander through the town, perhaps sing for a mug of ale each and find out what gossip stirs the inhabitants.' He looked up at the others as they dismounted. 'What do you think?'

'I could do with a wash,' said Jolint. 'If you threaded a little magic into your voice, you could perhaps earn enough for a room and a bath as well.'

Perian laughed. 'I don't know. I could sing more than one song.'

Elian stood in front of Perian, blocking his view. 'I know that voice. What is it you truly seek in this town? From memory, Lord Amonis lives in that castle there.' He swung about and pointed to a blocky structure that rose above the crowded dwellings. 'And from memory, if nothing has changed, he is no friend of the Shanahan.'

'Precisely. If the lords of the lands are turning, we will discover it here.' He looked up at Elian, whose shadow protected him from the glare of the sun. 'My senses tell me we should have a look.'

'As always, Perian, your senses rule the day.' Elian jingled a small leather pouch at his side. 'I think we can manage a drink each without the singing.'

Perian raised his eyebrows and stood quickly. The thought of a mug in his hand and the bustle of markets and tavern rooms should have lifted his spirits, but instead, a feeling of dread passed over him as he looked down at Crenonfelt with its ruff of makeshift housing about the outer wall. He suddenly began to wonder what it really was that drew him toward the town.

The road curved down from the hilltop and past a cluster of small farms before cutting across grassland. The closer they got to the gates, the more anxious Perian became. He pushed his mare to a faster pace. Images flickered through his mind, interfering with his sight, but they moved too quickly and overlapped each other, so he couldn't grasp what they were or even hold them in his memory.

Elian pushed his horse to Perian's side. 'What is it?'

'Wait for me,' called Jolint behind them. She came up on the other side of Elian.

'Turnell,' Perian said. 'He is here somewhere, I'm sure of it.'

Jolint looked around Elian. 'What of Radia? Are they in trouble?'

'I cannot tell. I just feel that something has happened.'

The gates were still some distance away, but close enough now to make out a guard leaning casually on the wall, talking to a woman leading a heavily laden donkey. Homes of the very poor pressed up against the wall and spread in a jumble a little way back from the road, but the stench that assaulted Perian's nostrils did not come from poor dwellings, nor from any sewerage line like the ones many towns directed beyond the wall. Posts stood on either side of the road like rows of rotting teeth at the edge of the grassland.

'I hope that isn't what I think it is.' Elian's voice was muffled by the handkerchief he had clamped over his nose and mouth.

But Perian knew that it was.

He pulled his horse in as they rode between the rows of severed heads balanced precariously on posts. He wanted to look straight ahead, away from the horror, but he couldn't. He searched each face, hoping he didn't know any of them, had never met them, and wondering whether he would actually recognise anyone if he did.

Then he saw Turnell's head at the end of the row.

It sat at an angle. His left eye rested on his nose like a large congealed teardrop, and his right eye stared glassily at Perian. His death fight began to play out in Perian's mind, but was stopped short when Perian suddenly threw up down his mare's shoulder. The horse stepped sideways into Jolint, nearly knocking her from her saddle and into a head without a jaw.

Elian pulled on the mare's reins and led them quickly back the way they had come. When they had crossed the grassland they pushed their horses into a gallop, stopping only when they had passed the last farm and gained the higher ground. Crenonfelt's grotesque greeting ran constantly through Perian's head. He slid from his horse and vomited again. *Poor Turnell.* He wouldn't get that pension after all.

He sat heavily on a stone marker by the side of the road and wiped his mouth with a clump of grass, rubbed his face with his hands and pressed the balls of his palms into his eye sockets. He waited for his eyes to clear, then looked back in the direction they had ridden to see if anyone had thought them suspicious enough to follow. The road was empty.

'That was memorable,' said Jolint.

'Too memorable.' Perian stared at her as she leant against her horse. She was pale and shocked. They all were. 'Did either of you see Radia?' he asked. 'I looked, but I cannot be sure.'

'No,' said Elian after a moment. 'Do you think he's in the town?'

Perian shook his head. 'I don't think so. We should keep going and I will check as best I can when we stop for the night.'

'That'll be useful!' Jolint spat. She studied her hands for a while, then looked over at Perian, her expression a little softer. 'But I agree. We can't go back.'

'Let's keep going,' said Elian. 'If you could look later, Perian, it will ease our minds.'

Or not.

10

Perian was unable to shake the images of putrefying heads from his mind. He had heard of such practices, but never seen them himself. That Turnell's head had been amongst them made it that much worse.

Whenever Turnell flickered into Perian's mind, so did visions of the battle that had taken his life. He and Radia had bumped into a deputation from the Shanahan on their way to Lord Amonis. They'd been exchanging greetings, Radia questioning the officer in charge, when they were set upon by a troop of Darna warriors. The town was full of them, Perian realised. The spectacle of heads, set out as a warning to disruptive travellers, had probably saved his and his friends' lives.

As evening approached, they stopped at a small travellers' inn. From a seat in the corner of the common room, his hand wrapped about a mug of ale, Perian watched Elian negotiate with the landlord for a room for the night. When the haggling was over, they followed him into a room off a landing at the top of the inn's narrow stairs. A single bed stood at the centre of the tiny room and a small table stood near a window that looked out onto the stables. He tested the bed and found it hard, but at least the sheets were clean.

'Two in the bed and one on the floor near the door should do it,' Elian said cheerily. 'We can take turns at the door.'

Perian walked over to the window and peered down at the stable boys playing dice in a corner of the yard. There was a big puddle to one side where they had washed down his mare, and as he stared at it, he found himself looking into Turnell's glazed eye again. The rheumy surface expanded, and Perian watched as Turnell greeted someone he knew. Perian had seen the officer at the palace. His face smiled at Turnell, but his eyes did not. Radia greeted the officer with a surly nod. The sorcerer didn't like him. Then, suddenly, fighting broke out; Radia vanished from sight, and the officer began shouting.

'Perian?' Elian called.

The puddle rippled again to reveal Elian's hands covered in blood, then a cloudless sky filled with white almonos.

When Perian turned back to face the room, he found Jolint and Elian lying on the bed side by side, their boots placed neatly on the floor. Jolint let out a deep sigh of contentment. He stood miserably at the door for a moment while Elian and Jolint grunted happily and snuggled together on the slim straw mattress. Then, with sudden decision, he threw a ward over the lock and leapt onto the bed between them.

Elian rolled onto the floor with a thud, taking the sheet with him. 'What are you doing? There's no room for you as well.' He stood, waiting for Perian to move, clutching the sheet to his chest.

'There's plenty of room. We used to sleep head to toe when we were young, remember —squashed in those tiny wagon beds? If you'll just remove your stockings, Elian, we'll all have a good night's sleep.'

'Yes, when we were young and a lot smaller and you weren't a monstrous Darna. And I will not remove my stockings.'

'Get in, Elian,' said Jolint. 'You can asphyxiate him with the smell of your feet.'

Elian muttered something no one could be bothered to listen to and threw the sheet over the two of them before slipping in beside

Jolint again, with Perian's feet between their heads. He turned on his side and bent one leg over Perian's stomach. Perian scratched the back of Elian's head with his big toe.

Elian took a swipe at the toe. 'You're a monster, Perian.'

Perian turned over on his side to give their legs more room and bent his head to keep it from hanging over the end. Elian was right. He was a monster, and he wished with all his heart that Gisela had chosen someone else to die and be reborn.

The following day their journey took them between fields of wheat and barley and through a seemingly endless woodland where the road became difficult to discern. After a short break, they found themselves travelling along a goat track where the ground fell away steeply to the left. Gnarled trees struggled sporadically beside the path and down the slope, bent like old men by the prevailing wind. The slender trail forced them into single file, their pace slowing to a walk. Perian found the plod of the animals monotonous and mentally dulling and struggled to stay awake – until he suddenly thought of Gisela.

Time to try again. Surely she will answer me this time.

He tentatively stretched his senses a little and called to her to see if she would respond. To his astonishment, he could see her clearly and instantly. She shone in silk robes; fine jewels sparkled about her neck, and a double-banded circlet sat upon her head, her blond hair looped through it in a style he did not recognise. She turned sharply to face him, the shock of his unexpected contact clear on her face. Irritation and anger quickly rolled across her features to replace her surprise.

'It's Perian,' he said. He was breathless with pleasure despite her bewildering reaction.

He expected her expression to flow into one of delight and welcome – joy at seeing him. But instead, her eyes darkened alarmingly. Her features hardened and her mouth twisted.

'I know,' she snarled, and then she repelled him with such force that he thought his mind would shatter into pieces.

Streams of colour whirled about the magic she thrust at him, dark emotive strands stinging him like the tendrils of purple jellyfish. Around the edges, not part of the flow, he could hear voices, urgent but soft with distance. Voices he knew, but could not place, except one: Cerister. He called her name and reached into the empty space left by the dissipating flow of magic.

Then he slid from his saddle and rolled down the slope.

Elian stood with his eyes closed, clearly trying to relax, but his hands opened and closed nervously by his sides. Perian watched him from a short distance away while he collected bits of wood for Jolint to build a fire. His head still hurt from the rocks it had encountered during his fall; his scalp was covered in lumps and bruises, and he had a gash across his temple that had bled profusely and accounted for his vision of Elian's bloodied hands.

'Do hurry up, Elian, before we wither from starvation,' Jolint said crossly. 'If the sun gets any lower I won't be able to see what I'm eating.'

'Don't nag me, Jolint. I haven't done this in a long time. I have to concentrate, form a perfect picture in my mind, and you're not helping. Go away.'

She sniffed loudly and dropped to her knees beside a fire pit she had been digging out. Elian turned and frowned at her.

That Elian had waited so long to take this step was a measure of how afraid he was, and Perian wished Jolint would be a little more patient with him. He knew how Elian felt. The biggest fear was that you couldn't do it anymore. Elian had loved to shapeshift; his greatest joy had been to soar above the trees as a large bird, stalk antelope as a wolf, catch salmon as a bear. It was the perfect skill for his fun-loving brother. Perian had once been the more circumspect, but in this life, half-Darna, he had been fun-loving too – until the day Fimian's sorceress had speared his tattoo with a feeble spike of magic and partially awoken his seer's abilities. Perhaps it was the skill that determined the personality.

Clutching his collection of twigs and bits of broken wood, Perian straightened to watch Elian again. Still no progress. He flicked a trickle of magic at the lower branches of a bush, making them rustle, and shouted, 'Quick, there's a biben!'

Elian's eyes flew open. 'Where?'

Perian pointed at the swinging branch. 'There, in that bush!'

Without another thought, Elian transformed into a large black wolf, common in the northern forests, and bounded off in the direction indicated.

Jolint laughed. 'He'll be cross when he comes back.'

It had been several hours since Perian's fateful contact with Gisela. He remembered gripping Elian's wrist as Elian lifted his head from the dirt, for support and to prepare him for bad news. But Elian must have sensed his fear and shock, for he had asked no questions. 'Later,' he had said, with that patient knowing Perian had always admired in him.

But now 'later' had almost come. And Perian didn't know how he was going to tell them – how to actually say the words. He had been rejected, and they had all been abandoned; cast off.

Elian wasn't gone long. He returned carrying a good-sized antelope, skinned and gutted ready for the fire, his face shining with his achievement as he hummed quietly to himself.

Perian sat close to the fire in the fading light and growing dampness, eating without appetite. His stomach had knotted, allowing him to swallow only tiny morsels at a time. When he realised that the other two had finished and were licking their fingers contentedly, he gave up and put his still-meaty portion down on a rock at his side.

'Tell us,' said Elian. He leant toward Perian and rubbed his shoulder encouragingly. 'Get it over with, and then perhaps you'll be able to finish your meal.'

Perian rubbed his hands together uneasily and stared out at the dark shapes of the trees that surrounded them. They moved and rustled in the wind, their shadows stretching and retreating in the gentle starlight. The firelight rosied the faces of his audience, hardening and then softening their features, and the crackle of burning wood punctuated the silence like a tapping finger.

Perian squeezed his hands together and told them of his encounter with Gisela. Elian and Jolint's expressions matched his own feelings, and his voice faltered as he told them of the emotive tendrils he had felt, and of hearing Cerister's voice, for which he had no explanation. He couldn't tell whether he felt better or worse once his brief tale had run dry.

'This is a Gisela I do not know,' said Elian at last. 'Our sacrifice – your sacrifice, Perian – has been for nothing if she has cut us off.'

Jolint sat perfectly still, her face tight and pinched with disbelief and growing anger. 'This doesn't make sense,' she said sharply. 'If things don't go as expected, you work with what you have and try for the same result, or a similar one from a different angle. Our mission was to stop the Darna pursuing our people and enslaving them, to infuse tolerance and acceptance so that we could live in peace in the ways and places of our ancestors, through your influence as a Darna prince. With the Darna in Rashinder, our people's situation has become worse. But if Shanahan Leren can retake his empire, then Rashinder, at least, will still be safe for our tribe. We must do what we can to help. And no matter the outcome, we should at least be asked to rejoin them, and they should honour our attempt.'

Tears suddenly warmed Perian's eyes. 'It is my fault. It is me she blames. I didn't see the possible parallel path and I didn't see what Grison would do to me. But she will probably take you two back.'

'No, Perian,' said Elian. 'Grison wasn't the one who branded you. It was Shimester, the old sorcerer. Maltha had him killed for it. Grison was the one who arranged for Esper to take you away.'

Perian's mind whirled. How could he have forgotten such a thing? He looked back with his mind's eye, but all he could see was Grison's face hovering over him.

'Don't look so shocked,' said Jolint. 'We did tell you, but you were very young and clearly only ever remembered Grison.'

'We were there, Perian. Think back,' Elian persisted. 'The ceremony was over – the one where you were displayed to the people with your promise of sacrifice painted on your chest. Grison had just completed your royal tattoo when he noticed that the mark upon your heart had not been washed off. He cursed the slave and took the cloth from her to wipe it off himself, and that's when he discovered that it was permanent. He was hysterical with fear and rage, and no wonder. If Maltha hadn't been coming down the corridor to find out why it was taking so long, if he hadn't seen Shimester leaving the courtyard, Grison would have been put to the torch. That's what you remember.'

Something shifted within Perian. His previous life, only recently recalled, and the present one collided in a confusing pattern, nearly driving him mad. He pushed them aside and got up to retrieve the skin of ale from between Elian and Jolint, squeezing the liquid into his mouth.

'It doesn't matter who did it; the result is the same. I didn't see it and we are now paying the price.' He took another mouthful of ale, wishing he were in a tavern where he could drink himself into oblivion rather than having to share one skin between three. He passed it to Jolint before he was tempted to finish it off.

Elian sighed loudly. 'I keep telling you, Gisela pushed you too hard.'

'In truth, I don't think she wanted to see any other way,' said Jolint. 'She jumped on what you saw and forced you to pursue it.'

'Let's put Gisela aside and assume her reaction is temporary. It would be foolish to dwell too much on something we can't change. In the absence of her leadership, I think we should determine our own actions and purposes from now on,' said Elian. 'She will contact you if she needs us.'

Yes, thought Perian bitterly, *if she needs us. If she can find a use for us.* They would continue as they were and trust that their path would unfold with more clarity. What else was there to do?

'I agree with Elian,' said Jolint. 'But what of these voices, Perian? You said they were urgent. And that one of them was Cerister's?'

Perian was grateful for a change in topic. 'I'm sure of it. But I couldn't understand what she was saying. I think she was warning me about something, but I don't know what it was.' He shook his head.

'If it was a warning,' said Jolint, 'she'll come to you again in some way.' She stood to rub the stiffness from her back. 'I'm going to bed.

My brain won't cope with any more discussion.'

As Elian had suggested, Perian tried to put Gisela from his mind, but it was difficult. By the wealth of her attire, he had to assume that the Farans had found another, more prosperous life somewhere – one that was safe, where the tribe was protected and the Darna could not find them should they bother with pursuit. It even occurred to him that Gisela might have found another seer who saw a different outcome. For the sake of the tribe, he hoped this was the case.

Now he, Elian and Jolint had to find another life for themselves. But there was one question that continually entered his mind: why would the Darna bother to pursue the tribe in the first place? Gisela had never questioned that aspect of his predictions. Why not? The only realistic answer was that she knew something she had not shared with them. But now, he would never find out what it was.

They travelled across the higher slopes of Porffer's Peak for one and a half days before turning down toward the plains. Perian didn't like the cold and spent the days shivering deep within his cloak. Despite his discomfort, the crisp beauty of the landscape made his heart sing – the majestic towering pines, the happy chirping of little birds going about their daily business amongst the dark green bushes, the wondrous sight of circling hawks in an azure sky.

Jolint rode ahead, with Elian just behind; Perian was the last to leave the track for the open plateau covered by tall, tufted grass. There was no reason to suspect an ambush, so they set out across the centre of the plateau with the mountain rising above them to Perian's right and crops sweeping across the flats to his left. It felt good to be out in the open again. A chill wind tugged at his tightly held cloak as he looked dreamily up at the cloudless sky.

He didn't notice the almonos until they had flown clear of the mountain peak and their movement caught his attention. Perian counted at least thirty small white dots that grew exponentially as they drew closer at an astonishing speed. He had never seen so many almonos together before.

'What are we looking at?' he asked as he rode up beside Elian, who, like Jolint, had stopped to watch. 'Even from here I can see they are too big.'

'Shapeshifters, if I'm not mistaken,' said Elian. 'I can feel them.' He kept his eyes on the approaching birds. 'Do you want me to join them, see what they want?'

'No. They'll make that quite plain soon enough, I think.'

He and Elian eased their horses closer to Jolint, who sat very still on her shifting mount, magic dancing about her fingertips. They watched the birds drop lower and lower in their spiralling flight until Perian could see all four of the distended eyes on each, looking down at them. Without landing, they flew upward as one and back over the peak in formation.

'Shapeshifters,' Elian confirmed at Jolint's questioning look.

'But whose?' said Perian. 'Grison doesn't have the power to command such a force.'

Jolint spoke quietly to her agitated steed to calm it. 'We can think about that later. First we should find cover.' She loosened her grip on the horse and galloped ahead of them.

The image of the almonos circled on in Perian's mind as he rode after the others.

They stopped for the night in a shallow cave that was clearly a regular resting place for travellers, judging by the assortment of items piled in a corner. Thankfully it was empty now. Jolint found a snug hollow in which to place her blanket, and Elian said he would take first watch, sitting on the horizontal trunk of a fallen tree that flourished despite being uprooted. Perian decided to join him for a while.

'Do you think you can listen to me while keeping an eye out for thieves, murderers and shapeshifters?' he asked.

Elian turned to him with a smile and a knowing look. There was an air of excitement about him – the same sparkle in his violet eyes that he got when facing a challenge or the hunt. His emotions washed over and through Perian, lifting his spirits, and he took Elian's hand and squeezed it tightly.

'Are you so keen to meet other shapeshifters?' Perian asked him.

'Yes and no. There were so many of them, and their form was perfect! How could I not be curious? Are they friend or foe? I would dearly love to know. If foe, I definitely want to know.' He cocked his head to one side and patted Perian's hand in a way he knew Perian found irritating. 'Now close your eyes and tell me a story,' he said in a sing-song voice.

Perian snatched his hand away. 'Don't forget to watch for the enemy. I don't want to die a second time. Not for a long while yet, anyway.'

He released his thoughts and let them drift toward the almonos that inhabited his mind. As soon as he focused on the birds, they began to circle in on themselves, and he followed them with his inner eye.

Someone he could not see pushed him into a hall the shape of a pentagon, filled with light so bright it hurt Perian's eyes. Tears trickled down his cheeks as he forced his lids open. The walls and floor sparkled with a whiteness that made him shiver, though he was far from cold. Figures moved at the other end of the hall, but their forms were unclear, hidden by a shimmering veil.

One of the figures separated from the other. He took only one step, but his distorted face suddenly appeared to be just a few feet away. Large eyes of glacial blue stared unblinking at Perian for a moment.

'Brother,' the figure crooned.

The voice was high-pitched and broken, but definitely male. The eyes were unfocussed, yet Perian felt him look closer —

'No! Not brother!' he screeched.

The words sliced through Perian like daggers; he cried out with pain and surprise, and the light exploded, leaving him in total darkness.

Elian's face suddenly came into focus above him. Words poured from his mouth and floated about in fragments. Perian reached out for him, struggling to free himself from his visions, but someone snatched Elian away, leaving Perian alone and desolate. No light penetrated where he was, no outside sound; all he could hear was his own breathing. He shivered in the frigid air.

Remaining very still, he reminded himself that this was not reality. Picturing the flying almonos again, he sought the pathway once more, and as before, they pulled him into the hall, but this time he grasped Elian, whom he now knew was at his side. Linked arm in arm, they faced the shimmering veil together.

'Brothers,' the distorted man crooned again in his shrill, faltering voice. A frown rippled between his eyes as he focused them on Perian. 'No, not —'

'Leave them!' thundered a deep voice.

The glacial eyes grew wide, and in a sudden flurry of movement Perian was flicked from his trance.

His chest heaved and his hands shook. He had never had his own visionary pathways snapped shut by another before, with the exception of his recent encounter with Gisela. Nor had he ever encountered someone who could voluntarily participate in his seer's trance.

Elian continued to gaze ahead into the night. He sat tensely at Perian's side, his elbows propped on his thighs, rubbing his thumb across his right palm. 'Who do you think this creature is? I feel chilled to the bone. I've come out in goosebumps.'

Perian snorted. 'I don't know why you're so worried. It's me he doesn't like.' He took a deep breath and realised he was unconsciously mirroring Elian's palm-rubbing. 'I know what you mean, though. A chill ran through me too. I have no idea who he is or who else was there, but he is the servant, not the master, I know that much. Why call me brother, then change his mind?' Perian ground his heels into the gravel just to make a noise and shift the charged air. 'Whoever they are, they know where we are and what we can do, and they are more powerful than us. Worst of all, they find us of interest.'

Elian groaned and put his head in his hands. 'As if we don't have enough to worry about. It doesn't sound as though they're offering to help rid Jasperen of the Darna or stop them from pursuing our people.'

'No, they want us. Or more to the point, I think, they want you.'

'How do you come to that conclusion?'

'Because I was rejected.'

'Isn't that a good thing?'

'It would be if I didn't suspect that I'm going to end up in a dark cell.'

Perian decided to scout about to see if there were alternative possibilities to being captured by a lot of almonos. His visions were fleeting and involved uneventful days of riding. Then he saw Radia enter a large cave filled with bloated bodies, both Rashinder guards and Darna warriors. Dried blood covered a floor heavily disturbed by violence.

He cut the vision off. They could explore the cave further tomorrow.

11

The cave was exactly as he had seen it – a great fissure high on the side of the mountain, obscured by large boulders that had long ago rolled down from the cliff face above. Even from below, the smell coming from the entrance made Perian gag. He wrapped a scarf about his mouth and nose and followed the other two into a large cavern now lit by Elian's mage lights.

Flies formed angry, buzzing clouds, protesting their disturbance as they inspected the bodies. Perian's senses told him immediately that neither Radia nor the Shanahan were amongst the fallen, and this was confirmed by the brief vision that began to play out before him. He left quickly, walking far enough away to be able to breathe freely again. Elian followed.

Jolint was the last to emerge, coughing violently and swatting at a host of flying insects that followed. She leant against a tree close to where Elian and Perian stood and shook out her scarf to free it of the stench.

'That was awful. I had to come out before I threw up.'

'I believe this is the tunnel Radia referred to, the one that leads to a hidden valley,' said Elian.

Perian remembered Radia saying he would find him in the valley. He had never heard of a valley hidden within the folds of the mountain, nor had Jolint or Elian. He thought it strange, since they were Farans, and he felt sure that they would have travelled all over Porffer's Peak and the lands either side, including the Deserts of Albys on the other side of the mountain. The quick flashes he saw of the valley told him that there had been a village – *had been*. Someone had burned it down, quite recently. He also knew with certainty that the Shanahan was not there.

'Radia said that this was Leren's secret, in case he ever needed to disappear for a while,' Jolint was saying. 'The Shanessa's cousin has a small holding there.'

'Not anymore,' Perian said softly under his breath.

Elian was the only one to catch the words. He turned sharply, but Perian was caught up with circling almonos again. They were driving him mad, and he wondered if he would ever be free of them. He was certain that the distorted figure was their source, but he couldn't understand how the man had such a clear connection to him. He wondered whether his power was such that any seer would be easy prey, but he thought not. There was a link between them. He hadn't wanted to admit it, but there was something familiar in their connection. Not safety, though – far from that.

Distant laughter tinged with madness filled Perian's head, and he threw up a barrier to block it out.

Jolint began to cover her face again and grasped her horse's reins. 'Let's keep going. We can lead the horses through, though they'll need a bit of persuading to get past the corpses and flies.'

Perian placed his hand on Jolint's shoulder to stop her. 'No. Let's not go there.'

'What have you seen?' she asked.

'He isn't there, I'm sure of it.'

'What have you seen?' she asked again.

'The village has been burned to the ground. There is no one there.'

Jolint stared at him for a moment, searching his eyes. 'Let's go anyway,' she said. 'No, there's more, isn't there? What is it, Perian?'

'Almonos. There are almonos there.'

'If it is as you say, there are bound to be almonos.'

That was true. Almonos were scavengers. But the ones Perian was thinking of were not.

Jolint hesitated, looking back at him, and he smiled at her. 'Give me a moment, Jolint. I need to think.'

He put a hand to his mouth absently. There was something wrong with his vision of the village. He thought back, remembered the distant laughter and saw himself block the intruder out, but this time, he also saw clearly a fleeting image of a different village. There was evidence of fire and battle, but nothing like the devastation that had occupied the main part of his vision.

With a start, he realised he had been manipulated.

He grasped his horse's reins tightly and wrapped his face before walking quickly toward the cave entrance. 'I have been played with,' he said to Elian over his shoulder. 'The man in the white room tried to interfere with my visions – rather successfully. If he does it again, I'll give him a smack that will make him regret it.'

The tunnel was wide enough for two men with horses to walk abreast. Jolint had pushed ahead and was already at the exit, blocking out the daylight, so Elian unfurled a few light bubbles from his palm.

'Can you move forward so I can see?' said Perian.

She moved outward to allow them through. They stepped out onto a flattened area of the mountainside, and Perian noticed that the ground had been worn to dust by pacing feet and disturbed by fighting. There was no sign of sentries. A wide path to his left led down to the village below, tucked neatly in the valley. Lush pastures and crops surrounded the houses and crept up the terraced slopes of the mountains. As he'd thought, there was evidence of a raid in the blackened remains of a few buildings on the approach to the village, but to his distant eye, there was little in the village centre to suggest a battle had taken place. People moved about as they would on any normal day. A bird flew overhead and disappeared into a stone shelter near the road.

'Is this what you saw, Perian?' asked Jolint.

Perian shook his head. 'Not exactly.'

'That was a message bird I saw flying past,' said Elian. 'Let's hope the welcoming party are nice people and not thugs.' He turned and studied Perian for a moment. 'In view of their recent experience, Perian, perhaps you should put your hood up.'

Perian felt himself redden, but he could see what Elian meant. Even a mixed-race Darna would likely unnerve the villagers. He did as his brother suggested.

The road zigzagged down toward the houses. In the distance, just as they reached the edge of the pasture, four men emerged from the stone shelter. Elian rode forward to speak with them, and Perian watched their animated discussion from beneath his hood. The villagers nodded, shook their heads and pointed in different directions as they spoke.

'There are two inns,' Elian said when he returned. 'The men recommended the first, Porffer's Rest. The battle within the valley was fairly brief, evidently, and they now have lookouts on the other side, but the Shanahan has moved on to seek refuge with Ishra in Wellorn. Radia missed him by a week and left yesterday. We can follow him tomorrow after a good meal and a night's sleep.'

The inn was crowded. People talked loudly to be heard over the general din and a group in one corner bent excitedly over a game of dice. No one paid them more attention than a quick glance, but Perian grasped Elian's arm as they stepped through the door.

'I don't like this place,' he said. 'I keep seeing us, bathing and eating, sleeping. Very deep sleep. Too deep.' The image of a cart jabbed at him sharply.

Elian clapped him on the shoulder before he could say any more. 'Perfect! That's all I hope for tonight. Relax, Perian, enjoy the small luxuries!' He pushed ahead to catch up with Jolint, who was asking about rooms, then looked back over his shoulder at Perian and waved him forward. 'They have rooms at either end of the inn – the ones in the middle have been taken by friends whose houses were burned down. Come, Perian, let's fulfil your very pleasing vision.'

Perian hesitated, but pushed his concerns aside at the looks of pleasure on Elian and Jolint's faces.

The innkeeper showed them into the room nearest the stairs. It was clean and comfortable, with two beds, a washbasin and a table that seated four; a straw wreath dotted with dried flowers hung on the wall above the table. Perian peered through the window, which overlooked the stables. There were a number of horses still saddled below.

When they had finished bathing, a man brought up their evening meal and a jug of ale. Steam wafted into Perian's face as he leant over his bowl to inhale the delicious smell. He plunged his spoon into the thick liquid with its unusually generous lumps of meat and thickly cut vegetables, and ate contentedly.

They ate in silence at first, all three far too hungry to think of anything more than the food in front of them. They mopped up the sauce with thick chunks of bread, then sat back to pick at the cheese on a side plate. Perian emptied his mug of ale and poured himself another. There were some benefits to travelling with a full purse. Whoever had packed that trunk had been very generous with coin.

'This is really good ale. I don't think I've tasted the like before. Perhaps we could just stay here rather than dash about the Empire looking for a defeated Shanahan.' He yawned and pushed his bowl aside. He was suddenly very tired – more tired than he could ever remember being. He rubbed his eyes to force himself awake. 'What do you think we should do? I'm becoming bored with chasing the Shanahan from one hiding place to another.'

Elian laughed and sat back in his chair, cheerfully rubbing his belly. 'We haven't exactly been chasing him from one place to another. This is the first setback we've had, although I admit the journey has been long, and more dramatic in places than one would wish. I don't relish another long trip. Wellorn seems a long shot. What do you think, Jolint?'

'That I need to go to bed and think about it all in the morning.' She rose clumsily and put her hand on the table to propel herself onto the nearest bed. 'Ale's too strong for me. Must be the long hibernation.' But her words were largely lost in the mattress.

Elian yawned and massaged his temples. 'Do you think you can control this person who interferes with your visions?'

Perian thought he was slurring his words. Perhaps the ale had been stronger than he'd realised.

'He is easily blocked,' he said in a halting voice. Like Elian, his speech was beginning to slur. He shook his head to clear his mind. 'I will know the difference between a true vision and one of his in future. His thoughts have a tang to them, if that's the right word …

We all have a personal redolence, a sense of who we are, and his has a touch of madness to it, like a spoilt child or a bully. Something about me confused him. I wasn't what he expected, but what that was, I could not say. But I'm not overly worried about him at the moment, more surprised.'

Elian pushed his chair back. 'In that case, I'm going to bed too.'

He attempted to stand, but slid to the floor instead. Perian tried to rise and help him, but his body wouldn't obey.

His vision blurred. His eyelids closed.

The sound of his head hitting the table was distant and painless.

PART II

12

Perian woke slowly to the sensation of being on a boat.

He knew he wasn't by the sound of wheels crunching noisily upon packed soil and the crisp night air brushing over his exposed left cheek, smelling of pines and the sweet tangy perfume of the white-flowered samarill tree. It contrasted starkly with the pungent odours of hay and animals that pressed into his nose from the boards beneath his face. His body rolled slightly from side to side and bounced on ruts and lumps in the uneven road. His hands were bound awkwardly behind him, putting pressure on his right shoulder. The bonds were not overly tight, and there was no numbness in his limbs, yet neither his legs nor his arms obeyed him. The magic that ran through the bonds was the most likely source of his paralysis.

He could feel Elian beside him, touching his back as they rolled with the movement of the speeding wagon, but when he opened his eyes slightly, all he could see was the wooden side of the cart and, when he rolled to his left, the glimmer of trees lit by mage lights that floated alongside them. Mingled with the sound of wheels was the rapid pounding of hooves on either side and up ahead.

His mouth was dry, and when he tried to swallow, he noticed that a thick cord had been tied about his neck. Soaked in magic as it was, he assumed it was to prevent speech, but decided to test it later. He ran a little magic into the cords that bound his hands to see if he could loosen them, and was punished for his effort with a searing pain that ran the length of his arms and jolted his heart.

Someone close by quietly suggested he should save his energy.

It wasn't long before the troop entered a tunnel. When Perian rolled to the left, he noticed that the mage lights had vanished and the light now came from clusters of luminous moss placed at regular intervals along the wall. The tunnel was smooth and wide, big enough for the cart and men on horseback either side. The guards wore long white scarves tied about their heads and knotted at the napes of their necks, with a length of narrow material hanging down their backs over loose hair. The guard beside him had dark blond hair, but he had caught glimpses of white and red hair on others. He couldn't see their faces clearly.

The sounds of talking and movement drifted down the tunnel from ahead, but also from the side tunnels they passed. At one point they rode into a great noise like that of a marketplace. The people stopped talking as they passed. The smell of spices and herbs filled the air – cinnamon, lavender, rosemary – and Perian strained his eyes to the left and glimpsed a wide domed roof painted with fruits and vegetables, antelope, biben, pigs and fish. He was right; this was an underground night market.

A rumble of excited chatter followed as they passed into another tunnel, but not long after, the cart stopped. Perian recognised the crunch of men dismounting and the calm, commanding voice he had heard on and off during their journey. Someone grasped his feet and pulled him toward the end of the cart, then lifted him out and laid him on the ground. One of the guards removed the binding about his ankles and pulled him to his feet with a quick movement that made his head spin. He wobbled a bit, but his legs held, and he stamped his feet to enliven the muscles. Beside him, Elian did the same, nodding to assure Perian that he was all right.

He looked around. Where was Jolint? The cart was empty as far as he could see. He swung his head back and forth, searching for her, until Elian caught his eye and shrugged. Perian's inability to ask the guards where she was filled him with fear for her safety. Then it occurred to him that they may have left her behind at the inn. She was probably still sleeping off the drug someone had slipped into their ale.

Setting his concerns for Jolint aside, he quickly turned his attention back to what was going on around him, and only then did he realise that they had been abducted by Farans. He could understand that Farans might mistake *him* for the enemy, but not Elian. He turned to Elian, forgetting for a moment that he was still unable to speak, but he didn't need to say anything. Elian looked as shocked as he was.

Unlike any Farans he had ever seen, these guards wore a uniform – the head cloth, and white thigh-length tunics bound at the hip with plain leather belts from which long knives hung. Loose white trousers were tucked into soft doeskin boots. They were shapeshifters, Perian was certain of it: the circling almonos.

With a gesture of their heads, their assigned guards urged them toward a smaller tunnel with an entrance decoratively framed in luminous moss. They used smooth sticks of dark wood to point the way – additional encouragement.

The hall they came to at the end of the tunnel was not as bright as the one in Perian's vision, and no tears appeared in his eyes. The high domed roof bore a picture of the sky, its blueness broken by a few puffy clouds and a small group of white almonos in formation. The guards stopped about a third of the way in.

'Kneel in the presence of our lord,' said one, and the guards pressed their sticks into the backs of his and Elias's knees. Perian tipped forward, unable to balance his painful descent with his arms bound, but recovered quickly and looked up toward the figures at the far end. Unlike in his vision, there was no concealing veil in front of them; they sat upon two thrones raised above the ground on a wide platform covered by a turquoise carpet. The older Faran, on the left, sat upright and commanding, but the other was more interesting. He sat crumpled in his seat, leaning to one side, two sticks resting on the decorative arm of his throne. His face was badly scarred and his large eyes stared at them, glacial blue. Those eyes alone told Perian that this was the man who had tried to manipulate his visions, and the unrestrained power about him confirmed it.

Perian threw up a barrier just in time to stop a blatant probing. The lord turned a sharp eye on his companion and tapped the man's hand sharply, and the probing stopped.

'I am Lord Aronaye,' said the older Faran, without getting up. He waved his hand at the man by his side. 'This is my son, Risenor.' His voice was deep and clear and it travelled through the hall so easily that it sounded as though he stood at Perian's side.

The name sucked all the energy from Perian's body, and he was glad that he was already on his knees. He felt Elian jump in surprise next to him.

Lord Aronaye. The man who sacrificed hundreds of innocent souls in the cruellest of ways at each festival, to appease his god and increase his tribe's wealth. For fun, Gisela had said. Perhaps he and Elian were to be the major entertainment at the next festival; Risenor would be ecstatic when they discovered that Perian was already branded for sacrifice. He began to vibrate with rising panic, and the images he had held at bay since entering the hall danced before his eyes, no longer controlled. His barrier evaporated.

At the lowering of Perian's shield, Risenor pounced, and the shock of his invasion brought Perian back to his senses. With a surge of anger he flicked back a mental bolt of lightning, and Risenor shrieked and jolted in his chair. His sticks fell to the carpet and rolled off the podium to clatter across the floor.

Lord Aronaye stood quickly, his face suddenly dark with anger. 'Stop, both of you!'

Risenor whimpered and held his hands tightly to his chest, his fingers curled into fists. His face twisted, briefly showing his teeth. Aronaye glanced down at his son, then slowly walked toward the prisoners.

'You are Perian and Elian.' His face softened with each step, and a smile played about the corners of his mouth. Risenor echoed their names softly in his high, broken voice.

Aronaye stopped close to Elian and gently stroked his cheek. Elian flinched backward, away from the caressing hand. Aronaye's action and the look on his face reminded Perian of his father when he had been captured at the Palace of Jasperen. But this man wasn't Elian's father, so what were his intentions?

Aronaye nodded at the guard. 'Take him to his chambers.' He looked back at Elian as the guard pulled him to his feet. 'I will visit you later.'

Elian turned large, frightened eyes at Perian as it occurred to both of them that Aronaye must intend Elian for a pleasure slave. Struggling despite his useless arms, Perian lunged upward and threw himself bodily at Aronaye.

The guard's stick cracked across his back, knocking him to the ground before he could reach his target and pinning him to the floor. Risenor made a sound in his throat that Perian assumed was laughter.

Aronaye remained perfectly still until Elian had been dragged from the hall, then cleared his throat and began to walk slowly around Perian's prostrate form, still held in place by the guard. Perian stopped struggling. He was beginning to feel like a beetle squirming beneath a collector's pin.

On the third turn, Aronaye gestured and the guard lifted his stick, allowing Perian to stand slowly. No one stopped him. He rose to his full height and Aronaye walked around him again, appraising him from head to toe before stopping to face him and placing his hand flat on his chest. Perian clenched his teeth, every muscle of his body taut.

Without warning, the Faran ripped his shirt in two. Perian lurched backward and into the guard, his face burning with a sense of helpless exposure. He thought he would explode from his terrible need to shout and strike out, but Aronaye ignored his obvious discomfort and ran his finger along the wings of the sygrilien several times, slowly and deliberately. Perian thought he was going to faint.

'Gisela has wasted your talents,' Aronaye said at last, looking directly into Perian's eyes, holding his gaze. 'She knows nothing of powerful seers and their special needs, or how to train them.' He did another circuit around Perian. 'There is much you should know, Perian, much that is your right to know, having sacrificed so much. But as an oracle, you must discover these things yourself. It is imperative that you see the truth.'

Aronaye shook his head slowly and stepped away. 'My guard here will take you to a place where you can do this – where you can allow your visions to run free, without direction or manipulation.' He glanced over his shoulder at Risenor. 'He will not be able to penetrate the walls of your chamber, nor will anyone else. You will be safe. Despite what you believe, I wish you no harm.' He waved at the guards and turned back toward his throne. 'I will know when it is complete. You can see Elian then,' he said over his shoulder.

Perian knew where he was going: a dark cell. The guard touched him on the shoulder, and when he didn't move, another guard took his other arm, and between them they forced him roughly from the hall. They marched him along a series of tunnels and down sharply descending steps until they entered a room devoid of furniture or decoration.

One of the men quickly opened a heavy door opposite the entrance. 'Two guards will be here at all times,' he said. 'Don't bother to scream or shout; no one will hear you. Nor will they hear if you bang on the door.'

He removed Perian's bindings. His release left him even more unsteady on his feet and he thought he was going fall, but before he could disgrace himself completely, the guard pushed him through the doorway into the dark hole.

'There's a water trough along the left wall and a bucket along the other,' he said as he pushed on the door. It closed with the wheezy thump of a hermetic seal.

Perian sank to the floor and wrapped his arms about his bent knees. He felt the bolt slide across, though he didn't hear it: no sound or light penetrated the thick darkness about him. His isolation was complete. He shouted at them to let him out, though he knew they could not hear. He shouted again, more for the relief of being able to hear his own voice than to serve any other purpose, but even that sounded dull within the blankness of his prison. His whole body shook with fear and desperation, both for Elian and himself.

He sat for a long time, or so it seemed, with his back against the wall, listening to his own breath. *Breath!* He wondered briefly where the fresh air came in, but it didn't matter; he was just grateful that it did. Herbs and straw had been scattered over the hard-packed ground, giving off a pungent aroma that was a reminder of life beyond the cell walls, and after inhaling the purifying scent of rosemary for a while, he stopped shaking and his mind began to clear. He realised that his eyes were closed, and opened them.

With no visual or auditory stimuli to distract him, Perian's mind tumbled from one thought to another until it came to a sudden halt on Jolint. Soon it would be morning, and assuming she had been left to sleep off the drug, she would discover that they were gone. What would she do? Aronaye had probably taken care of that in some way: lied to her, threatened her or evicted her. He had no way of knowing.

Then Elian's face filled his mind's eye. Elian's likely fate filled him with a dull ache of sadness and impotency. He could not help Elian any more than he could help himself, and he would go mad if he dwelt on it. At least they weren't destined for mass entertainment – not yet, anyway.

His thoughts lingered on the way Aronaye had looked at Elian – lovingly, but not licentiously, despite what he had first thought. It touched something deep inside him, a yearning that he hadn't been aware of before, but there was no time to dwell on this unexpected emotion. Without warning, that yearning burst into a flood of visions that rolled out rapidly and with exceptional clarity. He was used to being taken over suddenly, but nothing compared to the flood that rushed through him now.

He watched Aronaye play with three laughing little boys of four or five years old. The scene moved on quickly to Aronaye showing them how to use their small wooden swords and knives. With a shock, Perian realised that the boys were identical triplets, rare in any nationality and unheard of amongst the Farans. The scenes of domestic happiness filled him with an aching love and a desire so profound and agonising that he thought he would break apart.

His anguish cut the vision, its sense of comfort and love replaced. He could see himself and Elian struggling with lessons in a moving wagon, along with Jolint and Cerister. Juxtaposed as it was with the previous vision, he saw for the first time how isolated they were and how loveless their childhood had been, and he longed for the happiness of the triplets.

As though drawn by his desire, the triplets again filled his sight. They clung to the skirts of a woman who was struggling to hold on to all three at once as Gisela rushed toward them in battle dress. Two Farans raced past Gisela and wrenched the boys away from the woman. She let out a terrible cry of anguish that should have frozen the miscreants on the spot, and ran after them, her arms outstretched. One of the boys broke loose and ran back to the woman just as Gisela flung a lightning strike at her. The woman fell to her knees and tried desperately to push the boy away, but he clung on even as her clothes blazed about her.

Aronaye and his guards erupted through a doorway. He threw his cloak over the burning woman and beat frantically at the flames; Perian could sense a battle taking place just outside his view, but he knew without seeing that Gisela and the other two boys were gone.

The visions receded, leaving Perian panting and exhausted, consumed by despair. He sobbed loudly into his hands, wondering how neither he nor Elian had remembered this. Gisela must have blocked their memories. How else could they have forgotten and accepted her so completely? He had recognised the woman immediately: she was the mother of the triplets – Elian, Risenor and himself.

The little boy in her arms had survived, mutilated and deranged by Gisela's heinous act of cruelty: Risenor. And now he understood Risenor's confusion, and Aronaye's reaction to them. Aronaye was their father – or Elian's father, at least. He wasn't sure where he stood in that relationship anymore. He had another father. Yet he was still Perian, Elian's brother, Aronaye's son.

He shouted and raged at the injustice that had been done to them – done to him. He hammered his fists against the floor and the walls till they felt sticky with blood. He was still a part of his brothers, yet not.

He cried himself to sleep amidst the barrage of memories that had been blocked from his mind.

Later, he woke hungry. He shivered. For a long time he couldn't move. Eventually, on hands and knees, he slowly began to explore the cell. He determined that it was circular and had a circumference of approximately ten feet, and when he stood, he could touch the domed ceiling with his hands. The room reminded him of a large kiln. On returning to his knees, he discovered the trough with his forehead as he bent forward, and he drank greedily from cupped hands, then plunged his head beneath the cold water and rubbed his face vigorously. His knuckles hurt, reminding him of his previous frenzy. He had found no food tray during his exploration and wondered if they intended to starve him to death. He hoped not. There were many ways to die, and that wasn't on his preferred list.

Sliding down the wall nearest to the trough, he sat cross-legged on straw he'd scooped into a pile. He wasn't sure that he completely trusted Aronaye, but he did believe he meant him no harm. It occurred to him that this was a training cell, not a prison, and having stared into the black void for a while, with little else to distract him, he released himself to the images that hovered in his peripheral vision, thinking that he might as well see the extent of what he could only perceive as a spiralling queue. That was what Aronaye had put him here for. He had said, more or less, that Perian would not be released until it was complete, whenever that would be.

His isolation again brought about visions of a clarity he had never experienced. He felt as though he were two people: an observer, and at the same time a participant, fully engaged with what was happening as he watched himself walking slowly along an avenue of giant ferns. The tips of their fronds touched as they bowed under a tunnelling breeze. Early sunlight escaped the feathery leaves, dancing across a path of flat river stones, and he watched as Darna warriors walked solemnly behind him. He felt no threat, but whether he was a prisoner or not, he was unable to tell. Elian padded at his side as a wolf; Perian's fingers wound about his soft grey fur.

The scenes changed rapidly. He was in Jasperen Palace surrounded by Darna warriors, Rashinder's double-headed kroyer beneath his feet. Visions he had no time to comprehend flashed past in a stream, stopping briefly on a bloody battle. Then, suddenly, he found himself staring at … what? He wasn't sure. Spirits? Yes. Spirits of the dead, gathered in a group behind a barrier he could feel but not see. He stared, fascinated, as the spirits drifted about, some pushing their ethereal hands and tormented faces against the invisible wall.

The group swerved aside like a shoal of fish to make way for others that came up from behind, and to his horror he realised that he knew some of the latecomers. Two were the leaders of other tribes that had followed Gisela beyond Rashinder and into the Kingdom of Nor; they spoke to him, but he could not hear what they were saying.

Then Cerister appeared.

She pushed her way forward and placed one palm on the barrier, beckoning Perian closer. To his amazement, he was able to place his palm against hers. His heart expanded with a terrible need and he felt his longing for her travel through the barrier; she closed her eyes in response, and tears fell through her lashes to flow down her cheeks. Then she gathered herself, and stared into his eyes and spoke, so rapidly that he couldn't understand what she said. He asked her to slow down, but she seemed not to hear him. Her silent words continued to fly about him faster than his tired mind could grasp. Then, before she had finished and before he could ask her to say it again, she was sucked away, and Perian found himself alone in dark, empty space. Its vastness and beauty would have been pleasant at any other time, but Cerister's message continued to float about him as though the words were material things he was unable to catch.

He closed his eyes and willed himself to return to his cell, but instead he was overtaken by a new stream of visions. The Darna Empire spread out before him, ravaged by disease and famine. He saw the Deserts of Albys obscured by clouds of flying insects, and gasped in foul winds that came from the east.

On and on his visions rolled, until after what seemed like days or weeks, he woke up.

He slid sideways onto the floor, shaking and wasted, with no strength to stand or even crawl to the trough to relieve his parched throat. He lay there for an eternity, trembling in his distress, the wispy strands of his visions still floating through his mind's eye, but he didn't try to catch them or make sense of what he had seen. At least he hadn't been terrorised by the dark stranger, but he was too tired to wonder why.

Eventually he drifted into a blessed sleep without dreams.

13

Perian floated in a warm pool of violets. Soft flowerheads soothingly brushed his skin and strong, gentle hands lifted him through the air and placed his wet body on a bed of gossamer. The same hands patted his skin with more gossamer and he felt a groan of pleasure vibrate through his chest. Finally, he was placed on what he imagined was a white, puffy cloud. It crossed his mind that he might have died, but then, with a jolt, he remembered that dying wasn't like that. Where was he?

It didn't matter. Wherever it was, it was preferable to where he had been.

He was beginning to sink peacefully into nothingness again when the air stiffened and a voice he vaguely remembered tugged him back.

'How is he?'

'As you would expect, Master, still drifting between consciousness and sleep. He will improve with food and rest.'

Lord Aronaye came across the room to sit in a chair at Perian's bedside.

'Thank you, Rollamin. See to it. In the meantime, leave us.'

Perian snuggled deeper into his puffy cloud. Since his life wasn't threatened in any way, he had no desire to rush into a conversation, but when Aronaye put his index finger to the centre of his forehead, his eyes flew open involuntarily, and he was pulled back into full awareness with a speed that made his empty stomach heave.

'You did well, Perian. I didn't expect you to last three days.'

'Did you expect me to die? Or go mad?' Perian's voice cracked from lack of use. Or was it from shouting? He couldn't be sure.

Aronaye smiled at him. 'No. That I have never wanted. I checked on you every day and would have taken you out of the cell had I felt that you were near the end of your endurance.'

They remained in awkward silence for a while. Aronaye crossed his legs and fiddled with the edge of the sheet before looking directly at Perian. 'Shimester was my man in the Zamir's court,' he began. 'He filled your sorcerer's tattoo with a magical trace as a way for us to locate you and get you back. That the magic travelled to your sacrificial marking and made it permanent was entirely unexpected – and fatal for Shimester, as it turned out.'

Perian turned his head sharply toward Aronaye. 'Get me back so you could rip me apart personally?'

He immediately regretted his outburst. Aronaye put up his hand before he could say more.

'Let me finish, Perian. They will be here with your food soon, and I want you to know this now before we are interrupted.' Aronaye took a sip of water from a glass on a side table. 'Shimester recognised you as soon as he saw you, even as a babe. He could see Elian and the other two around you and he listened to you talking with your minds, and then aloud when you had speech. It was hard for us to believe that you were still my son – my Perian, reborn to a Darna Zamir. He listened to the stories Elian told you and tested you, asking questions that in your innocence you answered with the truth, although you did not appear to know where the information had come from. Sometimes you got your answers from Elian or one of the women. Through Shimester's questioning we also learnt what Gisela had done to you, and how she had used you all.'

Aronaye's words confirmed what Perian had already seen while locked away in his cell. A cold bitterness began to form within him, but his downward spiral into self-pity was halted by Aronaye's soft, compassionate voice.

'The sygrilien wings had already been painted onto your chest when Shimester placed his magic into your sorcerer's star. These finely painted wings are, as you know, symbolic, a gesture to show the people that even those of royal blood belong to the Sky God, through his intermediary the Great Sygrilien, and they sacrifice themselves for the Empire. No one believes it, of course; the wings are meant to wash off once the ceremony is over. But yours didn't, and Grison had to intervene to save you from the priests and their barbaric practices. Shimester was executed and you were sent away with your mother's slave, and without Shimester to release the signal, you were lost to me until the mark was activated in Lord Fimian's castle. I sent my guards out immediately to watch you and await our opportunity. That we found Elian as well was a blessing I had not expected. I had assumed him dead. I could hardly believe the reports that he was whole.'

Aronaye's voice caught, and he stopped his narration to stare down at his hands and the sheet scrunched up between them.

Frustration and anger boiled within Perian's chest. He was angry with Gisela, with himself, with everything, and most of all with his own impotency. And now, Aronaye's hypocrisy. He thought he would choke on his need to scream.

'A "barbaric practice", you call it.' He squeezed the words out through a clenched jaw and locked teeth. 'Yet you are also guilty of such practices.' His voice shook with emotion.

But the look on Aronaye's face was one of shock, rather than anger. 'What do you mean, Perian? What did Gisela tell you?'

Perian glared at him. 'She said that you raided nearby villages for sacrificial victims and strung them out by tens and twenties on festival days, and more in between if there was a drought or a famine, or even just if a member of your family fell sick.' Once the words were free they sounded ridiculous, and he felt foolish. But at the time, within the confines of their wagon, it had been terrifying and real.

'No wonder you both looked so frightened when I told you my name. But it's not true. The Farans haven't practised human sacrifice since the early days of the tribes, and even then it was only ever in times of drought. The Sky God with his voracious appetite for human flesh is a Darna invention, as is their reverence for the sygrilien.'

There was a soft knock on the door and Rollamin stepped inside, followed by two others with scars about their necks that marked them as nirilla slaves from the kingdom of Nirilla in the south, beyond the Deserts of Albys. They were tall and slender with overly large hands and feet, and Perian knew they would each have a double-twisted circle branded into their left shoulder. One carried a bowl on a tray.

Aronaye stood to leave. 'I have not told Elian the truth yet. I would like you to do it. He will believe you as he would not me. You will be allowed to see him when you have eaten and Rollamin here says you can.'

Perian had fallen into a deep sleep after swallowing his last mouthful of broth. When he woke, he thought he was alone. Muted light came from a single clump of moss that sat in a shallow bowl on the wall. The bowl was in the shape of a small, coiled snake, its scaled skin made of tiny pieces of rich green mosaic, and the room was shaped like a large pod, with his bedhead of plaited vines placed along the flat side. The peak of the domed ceiling was decorated with what looked like a knot of geckos, common in the desert regions.

He yawned and stretched. His body felt luxurious beneath the sheets – strong and well. It was amazing what a little broth and a good sleep could do to revive the body and mind. He sat up slowly and swung his legs over the side of the bed. There was an oval table with four chairs directly in front of him and to the right a mat with three compact cushions, and to his surprise, there was also a man sitting cross-legged on one of the cushions. He was one of the nirilla slaves who had attended him with Rollamin.

'You look better,' he said, smiling, then stood and bowed very low. 'I am Bellerin'a'marco, but everyone calls me Bell. I have been assigned as your personal servant.'

Perian hesitated. He'd never had a personal servant before, at least not since he was four. Bell smiled at him and waited. His genuine happiness was infectious and Perian glowed in response. He slipped from the bed and happily allowed Bell to dress him in the clothes he had laid out over a padded stand. When he had finished, Bell led him through an opening in the wall to the room where they had bathed him. There was a large tub at one end where the wall and ceiling merged in the shape of a scallop shell. To his right, Bell stood beside a long mirror in which he could see himself.

'We measured you while you slept. They need a little adjusting, but they will do for the moment, I think. The tailor will come by later to make alterations.'

Bell left to order food and Perian stared at himself in the mirror. He wore a long, sleeveless tunic of leaf green that covered loose white trousers. The tunic highlighted his green eyes and set off the darkness of his hair. In his heart he was Faran, but in his reflection, he saw only a Darna wearing Faran clothes. Then, as he studied his face, he could also see his Faran heritage in his olive skin, the fine structure of his face and the wideness of his slightly angled eyes, his lack of facial hair. So, neither one nor the other. As a Faran in his previous life, he had thought himself part of Gisela's tribe – all false. Who was he? Where did he belong?

He rubbed his eyes to ease his rising anxiety and confusion and turned back into the main room, where he sat quietly at the table until Bell returned with thick, warm soup and bread. His stomach gurgled at the aroma, and for a while he could think of nothing other than his hunger.

'There are no windows,' he said when he had finished, wiping his mouth with a napkin. 'Are we still underground?'

'This is a city within the mountain. There are no windows anywhere, but there are balconies in the upper section that overlook the valleys. It's morning now, so I have been instructed to take you to one that is in the way of the sun. Master Elian is waiting for you there, I believe.'

Perian's heart leapt at the mention of Elian's name, but then his spirits plummeted. It was going to be a difficult conversation, and as terrible a shock for Elian as it had been for him.

Sunlight sparkled through a curtain of glass beads a short distance from Perian's chambers. Past it, he could see Elian looking out over a waist-high wall; he turned at the tinkle of glass as Perian stepped onto the balcony threshold, shading his eyes from the sudden glare. A small frown creased Elian's forehead, then he took two long strides toward Perian and threw his arms about him. Perian basked in his sense of completeness, tight within his brother's embrace. They held each other for a long time before Elian pulled away and took Perian's arm, leading him across a mosaic floor depicting a pool dotted with water lilies to the balcony wall.

The balcony looked over a green valley dominated by mountains with high rocky peaks on either side. Nestled in the valley was the village of Ollamore, where they had stopped, tiny within the vastness of its surroundings.

'The valley and village are part of Silaven – Aronaye's domain – along with this underground city.' Elian spread his arm to encompass the mountain they stood on. His eyes shone with delight, yet the crease between his brows remained. 'What happened, Perian? Did they hurt you? I have been told nothing.'

A servant pushed through the beaded curtain, carrying a tray of refreshments – wine and small savouries. He placed them on a low table of carved black marble and left with a short bow. Clasping Elian's hand, Perian led him to the brightly coloured cushions that surrounded the table.

'No one has hurt me. They put me in a cell that I believe they use for training seers, a place where no sound or light penetrates. It wasn't pleasant, but Aronaye believed I had been badly trained and needed to relearn a few things. And after my experience there, I have come to understand that none of us were properly trained – or really, trained at all.' He sipped on his wine. Its tartness tingled across his tongue. 'In the cell my visions ran freely, and I was able to see the truth of what has happened to us. Who we really are.' He turned and looked into Elian's eyes. 'I have so much to tell you, but first, what of Jolint?'

'She continued on to find Radia. If she hadn't caught up with him after two days, she said she would return to Ollamore and wait for us. But she hasn't come back, so she must have found him.' Elian sipped his wine before continuing. 'Aronaye sent me down to speak with her the morning after we were taken. Jolint was beside herself. She thought we'd been murdered.'

'What did you tell her?'

'The truth – that we had been taken by Aronaye and that they'd locked you away somewhere. I told her I didn't feel we were in any danger, but we couldn't leave at the moment, and said that since Radia had only been gone a day, she should try to catch up with him and we would follow as soon as we could.'

Perian raised an eyebrow. 'How did she take that?'

'As you'd expect. But in the end I was able to persuade her. It was hard to see her go.'

Perian squeezed Elian's hand where it rested on his lap. 'I'm glad she took your advice. I feel our path will take us in a different direction to hers for a while.' And then he took a deep breath and told Elian about his visions.

Elian listened without interruption, and once Perian had finished he was quiet for a long time, staring absently at the surrounding mountain peaks.

'It is hard to believe that Gisela could do such a thing,' he said at last. 'Why?'

'I cannot tell you. Aronaye will need to explain that. But I thought much about our childhood in between the visions, and since. The more I think on it, the stranger it is. We were never alone, always locked in that wagon with Cerister and Jolint, or chaperoned. Can you really say that in all those years we ever got to know anyone else other than Garin? Ever mixed with the people? Do you recall the tribe at all? Were they happy and peaceful? Or were they aggressive and warlike? I have no idea.'

Perian lay back on the cushions to look at the sky, clear and blue, uncomplicated.

'She used us. She used me for my visions, she used you to spy on other tribes and even the factions within our tribe, and she used Cerister and Jolint to keep the renegade factions subdued and then to fight her battle. When I look back, knowing what I now know, I can see that she ruled an army, not a tribe. That man who lived in the cottage, Morven, even told us that. He said "the witch and her army". I knew exactly who he was referring to, yet I didn't let myself notice his description at the time. On some level, I think I already knew even before I died, but the knowledge wasn't something undesirable at the time. Who knows what really took place while we were growing up, and before we were sent on that final mission?'

'I know that when it went wrong she abandoned us,' Elian said.

'Why was the mission so important, and suddenly so urgent?'

Elian turned to look down at him, his face red with anger. 'As to urgency, I don't know. We never questioned her decisions that closely – you remember. But you know why it was important! She wanted control of the Darna, to stop them persecuting the remaining tribes and gaining a kingdom in which they could travel freely or settle as they wished. Our ancestral home, she said. She controlled you, and through your position as a Darna prince, she would have taken power. It shames me now to think that she manipulated us so completely – that we sacrificed our lives so willingly for her ambition. And what for? To inhabit the famine-ridden, disease-infested kingdom you saw in your vision?'

Perian closed his eyes as a bubble of understanding burst in his head. 'She didn't want the Darna Empire,' he said quietly. 'The prize was Rashinder.'

Elian's eyes widened. His brows knitted with a question.

'I told her,' Perian said. 'I saw it in a vision. That was when the questioning began. You remember. She dogged me day and night, and then suddenly she sent us off on one of those blissful camping trips with just a couple of guards. Jolint was stung by a bee and set a tree alight with the shock, and her arm swelled so badly that we had to return early. I always found it odd that we were kept back while one of the attendants went ahead to advise Gisela that we were coming.'

Elian nodded. 'And then she persuaded you to die and become a Darna prince, and Cerister and Jolint and me to lie in that tomb for years. She wasted Cerister's life. Faran against Faran, Jolint said.' He sighed. 'She took the other tribes by force or trickery, didn't she? There was always strife between the groups. That's why.'

The bitterness and hatred that accompanied Elian's words ignited Perian's own feelings; he found it hard to breathe and was forced to sit up and put his arms about his knees. 'She must pay for what she's done,' he rasped. 'But we must think clearly, and not let our anger interfere. First, I want to hear Aronaye's side of the story. Only then can we make an informed decision as to what we should do next.' He looked over at Elian. 'If he will let you go, that is.'

'What do you mean?'

'You're the only one of his three sons who is intact – not damaged by Gisela in some way. You are what I used to be and what Risenor should have been ... Would have been, if she had not burned him. If I were Aronaye, I wouldn't want you to leave, ever.'

'And I don't,' boomed a voice behind them. 'Nor you, Perian. As I told you before, even though you have another father now, you are still my son.'

14

Perian swung about to see Aronaye standing in the doorway. Elian stood abruptly. 'Have you been there all along?'

'I just arrived. I coughed, but you didn't hear. You have been here for many hours; I had hoped we could sit together for a while before the evening meal.'

Perian's throat tightened and his chest filled with unexpected warmth at the sight of Aronaye. He smiled and indicated that he should take a cushion. Servants followed Aronaye onto the balcony with trays of cheese and fruit, more wine and water.

'This is your private balcony,' Aronaye said once the servants had gone. 'It faces north and is sunny most days, and has a nice view over the valley and the village.' He curled his legs beneath him and leant over a plate of fruit, selecting a date. 'I see by the look on your face, Elian, that Perian has told you who I am and what Gisela did to you both.'

He paused, his features tightening slightly into an expression of deep sadness as he stared past the fruit still poised at his lips.

'Even after all these years, I'm not sure why she did it. I had seen her once or twice at the Winter Festival, when all the tribes came together, and then again at the meeting of leaders, after she replaced old Frish when he died unexpectedly. Why she was given the leadership, no one knew. Frish had four children of his own; it should have gone to the eldest. Of course the other leaders questioned her, but all the documents were in order and Frish's children did not contest it.

'You boys were five when we took you to the festival for the first time. You were the talk of all the tribes – so rare, so beautiful. All the sorcerers, both the powerful and respected and those not so powerful, came to our tent to see you.' Aronaye's eyes shone with the memory. 'To have three living triplets was a miracle, but to have three so powerful in the way of sorcery was a sign. The Magi had closed meetings to discern what such a sign meant. They spoke to you individually and together, but I was never privy to their findings. The Magi were always a secretive group.'

'But you're a sorcerer. Weren't you included?' interrupted Elian.

Perian also wondered why Aronaye had not been included in the meetings, particularly since it was his sons who were the focus of their interest.

Aronaye gave a short laugh. 'A weak one, as was Gisela at the time. Only the most powerful and wise are called to be members of the High Magi; a council of mages. They are the pre-eminent leaders of the sorcerers, and often advisers to the various tribes. They include and answer to no one. Whatever it was that the High Magi saw caused them to leave their tribes and wander off into the desert – even the Felfar mage, who had been my dear friend since childhood. No one has seen or heard of them since.'

'Gisela had little power,' said Elian. 'Someone else performed the magic required to preserve our bodies in that tomb while our spirits roamed free – a man I'd never seen before.'

Perian looked up in surprise. He had already died by the time the others were entombed, and Elian had never told him about it in detail. In fact, he knew nothing of what had happened to the others once he had gone. He had just assumed that their fate had been the same as his until he found them alive in the tomb beneath the tree. He couldn't think now why he had not asked.

'She took us all to the great lake beside Morlust's Forest,' Elian said. 'Only Garin and another Faran were with us. I was still holding Perian's hand when Gisela threw a rod of light into his heart.' Elian turned to look at Perian. 'The force of it threw me backward. You shouted with pain and stood rigid for a moment, clutching your chest. Then you were gone and your body was a heap on the ground.'

Tears ran down his cheeks as he spoke. Perian wiped them gently away with his thumbs, then grasped Elian's hand tightly to his chest.

'How did she explain that?' he asked, as calmly as he could. He found he was shaking. He hadn't remembered that bit, but his rosen bracelet would have shown it to him had he touched it – along with Gisela's true feelings and motives, buried in the magic she had hurled at him. He suddenly understood that the bracelet hadn't been placed in the cottage trunk as a trap after all. Someone had been trying to warn them.

'She said that you had completed your preparations, and she wanted to do it quickly before you had time to think too hard and become frightened,' Elian said in answer to Perian's question.

Elian looked back toward Aronaye to include him as he told them how Cerister and Jolint had been sent away to a battle that neither understood. Cerister had been mortally wounded there and the strange mage had taken the three of them to the tomb beneath the big tree. It was very old, but didn't appear to have ever been used. Elian, Jolint and Cerister had lain down on the slabs and the mage had put them to sleep; their spirits had then gathered and joined Perian, who already awaited his rebirth.

Aronaye's eyes widened at the mention of a mage, but then he shook his head. 'It seems to me that this mage did little. The real power was in your own awareness, and your ability to manipulate your disembodied spirits – a feat beyond my comprehension and that of many a mage, I imagine.'

A hint of memory stirred within Perian but would not come into focus. Even so, the mention of this man filled him with dread. 'What did this mage look like?'

Elian appeared surprised at the question. His eyes searched Perian's. 'Ordinary, save for the darkness about him. My height. His face and hands suggested that he had spent some time in the desert. His blue eyes were set deep within his skull, with great bushy grey eyebrows arched above them. He never removed his hood, so I cannot say what colour his hair was.' He tilted his head as if to question Perian.

Perian felt himself go pale, but he said nothing and shook his head. He was sure that this was the figure in his nightmares, both from his childhood and more recently. The cloak, the darkness – it all fit, and yet it could be someone else, since he never saw the man's face. There were ways to find out, though, now that he had a description. Next time this phantom appeared within a dream or a vision, Perian would uncover his identity.

They sat in silence for a while, then Aronaye stood and straightened his clothes. 'I will see you at the evening meal. I want you to meet your stepmother and your two half-sisters.'

Aronaye and his family had gathered on a balcony that stretched out from the dining room, a round room with the usual domed ceiling. Black lines stretched outward from the centre of the dome to give the impression of a tent. Painted scenes of mountains and green valleys covered the walls.

The family was engrossed in conversation, but turned as one when Bell announced the arrival of their two visitors. Elian entered first, followed by Perian, who banged his head on the lintel of the low doorway. Smiling happily, Aronaye strode forward to greet them, Risenor at his heels, but the three women left on the balcony stared at them as though in shock. Their attention was on Elian, and Perian could see why: he and the oldest daughter were so alike that no one would ever mistake them for anything but brother and sister. They both looked like Aronaye; Perian wondered why he hadn't already seen this resemblance in Elian.

The women's eyes turned to Perian where he stood still rubbing his forehead, and the mood shifted slightly. The older woman walked quickly toward them, to cover that initial reaction, Perian thought, and Aronaye introduced her as his wife, Lipheneli.

Perian's discomfort didn't dissipate, even when they sat down to eat on cushions around a low dining table. His legs were too long, the cushion too high, and in the end he had to sit on the floor to give himself more room. He felt out of place amongst these slender, graceful Farans with their light-coloured hair and long facial features. The women stared at his thick black mane, his long arms, the tattoos on his forearms, the knees that threatened to invade the personal space of those either side of him.

'You're a Darna prince!' exclaimed the youngest daughter, Millini.

The surprise in her voice was unmistakeable. Or was it distaste? Hadn't Aronaye told them? Perian's face burned hot. He put the offending arm beneath the table, and Risenor, who sat between Aronaye and his eldest daughter Patria, laughed in his squeaky way and showed his teeth again. Perian wasn't sure if it was by accident, due to his scarring, or a snarl. He suspected the latter.

To Perian's left, Aronaye patted affectionately at the knee that pointed at him like a blunt arrow. Lipheneli gave her daughter a cross, meaningful look, then asked Perian if he felt better. He smiled at her and confirmed that he felt quite well. After all, he hadn't been unwell, as far as he remembered – merely incarcerated in a dark cell and starved for three days.

But Esper's training in etiquette and easy conversation in any situation, with anyone of any social station, had missed this particular scenario out completely. He could think of nothing to say and concentrated instead on the display of food set out on the table until the women released him and focused on Elian, who blossomed under their attention. They asked him whether he remembered his childhood with Risenor and Perian, and it seemed to him that their reference to 'Perian' was in the past tense, as though he were deceased and not sitting at their table. Well, that Perian was deceased, after all. He was living evidence of that.

Then Lipheneli touched Elian's hand and said how wonderful it was to have him home. That she didn't extend this welcome to Perian too was like a blade to his heart.

He withdrew into himself and watched, drinking too much wine and eating his food too quickly, because what else was there to do? Nirilla servants arrived with more food and cleared away empty dishes. When they had filled everyone's glasses again, Aronaye took Perian's arm and led him to the balcony. The fresh night air lifted his maudlin mood, and he leant on the low wall to gaze down at the valley of pines below, then up to the mountain peaks on either side and, beyond them, the starry sky.

'It's beautiful,' Perian said. 'How have you managed to keep your city, the valleys, hidden?'

'Sorcery and illusion. I have gathered together the best in the magical arts – many from slave traders who were unaware of what they were selling.'

Perian grunted contemptuously.

Aronaye turned to look at him. 'I see you disapprove of slavery. So do I. There are no slaves here, Perian, even amongst the servants. Certainly, they were all chosen and purchased because I could use their gifts, but each is paid like any servant and free to leave if they wish. Very few do. Slavery changes a person for life, and it is hard to find happiness after. But here they are offered a new life where they are valued.'

Perian turned to face Aronaye and pushed himself upright with his elbow. 'Forgive me. I assumed they were bound to you. As you say, once a slave, always marked a slave. But Bell is a very happy fellow, and Rollamin is more than content, I feel.'

Aronaye smiled broadly. 'Yes, I believe they are. I thought you would benefit from Bell's happy nature. But as I was saying, some come from slave traders, some are invited, and some wander in from other tribes.' Aronaye sipped his wine in silence for a while. Loud laughter came from the room behind them and Aronaye glanced over his shoulder. 'It is difficult for them, as it is for you, Perian. You will all find it easier in time.'

Perian looked at Aronaye's face, so like Elian's. He wondered how long he would stay – and how long Elian would want to stay. Would he leave without his brother?

Aronaye leant forward to rest his arms on the wall and stare out at the valley. 'Stay with us a while, Perian. Learn to enjoy what a loving family can offer. If you will let me, I would like to train you, help you to tap into your full potential and control your visions so that you can see while remaining fully aware. Both as participant and observer.'

Perian thought about how free he had felt before his visions returned. If Aronaye really could release him from the constant uncertainty and crippling incapacity brought on by sudden and uncontrolled visions, he would take it.

'I would like that,' he said without hesitation.

'I am to take you to Lord Aronaye's chambers,' Bell announced when Perian emerged from his bath. He held out a robe for Perian to slip into. 'I believe you are to have breakfast with him.'

'Oh!' A tremor of excitement ran though Perian. It had been two days since their dinner with Aronaye's family. Perian had spent the time trying to relax and exploring the city and valleys with Bell as his guide, but his outings had been marred by his visions. Twice Bell had had to find somewhere to sit and wait patiently for Perian to recover, and another time he was forced to find a wagon to bring Perian home. His lessons with Aronaye could not come fast enough.

He had hardly seen Elian, whose days were taken up by training. He was receiving specialised instruction from various shapeshifting masters and enduring hours of rigorous coaching in the use of the long knife. On top of this, he trained with the elite Almonos Guards in the early hours of the morning. Elian was almost speechless with weariness in the evenings. Perian suspected that Aronaye had made sure he was kept busy so he had no time to mingle with the populace, since he was so obviously Aronaye's son. Aronaye would want to wait until Elian had decided on his own future before any formal announcement to the people. Despite all precautions, rumours whistled through the streets and hallways, according to Bell.

'Is Elian coming?' Perian asked now.

'No. He is already flying over the valleys and desert with the Guards.' Bell rolled his eyes. 'Thankfully, seers don't need to be airborne or sitting in time for the rising sun.'

Perian agreed with him. Much too early.

Bell led him past Aronaye's family quarters to his personal chambers further along the corridor. The main door opened onto a circular meeting room with a large, round table surrounded by simply carved chairs, their seats covered in an array of coloured cushions. It reminded Perian of a multicoloured daisy.

They continued down a hallway on the left, passing a small library and a servant's room. The door to Aronaye's study stood open at the end. Like Perian's bedroom, the study was shaped like a pod, but along the flat side were doors leading to a balcony. Perian stopped to stare at the ceiling. Palm fronds met overhead to create an umbrella of green as though the observer stood beneath the trees. Slender trunks peeked out from between the foliage along the walls and an irregular skirting of red and buff represented the sand of the desert.

On the balcony, Perian found his father seated at a low table covered in an array of food and surrounded by cushions. Aronaye smiled and pointed to a flat padded mat. The mat provided more space for his long legs, but Perian wasn't sure he would ever get used to sitting on the floor to eat.

They talked about general things over their meal – Perian's tours about the city and valleys, Aronaye's plans for a small garden – before Aronaye led the conversation toward Perian's training.

'Bell has told me of your occasional incapacitations,' he began. 'Since he was to care for you, I felt it only fair to warn him of what to expect,' he added quickly before Perian could feel betrayed. 'I asked him for his observations on these events, as an outsider, so I could see more clearly how to help you; and help you most certainly need.'

'And can you?' Perian closed his eyes and steeled himself for the answer.

Aronaye patted his arm. 'As I said, you just need to be trained properly. I am no seer, and I would have preferred that you be trained by a master as Elian is being trained. But seers are rare, and ours left with the Magi. I can most certainly help you with control, which is of course the first step, but for absolute mastery you will need to find another. Such things happen on their own, and a master will find you when the time is right.'

Perian hoped so, but control was all he hoped for at this stage.

'First, tell me what appears to trigger these visions.'

Perian sat for some time, trying to recall what had sparked the three most recent events. The first had been in the marketplace when he'd placed his hand on the side of a wagon full of second-hand clothing and inadvertently touched an old scarf. The previous owner's life and death had played out in his mind, followed by other things that were completely unrelated. The second had begun when he was watching young boys playing ball, and before the last, the worst, he had merely been looking at the sky.

When he had finished explaining, Aronaye nodded his understanding. 'You must learn to trust your visions, Perian. Trust that they will not hurt you.'

Perian was about to say that they didn't hurt him, but Aronaye put up his hand against the protest.

'Your hurt is not an injury. It is that you have no control, and that the visions have taken away your freedom and the small joys of your previous childhood, such as they were, and threaten to take over your future life. I would like to see you embrace your visions as they should be. At the moment you form a backlog that bursts through, as it did when you stared at the blank canvas of the sky. If you will be guided by me and can bear it, you will spend several hours a day in the seer's cell, allowing your visions to flow. In the cell there is nothing else to do, and you will not feel as though you are missing out on anything of interest. Then we will begin the breathing exercises needed to help you push through oncoming visions and hold them at bay until you can sort them out at your convenience. This will also help with scrying.'

Perian was a little alarmed at the idea of spending any more time in the cell. 'How many days will I have to visit the cell?'

'I believe you will come to love your visits to the cell; a place of tranquillity for seers such as yourself. We begin your lessons in three days.'

Bell showed him the way to the seer's cell later that morning. The passageway that took him to the spiral staircase leading down into the depths of the rock ran off the main marketplace, two levels down from his living quarters. At least he'd have no trouble finding his way back.

That first visit was a long and harrowing experience filled with battles and misery. This was made worse by the fact that he missed lunch and only just arrived back at his quarters in time for an early dinner with Elian. After Perian had listened intently to tales of Elian's exploits during their meal, Elian fell asleep in the middle of Perian's description of the hours he had spent in the seer's cell.

The next day was unremarkable and boring, since he had no visions at all. The third day was also uneventful until he bumped into a lady juggling two small children on his way out and had to rush back to his cell and close the door.

That afternoon he met Aronaye on the balcony of his study for his lessons in breathing.

'It is my belief that uncontrolled visions are, in many ways, similar to unwanted and deeply emotional thoughts that will not go away,' Aronaye began. 'So my advice will be the same as I would give any student who needed to control unwanted thoughts: when you feel your visions coming on, breathe deeply and slowly. As you exhale, relax your mind and shoulders, and at the same time imagine you are breathing into the vision, gently pushing it away. When you can, release the vision and watch until it is finished. You must always find time. Give it space to reveal itself. This is your gift. It must be seen. If you keep to your promise to set it free as soon as you have found a suitable moment, your visions will learn to trust you and wait.'

'You make it sound as though the visions themselves are intelligent.'

Aronaye shrugged. 'Perhaps. I think it is the mind taking some control of the wild, magical side of our nature. We sorcerers harness and direct our magic with our minds; I see no reason why visions are not the same. The mind and magic need to be trained as a dog is trained to fetch and a bird to take messages.' He uncurled his legs and stretched them out. 'Preparing to enter a deep trance is beyond my experience. But deep, centring breathing will, I believe, make you more receptive.'

After those first few days, Perian spent part of each day with Aronaye, practising his breathing technique and discussing any problems, and part in his seer's cell or reading the numerous books and scrolls in Aronaye's extensive library. In the evenings he dined with Elian, and often with the family.

Following that faltering first week, Perian's technique improved immeasurably. With every day he gained confidence in his abilities and more control over his visions. Once he had achieved a certain mastery over them, Aronaye helped him apply the same technique to scrying. He gave Perian objects to take into his cell so that he could follow the traces left upon them: a stone, a piece of jewellery, a woman's handkerchief. Everything he touched became a potential vehicle for information.

His scrying was not merely a way of determining potential futures, but a way of connecting to the whole fabric of existence. The world that Aronaye opened up for him was rich and always unexpected. Everything and everyone he came into contact with he saw in a new way, and a depth of compassion and respect for all things, both animate and inanimate, expanded within him. This was true rebirth, not just a change of body or circumstances: he had been reborn into a world of wonders he had never suspected was there, and as he shed his coat of anger and resentment and embraced who he was, with all his half-Darna, half-Faran attributes, his heart blossomed.

He and Elian had been in Silaven for nearly two months. Perian's many hours in his cell had already shown him he needed to leave, and he became increasingly anxious to pursue his destiny, whatever that may entail. He felt safe within his father's domain. It had allowed him to grow. But voices from his future whispered down the tunnels of time, and he knew he needed to be beyond Silaven's protection to give those voices clarity.

Elian had not yet decided on his own future, so Perian waited. If Elian decided to stay, he would go alone.

Elian began to have regular meetings with Patria – clandestine meetings, but ones that everyone knew about. Then one evening, as Perian and Elian stood upon their balcony, gazing at the stars, Elian announced that he was ready to leave.

'It's time to go, Perian. We've been here long enough and I know you are anxious to be on your way.'

Perian searched his brother's face to see if this was truly how he felt. 'What has brought on this sudden decision? You haven't fallen out with Patria, have you?'

Elian laughed and cocked his head to one side. 'No. I have learnt all I need to, and the tension between us has been resolved. I can now leave knowing that I will be welcome when I return.'

Perian speculated that the 'tension' Elian spoke of was to do with the leadership succession, but he didn't ask. Elian would tell him later if he wished. But no matter what came to pass in the future, Perian knew that he and Elian had a home to return to, and life amongst the Felfar was very appealing. A teasing love had eventually grown between himself and Aronaye's family, with the exception of Risenor. Aronaye's absolute love as his father still made him glow.

He had pushed his visions to see if they would return, but his desire was too great and the pathway had remained closed to him. He could wait; if it was there, it would reveal itself in time.

15

Silaven's street tunnels were thermally heated and only a sudden snowfall along the ranges, as seen from the various balconies, signalled one of the upper mountain's regular cold snaps. Time spent on their balcony dwindled to only fleeting excursions across the mosaic to the wall in order to admire this or that aspect covered in snow.

They had thought to wait for the snap to pass before setting out, but the icy chill was lasting longer than usual with no end in sight, so they decided to leave Silaven anyway. When they finally set off, Perian thought longingly of the warmth they had left behind. He and Elian rode against a bitter wind that whistled between the conifers growing in abundance over the slopes of the Middle Ranges. Despite his woollen shirt, padded waistcoat and thick cloak, he shivered and his teeth chattered uncontrollably. He could barely see from beneath his hood, pulled tight around his head. His ears hurt and he had lost feeling in his nose.

He consoled himself with thoughts of the warmer climate of the lower plains, which were not subject to 'cold snaps', and of the north, the direction in which they travelled. In the north, he recalled, there was very little difference between winter and summer temperatures and even deciduous trees rarely lost their leaves. Soon he'd be complaining of heat.

Day turned early to evening with the arrival of thick clouds that blocked the sun and its meagre source of warmth. 'Let's stop and build a fire before I f-freeze to death,' Perian stuttered. His breath came back at him from within his hood, hot and damp.

'Just another half hour,' said Elian. 'By then we should come across the first of the Silver River's tributaries. Aronaye said we would find shelter there.'

Perian looked up between the branches. The clouds were moving in obeyance to the wind and those that followed appeared darker than the ones currently travelling overhead. He hoped Aronaye was right, and that Elian's timing was accurate.

The omens were good. They arrived at the first tributary earlier than expected. There was an abundance of cover beneath a large rock overhang that ran deep enough to be a cave, and the rain clouds had held onto their load.

Perian brushed down the horses, warm against his frozen fingers, and gave them oats while Elian hunted for their dinner. He had only just finished setting up the fire when Elian returned with two small bren, skinned and gutted. They drank from a wine bladder that Bell had given them and watched their dinner drip noisily onto the fire with a sense of deep contentment. Perian's face and hands tingled from the heat.

A great streak of lightning sizzled through the sky and lit up the forest, followed by a sudden and tremendous clap of thunder that made the ground shake. Elian nearly dropped the hot bren leg he had been juggling. Within seconds, rain fell from the sky to the accompaniment of another rumbling thunderclap. The wind swirled and sprayed them briefly with a fine mist that settled into a determined downpour, rendering conversation almost impossible without shouting.

The noise isolated each of them within a wall of sound. Elian shrugged and licked the grease from his fingers, then lay down on his blanket. Perian watched him snuggle down beneath his cloak and close his eyes, his breath easing into sleep. *How does he do that with such speed and ease?* Perian was bone-tired from the cold and from riding all day, and he longed to rest. But he knew from experience that it would be some hours before he was able to drift into the deep sleep he needed, especially when the voices of a vision pressed upon him as they did at this moment.

He and Elian needed to know where they were going now that they had launched themselves into the world. Perian wrapped himself in his blanket and leant against the wall to stare into the cascade of rain that flowed over the ledge above. The fire flickered with the breeze and shadows beyond moved with the flame – mostly. He looked a little closer, but decided he had imagined the discordance.

A light trance came quickly once he had released himself to it. The path ahead was strong and consistent, and made him feel sick with fright. They needed to return to Jasperen.

He was overwhelmed by fate's stubborn consistency. All subsequent visions stopped, leaving a blankness he wished would swallow him up. No, that wasn't what he wanted. Things changed all the time. He just needed to take control and ensure that whatever the future held was through choice and not weakness.

As he began to slide back from his trance, a dark shadow crossed his vision and distant laughter rumbled with its wave-like movement. Laughter of the insane.

There was no mistaking who it was: the mage of his nightmares. The sound reverberated around Perian, hurt his ears and left him feeling weak. He froze, half in and half out of his trance state. Too shocked and afraid to continue his return, and to go back into a full trance would surely be unwise.

The laughter stopped suddenly. Perian returned to the cave and awareness at a speed that left him dizzy. The curtain of rain shimmered with an unnatural darkness, then all was still.

His heart hammered in his chest. He was limp and weary. He thought of waking Elian. But for what – comfort? Protection? To share? He gazed at his brother, smiling in his sleep as usual. How could he disturb such peace? It could wait until morning.

Nearly a complete moon cycle after leaving Silaven, Perian and Elian rode through the straggly outskirts of Jasperen. Perian had jumped at every loud noise and constantly stared into shadows for the first two weeks of their journey, convinced that the mage stalked him. But, without further overt sightings, he had recovered his equilibrium by the time they rode through Jasperen's outer township and on past the main gates.

Within the walls, the town was crowded and bustling with a confusing amount of activity, so they stopped at the first inn they came to: the Windy Path. Perian thought the name appropriate for their journey. They were given a modest room at the top of the stairs, with two beds backing onto the corridor wall, a washstand on their left and a shelf for clothes to the right. Opposite the door, a table and two chairs had been placed beneath a window that looked out over the main street. The noisiest room in the house, but conveniently placed. They would be able to see what was going on in the street and hear the comings and goings of the residents. The close proximity of the stairs would provide a quick escape – as long as the enemy weren't already on their way up.

They slept through much of the afternoon, until the noise from below drew them downstairs to eat and listen to local gossip. The room was crowded, hot and stuffy, filled with the smell of hard work and nervous energy. They found a space at the end of a table by a small paned window that looked out onto the roadway. The two men who shared their table were easily recognisable as travelling merchants by the soft, wide-brimmed hats on the bench seat beside them. One had a string of small square silk samples wrapped around his wrist like a multicoloured bracelet. The merchants' conversation was of little interest, revolving mostly around the dropping price of their wares, but they also complained of the bullying tactics of Darna buyers, and the silk merchant grumbled that his usual clientele had suddenly found his wares unacceptable.

Perian turned his attention to another table close by, where three women and a man were discussing the new slave market. He listened for a minute or two out of curiosity, but shut them out once he realised that they accepted and even sanctioned this addition to their city. Slavery had never been banned in Rashinder, but it had not been generally approved of. Social opinion seemed to have changed quickly since he and Radia had fled the capital, even amongst the lowly.

They were into their second mugs of ale when the merchants left and three men from the provinces swept onto the vacated benches. They nodded a curt greeting as they sat. One of the men pulled off his soiled headcloth and used it to wipe the sweat from his face, and another shouted for the waiter and waved his arm; the three sat in morose silence until a jug of ale arrived, then began talking in low, angry voices. Initially, Perian wasn't paying much attention to their conversation, until someone mentioned prisoners.

'Cruel to keep 'em locked up without knowing,' the man with the headcloth said. He absently rubbed the material over the table.

'Not knowing, you live in hope,' said a bald man to his left. He had a profuse amount of hair growth in his ears that reminded Perian of little nests. 'They let the servants go, I heard.' He looked up at the third man, who was unusually thin. 'You know if they've asked ransom, Willem? Lot of coming and going when I arrived two days ago.'

Willem clutched his mug with spidery hands before answering. 'Exchange, more like it. Demanded an offering of each lord in Rashinder, as I heard it. If none arrive by day afore solstice, the family member in the cell gets put up for sacrifice, or their neighbour's family member. As I heard it, as I say.'

Perian and Elian had encountered several soldiers of the Sky God on the road, but only then did Perian understand what they had been doing. The summer solstice wasn't far away, and Perian realised with a pang that this would be the first big sacrificial event since the taking of Rashinder. It would be a grand affair. Since just about every lord in the Empire would have attended, or been represented by close family, at the Shanahan's festival, this was a serious threat – one that most would comply with regardless of their opinion on sacrifice.

From the gathered victims, Grison, as the Zamir's representative, would choose those worthy of the Sky God; this dubious honour had been ceded to the Zamir by the priests in the early days, when worship of the Sky God had first arrived in Darna. Perian had always thought it was a sop to let the Zamir think that he had some control and a position of importance. In reality, the priesthood answered only to itself.

Later, Perian lay awake, listening to Elian's slow and regular breathing. He ached with exhaustion, and his muscles still twitched from the exertion of their long journey, but the tavern talk kept sleep at bay. Slaves and sacrificial victims competed on a seemingly endless wheel of misery.

Eventually he got up, pulled the blanket about his shoulders and sat at the table. The street beyond the window was empty, save the occasional stray dog that moved between the shadows. He didn't light a lamp; his thoughts were clearer in the dark, and the landlord had warned them that guards patrolled the streets at night, looking for excuses to disturb and search private premises.

His mind returned to the locals' conversation about the slave market. Such cruelty had not been approved in Rashinder before the Darna conquest. Gisela had always told him that the Faran people were actively sought as slaves – not just by Darna, but in all the other kingdoms too – but his mother had been Faran, and she hadn't been a slave. And Gisela's tribe had passed through many kingdoms without violence or abductions, as far as he knew; with the exception of the twelve she used to persuade him to die, that is. A lie and more lies that he and Elian had believed without question.

He shook his head in disgust at their naivety, wondering whether the other kingdoms even used slaves as Darna did. Perhaps. But he now suspected that Gisela had lied about the extent of slavery and demand for Faran slaves to frighten them; to keep them close and compliant. And she had used it to persuade them that his rebirth into Darna royalty was to stop the pursuit of Farans for slavery in their ancestral homeland. Did the Faran people even originate in Darna? Or was this another lie? He was sure now that her goal had been Rashinder; not for their tribe and all Farans, but for herself, and all her lies had been in pursuit of this.

His mind drifted to the Felfar and Aronaye's lands of Silaven. Presumably he, Elian and Risenor had been the reason for Gisela raiding Aronaye's camp, but was that all? What had she threatened Frish with to make him name her leader of his tribe, and his children to make them give up their rights? Aronaye's tribe, he knew, was considered first amongst the tribes. Had Gisela sought that position for herself through the abduction of Aronaye's sons? There were so many questions he had not asked when he'd had the chance; his mind had been so focused on improving his abilities, and on trying to fit in and accept who he was.

He returned to his bed and, finding sleep at last, dreamt of a man in a white robe bound at the waist by a thick belt. He had never seen a High Mage, but he knew that this man was one. The mage stared at him, motionless at first, then with a smile, he beckoned. His fading figure was replaced by a raven flying over miles of desert, followed by a large almonos. The Deserts of Albys.

Perian woke with a start, then slept erratically until morning, when he was roused by the smell of hot, watery porridge.

'Get up!' Elian called.

Perian pulled the blanket up over his head to block the foul odour, but Elian tugged on his bedding and pulled it away.

'Get up and eat. We can plan our day while savouring the delights of a Jasperen breakfast.'

Perian gave in and sat at the table to stare at the unappetising, salty mess in his bowl. He took a chunk of bread from the pile on a central plate and banged it noisily on the table. 'Yesterday's bread,' he moaned.

'You're meant to soften it in your porridge.'

Perian pushed the bread into his bowl. The porridge reminded him of the deadly mud pools of the marshlands, but he ate it anyway, and when he had finished, he leant back in his chair, picking at a grain husk that had jammed itself under his gum, thinking of his night visitor. The mage's appearance was clearly a summons, but why, he could not imagine. It would take weeks – months even – for him to travel back to Silaven and across the Deserts of Albys to find the High Magi, but Elian could do it in a few days. He had little doubt that the almonos in his dream vision was his brother.

'How would you feel about flying back to Silaven?' Perian asked.

Elian was gazing through the window, crunching contentedly on his rock-hard bread. He turned to look at Perian with wide, suspicious eyes. 'Why?'

Perian took his time in replying, choosing his words carefully. He decided not to mention his dream vision, nor the High Magi; he'd let the raven do that.

'There are some questions I failed to ask our father before leaving. I cannot say why I feel the answers are so important. I just feel that I need a better understanding of Gisela's intentions before we decide on our next move. We determine the future with the choices we make now, and I don't want to make any more mistakes.'

Elian took a deep and exasperated breath. 'If you hadn't made that mythical mistake, we would never have found Aronaye or learnt who we really are. I don't deny that it's been a difficult journey, but it's been preferable to living hidden in that caravan forever. For me, anyway. I can't speak for you or Jolint.'

A weight of guilt that Perian hadn't noticed he still carried lifted. He smiled at Elian, then laughed. 'I hadn't looked at it like that. But I agree – this journey has been far more interesting than life in the caravan. I am a master of our destiny, after all!'

Elian threw the remainder of his bread at Perian. It hit the window and fell to the floor with a thump.

Perian snorted. 'See how hard it is. Only good for donkeys!'

Elian laughed, but gave him a sideways glance.

'Will you go?' asked Perian. 'You'll only be gone for a day or two, and the food is better there.'

'Three days. It's a long flight and I'll need to rest.' He stared out the window again, a smile of pleasure slowly spreading across his face.

'See, you like the idea.'

'I do,' Elian admitted. 'So, what is it you're so desperate to know?'

'I want to know just how much of a threat slavery has been for the Faran tribes. Do the Darna actually seek Farans out for slavery, and persecute them more than the slaves of other races? Do other kingdoms do this too? Was Darna really Gisela's ancestral land? And I want to know more about the Felfar and Silaven. Why did the Felfar stop wandering as the other tribes do? Why are they considered the Head of the Tribes? But most of all, I want to know more about the High Magi. We know they left after the meeting at the Winter Festival, but what can he tell us of them before that?'

Elian threw his head back. 'Is that all? It doesn't sound very urgent or even necessary to me.'

'I doubt that it is, but I can't sleep for wondering. The same questions revolve around and around my head, and I need the answers so I can see clearly where we are heading.'

'And what will you do while I'm gone? It's too dangerous for you to walk the streets alone here. You must promise not to go out until I return.'

'I think I can manage that. Unless there's a raid on the inn, I should be safe enough here.' He swept his arm about to encompass the room. 'It's larger and more comfortable than a seer's cell, and at least I get fed!'

16

Perian spent most of that first day in quiet contemplation, but by evening he was already beginning to wonder how he would manage to stay locked up in one room for the duration of Elian's absence.

'Staying in our room is a non-negotiable condition of my agreeing to your, in my opinion, unnecessary request,' Elian had said. To ensure Perian didn't break this condition, Elian had pre-ordered all his meals and supply of ale, so he couldn't even punctuate the hours with a visit to the dining room.

He went to bed early and slept soundly until well after sunrise. A sharp knock was followed by the insipid smell of weak porridge drifting under the door. Perian scratched at his head and rolled over until he more or less slid from the bed, dragging the blanket with him.

From the window he watched the start of another busy day. People were already scuttling back and forth; everyone was in a hurry. Carts filled with goods passed by on their way to the market square, and young boys herded pigs or sheep toward the animal pens and meat market. Travellers and messengers weaved about the general flow. A group of Darna warriors crossed the busy street to peer in the window of the inn, then moved off, presumably satisfied that there was nothing of interest within. *If only they knew!*

One of the Darna warriors laughed loudly at something his colleague had said. It was a high, penetrating sound, so like the mage's hideous laughter that it sent shockwaves through Perian's body. He banged his head on the glass in an attempt to see the warrior clearly, but the group had moved away and he could see only their backs.

Badly shaken, he flopped back into a chair. His first trance after leaving Silaven filled his mind, even though he had not given it much thought recently. Strange shadows and the occasional distant whisper had dogged his journey until they were two days from Jasperen. The experience had left him on edge. He was only just beginning to relax. That the mage wanted him in Jasperen was obvious. But he was here by choice, he reminded himself, not herded here by another's desire.

He scrubbed his hand through his hair to erase thoughts of his tormentor, glancing about the room to anchor himself in the present and free his mind of its fear. His wandering eyes caught on Elian's knife, lying on his bed where he had left it the previous morning. He gathered up his empty breakfast bowl and placed it outside his door, then sat on Elian's bed with his back against the wall to enclose himself in Elian's essence, for comfort and to feel closer to his brother. He looked at the knife again as it pressed against his leg. On a whim, he picked it up and held it between his palms while concentrating on its owner.

The image of an almonos following a raven burst into his mind. He laughed out loud with the thrill of his achievement. He had hoped, yet not expected, to be able to scry Elian's movements in present time. But his initial excitement dwindled all too soon. He found that watching two birds flying was very boring.

He put the knife down and returned to the window to watch the activity in the street. He checked on their progress an hour later, but they were still flying. Being fearful that he would miss something of importance, he checked again several times during the day until the two birds at last entered the mouth of a wide valley. He saw a village nestled amidst green fields spread across the valley basin, with herds of domestic animals contained within fenced enclosures. The raven dropped closer to the ground. The people stopped to watch the birds as they flew to land on a high wall that surrounded a number of mud houses at the far end of the village. Perian counted ten houses. Most were small, probably just one room, with the exception of the one at the centre of the enclave, which was large and rounded, and another, on the outer rim, which he presumed was the servants' quarters.

A young man emerged from the large central building and watched the birds from the courtyard. By his dress – a blue sleeveless tunic over a calf-length sarong of a lighter blue – Perian surmised that he was a servant. He nodded at the raven and beckoned to the almonos, and Elian dropped into the courtyard, just in front of the servant, and shifted back to a man.

'I am Nessen,' said the young man. 'I have been instructed to see to your needs. If you will follow me?'

Nessen led Elian down a long corridor to an inner courtyard. At its centre a fountain swirled upward in a screw-like fashion, casting large droplets into a raised pond. Nessen led Elian to a scattering of cushions placed about a table and poured water from a jug of rose-coloured glass. He pushed a matching goblet toward him before disappearing through one of three doorways. A curtain of coloured glass beads covered the entrance and sparkled in the sun's lowering rays, reminding Perian of a gentle waterfall. Servants appeared bearing fruit and bread and a tureen of what looked like chilled soup.

Perian threw the knife into the centre of the bed and paced the room for a while. He was stiff from lack of movement and watching Elian eat just made his stomach howl. When he returned to his scrying shortly after, Elian had fallen asleep and Perian watched with amusement as he slowly slid sideways and woke with a start. Elian quickly sat up and dipped his fingers in the finger bowl, then got up to splash his face in the pond.

Elian was still studying something in the pond that Perian couldn't see when a slender Faran came up behind him. He wore the traditional desert wear of a long sleeveless tunic with a wide purple-and-gold brocade belt. His blond hair was short and clipped about a long beardless face, deeply tanned by the desert sun. He appeared youthful, but Perian thought he had the feel of an older man.

'They are strange little things, don't you think? The two-legged fish.'

Elian turned sharply. The man inclined his head by way of greeting, his hands clasped in front of him.

'They have been bred in these parts for hundreds of years. No one knows where they came from.' His deep blue eyes fluttered toward the pond, then back to Elian. 'I am Rolwen, once High Mage to the Felfar. You must be Elian, one of Lord Aronaye's triplets. You have grown well, and you look much like your father.'

'Yes, I am Elian,' Perian heard his brother say. 'I believe you were expecting Perian, but he does not have the gift of shapeshifting and we were too far away for him to get here quickly.'

Rolwen's smile was warm and friendly. 'No, Elian, we expected you. We have kept a close eye on the three of you over the years, and we knew you were in Jasperen. That is why you have been called, now that you are both in place, where you should be.'

A sudden rush of anger and indignation rose within Perian. They had been spied upon, their lives made a subject of study and discussion. Perian felt hot, his jaw rigid and his eyes cold.

He could see that the statement had shocked Elian too, but thankfully he said nothing.

'Now come and meet my companions,' said Rolwen. 'They are anxious to see you.' He turned his back on Elian, confident that he would follow.

Elian rarely lost his temper, but Perian could see that it was an effort for him to force his anger down. He was relieved when the moment passed and Elian managed to regain control. It was an honour to be called by the Magi, and important that Elian stay alert and listen carefully to what they had to say without his mind clouded by emotion.

They entered a large oval room with no windows and no decorative features on the walls. Illumination came from magical bubbles of light that clustered in the centre of a convex ceiling and shone directly onto what appeared to be a mosaic on the surface of a table. Seven High Magi sat around the table on delicate chairs of braided redwood sapling: six women and one man, excluding Rolwen. They stood and inclined their heads toward Elian as he entered, then sat again. Rolwen guided Elian to a seat at one end of the table and sat next to him.

When Perian looked closer, he could see that the table's surface was not a mosaic, but a detailed and colourful map of the known kingdoms and beyond. Elian sat in the south, by the Great Lake and Morlust's Forest where he, Jolint and Cerister had slept. Rolwen sat to his left, where Zyphire Mountain sloped down to the lands beyond King Albanal's Kingdom of Soluwi.

Three lines zigzagged across the kingdoms, red, green and grey. Perian traced the red line with his eyes: it travelled from the northern part of Albys to Silaven, turned north into the Kingdom of Wellorn as far as the main city of Carios, then turned west through central

Rashinder, curving northward to skim the upper border of Darna and continue west to the Kingdom of Nor. Then it ran south to Morlust's Forest, before turning back through Nor to the Kingdom of Soluwi. The green line began in Silaven and followed the red through to Nor and as far as Morlust's Forest, where it broke off; it started again in Darna, moving across the Central Ranges to the marshlands, then up to Jasperen.

It was not hard to figure out that the green line represented himself, and showed his journey back to the forest, on to Silaven and north again to Jasperen, where it ended. The grey was more circular but spiked out toward Fimian's lands and followed the green through Shadow Valley and back to Silaven. This, he was sure, represented the Almonos Guards – both in their initial search for himself and Elian, and their later one after Shimester's magic had been activated by Lord Fimian's sorcerer.

He looked back at the red line, which he now understood represented Gisela. This time he noted a black line he had missed at first glance. It started in southern Albys and travelled to Nor, where it joined the red and accompanied it to Morlust's Forest, then on through Nor to Soluwi. It left the red in Soluwi to return through Nor to Zyphire Mountain, then travel along the border of Darna to the southern tip of Rashinder, where it stopped. Who this black line represented he did not know. He thought he saw it move, but decided that he had imagined it.

His attention was drawn away from the map when one of the Magi began speaking. 'It is good to see you so well, Elian,' said a woman at the far end of the table.

Elian looked up, startled. Then he appeared to recall himself and thanked her. Perian noticed that there was an empty seat to her left, and it occurred to him that this was where the mage who had put Elian to sleep should have been, the one he suspected was his nightmare shadow. He glanced at where the black line now finished, then Elian spoke.

'Why have you called me?' he asked.

Elian had been gone for five days. Perian had followed him through his scrying on and off after his meeting with the Magi and knew he was back in Silaven. Allowing travel time and a day with Aronaye, Perian couldn't realistically expect him back for another day, maybe two.

Apart from spying on Elian, he had spent many hours in quiet contemplation. Under Aronaye's guidance, he had mastered the art of single-minded concentration, which was useful in a crowded inn on a busy street, but his appetite for contemplation was sated and he wanted to stretch his legs. The room became smaller and smaller with each day and each hour.

He peered through the window at yet another terrified sacrificial victim surrounded by household guards. Perhaps this person's lord had a family member still imprisoned, or was himself the one withering away in the cells. He wondered how they chose who would pay the price, but then tried to stop thinking about it. He knew how: the lord would pass the responsibility for choosing on to another. Politics being what it was, someone who was out of favour, a competitor or just didn't fit in could quickly find themselves tied to the saddle of a horse and on the road to Jasperen. But more often the sacrifices were servants or peasants, judging by their dress.

Suddenly, the need to escape his round of morbid thoughts intensified. He threw on his cloak and left the inn, following the road toward the main market.

Jasperen's marketplace was large and nearly circular, and while the early-morning rush had diminished, the area was still crowded with busy and distracted shoppers. He wove through the oncoming traffic and dodged around people who stopped suddenly to view something that had caught their eye. The movement of his cramped body and the pungent smells and noise were exhilarating, and he wanted to sing with the sheer joy of being out and about again.

He walked in pace with the tides of people to one of the roads that ran off the central market like the spokes of a wheel. Stalls bled into these side roads, and Perian was forced to join the throng at the centre of the thoroughfare to avoid stepping on the produce of small households spread out on hemp or reed mats. Smells from the occasional hot food vendor wafted from either side: sausages on a stick, hot potatoes wrapped in palm leaves or stew served in small terracotta pots. He ignored the aromas and turned down a narrow road to his right in search of the east market where they sold cheeses; here he bought yoghurt and honey, also served in small terracotta pots, and ate it with the spoon he kept in his pouch.

He walked north through the central vein that rose up through displays of materials, leather and weaponry both old and new. The market fell behind him and was replaced by small shop frontages – tailors and jewellers, haberdasheries and fine leather goods, saddles and whips.

When he reached the peak of the hill, he stopped to catch his breath and inhale the view. He could see all the way to Jasperen's magnificent harbour: the small Rashinder fleet was anchored a little way from the dock amidst a few other warships and the usual smaller boats that inhabited any great city's port. The Darna Empire's flag hung limply in the breezeless, humid air; the Empire's insignia was a bird's foot with overly large talons, its toes spread wide and raised as though to strike, against a blood-red background. Today, the flag looked like dripping blood, the threatening talons hidden within the folds of the material. Perian thought it might be a sign of some sort – the severed artery of Rashinder, the blood of its people dripping into the sea. But it was Darna's emblem, after all, not Rashinder's, so perhaps not. The design was meant to frighten the foe, but in Perian's eye it symbolised the grip the Zamir had on his people and the consequences of disobedience.

He rubbed his eyes. It was just a flag with no wind to unfurl it, not an omen.

Further along, to the right of the harbour, he could smell the fish market. He had wandered through there once or twice when he was last in Jasperen, usually early in the morning when he couldn't sleep. Today, though, he turned left instead, onto Prisoner's March, which led back along the rise toward the palace, where it divided either side of the palace walls. The left fork, Spangler's Boulevard, was where the wealthy lived – the city residences of various lords and the lesser nobility – but he continued right instead, along Prisoner's March, which ran along the harbour side of the palace wall and on to the large grassy common where the people held their holiday picnics and some grazed their sheep and goats. Beyond the common, he could see the edge of the woods into which he and Radia had escaped.

Darna warriors stood on guard at the back gateway. Perian pulled his hood close. One of the warriors stepped out as he approached and told him to move on, unnecessarily, since he hadn't slowed his pace. Just as he drew level with the gate, three priests of the Sky God stepped out and the warrior pushed him aside to let them through. The young priests scowled at him and made a sign to ward off his dark spirit. He returned the sign beneath his cloak.

Even though he felt refreshed and less oppressed than he had a short time ago, enclosed in his room at the inn, thoughts of the prisoners lingered in his mind, and he couldn't help wondering who the Darna had locked away. While there was little chance of entering the palace itself to satisfy his curiosity, he could catch the gossip at the Common Tavern, where the kitchenhands and lesser servants took their drink.

The Common Tavern was on the far side of the green, closer to the palace's grand entrance. He turned off into a street of lowly shops and the odd stall, where the tavern sat scruffily between a pastry shop and a second-hand armourer. The door screeched on hinges rusted by the salt air, and the hot, fetid atmosphere inside made his eyes water. He pushed through it and went to the bar to order a mug of ale, looking about for a seat while he waited. The tavern wasn't crowded, it being still early, but all the wall benches had been taken; like him, people preferred to be able to see who was entering and to have a wall at their back. He took a middle table near the hearth instead. Thankfully, no one had lit the fire.

He had scarcely touched the mug to his lips when one of the young priests he had seen at the palace's back gate burst through the door, followed by two of the Sky God's soldiers. Conversation and movement ceased as the priest scanned the stunned faces of the patrons, and Perian shrank down as far as he could without appearing to, hoping they hadn't miraculously recognised him.

Then the priest stopped his searching and his eyes narrowed, fixed in Perian's direction. The tavern heaved with a collective intake of breath. Shocked, Perian instantly lit up as though suddenly exposed to a blast from a furnace.

The priest pointed. 'There he is,' he said to the soldiers. 'Get him.'

They took a step forward. Perian flinched and gathered himself to run for the back door, but before he could fully react, there was frantic movement behind him. A man in the corner who he hadn't noticed before leapt over the tables and dashed between the occupied benches. The soldiers moved quickly to cut him off before he could get to the opening in the bar that led to the kitchen and presumably freedom, but the leading soldier tripped on someone's foot and the other fell on top of him. They scrambled to their feet and continued their pursuit.

As the soldiers vanished into the kitchen, the priest stepped up to the owner of the foot and lashed him across the face with his whip. Before the man could even put a hand to his injury, the whip curled about his neck and he was pulled to the ground. The priest stamped on his outstretched hand and left in a swirl of white cloak.

The door slammed shut and the tavern erupted. The man's friends picked him up and the barman's wife rushed to get water and a cloth to bathe the nasty gash the whip had left. Perian was still shaking from his fright when the barman announced that they'd got the fugitive. Perian gulped down his ale and signalled the waiter for another.

'Who was he?' he asked when the man arrived with his mug.

'An escaped slave, I heard.' He bent toward Perian and spoke in a low voice. 'Said to be awful cruel, the priests.'

Perian placed an additional coin on his tray and the man walked away. *Of course they're cruel,* he thought angrily. *Only a sadist would strap another man to a stone, punch holes into his lungs and leave him to slowly suffocate while being pecked to death by some damn bird.*

'Is that you, Perian?'

The voice hit him in the chest like an armoured fist. He had pulled his hood back to hear the waiter and forgotten to put it back up. He looked warily in the direction of the voice and saw a man in his forties, one of the palace servants. Perian remembered him. The man had often passed by his cage, carrying messages.

'Balon,' he said. 'My name's Balon. You remember me? I thought you was dead.' He left his friends and approached Perian's table. 'Last time I saw you, someone had put a torch to you. I can't see how you could have survived such a thing, even though that wizard Radia put the fire out quick enough.'

It occurred to Perian that he should ignore Balon, or pretend he had made a mistake, but the man had already seated himself, and his friends watched from a distance. He was studying Perian's face closely, looking for scars.

'It was an illusion,' Perian said quickly. 'The flames were a trick of Radia's. Very effective, I thought.'

Balon scratched his stubbled chin and studied Perian for a while longer. 'It left a great burn mark on the floor, though.'

Perian suddenly felt very strange. He had tried not to dwell too much on what Radia had said about him bursting into flames, but a burn mark was proof. 'I can't account for that. No doubt it was part of the illusion.'

Balon tilted his head. 'You should've stayed away. Darna warriors stalk the streets now and keep the people in their homes at night. Always on the lookout for those they can pick up and use for their infernal sacrifices. Poor sods in the cells grow thin from worry.' He shook his head and scratched at the table with a gnarled finger. 'None so noble now. Same as the rest of us in their fear.'

The mention of prisoners caught Perian's attention. He tried a little harder to look casual.

'I see by your uniform that the new regime has kept you on. Are they as cruel as I've heard?'

Balon drew into himself as though recalling a particular incident. 'Aye. Very cruel. Their fists and whips always at the ready. Treat us servants more like their slaves. That's what we all are now, really. Slaves.'

'I'm sorry, Balon. It's a bad turn of events. It was a terrible evening.' Perian matched Balon's mood as he phrased his next question. 'Have you seen the prisoners?'

Balon glanced at him.

'Just curious,' he said quickly, and was about to ask about the other servants he had met when Balon shook his head again and waved his hand as though to brush his distrust aside.

'Aye, I've been given the job of feeding them. Young, mostly. Lord Pathoyn and Lord Camus are still there. Never liked Lord Pathoyn, but Lord Camus was always nice to us servants.'

'Haven't some of them been released with the arrival of the substitutes?'

'No. They'll all go up for selection in any case, in my opinion.' He scratched at the table a bit more before looking over at Perian. 'You heard anything of what happened to the Shanahan?'

Perian stared at the man for a moment. There was something about the way he asked the question that signalled more caution. He shook his head but said nothing.

'You all got away together, as I heard it.'

'We were separated.'

'Ah!' Balon's head bent slightly as though to look at the tabletop, and he gave Perian a sidelong glance. 'The wizard would've joined his master, I'd have thought.'

This was more of an interrogation than curiosity. Balon served his new master.

'I can't help you there,' Perian said, and took a careful mouthful of his ale, watching Balon over its lip. 'We parted at Asper. I wasn't privy to his plans.' The Zamir would already know they had gone to Lord Fimian. 'What of the other staff? Did they keep everyone on?'

Balon seemed about to ask another question, but thought better of it. 'The kitchen's different. Everyone there got sent away. Many of the other servants too. Better off they are, I say.'

'But hard on them with no jobs to go to, I'd have thought.'

Balon agreed with a slight movement of his head. He put his hands on the table and pushed himself up to leave. 'Better get back to my friends. Good to see you, Perian. Where are you staying? Perhaps I'll see you again.'

'I'm leaving later today,' Perian lied. 'Going south to stay with my mother.'

Balon nodded solemnly and returned to his friends, and Perian watched them bombard him with questions. By the way they looked at him, he guessed that Balon was telling them about him turning into a human torch.

17

He didn't wait for them to leave; instead he pulled up his hood and left the tavern with a cursory nod at Balon. He walked calmly past the tavern window, then shot across the road to a street opposite and waited just around the corner.

The men came out too soon. Balon issued some quick instructions and they separated, Balon and another going up the road in the direction he had come, another heading toward the palace, and two more crossing the road toward Perian.

He ran down the road and slipped off to the right along a laneway at the back of the shops and slum tenements. A horse and cart blocked the way; he squeezed around the cart and past the irritated horse, which stamped at his sudden approach. The disturbance brought a shout from one of his pursuers.

Perian shot through an open gate and found himself in the busy yard of a chophouse. He ran around the cooks milling about outdoor ovens and apprentices bent to their tasks along marble-topped cutting tables, in through the back door, and zigzagged through the tables, benches and patrons until he was out of the front door. He crossed back over the road to a covered walkway at the side of the pastry shop that led to the stables. He flicked the stable boy more coins than he had intended and slipped into the darkness of the stall.

It wasn't long before he heard Balon's men run into the stable yard and breathlessly ask the boy if he had seen anyone run this way.

'Not seen no one,' the boy drawled sulkily. His broom scraped rhythmically over the cobbles.

'You sure?' growled one of the men.

Perian heard him jingle a few coins in his hand and was suddenly glad of his own generosity, even if it had been a mistake.

Finally, they walked away. The scrape of the boy's broom continued unfaltering. Perian slid down the wall and sat on the clean straw at his feet. The stable had seven empty stalls and was probably a common facility rented by the local businesses. That being the case, the stalls would remain empty most of the day.

'I'd stay there a bit,' said the boy, suddenly appearing in the entrance to Perian's stall. 'They're over the road, next to sharpener's cart.'

Perian tossed him a few more coins, which he caught with the ease of someone used to the odd flying coin. 'Let me know when they've gone.'

The boy smiled and turned to go. 'You'll need to be out of here by midday when old Thomas comes back.'

Perian settled down to wait. He didn't think the men would keep their positions long, especially if the sharpener was having a busy morning. The noise alone would drive them away. He dozed a little in the darkness of his hiding place amidst the comforting smell of horses; figures danced in his semi-conscious dreams, but most were horses and their drunken drivers, not visions. In the background, the sound of the stable boy going about his chores continued.

The boy returned in less than an hour. 'They've gone,' he said, 'but there are Darna warriors searching the shops now. You'll have to leave over the wall.'

Perian stood quickly. As he had suspected, Balon had taken on extra duties for his new masters. He probably spent all his time in the tavern listening out for suspected dissidents or runaway slaves.

He flicked one more coin at the boy and scaled the wall with the help of a barrel. Jumping down, he found himself on the common and completely exposed, but a quick glance across the open space told him that the warriors hadn't thought to search behind the shops yet. He pulled up his hood and walked quickly toward the buildings opposite, mustering all his self-control so as not to run or draw the attention of the odd person on the common tending their small herds.

It wasn't far, though it felt like miles, and soon he slipped into a street of humble dwellings where the unemployed loitered in small groups on front steps, watching suspiciously as he passed by. He slowed his pace and turned down a few more streets, until he suddenly found himself in the wealthy quarter, looking even more suspicious than he had in the poorer streets. The area was thankfully empty, save for the passing of one carriage containing occupants too busy talking to notice him and a driver who didn't care.

He felt safer once he reached the markets again. There were a few Darna warriors about, but no more than one would expect of an oppressive regime. He walked past the Windy Path, stopping further down in a shallow entrance to look back, but no one had followed that he could see, so he returned to the inn and slipped into his room, determined not to leave it again until Elian returned. He watched the street obsessively. If notice of his presence had reached the right person and travelled to the higher ranks, their search would be relentless.

That evening, though, he ventured down to the common room for a mug of ale and to listen for mention of any sort of disturbance. All seemed calm. No stories of raids, arrests or torture had reached the patrons yet. Perian thought about the stable boy, but assuming he had hidden his coins carefully, there had been nothing to suggest that he had lied to the men.

When he returned to his room, he spent a fitful hour or so watching the darkened street. Every bang or knock made him jump, thinking it was a raid. Eventually he lay on the bed fully clothed and closed his eyes on a vision he could no longer hold back.

Cries of battle filled the air – screaming and shouting, death and horror, the clash of metal, and his own voice yelling as he desperately tried to extricate himself from the vision. Then the sound of rushing feet on the stairs pulled him free of the images. Had he not been so confused, he would have been amazed that such a tiny sound could even be heard past the cacophony of his vision.

Seconds later, Elian burst through the door, shoved it closed behind him, and rushed to pull Perian from the bed.

'Get your satchel. We have to leave. Now!'

Hooded warriors dressed in black filled Perian's mind. They carried out night raids, silently moving from house to house, inn to inn, shop to shop, where, with extreme stealth, they would search each room, cupboard and attic, every stable and hayloft. He remembered Esper talking about them: Darna Ghosts, they were called, a special unit trained to hunt down miscreants, which was him at the moment.

'Where are they?' Perian asked as he followed Elian down the stairs.

Elian waved him to silence and slipped noiselessly behind the bar, into the kitchen and out through the back door into the stable yard. Perian closed the door carefully. A dog was cut off mid-bark further up the street – about three doors up, Perian thought. They were close.

Elian grabbed Perian's hand and pulled him through a hole in the back wall, into a small yard that stank of food waste and excrement. Elian tugged him over more walls and into more tiny yards with dubious contents, until they came to a break in the buildings. They huddled together on the corner, listening and straining their eyes in the darkness. Nothing moved.

Elian squeezed Perian's hand and slid out onto a street that paralleled the main road. Bent double and hugging the street-front, they ran until they came to a corner opposite the city's outer wall. Peering down to his left, Perian could see the lamps at the main gate, their weak light casting vague shadows over the cobbles and marking the unevenness of the wall itself. He dashed across the roadway on Elian's heels and into deep shadow on the other side.

They squatted in a dark, broken hollow of the outer wall. All was quiet, save the splash of the fountain near the gates, Elian's heaving breath, and his own.

'The gate is shut and heavily guarded. There's no way through,' Elian whispered into Perian's ear.

'How will we get out, then?'

'We can't. I had to fly over. I assume it's you they're looking for. The search is too extensive and specialised for it to be anyone else.'

Perian hunched his shoulders and put his head in his hands. He waited for Elian's admonition, but it didn't come. The agitation in his voice said it all.

'Think, Perian,' Elian continued. 'You've seen this. What must we do?'

He had. But he had put the vision aside, as he always did when the path ahead frightened him. He took a deep breath and reluctantly looked again.

'Perian. My brother. Whatever it is, it must be done.'

He lifted his head to face Elian, so close he could feel the warmth of his cheek. 'Only if you promise me that should it go awry, you will fly away and not return.'

Elian huffed, and Perian could feel his smile even though he could not see it. 'We'll see,' he said.

Perian shook his head, but he could not force his brother to leave. He would have to make his own decision. Instead, he lifted his arm and pulled at the knots securing his wristlet until it came loose, then did the same with the other. He slipped them beneath his belt.

'We must go to the gates with the first rays of the morning light. We must slip into roles, you as guide dog and me a half-blind seer.'

Elian remained silent, and Perian couldn't tell whether it was because he approved or because he thought him mad. *He* thought he was mad.

'With the rising sun, we will walk up the Palace Boulevard directly to the palace entrance.' He stared intently at the outline of Elian's face. 'What did the Magi have to say?' He wanted Elian to confirm what he had heard himself. He would tell his brother that he had spied on him later.

Elian shrugged. 'That you are one of the most accurate seers of our time. That what you have seen is the truth and it is imperative that you follow it to the end, even though it may seem destined to end in failure and death. That you, who can recall your previous life, are the catalyst and the stone around which the future will bend, for good or bad.'

'I sent you all the way to the Magi for that?' He gave Elian a shove with his elbow. 'You just made it up!' But Perian knew he hadn't, though he wished he had misheard.

'Only the bit about dying. No one mentioned death, thankfully.'

'Do you have answers to my questions?'

'I'll tell you later, when we're safe.'

'No, tell me now so that I can be certain of what I do.'

The faint glow from the gate lamps sparked briefly in Elian's eyes as he turned his tense face toward Perian. 'Gisela lied. Farans were never sought as slaves, nor persecuted. Certainly we were easy prey for slave-takers, moving about in small groups as we do, but no more than other travellers, isolated homesteads or small villages. Every kingdom has its slave-takers. The difference is that the Darna people rely heavily on their slaves: it's big business in the Empire, and a good trade for those without a conscience from other kingdoms. Aronaye said that to enter Darna or wander near its borders would be madness, and no Faran tribe went near it, not even the Northern Tribe under Gisela, as far as he knew.

'The Faran tribes didn't come from there, either. They originated in the Deserts of Albys and then spread wide to avoid starvation. One of Aronaye's ancestors discovered the deserted city under the mountain by accident. He sought permanence for his people – somewhere they could be self-sufficient and grow. The Felfar are looked upon as the Head of the Tribes because of their prosperity and power, but I think it has more to do with respect for Aronaye himself.'

Perian remained silent for a while once Elian had finished. Gisela's web of lies was astounding. There never had been a mission except the one that fed her need for power, riches and adoration. He pushed his anger down; he'd scream and shout another time. He was free of Gisela now and the mission she had set. The only one he was concerned with was the safety of himself and Elian. What the future held for the two of them, he did not know at present; he would face that as it came.

A slight glimmer caught Perian's eye. He thought he could see the edge of darkness beginning to lift and the stars in the east losing their lustre. His heart began to beat faster and his breath quickened. Part of him wondered what he was doing; he could still change his mind and hide or fight his way through the gates. But that was not the path he had been shown, the one his heart and the Magi knew he should follow.

He released his doubts and isolated himself from the building tension that radiated from Elian, settling his mind and body to focus on what must be done.

'You can tell me more about the Magi later. Now we must make our way to the gatehouse.'

He listened carefully for nearby movement before stepping out from their hollow. Elian followed, his hand upon Perian's cloak. Perian felt along the rough wall with the flat of his hand, his back as close to its surface as possible. His feet slid on the sharp stones, leaves and dirt piled against the wall by the road's traffic, yet made no sound.

By the time they were a few paces from the gatehouse, Perian could just make out small details along the rooftops. Three guards stood stiffly on either side of the closed gate. They had probably sealed off the city in his honour.

He stopped, pushed back his hood and flicked his cloak behind him so his arms were free. 'Are you ready, Elian? You should change now and follow my lead.'

'Are you really going to do this?' Elian sounded incredulous.

Perian released a short, rough laugh. 'The Magi said to follow the path. That's what we're doing. Change quickly, before it's too late.'

Elian's great wolf slid to Perian's left side.

'Here we go,' Perian said under his breath. He put his right arm across his chest in a sign of submission and greeting; the gesture also clearly displayed the tattoo indicating his heritage, and he hoped the Rashinder guards would recognise it before they pinned him to the cobbles with their swords.

The road from the main gate forked to either side of a large fountain. A mythical beast of mixed species spat water from the mouth of each of its three heads onto an array of prancing fish on white marble waves. The left fork led to the Windy Path inn and the markets; he walked evenly past the guards toward the right fork, the Palace Boulevard, and the grand entrance to the palace before the truly grand entrance within its walls.

The guards were a little slow, but spritely and aggressive once they got going. One of them shouted for him to stop and another stepped into his path.

Perian turned slightly unfocussed eyes on him. 'Step out of my way or I'll have you cut into pieces.'

The guard raised his sword and touched Perian's throat with its point. His eyes didn't once shift to the tattoo, which was beginning to glow shades of violet in the red light of sunrise. 'I said stop.'

'Step out of my way, you miserable Rashinder rat,' Perian spat.

Elian growled and the guard cowered slightly. But he stood his ground, flanked by the other two, who pointed their swords in Perian's direction, their eyes shining with excitement. The closer guard pushed his sword a little harder, so that Perian's skin dented inward. The wolf had frightened him. The other two spread out either side; one pointed his sword at Elian and the other stepped close to Perian and prodded him with a bludgeon.

'What you up to, walking about at this time of the mornin'? It's prison for those caught wandering about during curfew.'

'Maybe you's the one they're looking for,' said the other, without taking his eyes off Elian.

The guard with the bludgeon thrust his head closer with a smirk that released the gaseous stench of ale and garlic, making Perian blink. 'You'll get put in with the sacrifices.'

Just as Perian thought he'd have to fight his way out, the black-gloved hand of a Darna Ghost snapped over the arm of the guard pointing his sword at Perian's throat. The sword point jerked forward and up, leaving a small cut in the hollow of Perian's throat. The Ghost punched the man in the face and pushed him out of Perian's path. The other two guards scrambled back and noisily tried to hide their weapons.

Perian breathed a sigh of relief. Blood ran down the opening of his shirt, over his wrist and alongside his royal tattoo to spot his shirt below. He ignored it, and, with a slight nod at the Darna Ghost, continued his walk along the boulevard. The Rashinder guard would lose his arm for drawing the blood of a Prince of the Empire, even a wayward one like himself, but he tried not to think about that.

Ancient pesimine trees lined the white-stoned paving of the Palace Boulevard. Their tall, smooth black trunks formed a line of salute on either side and their umbrella-shaped canopy gave the impression of a covered walkway. Only the wealthiest lived along the Palace Boulevard, in extravagant mansions that sat within formal gardens.

The initial pink of dawn began to give way to a golden light that brightened Perian's path. Darna Ghosts, a nocturnal unit, lingered in the remaining shadows, awaiting the arrival of warriors to relieve them of their vigil.

Perian continued at an even pace, his eyes fixed on the road ahead and his face relaxed and neutral. The only outward signs of his emotional turmoil were the sweat that tickled his hairline and the fingers of his left hand, which moved rhythmically in the thick fur on Elian's neck. He found it comforting and a release for his tension.

Darna warriors emerged from the palace gates. Perian half expected them to charge him, but instead, they filed slowly down either side of the boulevard until the lead horses were on either side of him. The warriors waited, evenly spread, closing in behind him as he passed.

In his peripheral vision, Perian saw the Darna Ghosts slip away, handing their charge over to their daylight comrades. He felt, rather than saw, faces at windows and a small group of servants huddled in one of the doorways further up. He squinted in the brightening light as more people gathered in their doorways, having scrambled from their beds to watch the spectacle. He began to feel as though he was marching toward his execution and heard the beat of drums in the tread of horses behind him.

The glistening gates weren't far away now; it would be mere moments before he stepped through them. Beyond the gates, giant ferns replaced the pesimine trees, bowing to each other at the smallest air movement. Six Darna warriors stood stiffly just inside the gates, and they took their places on either side of him as he stepped into the palace grounds. He twirled Elian's fur about his fingers to steady the dizzy feelings of déjà vu he always experienced when the fulfilment of a vision was so exact.

As he came to the semi-circular steps leading up to the wide arched and scrolled entrance, Perian continued his constant pace without taking his eyes off the opening. While the entry was wide, the foot warriors were still forced back to allow Perian and Elian to enter side by side; they resumed their positions as soon as Perian was free of the threshold and walking toward the centre of the atrium. The floor depicted a large star in orange and blue, with the agitated, double-headed kroyer of Rashinder showing its sharp little teeth in the centre. The glass dome above gave off a clear light and sent little rainbows wriggling across the floor and hovering in mid-air.

Perian stopped between the two heads of the kroyer, and his entourage came to a halt as though attached to him in some way. He knew his father would greet him in the Audience Room, which was straight ahead. The vast doors, elegant in their simplicity, would open soon, and he would need to walk through them. Suddenly his hands were clammy; his jaw tightened, as did his chest, and his legs felt less certain. Then Elian leant against him and lifted his head to nose Perian's palm, and Perian's panic subsided into a sigh. What would he do without Elian's ever-present calm and support?

Someone quietly closed the main doors behind them, shutting out the warmth. The loud clatter of the bolt across the door marked the point of no return. He was committed to this path now, for good or bad, as the Magi had said.

18

The doors to the Audience Room opened. As far as Perian could see, there was no one there, apart from the slaves who opened the doors. They knelt either side, one hand on the door and the other on their chests beneath bent heads.

Perian walked past them, still looking ahead. A yellowy gloom fell around him as the doors closed with a soft click. The room had been cleared of the benches used on public occasions and supplicant days. The roof arched high on raked beams. He could see that the walls had once been covered in murals; someone had been hastily plastering them out, but had not yet completed the task. A vast bay window formed the backdrop to the raised thrones. It would once have shone brightly around the Shanahan and his lady; he presumed it now shone on the Zamir and his eldest son —

Halfway into the room, Perian froze at the sound of his father's voice.

He forced his breath to slow. Elian leant against him again, but despite Perian's mental preparation, the Zamir's entry was a shock. His father strode through the royal side door, still pulling his night-coat about him and tying a sash of gold silk about his waist. Perian's attention flickered briefly to the mural of a near-naked Rashinder fighter with a raised spear that covered the wall above the doorway. He wished it would suddenly come to life.

The Zamir held his expression rigid. His eyebrows locked together over glaring eyes, and his nostrils flared as though they might produce fire. Perian dropped to his knees as the Zamir stopped in front of him, and Elian crouched down at his side.

'Get up,' the Zamir growled.

As he rose, Perian inadvertently looked up and met his father's gaze. Even though his sight was a little blurry, he was aware of the shock that ran through the Zamir by the widening of his green eyes.

Without warning, the Zamir hit him hard across the face. His head swung sideways with the blow and he felt his lip split and spurt blood, but he remained steady on his feet. He didn't bother to wipe the blood, but let it flow down his chin.

The Zamir hit him again, then again, and again, each blow more forceful than the last, until the pain of the first was lost in a blur of agony.

Eventually Perian staggered sideways. Elian stood, having so far remained placid throughout the beating. Maltha slammed his fist into Perian's face one more time. Perian fell to one knee and Maltha kicked him in the ribs, forcing him sideways so that he had to put out an arm to support himself. The room spun nauseatingly around him and he fought hard not to faint.

'Find him chambers worthy of a prince of my blood,' the Zamir shouted at a slave who stood within the doorway. 'And a personal slave. One who has a sense of humour. He can remain here until you fetch him.' Then he turned on his heel and left the foyer in a flurry of gaudy purple and gold silk.

In a blaze of pain, Perian tested his jaw with little opening and closing movements to see if it still worked. He'd bitten his tongue and blood still filled his mouth; he spat it onto the floor and dabbed at his lips with the sleeve of his shirt.

'I'm all right,' he said. His tongue didn't work properly, and the words came out slurred and thick. Elian prodded him with his nose to indicate that he understood, then rested his head on Perian's bent knees.

Perian didn't move. He wondered if he would pass out if he tried to lift his head. He didn't bother trying to open his eyes; he knew they wouldn't oblige just yet. A brightly coloured display exploded behind his eyelids with every agonising beat of his heart, and his whole body throbbed. He'd known such beatings were painful from past experience, but he had forgotten just how much.

He heard the pad of bare feet, and a dark shadow hovered over him. He chanced a quick peek through a slit in his eyelids and found himself staring at a pair of enormous feet.

'I am Lono, your personal slave,' said the owner of the feet. His deep voice vibrated above Perian and confirmed his size. 'Will this beast at your side attack me if I help you to rise?'

Perian waved a hand to indicate he wouldn't, and Elian moved aside. Hands that matched the feet in size grasped Perian strongly beneath his arms and lifted him until his feet gained uncertain purchase on the marble floor. He wavered dizzily, trying to clear his head enough to stand unaided, then put his hand on Lono's chest and pushed him aside. Lono did as he was bid, but thrust his left arm firmly under Perian's right.

'When you are ready, my Zameel, I will lead you to your chambers.'

The slave urged Perian forward, and the two shuffled in a semi-dignified manner through the doorway so recently used by the Zamir. Lono gently bent Perian's arm against his chest so that his tattoo of heritage was on display for the benefit of anyone they might encounter. They passed side passageways until they reached a great spiral stairwell that wound upward beneath a painted hunting scene. Warriors at the bottom of the stairs stood to attention as they approached, and Perian waved his left hand to indicate that they could relax. He concentrated on each step, careful not to trip. He didn't want word to get about that he was a whimpering mess who had been beaten into submission by his father, even though that was how he felt.

On the second landing, he was forced to stop to catch his breath and lean on the balustrade. He could see a fuzzy pattern on the mosaic floor below and made a note to look at it more carefully if he were ever let out of his rooms.

'Do you need assistance, my Zameel?'

The voice came from above them, and the words were earnest, though Perian was sure he could sense a hint of amusement. He could do little more than ignore it. He felt like laughing himself, in a macabre way.

'One more floor,' Lono whispered.

Perian's feet had scarcely touched the final landing when two warriors appeared and stood to attention, pulling their spears upright and touching their right fists to their chests. Perian held his head high, openly displaying the wreckage his father had wrought upon his face as though it were of no consequence. His post-beating confusion had begun to lift, so asserting himself wasn't so difficult. To their credit, both warriors looked straight ahead and their features didn't change, as far as Perian could see. Nor did they flinch away from the wolf.

Lono turned down the corridor to his right and went through a door at the far end. He led Perian through an oval-shaped vestibule into a large room dominated by a four-poster bed, its curtain of yellow silk rolled up. Perian looked longingly at the bed, but Lono pulled him toward a group of padded chairs placed loosely about a large hearth that was set up ready should the weather turn chilly. He eased Perian into one of the chairs, then disappeared through a door at the opposite end of the room.

With Lono out of the way, Elian padded up beside Perian and put his head on his lap. *That wasn't so bad!* he said with mock cheerfulness.

'Do you want to change places and rethink that statement?' Perian lisped. It suddenly dawned on him that no sound had issued from Elian; nor had he ever spoken to him while in animal form before. The shock was so great he almost forgot how much his face hurt. 'I didn't know you could do that!' he hissed through clenched teeth and swollen lips.

Nor did I, Elian replied, as surprised as Perian. *Say something to me!*

Perian concentrated. *Can you hear me?*

If you're saying anything, I'm not getting it.

Perian let out a frustrated sigh and patted Elian's head. 'We'll have to practise.'

The sound of splashing water came from the other end of the room. A bath! Perian could think of nothing he wanted more. When the splashing stopped, Lono reappeared and removed Perian's boots.

'I am the only slave assigned to you. You have no dresser or washers, so I will perform these tasks for you,' Lono said. He stretched out thickly muscled arms and eased Perian from his seat. His short brown hair was dark and thick, and he had a firm, square, honey-coloured face, wide cheekbones and a straight nose that flared slightly at the base.

'I can take care of myself,' Perian slurred.

'It is not seemly that a Zameel should do such a thing. I will help you, if you deem me suitable.'

Lono's dark eyes flashed wide and Perian noticed for the first time that his hands were rough and calloused. Perhaps serving him might be preferable to whatever Lono had been doing before. He briefly wondered what would happen to the slave if he were not deemed suitable. He would ask him another time.

'You seem to me to be very suitable, Lono. Let us proceed.'

The tension that had stiffened the slave's body released with a near-audible sigh, and he led Perian, wheezing and groaning, to an oval tub of smooth, polished black stone. Elian stood in the doorway to watch as Perian was stripped of his clothing and stepped awkwardly into the warm, scented water.

A strangled, high-pitched sound issued from his throat at the enclosing warmth. Every muscle sang and expanded into the delicious heat as the spirit sings and stretches toward the sun and stars. Tears of relief stung his swollen eyelids and he lay very still, savouring the moment, while Lono waited patiently beside the tub, as did Elian, who had sidled up close to the slave's side.

Finally, Perian pushed himself up, splashed his face with water and gave Lono a careful nod. Even the movement of the soft sponge hurt as it passed over his ribs where his father had kicked him, and Lono dropped it twice in his attempts to be careful. When he had finished his sponging, he turned to a tray holding a bowl and a pile of smaller sponges. He dipped one of the sponges into the bowl and the smell of yarrow burst into the air. Perian lifted his head, as much to inhale it as to give Lono access to his face, and Lono bent awkwardly over the tub to gently dab the herbal infusion over Perian's injuries.

'This will ease the pain and cleanse your wounds. It is good for bruising,' said Lono. The spicy smell alone made Perian feel better, and the sponge cooled his overheated skin.

When he had finished his bath and been patted dry, Perian stood in the doorway of the bedroom watching Lono sort through clothing and lay items out on the bed. Darna clothing: a finely woven cotton shirt, a calf-length silk tunic of deep blue, and fine cotton trousers the colour of amber. Embroidered slippers went onto the carpet near the bed. Lono retrieved his bowl of yarrow to bathe Perian's bruised ribs, then helped him to dress.

'Get me something to eat, Lono. Something soft that I don't have to chew.' He motioned toward Elian. 'My wolf here will eat the same as I do, so bring breakfast for two.' When Lono was at the door, Perian called out to him: 'You must always knock and wait for permission to enter. Never come through that door unannounced.'

Once Lono had gone, Perian glanced at himself in a long mirror placed near the wall and touched his face. Behind him, Elian changed back to his normal self and sat on the side of the bed, watching as Perian eased himself into the chair he had occupied before his bath. Hopefully his father would leave him alone for the day.

'Well, that was interesting,' said Elian. 'How do you feel? You don't look your best.' He slipped from the bed and walked up behind Perian to gently rub his shoulders. 'Did he break any ribs?'

'No, but it still hurts to breathe.'

'What will we do now?' Elian asked.

'Wait. My father will come for me, or send for me, eventually. We can explore the other rooms later, but for the moment I want to rest and eat my breakfast.' Perian turned awkwardly toward his brother. 'You must change back the instant he knocks at the door.'

Seven days later, just after dawn, Perian woke with a start to a loud banging on the door. He lurched from the bed and threw his night-coat about him as men swept into his vestibule, and Elian shifted quickly and sat up on the bed, his ears alert.

'Here we go,' Perian said. His voice trembled slightly with the rapid movement of his blood. 'The game has begun.'

'Wake the Zameel,' said one of the men, loud enough to be heard throughout the palace. 'The Zamir wants to see him.'

Perian lowered himself into one of the large, soft chairs by the hearth and tried to look relaxed. Even so, Lono's knock on the door made him jump.

'I know. I heard,' he said to Lono without looking at him. 'Tell them to wait outside while I dress, then come back quickly to assist me.'

Elian jumped from the bed and came to Perian's side, laying his head on Perian's lap.

'It will be all right,' Perian said. 'Far from pleasant, but we will survive, I believe.'

Why are we doing this, Perian?

'Because we were trapped, remember? And this is the advice you brought back from the Magi – follow the vision I was avoiding. Now you begin to see why I was avoiding it.'

Lono quickly selected his clothing, spreading it on the bed for Perian's approval: shirt and slender trousers in fine white cotton, and a thigh-length tunic of deep red silk, its bottom edge embroidered with the three-pronged claw of Darna in gold thread. Its close repetition reminded Perian of waves. Short, tanned boots completed his outfit.

Lono wrapped a light grey silk sash about Perian's waist and stood back to admire his choice of attire. A smile eased onto Perian's face as he watched Lono; he was built like a blacksmith or a warrior, yet here he was fussing over bits of clothing. Then the thought passed, and

Perian rearranged his facial expression. He liked Lono, but he needed to remember that he was a slave and would be vulnerable should the Zamir, or others, choose to use him. He could not be trusted. Not yet, anyway. Perian couldn't afford to let his guard down and slip into a sense of camaraderie.

He gazed at himself in the long mirror while Lono stood on tiptoe in an attempt to brush his thick black hair. His eyelid was no longer swollen, nor were his lip and jaw, but his eyes were still a nasty shade of purple that had just begun to yellow about the edges, and his jaw bore a motley pattern of yellow and brown that had faded somewhat. It was still very evident that he had recently taken a heavy beating.

He turned down the open neck of his tunic and ran his hands down his chest to smooth a few wrinkles. 'That'll do.' He looked down at Elian. 'Let's see what he wants.'

Slaves in tunics of soft, flowing burnt-orange cotton crouched outside the grand double doors that led to the Zamir's private chambers. They stood as the warriors approached, and one slipped through a door at a nod from the officer at Perian's side. The other looked at the floor, but not before glancing at Perian's face and royal tattoo.

His companion returned swiftly and the doors opened onto an oval-shaped vestibule. The four visitors crossed a white-tiled floor and went through another set of open doors opposite, into the perfumed presence of the Zamir.

Perian's eyes passed over his father and focused on the floor as they stopped a third of the way into the expansive room. Even though Elian had not been permitted to accompany him, Perian's fingers twitched, reaching for the comfort of his fur, and he tried to imagine Elian by his side to calm his nerves and quell his rising fear. His father sat impassive upon a large, ornate throne that had been placed on a high dais. When he heard the doors softly close behind the departing warriors, Perian bent to one knee to await his command.

The smell of freshly cut timber and beeswax wafted across the floor from the dais, which was out of place amidst the subtle tones of the room. Perian could just make out a pair of feet on the green carpet that covered a large portion of the white tiles and realised for the first time that Grison stood at the Zamir's right.

He remained perfectly still for a long time before he heard the rustle of the Zamir's clothing. Finally his father spoke, but not to him.

'We know he has the power of a sorcerer, but Shimester believed he had the gift of a seer too. See if this is true, Grison.'

Grison shuffled forward. Perian watched his soft-booted feet walk to his side and forced his panic down, remaining still. His hair bristled, and a bright light exploded into his skull as Grison's fingers touched his head. Despite his best efforts, he instinctively pulled away in shock. Grison made a clucking sound through his teeth and returned to his position next to the dais.

'Well?' the Zamir asked quietly.

'He was right, my Zamir. The boy has the gift of sight.'

'How much of a gift?'

'It is as he said: exceptional, as far as I can tell. But he has yet to prove this.'

A grudging admittance, Perian thought. He made a mental note to be very careful of this man.

'Leave us, Grison. Wait for me in the library, and make sure that witch is with you,' said the Zamir.

When Grison had gone, he stepped down from his dais and walked toward Perian.

'Stand, Tanais. Let me look at you.'

A bolt shot through Perian. For the briefest of moments, he had thought his father was talking to someone else; he had all but forgotten his Darna name.

'Stand, Tanais. I will not hit you again unless you give me cause.'

The tone of his voice helped Perian unscramble his head. He stood slowly and looked directly at his father. They had the same deep green, almond-shaped eyes, but Perian's were not as angled as his father's and other Darnas'.

'You have grown into a fine-looking man, Tanais. It seems to me that you have acquired the best of both races. Your beardless chin is unfortunate, of course, but since you are unlikely to become a warrior, it probably doesn't matter. Do you still bear the wings?'

Perian nodded, and his father asked to see them. Perian undid the sash so carefully wound about him and tied by Lono, then removed his tunic. When he lifted his shirt, his father touched the tattoo with two long fingers, then let his hand drift down Perian's chest in a caressing way, cupping the ribs at his side. Perian's stomach heaved and it took all his control not to shrink away.

The Zamir sighed and removed his hand. 'If you prove to be all that Shimester and Grison believed, you will be my official seer, Tanais. For the time being you may consider yourself my prisoner and will remain in your chambers until I call for you. Your life has not been your fault, but you are a man now and may make your own choices. Perhaps you will come to love us, and things will change.'

The word 'love' triggered thoughts of his mother and a faint hope that he may see her again. A question he hadn't intended to ask suddenly burned in his heart and burst from his mouth. 'Does my mother live?'

The Zamir shook his head. 'She died in the plague that passed through Darna three years after you were sent away.' He studied Perian a little longer, then gathered himself with a loud intake of breath. 'Put your clothes on, Tanais, and we will join Grison in the library.'

19

The library smelt of books even above the mingled perfumes of his father, Grison and a woman Perian didn't know. Books lined the walls, save one that bore a wide leaded window. He remembered Elian saying that the Shanahan had been a scholar, not a warrior.

Grison and his companion had been sitting on chairs near the window, but they stood immediately and bent one knee briefly.

'Welcome, Erely. It's been a long time,' said Maltha.

'It has indeed, my Zamir.'

Tall for a Darna woman, who were generally a good head shorter than the men, Erely wore a silk tunic the colour of the sun, with pale green trousers peeping out from beneath its hem. Her hair was bound back into a single braid. Perian noticed strands of grey within the black, but her features were quite youthful, as were her brown eyes. A simple sorcerer's star twinkled on her left forearm.

She studied Perian for a moment. 'Is this the young man?'

'Yes, this is my son, Tanais, my fourth and youngest. Grison has told you what we require?'

She inclined her head and smiled. 'Yes. It is as usual, I believe.'

'Very good. Let us begin.'

Maltha placed the flat of his hand on Perian's back and urged him toward one of the chairs. Erely and Grison waited for the Zamir before resuming their seats.

'I assume this is some sort of test,' Perian said, more to assert himself and establish some kind of power balance in his favour than because he needed confirmation. The Zamir didn't really have to explain what was going on. But he wasn't sure why Erely was there. She had the sorcerer's star, yet he could feel no overwhelming power about her.

'Yes. Grison will ask you to look at something, and you will tell me what you see.'

He made it sound so easy. It didn't really work like that, and if Grison had any knowledge of seers, he would know this. Or perhaps Erely did, and that was why she was here.

At a nod from the Zamir, Grison pulled a brooch from amongst a small collection of objects by his chair leg. So, they wanted him to do a bit of scrying. Not so hard or taxing. Perian closed his eyes and deepened his breath, swirling the air about his lungs in a circular way by concentrating on his left lung with his intake of breath and on the right as he exhaled, an exercise that quickly brought about a meditative state.

After a few breaths, he mentally isolated himself from the others and took the brooch from Grison's hand. The delicate silverwork formed a small flower with a tiny piece of red glass at its centre, and leaf stems bent inward on either side to accommodate the pin that would attach the brooch to a person's clothing. A sense of Grison prickled across his fingertips. He was tempted to look at the man, but there would be time enough for that later. Better to concentrate on what they wanted for now. He allowed his senses to go deeper.

The Zamir moved in his seat. Perian ignored him. If his father wanted to see what he could do, he would have to be patient.

Slowly, the image of a young woman appeared. She looked strikingly like Maltha, but she had dark eyes ... One of Maltha's daughters. His half-sister. She placed her hands over her swollen belly and rubbed the mound lovingly.

Then the scene changed, and she was screaming. Women rushed about her. A small boy holding her hand filled Perian's vision. He was strong and healthy.

Perian handed the brooch back to Grison, who stored it away on the other side of his chair.

'The brooch belongs to my half-sister. She is currently about seven or eight months pregnant. She will have a healthy boy. Both are safe.'

Erely nodded and smiled at a nonverbal question from the Zamir, and Perian realised why she was there: she was a truth-seer. They wanted to know if he lied about what he saw. He wondered what other questions they had for him that he might lie about, but it didn't matter; he didn't think his father would be interested in the movements of the Farans. Maltha was ignorant of Silaven, as far as he knew, and of Elian's presence. But should his visions turn to them, he could distort the truth if necessary.

'Very good, Tanais. Proceed, Grison.' The Zamir crossed his legs and placed his hands on his knee in a more relaxed position. It hadn't occurred to Perian that his father might have been worried that he would fail.

Grison dropped a man's ring into Perian's outstretched palm, and a fierce battle burst out all around him. He stiffened and heard his own raspy intake of breath. Pain surged through his body and he threw the ring back at Grison.

'This person is dead. There is nothing to be gained from reading a dead man's ring.'

'Take it,' said Grison. 'Look again.' A distorted smile crossed his face, as though he were enjoying himself.

Perian did as he was told. Tiny bits of blood spotted the ring's exterior and congealed on one edge. The metal pulsed with screaming, but whether it came from the wearer or others he could not tell.

'The owner of this ring was of Rashinder, probably a minor lord. Most of the blood is his, but it is sprayed with the blood of his Darna victims too. He fought well and hard to protect his Shanahan and his empire. He was taken alive and tortured to death.' The feel of the ring disgusted him, and again he threw it back at Grison. 'I cannot tell you who he was.'

'That is good enough,' said the Zamir after a nod from Erely. 'I think we can try the other now.'

Perian resisted the urge to look at his father. Now they had come to the real issue – the reason for this test. His palms moistened and his nerves began to jangle again.

Grison pulled a small scroll from his pocket. There was a hole at its edge where the seal had been torn off, and Perian's light trance deepened as he touched the parchment. He slid his finger beneath its curled end and ran it over the lettering hidden beneath. Images moved quickly, leaving him with little option but to describe his vision as it unfolded before him.

'This was written by a Rashinder traitor. He is currently hidden within the Shanahan's entourage. A young lord, if I'm not mistaken. Something of a dandy, but I do not know his name.'

The Zamir moved again, releasing his crossed leg to the floor in sudden intense concentration. Perian struggled for a moment with what he saw and how much to reveal, but Erely's silent presence bore down on him, so he decided to worry about his loyalties later.

'Leren is dead. Edun, his oldest son, is Shanahan now. He and Radia have negotiated with Queen Ishra to retake Jasperen. Ishra's troops march to the border.'

The air bristled about Perian. He had assumed that the letter contained at least some of this information, but from the shocked reactions of the Zamir and Grison, it had not.

'Are you sure?' His father looked at Erely.

'He speaks the truth,' she said quietly.

The Zamir turned back to Perian. 'How far are they from the border?'

'I cannot say. I cannot be sure whether I see the future or the present.'

'You must,' said his father with a touch of anger, before Grison intervened.

'This is the way of such visions, Maltha. Look again, Tanais.'

Perian closed his eyes to recall the vision as best he could. He knew he would never recapture its clarity, but it might be enough to study the background, as long as a new set of images didn't intervene.

'It is the present,' he said excitedly, 'or very close. It is near midsummer by the angle of the sun; the trees are still in full leaf, and the white missen that stands in the centre of Ishra's garden is in full bloom.'

'Well done,' Grison said, so softly that Perian barely heard it.

Maltha stood abruptly and called for his warriors. 'Valia, call the generals to meet me in the Council Room immediately.'

Valia bowed deeply and vanished through the doorway. Grison and Erely had stood at the same time as Maltha, but Perian was still rubbing his face and recovering from his trance when the Zamir turned his attention on him.

'You have done well, Tanais. Now return to your chambers with the warriors assigned to you. You are still my prisoner and may not leave your rooms unless I call for you.'

Lono was standing near the door when Perian burst into his chambers – *waiting to serve my every desire,* Perian thought miserably.

Lono dropped to his knees. 'How can I serve you, my Zameel?'

'A drink. I need a drink. Bring me some wine. Three bottles should suffice.' Lono flicked him a look of surprise. 'And breakfast, Lono. I'm starving.'

Perian slammed the bedroom door and strode past Elian as he changed back to human form. He fell rather than sat onto a chair by the hearth, dropping his head back on the headrest.

'You've been gone for ages. I began to think he'd killed you this time. What did he want?' asked Elian anxiously.

'He wants to use me. My sight, that is. I had to go through a few childish scrying tests, and then a full trance came upon me.' He released the hand that gripped the chair's arm and rubbed the soft red velvet for a moment before looking over at Elian, who had taken the other chair. 'Shanahan Leren is dead, and Radia has persuaded Queen Ishra to help the new Shanahan, Edun, retake Jasperen. They march to the border as we speak.'

Elian shrugged. 'That's good, isn't it?'

'No, it isn't,' said Perian. 'There's something wrong. Unless Edun can muster a substantial army from within Rashinder and prove his ability to Ishra, why would she risk her own men in war?' He stretched his legs out in front of him, one ankle resting on the other, and arched his fingers before his lips. 'I didn't get the impression that there was much active support from the lords we encountered on our way to

Silaven. And Maltha still has half the sons of the landed gentry in his cells. I'd love to see just who he has in there; I'd probably recognise most of them from that training session where Lord Bellam drummed into his wandering minstrels who was who and how to address them all.'

'Pity he didn't warn you about the women's quarters,' said Elian. Perian shot him a look of disapproval.

There was a clattering at the front door. Elian just had time to shift into animal form before Lono knocked and Perian told him to come in.

'Put it all on the table, Lono. You may return to the kitchen for your own breakfast – or is it lunch? I can serve myself.'

Elian shifted back as soon as Lono left, and Perian poured wine into a glass goblet and drank a large mouthful while Elian cast a ravenous eye over the delights spread across the table: boiled duck eggs wrapped in smoked ham, a variety of cheeses, fresh bread still hot beneath its napkin cover, and a bowl of thick soup. They fell upon the feast as though they hadn't eaten for a week.

There was a noise at the door and Elian looked up nervously, his slab of bread dripping soup across the table.

Perian shook his head. 'This can't continue.' He split a duck egg in half, accentuating his frustration.

'What can't?' Elian asked through a mouthful of bread.

'Having to eat in here. Shifting back and forth depending on Lono's movements. I am a prisoner here, and so are you. My father has no intention of changing my situation in the near future. Understandably, he doesn't trust me. He will, but not yet.'

Looking alarmed, Elian swallowed his bread, which was still a little too lumpy for comfort. 'What are you saying?'

As he turned to look at his brother, Perian's eyes caught on a small table by the window. He was sure it hadn't been there when he left, but it took a few moments for him to realise what was wrong, apart from it being there at all. Playing cards were scattered on its surface, and although they had been shuffled about as if in frustration, a suspicious eye could still tell that there had been two players.

Elian's gaze followed Perian's, and he shrugged. 'Lono came in without knocking. I was sleeping,' he added before Perian could ask.

Of course. Why would Lono bother to knock with his master gone? Perian sipped calmly on his wine and stared at the tabletop, wondering how long it would be before Elian was discovered by someone other than Lono. He was a fool to have endangered his brother by bringing him into the palace, but there had been no time to think of different scenarios. Elian had always been at his side in his visions and he had seen no harm coming to him, but he would need to be more vigilant in his searching of the future now.

Perian filled the awkward silence. 'We would have been discovered at some point. But it is very dangerous for Lono, and for you. The life of a slave means nothing to the Darna, especially the Zamir and the royal household. And we can't actually be sure that Lono doesn't have to report to the Zamir or to Grison. If he is found to be lying, they will cut out his tongue, if not take his head.'

Elian's eyes widened. Perian could see that the possibility that Lono could be a spy had not occurred to him.

'Cheer up,' Perian said at last. 'He is my personal slave, and slaves are privy to all sorts of things people wouldn't want anyone else to know. You may speak with him as an equal, but I cannot afford to deviate from my role even a little bit, for my safety, yours and his. My father has no reason to suspect that I am up to anything, other than possibly escaping these rooms.'

Perian's head had begun to swim pleasantly from the wine. He took another egg and dipped it into his soup. The thick liquid spread across his tongue and oozed out of the corner of his mouth to run down his chin, and the aroma of tomato and rosemary wafted into the air as he captured the stray morsels with his tongue. 'You've told him nothing, I assume?'

'Of course not,' Elian said. 'But then, I know little to reveal. You haven't exactly confided in me what you've foreseen.' He looked down at his palm, rubbed red by his thumb.

The hint of resentment in his voice surprised Perian. 'There's little to tell – it's all so sketchy. All I know myself is that this is where I should be and that I must reinstate myself within the royal household. I keep nothing back, Elian.'

He was about to ask Elian to describe his visit to the Magi when the outer door opened and closed. Lono had returned. Elian looked up nervously, and Perian wiped his mouth with his napkin, dipped his fingers in the finger bowl and called for Lono. He rushed in, and with only the briefest look at Elian, he knelt by Perian's chair, his head on the floor.

'You have no reason to fear me,' Perian said. Lono kept his eyes down. 'I don't want to know if you are expected to report on my activities to Grison or my father, or even if you are questioned by them.'

Lono looked up as though to deny such activity, but Perian raised a hand to stop him.

'I am a Darna prince and you are my slave. You must never forget that, despite any informal relationship you may have developed with my companion. You will accord the two of us the respect required while I am present, and what goes on in my chambers must not go beyond these walls. Having said that, I have no wish for you to lie if questioned. If you are asked a direct question, you must answer truthfully. Your life will depend on it as Elian's and mine will not. Is that understood?'

'Yes, my Zameel.'

'This is not your fault. It is not our fault. It just is,' Perian continued. His voice was harsh and louder than he had intended, and in the brief moment while he took a breath, he wondered what had become of him. In less than a few months, he had turned from a carefree, happy wandering minstrel into a tyrant. Why couldn't he be more like Aronaye? He could feel Elian's angry eyes burning into him, but thankfully, his brother said nothing.

Perian brought his attention back to the man still bent before him. 'Are you literate, Lono?'

'Yes, my Zameel.' The words were clear and prideful, even though his forehead was still pressed into the carpet.

'Good. Go to the study and select a book of your choice. Not one you think may please me. Choose a paragraph and copy it in your best hand, and wait for me.'

'Yes, my Zameel.'

Lono rose slowly, bowed and left, careful not to look at anyone. When the door closed behind him, Perian sat back in his chair and drank a full glass of wine before pouring another, which he knew was probably a mistake. Only then did he look at his brother. Elian was white with anger and shock.

'I thought I knew you, my brother, but I don't. How could you talk to another human being like that?'

Perian stared into his glass. His hands shook slightly.

'I don't know. It will be all right. When this is over I will free Lono and he can return to his life. But in the meantime, he must not slip up. The officer at our door will notice any change in attitude, and my father will send Lono back to whatever miserable chore he was engaged in before he was given to me. Or worse, kill him. I believe I have just saved his life.' He directed his gaze at Elian. 'I am not insensible to his plight, but I must follow the path I have been given, and Lono is better off here with us than he would be otherwise. He's built for the mines, and that's probably where he was before we came.'

Elian's anger diminished, and Perian could see that he finally understood.

'I'm sorry, Perian. I am sorry you have found yourself in this situation.'

Perian turned his glass about in his hands and watched the refracted rays of the sun spread into a colourful aura across the table. 'As I said, it would have happened at some point, and in truth it's a relief that it has. Let's move on.' He leant across the table and took Elian's hand in his. 'You must promise me that if you are discovered, you will fly from the nearest window and return to Silaven.'

Elian looked up, startled. He tried to pull his hand away, but Perian held it tight.

'Promise me.'

Elian nodded his assent and put his other hand over Perian's. 'Let's hope it doesn't come to that. Who are you going to write to?'

'No one. But I'm interested in what Lono finds pleasurable and I want him to read to me. It will give me time to think.' He grinned. 'And if it's very boring, I can at least catch up on my sleep!'

20

The study was the smallest room in Perian's chambers. Shelves crammed with books covered half of one wall; on the opposite, two plain metal sconces hung over a reclining chair with three cushioned chairs about it. Daylight shone on Lono through leaded windows as he sat at a small desk to one side, still engrossed in copying the paragraph he had chosen. The index finger of his right hand pressed upon the page of his book, and he carefully guided his quill across a sheet of paper with his left hand. The process looked awkward.

Perian was at his side within a few long strides. Lono looked up, startled, and slid from the chair to his knees, his quill still between his fingers.

'Be seated, Lono, and let me see what you have written so far.'

Lono stood and handed Perian the sheet he had been working on. Long, elegant strokes glided across it, angled as though frozen in an attempt to flee the page. Perian touched his finger to the black strokes, then pulled it away quickly as a large, wood-panelled room began to open in his mind. He didn't want to see Lono's previous life, or what he had once been. His perfect script told him enough: Lono was an educated man, perhaps a scholar.

Esper, his foster mother, had been a scholar. The youngest daughter of Lord Perni, before Perni had been executed as a traitor and the Zamir had taken his lands and sold his family and household into slavery. Esper had always maintained her father's innocence and said that the Zamir merely wanted their lands. When Perian's mother had produced a son, the Zamir had given Esper to her as a gift – a slave who would become Perian's tutor eventually. As it turned out, she had been more than that to Perian. Esper was the only mother he knew. She would be disappointed if she found out that he had returned to the royal household.

The paragraph Lono had chosen was a quote from Higrean, a well-respected Darna philosopher who had lived some two hundred years before. Perian scanned the text, enough to see that Higrean was holding forth on the moral obligations of all free thinkers to oust the scourge of prophets and priests, especially those who demanded blood sacrifices. Either his argument hadn't been very good, or no one had paid attention.

Perian returned the paper to the table and turned to the wide, padded bench in the window alcove, beating a green velvet cushion as much to expel thoughts of sacrifice as to push it into a comfortable shape. He fell against its feathered softness at an angle that permitted a view from the window. It looked over the front courtyard and down the middle of the boulevard. Perian decided that, with their view onto the comings and goings of court, his chambers would most certainly have been home to one of the Shanahan's brothers.

He craned his neck up a little further to watch the slaves running back and forth beneath him, going about their daily chores. Thankfully, he didn't recognise anyone, but he felt sure the day would come when he did. He wondered what he would do: look away, greet them with a wary smile of sympathy, or ignore them and walk by without recognition as his station required? Probably the latter. To engage with them would give them hope, and he had no hope to give.

Two warriors with satchels over their shoulders rode out in a great hurry; those would be the messengers going to the border with Wellorn in response to his vision. A pigeon flew past shortly after, heading in the same direction. The birds had roamed wild once, but now they existed only in captivity for the purpose of relaying messages. Any rogue pigeon was killed, and no doubt eaten.

He suddenly remembered Lono, still sitting motionless at the table. 'What book did you choose, Lono?'

'*A History of the Known World, Volume Three: Darna.*'

Perian glanced up at him suspiciously.

'I am interested in all history, yet I know little of your people, my Zameel.'

Lono's reference to 'his people' made Perian's stomach turn. But Lono's choice was a sensible one, considering he could expect to spend the remainder of his life amongst them.

'Read to me, Lono. You may choose whichever chapter pleases you.'

Perian found their incarceration more tolerable now that they didn't have to live in one room. They moved all the furniture in the living room to the outer walls, and mid-morning was taken up by exercise and mock fights with Elian to ensure their muscles remained strong and their reactions automatic. Apart from exercising, Perian read most mornings, and when he didn't need his attendant's services, Lono was free to continue his studies of Darna history in another room. In the afternoons, Lono read to him from a rather thin book on Wellorn battle tactics. Elian usually dozed on the couch.

After a few days Perian noticed an increase in the number of message birds flying back and forth. There hadn't been time for the riders to reach the men the Zamir had sensibly posted along the border, which suggested that Ishra's army was already in sight. A group of five riders lined up before the entrance, and one of the Zamir's generals approached them and handed out scrolls. Perian couldn't hear what was said, but the riders left and rode down the boulevard at a canter. He followed their progress through the outer gates until they disappeared from his sight, but he saw enough to know that they didn't go in the direction of the border.

On the same day, a group of priests of the Sky God crossed the courtyard and disappeared through the entrance somewhere beneath him. Their presence puzzled him for a moment, until he realised, with a slight shock, that the solstice was almost upon them. He turned back to Lono, allowing the slave's voice to fill his mind. He wasn't really listening, though. He was waiting for the inevitable knock on his door.

It came less than half an hour after he'd seen the priests leave again. Elian shifted into the wolf automatically, Lono dropped his book, and they stared stupidly at each other for a moment. A second, louder knock came too soon after the first.

'Answer the door, Lono, before they burst in.' Perian stood and brushed his clothes down, as much to calm himself as to look presentable.

Lono hurried through the door.

'Get the Zameel, you lazy bastard,' came the familiar harsh voice of the officer.

He's having a good day! Elian mumbled into Perian's mind. Perian ignored him and walked calmly from the study before Lono had time to turn about.

'Thank you, Lono,' Perian said as he glided past the slave, who had dropped to his knees. 'I'm all yours, officer.' He inclined his head by way of greeting, but the officer had already turned on his heel and was walking quickly toward the stairs.

Perian's personal guards waited anxiously for him to catch up with the receding figure before falling in behind him. Perian raised his eyebrows, startling them with his informal gesture, and a warrior with a thin beard and broken nose shook his head slightly in response.

Sounds of unusual activity rose to greet them as the four men descended the stairs. The officer swung off to the right on the first floor, suggesting that Perian was being led to the library again. They were within a hundred paces of the door when a younger version of his father stomped from the room into the corridor. He closed the door quietly, but the whiteness of his knuckles and the twisting muscles along his arm suggested that he exerted great control not to slam it. He turned his attention on Perian's party as it came to a sudden stop; the officer placed his right arm across his chest and bowed his head, as did the two warriors, but Perian merely inclined his head. He would have extended his hand, but the look on the man's face didn't encourage such friendliness.

The two princes stared at each other for a moment. This new half-brother was shorter than both Perian and his father, with thick dark hair that hung loose below his shoulders. The kinks in his shiny mane suggested that he usually wore it in a thong that had gone astray. His green eyes flashed with anger and he held his square jaw tight beneath a thick brush of beard.

The prince stepped past the officer and came to stand so close to Perian that his sour breath made Perian's nose wrinkle. 'I'm next in line,' he snarled. 'If the old man dies, I'll have your head on a spike before his body's cold.' Then he stomped off toward the stairs, ramming Perian's shoulder as he passed.

Perian watched his half-brother disappear down the stairwell before entering the volatile atmosphere of the library, where his father paced the rug at the centre of the room. The gold trim about the hem of his long black vest flew out behind him and flicked around his legs with each turn. The flush of anger and impatience upon his face didn't bode well for a friendly interview, and Perian braced himself for an angry verbal – or possibly physical – assault. He wondered if part of his vision had proven untrue.

'Sit,' Maltha barked before Perian had time to drop to one knee.

Perian took the seat he had used before and waited with his hands open upon his lap. Maltha paced back and forth a few more times, then stopped to shout for Grison, his fists clenching at his sides. Perian sat very still and looked straight ahead. The marks of his previous battering had scarcely faded, and he didn't want new ones.

The faint whisper of rushing feet finally came from the corridor, culminating in Grison's noisy entry, followed by Erely's lighter step. The Zamir indicated that they should sit quickly with a slight movement of his head. He was calmer now, and Perian noticed as he sat by his side that whatever had occurred between father and older son had been put aside for another day.

'You know why you're here, Tanais. Put yourself in the mood to earn your keep, and quickly.'

Grison chanced a disapproving look at the Zamir before addressing Perian in a voice forced to calm. 'What your father is saying is that you should try to relax and prepare yourself to receive your visions.'

Perian was distracted for a moment by his father's fingers tightening about a knot he had created in his tunic as though it were Grison's neck, before he released his grip quite suddenly and nodded at Grison.

'Your previous predictions were correct,' said Grison, 'as you have no doubt observed from your window. If you can, we would like you to look further into the coming exchange with Ishra's army.'

Perian looked into Grison's expectant face. The fear and need in the man's cold grey eyes spread rapidly over him, increasing his own anxiety, and he wriggled into his chair to hide his nervousness. What would he say if he saw defeat?

The truth, he told himself. Erely would know if he lied or held anything back.

'Do you need something to touch?' Grison asked.

Perian shook his head. The tension in the air and their concentrated thoughts were quite enough. He breathed deeply and withdrew as best he could, closing his eyes to block out his audience.

At first nothing came. He could feel the minutes ticking by and his father's impatience growing, and he sank deeper into himself and willed his mind to look at the forthcoming battle.

The field of slaughter came upon him suddenly. His instinctive shout of horror rose above the sound of battle and distracted him enough to pull him back from the action. The clarity of his surroundings wavered with his thundering pulse, but both settled as his initial panic subsided. He cast his seer's eye about to look for markers on which to hang the battle's progress. Without listening to the words, he began to voice what he saw.

'The battle is fierce but appears almost over. Queen Ishra herself marches at the head of her troops. She has crushed your border warriors like grass in a field. I see Sun Mountain in the background and great columns of smoke rising from the north-east. She must be at least twenty miles inside Rashinder.'

Perian paused as the vision faded. He was still gripped by his trance. No one in the library moved. Burning cottages and fields, slaughtered animals, flashed in and out of his sight, accompanied by the sound of screams and the bellows of triumph. Then, at last, he entered another scene.

'She has pushed as far as the Silver River. They have been brought to a standstill by the river and the sight of a large Rashinder army on the other side, led by Darna officers. Darna warriors are in the forefront. A Zameel wearing the royal colours is talking with his officer. The officer is moving forward with the staff-holder and his arm is across his chest. I believe he wishes to talk rather than fight. Ishra herself goes to meet him as he crosses at the shallow point of the river. They face each other. The Darna officer is saying something to her.'

A single arrow flew through the air and lodged itself in the Zameel's throat, and Perian's account came to a sudden halt as his body froze. Before anyone in the vision could register their shock, Ishra drew her long sword and severed the heads of both officer and staff-holder with one pass of its blade. Perian's body was suffused with heat and a blank whiteness overtook him.

He came to with a jolt when his shoulder hit the floor. Grison was at his side immediately, holding his head and asking what he'd seen. Erely gave him some water from her glass.

'You must not try to negotiate with her,' Perian shouted. 'Push your troops to get across the river first or wait for her on the other side. She will not parley. She will trick your son.'

The Zamir was about to say something, but Grison put up his hand. 'Why, Tanais? What did you see?'

Shakily, he described the vision. His father turned pale and asked him to go over it all again and add any further details he recalled.

When Perian could give him no more, Maltha rose quickly and left the room, and it was not until Perian heard the door to the library slam shut that he reseated himself and put his head into his trembling hands. Grison patted him on the shoulder and left to follow the Zamir.

The room was suddenly quiet and empty, except for the vaguely disturbing presence of Erely. Perian lifted his head slowly to chance a look at her. She smiled at him.

'You did well, Tanais. You are indeed all that dear Shimester thought you would be.' She handed him the glass of water again. 'Now, if you feel strong enough, I would like you to do a little scrying for me, too.'

She took a small handkerchief from her pocket and unfolded it. In its centre sat a man's gold ring. At its widest point, small rubies formed the shape of the Darna claw. The stones were so dark as to appear black.

Perian glanced at her again, then took the ring tentatively between his thumb and index finger. The deep red stones sparkled as they caught the light.

A sharp pain erupted in his belly and spread to every part of his body. He felt his blood turn black and spewed the stuff over already-stained silk sheets, once pale blue. His lungs were filled with pitch that burned and stank of rotting flesh. As his head rolled to one side, he glimpsed a young woman, motionless and covered in her own vomit. Blood filled his throat again, and slowly, without strength enough in his lungs to cough for air or even move, he drowned in his own fluids.

While all-consuming and debilitating, the vision was brief. Perian had dropped the ring seconds after picking it up as he fell to his knees at Erely's feet. Every part of him shook, and he noticed he had drooled onto the rug. He wiped it with the hem of his tunic and ran his hand across the sweat on his forehead.

'Poison,' he gasped. The intense pain had receded, and he felt faint with relief, but when he looked up at Erely she was ashen, her chin quivering for control. 'A cruel way to die,' Perian whispered. 'No one should die like that.' He got up and staggered to the door. 'Who was he?'

'My nephew,' she said, without looking up from the ring on the floor.

Perian hesitated for a moment. 'I'm sorry. Can I get the guard to fetch someone?'

'No,' she snapped, then snatched up the ring and returned it to the handkerchief. 'You will mention this to no one, Tanais. Your father and Grison will find out soon enough.'

Perian nodded and left, walking quickly past his startled guards to have the satisfaction of hearing them run to catch up.

'Wine, Lono,' he shouted at the figure that burst from his bedchamber. 'A sealed jug, not one of the open pitchers the cellar master usually gives you.' He wasn't going to take any chances, having just experienced a man's horrific death by poison.

As he entered his room, his eye caught the hastily discarded cards on the table before settling on the wolf, expectant on the rug by his bed. He'd deal with that particular issue later, but for the moment he needed to make sense of what had just occurred in the library.

He threw himself into what had become his favourite chair and stared at the fireplace. It annoyed him that he had already fallen into a routine on returning from his sessions with his father.

He heard Elian's soft pad across the carpet, but it was his brother's human form that sat opposite. 'We won't play cards again.'

He knew it. Elian could read his thoughts! Perian wondered why he found their card games so irritating. It wasn't because he couldn't join in and have some fun for a change – at least, he didn't think so.

Then he realised with a jolt that he was afraid. Terrified, in fact, that Elian might have to leave, or worse, that he would be caught and taken away. Hurt, or even killed. He shook his head and glanced at Elian with a look that pleaded forgiveness.

'It is fear that influences my thoughts and actions, and my words,' he said. 'I couldn't bear to lose you, Elian, or think of you getting hurt.'

'Nor could I.' Elian snorted. 'I've gone off the game anyway. Lono keeps winning and I've run out of the pieces of stick we stole from the fire.' He moved his chair closer to Perian and took his hand. 'Why the sealed jug? Has something happened?'

'You could say that. I witnessed – no, experienced – a terrible poisoning.' Something began to unravel within him as he spoke. Tears welled up to heat his eyes and his throat caught so that he could scarcely breathe.

Elian shifted forward to the edge of his seat and slid an arm around Perian's shoulders to draw his head close. Perian sobbed against his chest, releasing all his pent-up fear, anger and anxiety in a great spluttering waterfall of tears. Elian gripped him tighter and put his face against Perian's thick black hair.

'We'll wait until Lono returns with the wine. Then we'll share your insights, as we always do.'

Perian dragged himself away from Elian just as Lono returned and knocked on the open door. Perian averted his face slightly. A feeling of emptiness opened up within him. His face felt blotched and swollen. He listened to Lono pull the cork and pour the wine into two glasses. Elian took them from him and handed a glass to Perian as the bedchamber door clicked closed.

Perian found it easier to describe his experience now that the worst of his emotions lay in a sodden patch on Elian's shirt.

'It was an act of extreme cruelty. Even slitting the man's throat would have been preferable, and that's not really to be recommended. At least, I can't imagine it would be. There are plenty of quicker poisons, and several that take their victims peacefully in sleep. What that man experienced was born of malice and hatred.'

'Who was he, Perian? And what of this Erely?'

'Erely said he was her nephew. Her face displayed great grief, yet her eyes said something different. It wasn't that they were cold, more that she expected the news, or already knew about it. Perhaps it was the nature of this man's death, and his lady's, that caused her grief.'

'Do you think she was warning you with her request?'

'Well, it has certainly done that. But no. I think she wanted confirmation – either that it was done, or how it was done. As to who it was, I'm not sure. I suspect that he was another of my half-brothers, but I cannot be certain. I think it is time I found out more about my family tree.'

He remembered Esper drawing one up and lecturing him on his family history, pointing out the Zamir's children, where he fitted amongst them, and the familial relationships at court. He now wished he had taken more notice, but he had found it boring and spent the time wishing it were over. He could see the winding connections in his mind's eye, but could not bring them into focus enough to make out the names; they had covered several sheets and had looked too complicated for him to bother with at the time.

'Lono would probably know. It's the kind of thing that's important for a slave to memorise,' Elian said.

Perian nodded. 'Call him in.'

Lono was kneeling at his feet so quickly that Perian wondered whether he had been listening at the door.

'Get up, Lono, and tell me about the royal family – the names of the Zamir's children, their order of birth and where they are now. I assume you know all this.'

Lono's demeanour remained unchanged, but his eyes showed his surprise that Perian didn't already know. 'Yes, my Zameel. I know much of what is going on.' The offer of information was not lost on Perian, but he let that lie for the moment and nodded for Lono to proceed. 'The eldest son is Soas. He and his wife remain in Darna's capital, Loren, in the Zamir's stead. The second son is Valamer, who came to Rashinder with the Zamir, as did the third, Saphrax, who now leads the warriors against the invading Wellorn army. Then of course there is you, my Zameel, the youngest.'

'And the daughters?'

'There are five. All married. Intha, Nanda and Lieva are all here in Rashinder, married to Rashinder noblemen. Amalase is the wife of King Arnden of Nor, and Untha is married to the Zamir's cousin, Vorten. She remains in Darna as she is with child, but her husband has accompanied the Zamir.'

Perian stared at Lono. Suddenly he understood why there were so many Rashinder troops facing battle with Wellorn, and why there had been a traitor within the Shanahan's entourage to slam the door in Radia's face when they were escaping the invasion. His father had been planning this invasion for more years than Perian had imagined, and he had no doubt that the noblemen Lono had mentioned were highly placed within the hierarchy of Rashinder.

He cast his mind's eye over Esper's drawing of his family tree again. There had been more than nine names listed under Maltha's.

'The Zamir has six wives, I believe,' he said. 'One would have expected more children to survive. Was there some illness that swept through the country, or an hereditary defect that you know of, Lono?'

'I cannot say, my Zameel. But I have heard that the mortality rate amongst the young males of the Zamir's seed is unusually high.'

In other words, it was common knowledge that they were being done away with, but no one was saying it outright. 'And do you know anything of a woman called Erely, who my father refers to as a witch?'

Lono's eyes flashed with recognition. 'She is the aunt of the Zameels Soas and Valamer – their mother's sister. I understand that she is unmarried.'

Perian suddenly felt weak and hollow. It must have been Valamer he had met outside the library. His nasty little comment suggested that he already knew of Soas's death and had stupidly implicated himself. Perian wondered how long it would be before Valamer realised this and began to take steps to eliminate him. He would have to be very careful – and mindful of what he ate and drank.

'What else have you heard about her, Lono?' Elian asked.

'I know only that she is a truth-seer. She is there at the interrogations of all the royal slaves.'

'They interrogate you all? Regularly?' said Elian. 'Why would they do that?'

'Only the personal slaves who attend the royal family. The Royal Slave Master is careful to deal with only certain merchants he knows he can trust, but we are always questioned to ensure the family's safety. Everyone's life is at risk if a slave turns traitor.'

'I had no idea it was so complicated, keeping slaves,' said Elian; he started to ask another question, but Perian stopped him with a look and dismissed Lono.

'You can ask him about his life history another time, Elian,' said Perian once Lono had gone. 'In the meantime, we, or I, have a problem.'

21

'I hope you're not expecting Lono to taste your food for you,' Elian said when Perian told him of his encounter with Valamer.

'Of course not. We'll have to rely on his care and that wolf nose of yours.'

Elian sat back in his chair and crossed his legs. 'Well, that sounds foolproof!'

'What else can we do?' Perian shrugged and told Elian of the meeting of armies across the Silver River. 'The majority were Rashinder men, but even including the houses whose loyalty my father has secured through marriage, that does not account for the numbers.'

'The rest he's probably blackmailed into service using his hostages.'

'That's what I thought,' said Perian. 'He would also have placed his daughters with men of influence over smaller domains. Not wholly reliable, but enough to make a good show of force.'

Elian rubbed at his eyes and the worry lines that creased his face. 'Did you notice Radia, or Edun and his men, amongst the Wellorn troops?'

Perian thought for a moment, trying to recapture what he had seen. 'I was concentrating on Ishra, but if they were there, their presence wasn't obvious.'

Suddenly he felt tired. He wanted to sleep and forget about the fate of Rashinder for a while.

'I cannot think about it all anymore, Elian. I am tired to the bone. The day is not over and my feeling is that I will be called out again before evening comes.'

He rose stiffly and lay upon his bed, but he could not sleep. His mind would not rest and his body remained tense. After a while, the bed dipped as Elian sat on its edge.

'I'm sleeping,' Perian mumbled.

'No, you're not. Your eyes are still open.'

Perian squeezed his lids tighter, but they opened again as though on springs. Soas' suffering and Valamer's venomous words ran through his mind in a constantly repeating stream.

Then a vision severed them.

He found himself watching his door implode. Men spilt in through the opening, followed by screams and the smell of blood. Before he could see who the invaders were, the scene changed rapidly, like a volley of picture cards, one after the other. He saw fighting and blood on the stairs – and himself, with his hands bound behind him, Valamer's personal warrior pushing him along in the dark.

He sprang upright with shock, then cursed himself for inadvertently breaking the connection. There it was, then. Valamer would come for him and he would disappear. There could be no witnesses, so Elian and Lono would disappear with him – into a deep hole, no doubt. It would be a brazen attempt on his life. But he knew Valamer felt safe in the knowledge that his father would not kill his own son.

For the first time, it occurred to him that the Zamir had no brothers that he was aware of, which was unlikely considering the number of wives Darna rulers usually took. No doubt his father had done the same as Valamer in his youth: removed any competition to his rule in the form of both older and younger brothers.

Elian had been talking quietly, but stopped when Perian sat up, and Perian had to ask him to repeat what he had been saying.

'I was just suggesting I take a little trip to check on Jolint. Find out what's happening in Wellorn.'

Perian stared at him, again wondering whether his brother had read his thoughts. He decided not, but seized the opportunity to remove Elian from danger anyway. 'What about your nose? Am I supposed to starve while you're gone?'

'Always thinking of your stomach,' Elian laughed. 'You and Lono will just have to muddle along as best you can. I'm fairly certain that one of your fingers immersed in your food will tell you more than my super nose.'

'Well, that will look good if I'm invited out for dinner. And how am I supposed to look superior in front of my slave with my fingers in the stew?'

'You see, you're perfectly safe. No one is going to invite you for dinner and no slave has any respect for their master anyway. Lono already knows you're an ill-mannered, lazy sod.'

Perian launched himself at Elian, but Elian jumped up quickly and Perian slid to the floor in a tangle of slippery sheets.

As they returned to their seats at the hearth, Perian studied Elian's face. The violet eyes that shone with amusement, the long face and delicate nose, the long blond hair that hung loose about his shoulders, the slender body at ease with one leg over the other. He wanted to soak in every part of his brother so that he could hold them in his memory and heart once Elian had gone. Later he would seek a vision in the hope that his path – their path – had not changed too much, but not now.

Elian's smile faltered. 'Don't look so serious. I'll be back soon with my report.'

Perian paused before replying. 'No, Elian. You can tell me what you learn from outside the palace. Stay in town so you are close, but for the moment, you are more use to me beyond these chambers.'

Elian slowly uncrossed his legs and leant forward accusingly. 'Why?'

'Soon I will be incarcerated. At the moment I cannot see what will befall you or Lono. All I can say is that if you are imprisoned with me, we are both lost. Hopefully, necessity will unlock my inability to respond to your communication.'

'Did you just see that, or have you been keeping this from me?'

'I just saw it, a moment ago. There is little – nothing – I keep from you, Elian.'

Elian sat back in his chair and let out a long breath that whistled slightly between his teeth.

'You must go now, Elian,' Perian insisted. 'It doesn't matter who sees you fly from my window. You will be gone and safe, and there is nothing anyone will be able to do about it.' Elian searched his face as he stood and held out his hand to draw Elian to his feet. 'Please, Elian. Go now before I relent and plead with you to stay.'

Elian threw his arms about Perian and held him so tightly, Perian's breath would not come.

'The pathways of possibility are moving so fast, none dominant for long in any major way. Yet, so far, I have not foreseen our deaths.'

'You'll tell me if you do?'

Perian pulled away from Elian's grip and held his face between his hands. 'Of course. What's the point of being a seer if you can't rearrange fate?'

Elian laughed and squeezed Perian briefly before walking toward the window. 'Say goodbye to Lono for me, and let me know if you want me to drop food through the barred window of that cell of yours.'

He flung open the window and stepped back to change into a sygrilien; then, letting out an almighty screech at Perian, he hopped onto the sill and flew off across the rooftops.

Perian leant out through the opening to watch Elian's progress until he was a dot vanishing into the verdant canopy of the forest beyond the walls. Elian's screeching had drawn the attention of the people in the streets and the guards about the palace. The raucous noise of such a large sygrilien would be cause for gossip in the taverns and concern for the Darna. It amused him to think that the sighting would send the priests into a frenzy of discussion about what it meant, especially so close to the solstice.

The solstice! When was it? A different kind of panic constricted his chest and stomach. 'Lono!' he shouted.

As usual, Lono was quickly at his feet. It still surprised him. How he longed to be the person he only vaguely remembered, sitting in a tavern with a mug of ale in his hands and yesterday's bread and cheese on the table, instead of a prince with a slave.

'When is the solstice?'

'Tomorrow, my Zameel.'

Tremors ran through Perian's body in overlapping waves. He took a moment before asking Lono what time the ceremony would be held.

'At the usual time, my Zameel. Dawn.'

Of course; he remembered now. If the birds didn't finish the poor souls off, the midday sun would. What a horrible way to die. On par with poison, no doubt.

He had just fallen into a deep sleep when he was woken by shouts outside his door and the startled presence of Lono in the doorway. At first he thought it was Valamer's man, but no one was breaking the door down yet, and through the muddle of waking, he began to understand what the interruption was about.

'Soldiers of the Sky God are demanding that you go with them to see the priests,' said Lono.

Perian lifted his head. Lono stood with his hand against the doorjamb as though to support himself, his eyes getting wider by the second. Belatedly, he fell to his knees. Perian stared at him blankly.

The shouting grew louder. 'We answer to the Zamir, and he determines where the Zameel goes,' bellowed one of Perian's guards.

'The priests have summoned him. He must attend,' shouted one of the soldiers. 'He is only a half-blood and not safeguarded by the Zamir.'

'Tell them to go away,' Perian shouted irritably over the noise from the corridor, just as the sound of a scuffle arose from beyond the vestibule door. The distinctive *zing* of a drawn sword sang above the curses and movement.

Perian rubbed his eyes and slid from the bed, yawning and scrubbing at his hair. Apart from the noise, the arrogance of the soldiers was beginning to annoy him.

The shouting became more intense. Someone would die if he didn't hurry.

He strode past Lono and pulled open the door to his chambers; one of his guards fell backward through the opening, his sword arcing through the air, and Perian found himself facing the blade of the priests' man.

'Put that away,' Perian shouted. 'Half-blood or not, I am not under the jurisdiction of the priests, or the Great Sygrilien, for that matter. I have no desire to see, speak or come within half a mile of your demented, sadistic superiors, and I do not leave these rooms unless requested to do so by my father, the Zamir. He would cut out your tongue for calling one of his blood a "half-blood". Now leave my chambers. I'm trying to sleep. I've had a tiring morning.'

Perian's guard scrambled to his feet beside him. The soldier of the Sky God did not move, and nor did the sword he pointed at Perian. His two companions stepped to his side.

Perian wasn't gifted with powerful sorcery, but he had enough, especially when so roused, to get a small advantage. He swept his arm about, releasing all his anger and frustration through his fingertips, and a satisfying light crackled and sparked, knocking the soldiers backward against the stair rail. They slid to the floor and their weapons clattered on the tiling. One sword tapped its way down the stairs.

Perian turned to his startled guards. 'Remove their weapons and take these arrogant sycophants to the main entrance. You can throw them into the courtyard with as much force as you wish. But you don't have long. They will revive soon and start their bleating all over again, at which point I might really lose my temper.'

He wasn't sure he could muster up another strike, but the soldiers and his guards didn't need to know that. His guards jumped to attention and Perian slammed the door on two men more than eager to do his bidding.

'May their god suck them dry,' Perian hissed as he stomped past Lono, who still knelt in the bedroom doorway. 'More wine, Lono, and hurry, before the next caller comes.'

He pumped cold water into his tub and splashed it over his head and face. He couldn't find a towel, so he flopped into his chair by the hearth and let the water trickle down his neck, soaking the front of his nightshirt. His heart still thumped with a mixture of rage and fear, and he scratched absently at the wings on his chest. The last thing he wanted was to face the priests. But they had no way of knowing that he was marked, and when he had calmed down a little, it dawned on him that it was Elian's sygrilien they were concerned about, not his tattoo. He let a smile creep over his face. The sighting had rattled them after all.

By the time Lono arrived with his wine he was calm again. Lono placed the tray carefully on the small table at his side and filled a glass before kneeling at Perian's feet. Perian took the glass slowly and drank most of its contents before looking down at Lono's bent head.

'You will sleep with the other slaves tonight, Lono. I want to be alone,' he lied.

Lono's head shot up, only briefly, but long enough for Perian to see the alarm in his eyes.

'I am not dismissing you,' Perian said softly. 'I merely want you out of the way tonight. I want no other slave to serve me. Make sure you tell them that, should you be questioned. Is that clear?'

'Yes, my Zameel.'

'Now, return to wherever you go when you're not here and wait for the next callers. The priests will not have given up. They will merely change their method of approach.'

Perian lay on his bed fully clothed, waiting for Valamer's men to break down his door, but no one came. Even the priests hadn't bothered to come for him again, and while he was thankful for that, he was also intensely bored. He had even left his bedroom door open to ease his loneliness with the muffled sounds of the guards talking. Once or twice he had crept into the vestibule to eavesdrop in the hope of hearing some interesting gossip, but they seemed obsessed with the coming sacrifices. The sooner Perian could forget about tomorrow morning's event, the better.

He estimated that it was about two hours before dawn when the sounds beyond his door became a little livelier. A light glittered in the front doorway, and Lono crept in very quietly.

'What do you want, Lono? I told you to sleep with the other slaves. Do they snore too much for you?'

'I was ordered to prepare you for the dawn ceremony, my Zameel.'

Perian sprang from the bed, his hand going automatically to the tattoo on his chest. 'What do you mean, "prepare me for the ceremony"? Who gave you this order?'

Lono closed the door quickly behind him and strode toward the bed. 'No, no, my Zameel. They wish you to attend, not take part.'

Perian sat back on the edge of the bed and put his head in his hands. Blood raced painfully through his body at the command of his pumping heart that refused to slow down.

'Forgive me for frightening you, my Zameel,' Lono said as he quickly lit the wall lamps. 'Should I run your bath so that you can be cleansed for this special occasion?'

'Whatever is usual, Lono. I am in your hands. I know nothing of these ceremonies.'

'Then I will talk you through what will be expected of you,' Lono called over the sound of rushing water.

Perian was still too shocked to play the game of master and slave, and he allowed Lono to lead him to the bath and sponge away the sweat that had coated his body.

'Master Grison gave the instruction. I have witnessed many of these ceremonies.'

Perian let out a groan. 'I don't have to give a speech or do anything, do I?'

'No, there are no speeches, thankfully. You will follow in the Zamir's train as a member of his family. I cannot tell you where you will be placed. Probably next to Zameel Valamer.' Another groan escaped Perian, but Lono ignored him and continued, 'There will be seats placed in view of the sacrificial stones, above the crowds of worshippers. When the sacrifices arrive they will be chained to the stones, which you must watch, and when the edge of the sun appears above the horizon, the Voice of the Sky God will release the life of each sacrifice by puncturing their lungs with the sacred fork. Once the last sacrifice has been released to their god, the crowds will be ushered away and the royal family will follow the priests from the scene, leaving only the Voice behind to receive the blessing and wisdom of Tarse.'

The whole thing was going to be horrible. Why couldn't he and Elian have been trapped after the solstice rather than before?

Lono was tying the royal gold-threaded sash about Perian's waist when someone knocked on the door. He stepped back and gave Perian a look of satisfaction before attending to the visitor.

Perian studied himself in the mirror. They hadn't had a mirror in the wetlands of his youth, and it still amazed him to see the whole of himself rather than just his head on the surface of still water. There was little evidence now of his beating – just a touch of darkness around his left eye – and his features were finer than those of his half-brothers. Lono had dressed him in the robes appropriate for such a ceremony, and he ran his fingers about the high neck of his long coat of soft white silk. Bright, ruby-studded buttons ran the full length of the coat and had taken Lono an age to do up. Beneath the sleeveless coat was a sheer white shirt, and Lono had gathered its billowing gossamer sleeves and bound each above the elbow with a ruby-encrusted armlet in the shape of a hooked claw. Short doeskin boots of the lightest tan peeped out from beneath his coat. All this was completed by the wide royal sash.

He was startled by the appearance of Officer Valia in his mirror. Valia bowed low when Perian spotted him. He had a look of amused approval, Perian thought. He turned and nodded at the officer as he walked past him toward the doorway.

'Let's get this over with,' he said, then took a deep breath and slowed his pace to allow Valia to catch up before descending the stairs. He needed to calm down and hold his tongue. Devotion to the Sky God was the religion of the Darna people, and he should be more careful not to offend.

Perian's family had gathered in the Audience Room. It was the first time he had seen all of them together. They were all dressed the same, and his father was in discussion with Grison and another man Perian assumed was Vorten, Maltha's cousin and son-in-law. Valamer stood alone, at a distance, tapping his foot on the mosaic eye of a coiled kroyer. Four women stood in a cluster. Perian assumed they were the wives his father had brought with him. They also wore white robes offset by ruby-encrusted jewellery that hung from their ears, necks and noses, but strangely, they wore no rings.

Grison left and Valamer joined his father. The Zamir looked briefly at Perian and made a clicking sound through his teeth. A bowstring twanged inside Perian, and he automatically smoothed his hair and stroked the braid that touched his left shoulder. He gazed down self-consciously at his clothing. Everything seemed to be in order.

With a glance at Perian, Valamer took his place behind the Zamir. Perian moved up behind Valamer, and the women moved silently to take their position at the rear. He thought of Jolint and Cerister; they wouldn't be so content to walk behind their men.

Cerister. *I haven't forgotten you,* he said to the figure that formed in his mind. He recalled his vision: her hand against the invisible wall, the distraught look upon her face. She had not come to him again, so perhaps it had been a farewell gesture rather than a warning.

22

For the sacrifices, the priests had chosen a cluster of large rocks that jutted out high over the sea on rolling downs, east of the city walls – the Whales' Breach, they were called, due to the way they arched toward the ocean like enormous sea creatures diving into the water. Below, waves crashed and wailed through a hole worn into their base. Large, flat oval boulders, appropriate for sacrifice, had been hauled onto even ground, forming an eerie silhouette against the moonlit sky.

The royal family filed from their carriages and took their places on seats along a platform lit by torches, not far from the rocks. The priests were already there, standing in a group at one end, and Perian detected Grison's handiwork in the unnatural brightness of their headbands.

He stared in confusion at the large crowd that had gathered below, stretching into the darkness, its excited and expectant chatter shattering the early-morning peace. The wealthy stood together in three rows at the front, cordoned off from the riffraff by armed warriors. Whether they were there by choice or social pressure, he couldn't tell, but the majority were ordinary townsfolk, farmers and visitors from further afield, come to be shocked, horrified and delighted at the same time. The scene reminded him of the conversation he had overheard at the Windy Path when he and Elian had first returned to Jasperen, in which the merits of the new slave market had been discussed. Now the populace was showing their approval of human sacrifice. Perian looked away from the crowd. He didn't want to think about it.

He sat between one of the Zamir's wives and Valamer. The heat of Valamer's anger burned into his side, but he didn't know whether it came from having to sit next to his beardless half-brother, or some private disapproval of the ceremony. Perian noticed that many in the crowd pointed at him, and suddenly he felt conspicuous and naked amidst the thickly bearded Darna men.

A disturbance in the crowd to their left signalled the arrival of the victims, chained to the bars of a horse-drawn carriage. Simple metal sconces on the corners of each cage held torches, and their upward light made a grotesquerie of the terrified faces.

Like everyone else, Perian was curious to see who had been chosen. He couldn't help himself. He leant forward to look at the seven healthy young men and women whose lives were to be cut short. By their clothing, Grison had chosen mostly from amongst the poor sent in by landowners. Only one did he recognise: a young nobleman who still wore the tattered remains of the silken finery he had sported at the festival, no doubt the son of a minor lord who had many other children and had refused to comply with the priests' demands. Or perhaps he had refused to submit to the Zamir in his own right. Of them all, he was the only one who looked thin and malnourished.

The cart stopped not far from the stones, and the level of excitement amidst the throng rose to a new level as a faint glimmer of light appeared along the horizon and the Voice of the Sky God began a piercing wail from his position near the stones. The unusual sound startled Perian. Lono hadn't mentioned it in his brief description of the proceedings. The wail soon changed to something more like a hoot with each inward and outward breath. The other priests joined in with the Voice, then the mesmerising sound was taken up by the crowd.

The air throbbed with pulsating sound and Perian's head began to swirl. He felt as though the hooting went through him and pushed him back and forth. He wanted to scream at its intensity, to stand and run away from it. But he couldn't. He gripped his seat with his hands and hoped that he wouldn't pass out.

A soft pink coloured the hills to the east, rosying the cheeks of the already flushed chanters. Perian turned his head a little to look out to sea, away from the nauseating sight of mass euphoria, and found himself staring at the sacrifices. They were led forth in a solemn procession and stripped of their clothing before being laid over their individual stones. That none fainted or tried to run suggested that they had been drugged to make them compliant.

Beyond the victims, the sygrilien were already gathering, and it occurred to Perian that the priests had been training them to come to this spot for weeks with morsels of meat. They floated on the wind, their blue heads and beaks moving as they screeched above the chanting.

A nudge from Valamer brought his attention back to the crowd, which had begun to vibrate in time with the priests' hooting. Perian vaguely wondered if they really were swaying or whether he was hallucinating. Sweat broke out in droplets over his face; his mouth filled with moisture and his eyelids drooped a little. He wondered whether he would vomit first and then pass out, or the other way around.

He stared out into the distance, over the top of the crowd. A large white spot hovered within his vision, and for a moment the pulsing and hooting faded away as he tried to concentrate, but he found it hard to focus and dismissed the spot as part of his hallucination.

Wake up, Perian, or you'll miss the show!

Elian's voice struck him like a slap on the face, and suddenly he was fully alert, his nausea forgotten. The object was speeding toward the gathering, rapidly growing into an oversized sygrilien. Elian – it had to be!

Perian's whole body lit up with excitement. He wanted to laugh out loud and fly into the sky to join his brother, but the first was likely to suggest that he was either mad or complicit, and the second was impossible.

By this time, the victims had been chained down. The Voice thrust the sacrificial fork high above his head, triumphant, with such a look of rapture upon his face that Perian's stomach turned.

Elian's vast body turned pink in the rays of the rising sun, and his long blue neck an unpleasant mauve. His screeching drowned out the priests' throbbing hoot, which slowly dissipated as he flew low over the crowd. Beyond the deafening sounds, Perian could hear the real sygrilien responding as they coalesced into a noisy, shifting group that drifted cautiously closer and closer.

Elian swept over the sacrifices, who woke in unison with his approach as though from a dream, then up into the group of sygrilien, causing them to disperse. The victims screamed. The sygrilien screeched and the hooting chant faltered. Still holding the fork high, the Voice fled to the platform, surrounded by his priests.

Elian turned about and flew straight at the platform, toward the seated figures. His enormous wingspan alone was terrifying, but his open beak showed that this was not just an aerial display of power. Admiration and love flooded through Perian.

The Zamir stood, which was a stupid thing to do, but he wasn't Elian's target. Instead, the sygrilien swerved to the side, toward the priests. Several toppled from the platform as they stepped back, but others moved forward to surround the Voice, who had dropped the sacrificial fork. Their actions did nothing to sway the bird from his purpose: Elian thrust his great claws forward as he neared the huddled group without slowing in his approach.

The courage of the Voice's priests deserted them as Elian drew closer, and they threw themselves from the platform, leaving Elian to sink his claws into the face of the screaming Voice unhindered. The man fell backward to the floor with Elian still attached, and Perian turned his head away when he realised that Elian was plucking out the Voice's eyeballs with his beak while shredding his tongue with the foot he had managed to shove into the man's open mouth. He remembered Elian once saying that he often had to fight back the instinctive nature of the beast he transformed into. In this instance, he clearly wasn't bothering.

Neither the soldiers of the Sky God, nor Grison or the Zamir's warriors, moved. The sygrilien were sacred; it would be a death sentence for anyone who killed or maimed one.

Warriors swarmed onto the platform to surround the Zamir and his family and usher them back into their carriages. Not surprisingly, most of the crowd was running back toward the city wall, but some remained, mesmerised by the spectacle. Perian turned to look back just as the sun popped its glorious head above the horizon. The priests' men were dragging the sacrificial victims back into their cage and preparing to leave.

Perian looked back one last time from his carriage. Elian was flying east, toward the sun and Jolint. Toppled chairs lay like broken bones across the platform, with the Voice alone and unmoving amongst them, a bloody mess. The only other person left on the platform was Grison. The whole attack had taken just a few minutes, and only now was Grison beginning to surface from the shock. His eyes drifted toward Perian as he clambered into his carriage. Their gazes met for a second before Perian looked beyond him.

The expectant sygrilien were moving in from the sea toward their daily feed, which today would be the Voice. Perian pointed; Grison turned to see the white cloud of birds approaching and began to shout instructions. Warriors swept the Voice of the Sky God off the platform and into his carriage. The sygrilien screeched their disappointment and flew low and threateningly over the remaining crowd.

The return journey was conducted in frigid silence. The Zamir stared out at the crowd as it parted before the speeding carriage. Perian expected jubilant cheering and possibly a few fists raised in anger, but most were too intent on escaping the birds that still flew about in hopes of the odd morsel of flesh. There were no taverns along the boulevard, but Perian knew the city's drinking holes would already be full to capacity. This was meant to be a religious holiday, but he doubted that any Rashinder tavern-keeper would lose a day's trade over a few sacrifices, and then there were all the out-of-towners who had come in for the entertainment.

The royal family was ushered into the Audience Hall, surrounded by a swarm of warriors. As soon as the Zamir stood over the coiled kroyer at the centre of the hall, he spun on his heels and glared at his two sons.

'You two, stay. Everyone else, out.' His voice was quiet, but forceful, and before Perian could catch his breath, they were alone.

The Zamir moved his foot about as though trying to find the right beat, casting his eyes around the room. Perian scarcely dared to breathe. He desperately wished he were somewhere else. He was certain his father would strike him. Each time Maltha's head swung his way, he wanted to duck. Valamer held himself stiffly beside him.

After what felt like long minutes, the Zamir looked Perian full in the eye.

'I have no love for the Voice. He is an imperious worm who dares to challenge my authority. I hope he lives and suffers for many years to come.' He looked down at the green mosaic tile he was prodding with his toe. 'But I have little doubt that you are involved in this fiasco in some way, Tanais.'

Perian opened his mouth to deny any connection to the incident, but quickly changed his mind.

'I do not wish to know your reasons,' the Zamir continued. 'But be aware that this is a disaster not just for the Order of the Sky God, but also for our sovereignty. That the messenger of the Sky God should turn on its servant on the day when we were to give thanks for our conquest undermines my right, our right, to be here. You will both go to the library and wait for me there. I want Grison present when we discuss how to deal with this situation.'

Grison was already in the library, seated in the same azure chair he had favoured on previous occasions, looking pale and shaken. Perian sat opposite him, but Valamer hovered about the oval table instead.

'Does he live?' Valamer asked.

'Yes.' Grison shuddered. He sipped from the mug of ale he held tightly with both hands. 'He lost both eyes, though the creature didn't eat them. I nearly trod on one as I left the podium; the other had rolled off the edge. The physician says he will need to amputate his tongue, and in future he will only be able to suck his meals through a straw.' Grison looked hard at Perian, then at the door. 'Where are your guards, Tanais?'

'He doesn't need them,' Valamer said. 'He has me.'

'Then you should wear your sword, Valamer. The priests blame Tanais. It will be very difficult to keep them off him. There are already rumblings of retribution. Maltha will resist them, of course, but they may pay someone to do it for them.'

Of course. Elian hadn't thought of that, had he? A large sygrilien had flown from Perian's window only yesterday. Who else had a trained sygrilien, as they would see it, of that size? He was bound to be the main suspect. And it was a crime punishable by lifelong servitude to capture a sygrilien. If they discovered his sacrificial mark, too, he would be the main entertainment at the next ceremony. They probably wouldn't even bother with the other victims.

'From what I heard, our Prince of Flame doesn't need any protection.'

Perian jolted at Valamer's reference. 'The men exaggerated,' he said quickly. 'I am not a powerful sorcerer.' He immediately regretted his words; he had just admitted a weakness to his enemy.

'Where did Father get this one?' Valamer spat.

Grison looked up as the Zamir entered, slamming the heavy door behind him. They all jumped. Perian noticed blood spatters on the hem of his father's robe as the Zamir stomped across the floor and sat beside him. Grison quickly poured ale into a mug and passed it to Maltha, and the Zamir held the mug so hard that Perian expected the pottery to crack at any moment and cover them both with its contents. He reached out to grasp the only mug left on the tray.

'That's for Valamer. We want your head clear,' said Grison,

snatching it up and passing it to Valamer, who wasn't concentrating and nearly dropped it.

'If the priests don't stop their demands, I'll brand every one of them and place them on the rocks myself, one at a time,' said the Zamir. His shoulders were hunched. He looked older, tired, and his words had lost their usual force. Without turning his attention from the amber liquid in his mug, he quietly asked Perian what was happening in Darna.

So this was at the heart of his father's demeanour. He had heard something, a rumour perhaps, even if the official pigeon hadn't arrived yet, which was unlikely.

Grison reached into his pocket and pulled out a piece of yellow silk, which he unfolded to reveal a lock of black hair. Grison offered it to Perian, who shook his head. He didn't want to experience that death again.

'It belongs to Soas?' he asked. The look in Grison's eyes told him it did. Perian waved the item away. 'Then it isn't necessary. I have already foreseen his fate.'

His father looked at him questioningly, as did Grison. Valamer turned slowly to face him. The look of surprise on his face told Perian that Valamer hadn't known he was a seer, and that gave him a feeling of satisfaction. He couldn't prove that Valamer was behind his brother's demise, but he hoped he was very worried.

'I do not necessarily need items to touch. My visions mostly come of their own. Do you not want to wait for Erely?'

Grison looked long at Perian, but it was the Zamir who spoke. 'No, Tanais. Please, just tell us what you have seen.'

'Your son and his wife are both dead by the same hand.' Perian glanced at Valamer; he leant heavily against the table, his face ashen and eyes wide. Perian heard his father's breath quicken, then slow again as he regained control.

'How?'

'Poison,' Perian said quickly, hoping he wouldn't ask for details.

'How can that be?' Valamer blurted. 'He had a taster, surely?'

Ah. He was going to steer the blame onto the slave. *But the slave is merely a puppet. How clever are you, Valamer?*

Quite suddenly, the Zamir stood and left the room without a word. Perian and Grison both rose from their chairs automatically, then sat again at the sound of the door closing. Valamer walked slowly to the Zamir's chair and flopped down, letting his empty mug swing from his finger by the handle. His closeness made Perian uncomfortable, and he shifted as far away from him as his seat would allow.

Grison leant forward, placing his hands on his thighs as though he were about to rise. He jutted his thin, pinched face toward Perian and pierced him with his rheumy eyes.

'Details,' he hissed.

'You should catch this villain and put him to the irons,' Perian spluttered. 'Soas died slowly, in agony, drowning on his own bloody vomit. I know little of poisons, but I do know that such a death is unnecessary. There are plenty of poisons that are —'

'Enough,' Grison interrupted. 'Who else was there?'

The question took Perian by surprise. He had been too caught up in the dying man's last moments to notice. He looked toward Grison, his eyes shifting back and forth as he tried to survey the scene of his vision.

'I don't know. His pain was all I saw.'

'Go back in,' Grison commanded.

'It's not that simple.'

'Try.' Grison looked as though he would burst. A vein stood out on his left temple, and his colour was blotched.

Perian closed his eyes and drew on his memory of the terrible event. Images moved about, but they were too far away to pull into a coherent form. He was afraid, and his audience was too distracting.

He shook his head. 'I cannot.'

'You must, Tanais. This slaughter must stop. We need to know if there was anyone else in the room, and if there was, who were they and what were they doing? Any information you can provide would help.'

'Whoever was in the room might not be the poisoner,' said Valamer.

'No, but what they are doing might still tell us something.'

'You think they watched?' asked Perian incredulously. He stood suddenly, not giving Grison time to answer. He needed to get back to his room, away from these men. He needed to think. 'I will try again in the peace of my chambers. The pressure of your expectation is too disturbing. My slave can take notes should I be successful.'

Grison turned a pale and gaunt face up toward Perian and took a deep, wheezy breath. 'Very well, Tanais. Send a guard for me as soon as you have anything at all.'

23

Two of Valamer's personal warriors escorted him back to his chambers. One was to stay as additional security on top of the guards he already had. When the guards opened his door, Perian swept past Lono, who was kneeling in the vestibule.

'Lono, bring me something simple to eat and some water.' He wasn't sure that food was a wise decision, but now that he could relax a little, he found he was hungry. He had been ushered from his rooms without breakfast, after all. Better to eat than be distracted by hunger.

He was sitting calmly at the table near the window when Lono returned with a tray of food and jug of water.

'Fetch your quill and paper, Lono.'

Perian tried to eat slowly, but the sight of cheese and dried fruits nearly caused an eruption in his belly. His mouth was still full of dried apricot when Lono returned, so Perian gestured to the seat opposite. Elian's seat.

'I suppose you've heard about the aborted ceremony?' he mumbled through the remnants of the fruit.

'There was talk in the kitchens,' Lono replied. 'The guards were visited by some of their companions and I could hear what they said through the door. I gather Master Elian upset the proceedings and injured the Voice?'

Perian could feel Lono studying him to see if it was safe to laugh. He looked sideways at the man. 'He was magnificent. It was horrible to watch, but a sight I never thought to see. The Voice is blind and will never eat solid food again.'

Lono's eyes widened, and a smile crept across his face. 'He deserves it,' he said suddenly, with feeling. 'They are all cruel men.' Then he caught himself and looked down, but when Perian didn't chastise him for expressing an opinion, he continued: 'The priests will blame you for this, my Zameel. Is this why there is one of Zameel Valamer's personal warriors at the door? There has been little conversation amongst the guards since his arrival.'

Perian nodded. 'Yes, they will blame me. Let's hope that my father can override them.'

They had crossed the line, he and Lono. Smoothly and naturally, equilibrium had triumphed over slave and master. He couldn't help it. He was lonely, and he liked Lono, and slavery was, after all, an abomination. He just hoped that they could keep up the charade when others were around. Not that he had many visitors, thankfully.

Lono picked up his quill and twirled it between his fingers. 'You want to write a letter, my Zameel?'

Perian stirred from his thoughts and watched the bright stripes of Lono's quill form smooth circles of colour with the speed of its movement. He had to do as Grison asked. If Valamer was ridding himself of any possible challengers, Perian would now also be on his list of victims. He needed to shine a light on the man's activities before that happened.

'Come, Lono, we have work to do.'

He left the table, settled himself in his red chair and instructed Lono to take the chair opposite once he had closed the doors and drawn the curtains against the day.

'Bring that small table on which to rest your paper. You will make no sound but wait patiently. This may take some time. When I begin to speak, you will write down every word, even if it doesn't make sense to you. Should I become agitated and distressed, you will call my name very softly until I stop, but you must not touch me. Do you understand?'

Lono nodded as he pulled up the small table. He placed the paper carefully on its surface and removed the cap of his inkpot. Then he settled into the chair with his quill in hand.

Perian stared at the empty mantelpiece, took the deep, slow breaths needed for a controlled trance, and closed his eyes. He continued to stare, but this time it was into the blankness of his eyelids. His breath rasped against the tightness of his jaw until he released the muscles, and soon the movement of air against his windpipe, the expansion and release of his ribcage, the movement of the twin pumps, heart and lungs, were all that existed for him within his self-imposed darkness. Shapeless thoughts sped past like comets travelling across the night sky, and other scenes pressed for attention about the edges of his awareness.

'Later,' he said to the flowing mists as he pulled his sight further inward and turned it toward Soas's last moments.

This time there was nothing to pull him in uncontrolled, but even as an observer he found the man's suffering deeply disturbing. He approached slowly. He wanted to scream; he wanted to cry; but above all, he wanted it to stop, even as he heard his own voice rumble dispassionately, describing what he saw.

He turned his awareness away from the victims to look about the room. It was empty! But Soas's strange screams were deafening. Surely someone had heard. Why weren't they at his bedside? Where was the ever-present slave?

When Soas began to choke, the scene faded. With nothing more to be gained by reliving his earlier vision, Perian opened himself to the moving mists, allowing them to flow into his mind. They came in a rush that made him gasp.

Elian came into view. He had changed from a sygrilien into an almonos and flew with ease over deep forests, fields rich with produce, lakes and deserts: Wellorn. The moment was thrilling, but passed too soon. The scene changed. Elian sat outside what appeared to be a pie shop. Perian assumed it was somewhere within the city of Carios, where Queen Ishra of Wellorn resided in Toolery Castle. He appeared to be listening to the conversations around him, but then his expression changed to one of amazement and delight. He stood and stretched out his hand toward someone Perian couldn't see, but the look on Elian's face and his actions suggested that this person was out of place.

The scene changed again before the person came into view. He saw Elian and Jolint together in a small room, deep in discussion, holding hands, their faces joyful with each other's company even as the set of their jaws showed the seriousness of their exchange. Jolint raised her hands to touch Elian's arm and her sleeves slipped down with the gesture, revealing silver metal bands entwined around both wrists. The filigreed metal wound about her lower arm almost to the elbow and around her thumb, curving back in toward the wrist. Perian had never seen such things before, but instinctively knew they bound her magic and left her defenceless. Jolint was a prisoner, not a guest. This confirmed that Ishra was trying for Rashinder on her own behalf.

A ferocious battle quickly replaced them; cottages burned and blood seeped into the fields. At first he assumed this was the battle taking place between Ishra's men and Rashinder, but as he looked more closely, he realised that he recognised the rolling hills of Western Darna, even though their colour was wrong, and that the invading army wore the black uniform of Nor.

The shock weakened his trance and he began to surface. Using all he had learnt in Silaven, he clung to the edges of the vision, but another imposed itself, and Perian found himself looking into the eyes of a mage.

The man stood tall on the crest of a hill. His attire was that of a traveller, and his brown cloak flapped and tugged for release behind him; his sun-weathered hands were woven together before him. His blue Faran eyes gripped Perian as he tried to pull away, and laughter issued from a mouth twisted with success and power.

In that moment, Perian knew who his real enemy was. Not Gisela or Valamer, but this renegade mage who had put his brother and friends into their deep sleep beneath the ancient tree: the dark shadow that had stalked his childhood dreams, turning them into nightmares.

Perian heard himself shout as he emerged from his trance too quickly. Even fully alert, he could feel the mage's eyes penetrating into his mind, and he gathered all the power he had and thrust the image away with a blinding force that propelled him backward in his chair, nearly toppling it over.

He ground his knuckles into his eye sockets. Intuition told him that all these visions intertwined. He viewed them all again, but could not see the connection. Why would the mage choose now to make himself known? Was it a threat, or was the mage playing with him as Risenor had? Were these visions really his, or something the mage had created?

He glanced at Lono, still silent and patiently waiting. When his trembling subsided, he took a sip of water, then looked carefully at each of the visions and tested their quality. No, they were his; the mage had merely broken in to make himself known. The question was: why?

The angle of the light through a gap in the curtains told him that the morning had passed. As usual, he had been in trance for longer than it seemed. Pages covered in a frenzied scrawl were scattered across the small table and surrounding floor.

Lono followed Perian's eyes to the table. 'I have numbered the pages, my Zameel,' he said defensively.

'What did I say in my first vision?'

Lono shuffled the papers until he had them in order. 'You talked of the terrible screaming. You said the noise was deafening, yet no one had come. Even his slave wasn't there.'

Perian closed his eyes so he could visualise the scene clearly as Lono repeated his description.

'*The Zameel's lady is already dead. Her vomit is smeared across the pillow and encrusted on her long black hair. Her fingers and toes have turned black. There is a purple-and-red patch on her upper chest. She wears a cotton nightdress that she has shredded in her struggle and rucked up above her waist. Soas is naked. His body is moist and soiled. Blood oozes from scratches to his stomach and chest. Like his lady, he has a red-and-purple patch, but on his palm. His fingers and toes have a bluish tinge that will probably turn black with death. The sheets have been pushed over the end of the bed, suggesting that the first sign of their poisoning was a fever.*

'*Oil lamps on the walls cast dark shadows around the furniture, but they are not so large or dark as to hide a man. Beyond the bed there are two doorways. One presumably leads to the other rooms, or perhaps a corridor, and the other to a bathing or dressing area. To the right of the bed, on Soas's side, stands a large cupboard with fretwork on the sides, and beyond this, two glass doors open to a balcony. The curtains are partially pulled back, and moonlight glistens across the stonework, spilling into the bedroom, broken only by a slender moving branch. The moon is either full or nearly so by the brightness of its rays. There is a pot beyond the curtains, but I can see no human silhouette. By earth and sky, it is hard to concentrate with this screaming harmony shredding my nerves!*

Perian lifted his hand to stop Lono's recitation. Since when had anyone screamed in harmony? He looked again at his vision, and this time, rather than blocking out the sounds of agony, he listened more carefully until he was sure the sounds came from different sources. The woman was dead, so there was another.

At that moment, the slender branch moved, its shadow curling and uncurling in a slow ripple. He'd seen that shadow before. He knew its source.

A smile crept over his tense features, and a laugh issued from his throat. He clapped his hands in triumph.

'Lono, go ask one of the guards to get Grison and tell him I have his answer.'

Grison swept through Perian's door shortly after, followed by Maltha and Valamer. Perian hadn't expected them all, but he gathered in his surprise and fell to one knee.

'Get up, Tanais. You are my son; not every occasion requires you to kneel.'

Perian ushered them nervously into seats and looked through the vestibule at Lono, who still knelt by the door with his head pressed hard to the tiles, waiting for someone to tell him he could rise.

'Wine for myself and my guests, Lono.'

Perian took the empty seat next to his father and glanced around at the three men. They all looked tense and expectant, but his father was paler than the others, a little flushed about the cheeks. No one spoke. Lono produced their refreshment almost immediately, having raided the little store of wines he kept for just such an occasion; he poured the wine and placed the small table so that each man could reach it comfortably, then left.

'Do you have moon-crested monkeys at Loren Castle?' Perian asked over the rim of his glass.

Grison looked up in surprise.

'You're not suggesting that a monkey poisoned Soas?' scoffed Valamer.

'Yes, and yet no,' said Perian.

The Zamir sucked air in through his teeth. 'Tanais, please don't drag this out. Just tell us what you know.'

'It was a serious question. I believe there was a large moon-crested monkey on the balcony at the time of my half-brother's death, and it was doing what all moon-crested monkeys do – calling to the moon. At least, that's what they say. What it's really doing, one wouldn't know.'

Valamer looked up, the sneer gone from his face. 'Areagne had one, a large one. Gave me the creeps, but she loved it and Soas tolerated it.'

The atmosphere shifted, becoming more focused. Perian had everyone's attention.

'It will disappear now, and everyone will think that it has left because its owner has died.' Perian sat back and sipped a little wine, but didn't smile, although he wanted to. 'There was no one there for Soas's last agonising moments, not even his slave. I couldn't understand this, because his screams were so intense. That was, until I realised there were two voices screaming, one at a slightly lower pitch. No one could hear Soas because of the monkey screaming on the balcony. It was a full moon. The whole castle would have been expecting it.'

'This is no doubt what the killer wanted, but it doesn't tell you who the killer was,' said Grison.

'It does when you consider that the monkey was only one of its guises. I am fairly certain that Zamella Areagne's beloved monkey was a shapeshifter.'

Maltha stared at Grison, who closed his eyes and put his hands to his face.

'Unfortunately, this does not tell us who his or her master is, but I believe it will be someone working at a distance.' Perian wondered if Valamer was getting worried yet. If he was, he wasn't showing it.

'How do you think the poison was administered? The only connection you have made with the killing and the monkey is the successful covering of Soas's cries,' said Valamer.

'I know nothing of poisons,' said Perian, 'so cannot be sure what was used to kill them, but I suspect it may be the work of a highly venomous spider or a small snake. Soas and Areagne both had a red-and-purple rash, blistered like a burn, here on Areagne's chest' – Perian put his fingers to his chest, just below his throat – 'and here on Soas's palm. This would make sense if he attempted to brush the creature off her or kill it. But the poison must have taken effect instantly, otherwise he would have gone for help. The monkey could easily have carried the thing in a small box, which it discarded or took with it. A present for its mistress, perhaps!' He looked at Valamer and Grison in turn. 'Areagne's fingers and toes had gone black, and Soas's were going the same way. This may indicate what killed them to those with knowledge of such things. If I am right, the spider, or whatever it is, may still be alive, or there may be more than just one, in which case there will be more deaths.'

The men said nothing. Maltha stared down at his hands. Grison's eyes were closed. Valamer was the only one looking at him. The muffled sounds of normal life drifting in through the windows and the guards' chatter in the corridor accentuated the silence.

The Zamir's clothing rustled with his movement. 'Is there anything else you can tell us, Tanais?'

'No. I'm sorry.'

'Valamer, send word to Loren. If that monkey is still around, it must be killed on sight,' said Maltha.

Valamer stood, bracing his lower back with his hands as he stretched, then strode toward the door. Perian was only vaguely aware of his intended departure, too busy going over all that he had seen, but he looked up when Valamer began to open the door.

'Wait.'

Valamer pushed the door closed again impatiently.

'There is something else. Nor will invade, or has already invaded, the western hills of Darna. They do not appear to have a vast army, but there are certainly many more men than are required for a quick raid. They know your army is divided and are testing your strength.'

Valamer reddened with sudden anger. He strode back toward them and confronted the Zamir, his words bursting forth in a torrent: 'Just how accurate is this seer? Can we actually trust everything he says? Surely he lies. Once a traitor, always a traitor, never to be trusted.'

The Zamir shot up faster than Perian had thought possible from his limp and defeated position, and his colour rose to match Valamer's. 'You dare to challenge my judgement? You are a child compared to Soas and Saphrax. I would have left you in Darna had I known that the one who remained would die.'

Perian found himself trapped between the two angry men, their clenched fists either side of his head. He looked over at Grison, who just sighed in resignation and placed both hands on his knees.

'Please, both of you, sit down. This will not help our situation,' said the shaman. His voice was soft, but it calmed the two glaring men. They continued to stare at each other and their fists did not loosen, but they said no more. 'Sit,' Grison said again, more forcefully.

An angry silence ensued, and Perian noticed that the chattering from the hallway had ceased. Valamer thumped into his chair. The Zamir stood for a little longer, then lowered himself into his seat.

Grison waited until the prickle in the air had subsided before speaking again. He glanced at Maltha, then turned his attention to Valamer.

'Tanais passed the tests we gave him in Erely's presence. It was he who warned us of Ishra's invasion and her treachery. Without his visions, I believe Saphrax and his officer would now be headless and our troops devastated. As far as we can judge, he is unusually talented and accurate, and he has shown no sign of disloyalty.'

By his demeanour, this was not what Valamer had wished to hear. His green eyes drilled into Perian, and a chill rippled along the length of Perian's spine. He wondered what this man would do to him when he eventually came for him in the night.

'What are your wishes, my Zamir?' Valamer asked tartly.

'Send the message as before and get them to find out what is happening on our borders.'

With a curt nod, Valamer left.

The Zamir sat upright, taking control of himself. With a large intake of breath, he pushed himself to his feet, and Perian and Grison did the same, but without looking at either of them, the Zamir turned and followed Valamer. Grison hesitated a moment before following too, but stopped in the doorway to face Perian.

'Thank you, Tanais. Let me know the minute you see anything more. Some good news would be appreciated, but I know that is not in your power. They are always like this. Do not make the mistake of thinking that Maltha means what he says.'

'Just one thing, Grison. I remember the hills adjoining Nor as being lush and the fields rich with crops, but in my vision I saw only a brown and scorched landscape. Did I see wrongly, or has something happened?'

Grison shook his head. 'Drought. Our southern crops have failed, and disease spreads from the lower hills and Nor.'

With that, he left, and Perian found himself feeling strangely empty and alone.

24

Perian and Lono spent the rest of the day in the study. Lono sat at the desk, reading quietly to himself, while Perian lounged on the couch, trying to read a book on sea monsters. But he dozed off more than he read and found himself going over and over the same paragraph. When the book slid to the floor for the fifth time, he gave up and stared at the ceiling.

Apart from the extra activity in the courtyard, they had only been disturbed once: there had been a confrontation in the corridor when the soldiers of the Sky God had tried to force entry. To his relief, they had been successfully repelled by his personal guards and Valamer's man. He wondered dismally how long it would be before the priests' men doubled their numbers and overcame his protectors. He couldn't decide which would be the worse fate – kidnap by the priests or by Valamer.

'Which would you prefer, Lono,' he said, 'abduction by the priests, or by Zameel Valamer?'

He sensed a sudden stiffness in Lono, even though he could not see him from where he lounged. It took a moment's hesitation before Lono replied, 'Zameel Valamer.' Then he swivelled on his seat to face Perian. 'Why would the Zameel want to abduct you? What for?'

Perian shook his head and closed his eyes to sleep again. He'd let Lono work that one out for himself.

Lono's voice broke into his sleep, and when he opened his eyes the room was lit by oil lamps. Darkness filled the windows and the smell of roasted meat wafted in through the door.

'I have placed your evening meal in the dining room,' said Lono.

Perian shook his head to clear it and swung his legs to the side of the lounge. He must have slept for hours. 'You must leave,' he said to Lono. His voice was slurred and thick.

'But, my Zameel —' Lono protested.

'Leave, Lono. You will be safer with the other slaves.'

Lono jolted. He opened his mouth to protest again, but Perian cut him off.

'Leave, I say!'

Shocked and uncertain, Lono fell to his knees, his head to the floor, then left with silent speed.

Standing alone in the room that had held such homely comforts only hours before, Perian ground a fist into the palm of his other hand and wondered at what point he had acquired the dominating tone of voice that could frighten the wits out of helpless men. It disgusted him.

He wandered into the dining room, shutting the study door behind him. He had no appetite, but forced himself to eat the meal slowly. If Valamer came for him tonight, he couldn't be sure when his next meal would be. When he was done, he snuffed out all but one of the oil lamps and dragged a chair to the window. The stars winked brightly above the outlines of mansions and treetops. Memories of his travels and nights around the campfire with Elian and Jolint filled him with longing, until the stars wavered in his moistening eyes and he cast his sight lower, into the mundane darkness of buildings and walls that held no memories.

Shouts and the clash of metal woke him with a start. He lifted his head from his chest, rubbed at the ache in his neck and peered out through the window. Dim moonlight showed the activity outside: warriors ran this way and that across the courtyard stones, and sporadic fighting was taking place below him, but the main battle was out of sight. He could hear shouting within the palace itself, and the tread of heavy feet upon the stairs outside his room.

Perian stood at the sound of more shouting just beyond his door. They had come at last. He clasped his hands to stop their shaking and waited.

But when the door burst open, it wasn't Valamer's men who stood in the doorway with fresh blood dripping from their swords onto his carpet. It was soldiers of the Sky God.

Power flowed through his hands instinctively. The first three men fell back, clutching their chests and bellowing, but those behind pushed on through the door, shoving their fellow soldiers aside. Perian saw no fear or astonishment on their faces, only manic determination. He had heard that in the past the soldiers were given a holy liquor to drink during a ritual ceremony before battle, and the look in these men's eyes suggested that the stuff was laced with something stronger than alcohol.

He had depleted his pathetic store of power in that one strike, and with his small advantage gone, he stood powerless as the four men jumped on him. Their combined weight pressed him into the floor. They shackled his hands behind his back. Perian had barely regained his feet when a man still clutching his chest stepped forward and sank a fist into his stomach. He doubled over, and his knees crumpled. He would have slipped to the floor again had he not been so tightly held.

Fire spiralled out from the point of contact, making him nauseous. Perhaps dinner had been a wasted effort. He'd aim it at their feet if it came up any further.

Almost before he was upright once again, the soldiers were half pushing, half dragging him from the study. His personal guards lay bleeding on the landing. Lono looked up from where he knelt and caught Perian's eye briefly. Perian shook his head, very slightly, and Lono did not move.

Someone put a cloak around him and pulled the hood up over his head to hide his face. A hand shoved him forward with unnecessary force and he nearly slipped on the first step. The stairwell echoed confusingly with the sounds of clashing swords, grunting and heavy boots, and just as they completed three quarters of the first spiral, Perian saw Valamer's man lying broken and bloody on the floor of the atrium.

The soldiers hustled him through to the grand hall where it had all begun, for Perian at least. They rushed past clutches of men fighting and the bodies of the fallen. He tried to flick his hood back with a quick movement of his head, only to have it pulled down again sharply and receive a fist to the shoulder. A cool wind swept around his face and billowed the hood out anyway as they rushed him through the conservatory and into the night, where the moon duplicated the battle with long shadows.

They moved quickly to the right, past the cockerel bush that nodded at him in the gusty wind. Their feet shuffled over gravel pathways and through a long arbour filled with the scent of wisteria. Perian peeked around his hood with one eye, looking for the gaps between stocky trunks, but all he could see were quickly moving legs and feet that stomped in a way quite unlike the graceful movements taught in training.

Someone beyond the wisteria walls shouted something he couldn't understand, and the movement became more frenzied. A small group of men left the melee, running right and left. When they appeared at one end of the arbour, the priests' men stopped suddenly and jerked on Perian's shackles. A thick arm wrapped itself about his chest and pulled him into a close and suffocating embrace. His sight was still limited by his hood, but he could feel the knife the soldier placed at his throat. The man's rapid breath puffed across his neck.

He could tell by the way his captors shuffled about that warriors also blocked their exit at the far end of the arbour, so when his hood was snatched off his head, it took just a moment to make sense of the scene. As he'd thought, warriors approached slowly from either end. He forced himself to calm down and concentrated all his energy and will on the knife. A simple matter of melting the weapon, he thought without conviction. Nothing happened. He nearly burst with frustration —

When the blade unexpectedly sparked and flared, it took both Perian and his captor by surprise. Not melting, but hot enough. That he could manage even that was a measure of his fear. The man screeched and dropped the blade. Perian shoved back hard against him until he overbalanced, then dove for a gap between the wisteria trunks.

He pushed with his feet and knees to wriggle his way into the opening. His feet slid on the loose gravel, slowing his progress, and his panic grew. Someone grabbed his feet and tried to pull him back. He kicked out hard, hitting them in the face. With his feet free again he pushed even harder, careless of his bruised knees and chest and the choking dust storm his movement caused.

He was nearly clear of the arbour when his face came level with a pair of bare feet. Strong arms heaved him upright.

Lono. Perian could have kissed him.

'This way, my Zameel,' Lono shouted above the clamour. He pulled Perian's hood over his head, gripped him firmly about his upper arm and pulled him back toward the palace, dodging clusters of struggling men and those lying still or groaning upon the grass. With no way to balance himself, Perian skidded and tripped, and would have fallen without Lono's firm hold.

They slid into the deep shadow of the palace and through an open doorway to a set of descending stairs, lit only dimly by the widely spaced lamps along the wall. Perian had expected Lono to guide him away from the battle, across the common and into the forest beyond. He pulled up hard on the first step.

'Where are you taking me?' His throat was dry with dust and fright, his voice a husky whisper. But he knew where Lono was taking him; he'd been here before.

'To safety,' was all Lono said. He urged him on with a gentle push.

Perian still hesitated for a moment before doing as Lono bid. He didn't like stairs that descended into the bowels of a building. Like these ones, they usually led to cells and rumoured horrors.

These steps were worn by years of use, and the walls were damp and mossy. The smell of unwashed bodies and misery rose to greet him as the stairwell screwed its way downward, and a soft mumble of many voices drifted up with the stink. He hesitated again, only to be urged along by his guide's gentle hand. Finally they came to a landing that opened wide, where their way was halted by a barred gate. Lono eased him toward more steps on their right that descended even further into the depths. He didn't need to touch the walls to know who had passed before him and what lay below; blinding terror radiated from the stone on either side of him, and even the moss hadn't ventured into this well of hopelessness.

He must have slowed down. Lono urged him forward, but Perian stopped, one foot hovering over the next step. 'This leads to the torture chamber, Lono.'

'Yes, my Zameel. You will be safe there.'

Perian turned as best he could, but his head merely swivelled inside his hood. With a flick of his head, he was soon free of it. Lono's face was tight and worried, but he quickly tried to rearrange his expression, moving his lips into a smile.

'You can't be serious! How could anyone be safe in a place used for such atrocities? Get a key, Lono, and release my hands. I'll find my own way out of this —'

Without warning, one of Valamer's warriors appeared behind Lono. His presence took Perian's breath away; he hadn't heard the man's footsteps on the stone. He shouted a warning at Lono, and the slave turned sharply, loosening his grip on Perian in the process. Perian's heel slipped from the step with the sudden movement in such a confined space, and with no means of stopping his fall, he crashed against the curved wall and bounced forward, hitting his shoulder on the tread and grinding his vertebrae and head over the next two steps before he was finally able to jam his feet against the stones.

He didn't have time to worry about how much it had hurt. He shook his head to dispel the dizziness and scrambled to his knees.

'Thank you, Lono,' the warrior said. His deep voice vibrated along the close walls. 'I'll take care of it from here.'

Lono had taken a step down to help Perian stand, but turned back at the sound of the warrior's voice and nodded, giving Perian only the briefest of glances before walking back up the stairs and squeezing past the warrior, who didn't bother to make way for him.

'Go back via the kitchen. It's nearly over and the kitchen is clear. You'll find him in the Audience Room.'

'Find who?' Perian yelled before he could stop himself, but no answer came from the shadows.

Lono had betrayed him.

He had never once thought that Lono was leading him into a trap. Yet again he had been deceived by someone he trusted. He fell against the wall, depleted; emotionally stripped bare, empty, and exhausted by the heaviness of self-pity and anger he had no will to fire up.

The warrior stared down at Perian. A deep cut on the man's forehead trickled blood toward his left eye and caught on his bushy eyebrow. He brushed it aside with the back of a grimy hand.

'Get up and keep walking. Hurry. I should be with my men.'

He clenched his left fist at his side. The other hovered over the hilt of a dagger slipped into his belt. Perian noticed for the first time that the warrior wore his hardened leather armour over a bare chest, and his naked arms were covered in gashes, which bled into the remnant blood of others around his wrists and hands. They had been taken by surprise.

Perian hurriedly struggled to his feet, using the wall for support. He didn't want to be touched by the man's hands.

They continued downward for another two turns of the stairwell, where the space grew even more tight and oppressive. Light cut across the steps on the next turn and spread wide to reveal a room in which two guards waited. They stood quickly as Perian stepped through the door. One was a small man with a pointy face. Severe acne had left his cheeks with scars that were unsuccessfully concealed beneath a sparse beard. The other, a larger man with a round face and enough facial hair for the two of them, showed signs of inactivity about the waist. Their eyes widened in surprise, glowing yellow with the reflection of the lamps; clearly they hadn't known who they would be guarding.

The warrior pushed Perian on. The room was long and wide with a small table and two benches along the wall to Perian's left. Along the opposite wall he could see three cells, all with barred fronts. He could just make out two wooden doors further along, where he assumed the nasty business happened, but at least he was spared that; instead, the warrior pushed him unceremoniously into one of the cells. There was no light within, and the darkness felt thick. He spun about, frantically searching for a way around the large Darna, who had placed himself in the doorway.

'I can't stay here,' he said. His throat was so dry, so tight, that his voice sounded more like a squeak.

A humourless smile rippled within the warrior's beard. 'I don't think the Zameel had torture in mind,' he rumbled, 'but then, that depends on how he'll be feeling at the end of the fighting. Maybe he'll need a little outlet.' He laughed out loud, then grasped Perian by the shoulders, turned him about and pushed him further into the semi-darkness.

'I'm of r-royal blood,' Perian stammered. 'How dare you even touch me!' He sounded pathetic even to his own ears.

'Here.' The warrior tossed a key to the smaller of the two men. 'I'll hold him, you unlock the cuffs.' When the guard had scuttled back to his companion, the warrior stepped closer to Perian. Whiskers prickled the back of Perian's ear. 'You'll be safe in here, Zameel Tanais.

There's an assassin on the loose in the palace, but they won't bother with the cells.'

Perian opened his mouth to ask who had been assassinated, but the man had already turned his back and marched out and up the stairs, stopping only briefly to shout back at the guards: 'Guard him well. Don't listen to anything he says, and don't stand too close! You'll regret it if he's not here when I return.'

The plump guard closed the cell door and returned to the table, where the two men talked in a whisper. From the snippets Perian could hear, they knew no more than he did, so he gave up straining his ears and slowly turned to look about his cell. He knew he could probably manage to open the lock, since as far as he could tell Grison hadn't been down here to fix it with magic – not yet, anyway. He'd wait for the right moment, when he was calmer and had had time to assess his situation. When the guards had grown complacent. When the priests' men had been contained.

The only light came from the lantern hanging above the guards' table, but even though it scarcely penetrated his cell, Perian could still tell he was the only object it contained. There was no pallet or straw for him to rest on, no stool or bucket. He was too afraid of what he might see to touch the walls with any part of his body. After turning this way and that, grinding his foot into the dusty floor to see just how dirty it was, he finally sat in what he thought was the middle with his knees pulled up tight against his chest.

A cold breeze pushed through the cell bars, carrying the whispers of the guards. He could hear no other sound. He was reminded of his cell in Silaven, dark and quiet, and he wondered how far beneath the surface he must be that he could not hear even the slightest sound of battle. Perhaps it was over, though he doubted that.

But the dangers of the last few hours were over, for the moment at least, and his intense fear and panic had subsided. He released his knees and moved to sit cross-legged, placing his hands gently in his lap. The guards had started a game of dice, but even their whooping and muted shouts slowly became distant, as did their light.

At first, he didn't realise he had slipped into a trance. Only when he heard someone groaning and weeping, their chains rattling with their rhythmic movement, did it occur to him that he sat in complete darkness. He gathered his senses, alert now to everything around him. Whoever it was, they were close and familiar. No, more than familiar. Was it himself that he could feel, squatting in a corner? He knew the figure so well that if not himself, it must be …

Elian! The shock nearly severed him from his vision, but he had to see what was unfolding. He sighed, slowly and purposefully, allowing his emotion to drain away so he could think. What was Elian doing in a darkened room and in chains? Where was he? Wellorn or Rashinder? Jasperen, even? And where was Jolint?

He jolted at the thought of her, and his vision shimmered again. Blood pounded through his ears and body so hard he could scarcely hear or see, so he forced himself to be calm, to concentrate and release.

He waited, patiently allowing his senses to penetrate every part of Elian's surroundings, while Elian continued to groan and weep, unaware of Perian's presence. Gradually a pale light crept across the rough floor of the cell. A woman stood at the door and leant casually against the architrave, staring toward the crouching figure, her arms crossed and a look of disgust upon her face. Although he hadn't seen her, he knew without a doubt that this was the person Elian had met at the pie shop in Carios, the person out of place.

There was someone else there too. Someone he recognised. Their form wavered in the feeble light, showing Perian only their back, but as understanding began to develop in his mind, the figure turned sharply to look straight into his eyes and burst into a sneering laugh.

The mage.

'I have your snivelling brother. I assume you want to keep him. I will be with you soon, Perian, to take Grison's place as your protective sorcerer; he can't save you, nor can he save you from the other. You will be my puppet prince after all. Prepare yourself.'

Elian leapt up suddenly, straining at his chains. 'Perian,' he shouted. 'They've killed Jolint! She —'

The streak of magic that flashed from the mage's fingers cut him off, and he dropped back into his corner like a broken doll.

The mage laughed again. 'I will be with you soon, Perian, and we'll have a nice little chat.' He spun in the darkness and vanished.

Perian suddenly twisted and whirled in an ethereal wind, a leaf in an autumn gust. Scenes he could not capture rushed past in a line of faint light, into which he screamed a warning to Elian, while trying desperately to still his own panic. With all he had, both heart and mind, he willed his message to reach his brother.

Something hard slammed into his back. Small worms of colour briefly danced before his eyes and pain surged through his head.

'You all right in there?' came the voice of one of his guards. A chair scraped, and feet shuffled toward his cell.

He heard himself groan and mutter something that he thought was 'yes', and the men returned to their game. He found he was lying flat on the dusty floor; he unravelled his legs and straightened his twisted back, then sat upright, tentatively touching the back of his head where it had made contact with the floor. A small lump had formed, but the skin was unbroken.

He recalled his visions and let them run through his mind again, once, twice, then stopped abruptly. His head felt near to bursting, and he rubbed his temples vigorously to ease the tension. He could remember no echoing response from Elian, and he had no idea whether he had, for once, succeeded in reaching him.

He sat quietly for some time then, reorienting himself to the present, concentrating on the voices of his guards and the soft tap of dice upon the wooden table. His body felt weak and fragile with the flood of emotions that washed through him, wave after wave of dread and helpless terror. He had failed them. In the end, he had failed them. He had not foreseen Jolint's death or Elian's imprisonment. What was the point of being a seer if you only saw the tragedy after the event?

He forced himself to stop. Had it been after the event? What was the timeframe? Was it possible that the line of faint light was in the present? Had the first vision been a possible future? He felt sure that it was, but how could he tell?

He clung to hope as though it were a floating log in an angry ocean. He would – he must – clutch that hope to his heart, or he would go mad and die without knowing.

Hurried footsteps on the stairs and the clatter of the guards' chairs against the wall dragged him from the depths of his torpor, but his eyes remained closed and his clammy body continued to shake violently.

'Let me through,' came a gruff voice.

It was Grison. Grison the protector. How could that be? Protector from what? And who was 'the other' the mage had mentioned?

He forced his eyes open as the lock was released and Grison rushed through.

'Tanais. Are you all right?'

The look of concern on the shaman's face startled him. This wasn't the Grison he thought he knew. His mind jostled frantically between conflicting views, his long-held fear of the man still prominent despite what Elian and Jolint had said about the sorcerer seeking to save his life. What if fate had changed and Grison was here to kill him at last, his expression merely a mask?

Grison sank to his haunches just in front of Perian and searched his face. 'Tanais, you must come with me now. You are in great danger. There is a very powerful mage called Armin on his way to the palace. He comes to kill Valamer and enslave you for his own purposes. Only if you and Valamer are together do I have any hope of protecting you both.'

Perian stared at him. 'How do I know you won't kill me yourself? That this isn't some pretext to get me out and mislead my father?'

'Maltha is dead,' said Grison baldly. 'That's what the fighting was about.'

Perian stared at him, frozen. He'd had no love for his father, but he had not wished him dead. And who would stand between him and the priests, or Valamer, now?

Grison put his hand on Perian's shoulder, bringing his paralysed mind and body back to life. Perian pulled away, still uncertain. 'Why would this mage want to enslave me?'

'Don't play with me, Tanais. I know all about Gisela's plan to control Rashinder through your rebirth. Did you think I would not have heard your childish conversations with your spirit friends just as Shimester did?'

'How do you know about the mage?'

'I didn't.' Grison's voice softened again. 'The Faran Magi sent me word not half an hour ago that a renegade sorcerer was on his way, and that I must do all in my power to protect you – and also Valamer, if I could.'

Perian's thoughts had just begun to settle, but the mention of the Faran Magi sent him into another spin. He knew his eyes had widened but hoped his jaw had not dropped. 'Why would the Magi talk to you? You're not a Faran.'

'No, I'm a sorcerer. Sorcerers are not bound by kingdom or race; they are a race of their own, which is something Gisela never taught you. The person you see before you is a Darna, but the star upon my forearm shows that I am part of a greater calling. Why else do you think I had you sent away from the clutches of those infernal priests?'

'And Shimester?' The words came out sharper than he had intended.

'I could do nothing for him. Your father's rage was such that I had no chance to intervene, even if it had been in my power to do so.'

Perian knew this was true. His father's flashing temper had been impossible to stop; no voice, of reason or otherwise, could penetrate such fury.

'Come, Tanais. The fighting is almost over, and they are waiting for us in the Council Room.'

'I know this mage you speak of,' Perian said as Grison began to stand. 'He has invaded my visions and taunted me. I would be very pleased to see you destroy him.'

He pulled his cloak over his shoulders and stood beside

Grison, and to his surprise, realised that his doubts about the man had evaporated. He could not continue alone; he desperately needed to trust someone, and his enemy had marked Grison as his protector, so perhaps he was. With a nod at the shaman, he tugged his hood over his head and they left for the Council Room.

25

Below a vast, curved ceiling of gold and silver, some twenty men, mostly officers, sat around one of two large, solid tables. Many were bleeding. All were dirty and exhausted. Slaves moved silently across the richly coloured Soluwi rugs and polished floorboards that shone with the light from the large diamond-leadlight windows. They carried dressings, bowls of water, wine and food. No one spoke. The sullen atmosphere dulled the room's glory and the beauty of its contents.

As Grison took Perian's arm and led him toward the fireplace, where Valamer stood with his elbow on the mantel, Perian looked for the warrior who had escorted him to the cells, but he was not there. He hoped the man still lived.

His breath caught when he saw Lono kneeling by the corner of the chimney wall. He didn't look up as Perian approached.

'We're here,' said Grison. 'You should get rid of the rest. They will make no difference to the outcome, whichever way it goes.'

Valamer lifted his elbow slowly from the mantelpiece and turned to the table. 'Leave us. Go back to your men.' He nodded to a tall blond warrior with a bandage around his upper arm. 'Wisen, you take charge until Doran recovers. I want a double guard on the door and at either end of the corridor. No one is to enter this room unless I call for them. Only Lono may come and go. Is that understood?'

'Yes, my Zameel.'

When everyone had gone, Valamer sauntered over to the table

where jugs of wine and plates of food still remained. A signal Perian didn't see passed between him and Lono, and the slave got up, poured Valamer wine, then knelt again just beside his seat.

Perian stared at Lono for a moment. This was the same man who had laughed and joked with Elian, whose company he had enjoyed. It was all wrong. His anger had gone, although his disappointment lingered still. He vowed again that he would do something about Lono's situation, but it would have to wait for now. Shaking his head slightly, he took a seat on the other side of the table. He didn't want the sight of Lono to distract him.

Valamer broke the heavy fog of silence that had stilled the air. 'So, you wanted the throne after all. I wondered why you came back after all those years. But I'm still here, and you can't have it.'

Perian stared at Valamer, stunned by the accusation. He didn't want the throne. He never had. But then, why *was* he here? And as he asked himself the question, the answer finally came to him with clarity. It was obvious; he had known all along.

Armin intended him to replace Valamer, or his father, as Zamir, just as Gisela had – but the true purpose of his return, the one the Magi intended and the one he had followed, was for him to sit at the Zamir's side as his seer and guide.

He wasn't sure he wanted that either. The man before him was a murderer of siblings, and so had his father been. He continued to stare, trapped between the two truths and unable to speak.

At last, Grison spoke for him. 'I don't think that was Tanais's intention, nor that of the Great Magi I spoke of.' He was still standing at Perian's side, though Perian had forgotten him, and now he put his hand on Perian's shoulder. 'Tell him, Tanais. I can see you finally understand.'

Perian ignored him, though Grison's touch brought back his ability to move. 'I have merely followed my visions, as instructed by the Magi. I take no pleasure or satisfaction in what I now understand, which is that I am here to work beside you as your seer – to help you follow the path that fate has laid out for us all. But it will be hard to sit comfortably at the side of someone who rises to his position by murdering his siblings.'

Grison pulled his hand from Perian's shoulder as Valamer's face blanched and he sprang to his feet, all his pent-up rage and violence about to unleash. 'I'll have your tongue out for that!'

Perian froze. He had said it at last. But then Lono's head bobbed above the table with a look of such astonishment that Perian began to lose confidence in his allegation. Maybe he hadn't thought this out properly. Maybe had been too quick to find a reason to dislike Valamer.

'Sit,' said Grison firmly to Valamer. 'And think before you accuse, Tanais.' His anger spread outward like a hot wind, less violent than Valamer's, but more threatening.

Valamer glanced at Grison, then returned to his seat, but leant as far across the table toward Perian as he could. 'Which brother's death do you accuse me of? All, or just Soas?'

Perian opened his mouth to say *all*, but stopped himself as his mind finally began to work past his prejudice. That was not possible; Valamer would have been a child when the first of his brothers began to die. Even he could see that now. Soas, then? The image of the shapeshifting killer formed in his mind. He already knew Valamer did not have the power to control such a being.

He looked away from Valamer's reddened face and gazed at

the table's edge, where he had seen Lono's startled eyes. He knew who the murderer was and why the killings had started.

Armin had been clearing the way for his own ascent through Perian.

'Forgive me,' he said at last. The words clawed at his throat, but what else could he say when he had just mistakenly accused the future Zamir of killing his brothers? He looked up into Valamer's eyes, just briefly. 'I understand now. It was the work of the renegade mage, Armin, and I – I was the cause. My rebirth triggered all that has befallen the house of Maltha.' He spread his hands on the table and rested his forehead in his damp palms.

Grison's hand gently touched Perian's back. 'This is not the time for accusations or regret over a past that none of us foresaw or had a hand in. The mage will be upon us soon, and we must work together if we are to destroy the true architect of this plan. I do not fully understand the motives of the Magi, but I believe this all started with something you and Risenor told them when you were children – a joint vision that forced the Magi to try diverting fate from its intended path. We are now at the apex of that plan, and we must not fail.'

'It is your fault that our father is dead.' Valamer's accusation burst from him, full of contempt and hatred.

His words hit Perian like the blow of a mallet. He lifted his head as though on a spring and, curling his hands into fists, brought them down onto the table with a bruising force. He wanted to shout that it was not his fault, but his defence faltered at the sight of tears welling in Valamer's eyes. Grison had been right; the relationship between father and son had not been as it appeared. Valamer had loved his father. What could he say?

He released his hands and placed them back on the table, palms down. He could feel the sweat forming beneath them, and perspiration upon his brow.

'I did not know our father, but I would never have wished this for him. My brother, who Grison or Lono will have told you about, acted in innocence, not understanding the consequences of his actions.' He stopped himself from saying more.

Grison sighed and took the seat next to Perian. 'He speaks the truth, Valamer. You have to admit that even Maltha found the attack satisfying. This revolt has been a long time coming and might well have had the same result with or without the actions of Tanais's shapeshifting brother.'

Valamer snorted and wiped his eyes on his sleeve. 'We all found it satisfying,' he said. 'If only he had listened to me. He should have seized the opportunity to neutralise them, rid the sect of the fanatics and the overzealous before they had time to organise themselves.'

'I agree,' said Grison. 'But he didn't, and he paid the price for his inactivity. And now you are Zamir, Valamer, and you must live to lead your people. Saphrax is not suitable, and as a seer, Tanais is incapable. You are the only hope for Darna, against Ishra and now also King Arnden of Nor.'

Valamer stared at Grison, then shifted his gaze toward Perian. His anger flared again briefly. 'I would give you up to this mage gladly if I thought it meant he would leave and the bloodshed would stop.'

Perian wanted to say he would go gladly, but he couldn't. The thought of being in the hands of Armin terrified him. 'That may come to pass anyway,' he said instead. He could not keep the fear and hopelessness from his voice, and the words trembled within his throat.

Valamer continued to stare at Perian for a while, until Perian looked up and into his identical green eyes, the eyes of their father. Perian thought Valamer jolted slightly, his shoulders relaxing, and he saw, in that brief moment, the commonality between them, the invisible cord of connection. This was his brother. Not a brother in the way that Elian was – that was something far more – but a sibling nevertheless. He thought Valamer had seen it too, but he said nothing.

Valamer stood abruptly and went to one of the glass cabinets that lined the walls. Swords of similar sizes but varying shapes hung on double pegs at the back of the cabinet. He gathered up knives from a shelf, five in all; two had handles carved by a master, and the rest were quite plain. He strode back to the table and slid two of the plain knives over to Perian. Once he had reseated himself, he nudged Lono to sit up and handed him the two with the decorative yet serviceable handles. Lono slipped the knives into his belt and put his head down again, but not before Perian saw a smile creep across his face. Valamer's meaning was obvious, childish even, but it made Perian smile also. The other knife Valamer slid into his own belt, and suddenly Perian's spirits lifted. Perhaps they would fight together after all.

He slipped his own weapons into his belt and boot. Grison was about to say something when the doors opened behind them and —

Perian blinked. *Lono* stepped through, closely followed by another man of medium height whose face was covered by the hood of his worn brown cloak. Grison turned in his seat, and for the briefest of moments, they all stared at the two men in confusion. Out of the corner of his eye, Perian saw Valamer put his hand down to touch Lono kneeling at his side, as though to reassure himself that he was really there – but Perian knew exactly who had walked in the door.

He grasped the knife he had just thrust into his belt and threw it into the shapeshifter's neck before the man's master could stop him.

The dying imposter fell backward onto the mage behind him, knocking him almost back through the doors. Valamer shouted for the guards, but it was too late; at a twitch of the mage's hand, the double doors slammed tight, and they heard the lock click and the wooden bar fall with a thud into its holder.

The figure in the cloak flung his servant's body aside. Perian was surprised to see that the shapeshifter wasn't a Faran, but someone quite small and very ordinary in appearance, apart from the knife protruding from his throat.

Two knives whistled past Perian's ear, only to be diverted mid-air by the mage. They skittered across the floor. Grison's chair fell back at Perian's feet as the shaman stood and twisted, releasing a powerful electrical force that drove the mage back onto the door. A cacophony of sound exploded from the corridor as men ran toward the Council Room and others banged and pushed at the doors.

Armin leant against the door and howled like a demented animal. Then he howled again while twisting his hands about one another to form a plume of foul brown fog that began to roll toward the four men still around the table. Grison's attack faltered under its advance; he tried to change tactics and sweep the mage aside, but Armin didn't move, only roared with laughter.

Valamer leapt onto the table behind Perian and threw his second knife, but like Grison's magic, it vanished into the rolling brown fog.

Armin waved a hand of crackling light at Valamer, as though flicking off a troublesome fly, and Valamer fell backward into the weapons cabinet. Glass showered across the carpet, wood splintered, and metal clattered to the ground all around his limp body.

Perian grabbed the knife from his boot and rushed at Armin: a foolish move, he realised detachedly, but the best he could do with all so quickly in disarray about him. Lono had scrambled over the table and was just behind him. Perian sucked in air as he approached the thickening brown fog, and heard Lono do the same. The stench of the stuff was awful, like slow and putrefying death. Perian felt confused and dizzy. Bile shot up his oesophagus so fast he thought he would be sick on the mage even if he couldn't get his knife in.

Then everything changed. The fog vanished. At the corners of his eyes Perian saw Lono and Grison fall. He continued on, building momentum, his knife raised ready to plunge into whatever part of Armin he could get to —

The mage's hand twitched in his direction and his insides turned to liquid. Fire surged through every part of him, stopped him in his tracks and held him rigid, his jaw clenched so he thought his teeth would shatter. Every nerve shrieked, line upon line of searing agony beneath his skin. He heard himself scream through his closed mouth. His legs gave way. But even as he fell to his knees, his body remained stiff, each muscle so taut he feared his bones would snap.

Armin twirled the flickering lights about his fingertips, each tiny movement tweaking this muscle or that and forcing another stifled scream from Perian, until at last he lay shuddering on the floor.

'I told you I would be here soon, Perian. Stop fighting what you cannot win. Let's get this over with.'

The flickering eased, yet Perian remained rigid and unable to move. Armin pushed himself away from the doors and began walking toward Lono and Grison. Then a groan issued from the other side of the room and knives clattered against one another. Valamer. The sound caught Armin's attention, and with the mage's mind elsewhere, the pain in Perian's body eased a little and he found that his limbs obeyed him.

He pushed himself up and forward to grab at the mage's ankle as soon as he came within reach. But Armin swerved aside and Perian landed on his face with his arms outstretched. The mage cursed and intensified his hold. Perian howled, convinced his body had burst into flames again. The battering on the door became more urgent.

Through the fog of his agony, Perian was vaguely aware of Valamer moving. A killing light flashed about Armin's right hand. Even with his face pressed into the carpet, Perian could see Valamer standing amidst the shattered remnants of the cabinet, staring grimly at Armin and awaiting his final strike.

Determination hardened within Perian. *It cannot end like this; I will not let it.* Death was preferable to becoming the slave of this mad mage.

Sucking in air, he strove to move past his pain and force life into his limbs. He surged to his feet, and with a strength that amazed him, he knocked the mage sideways with his elbow and stepped in front of Valamer as a human shield. Armin's magic shot wide, scoring a line through the gold-and-silver ceiling and shattering the decorative cornice at the far end of the room.

Armin recovered with ease and Perian rushed at him, striking the mage in the face with his fist. He would have broken his nose if Armin hadn't shoved his fingers into Perian's diaphragm and released needlelike icicles through his body. The shock was so severe that Perian's scream died in his throat. Behind him, he heard Valamer scrambling for a weapon.

Perian's knees began to crumple. He angled his body and dropped his dead weight onto Armin, pushing him back and pinning him down to give Valamer a few extra seconds to find a weapon and strike. Armin cursed beneath him and flicked Perian off as if he weighed nothing. He rolled helpless over the displaced weaponry. Swinging sideways, Armin sent out a pale blue plume with an awkward twist of his wrist, pushing Valamer back into the cabinet.

Perian's anger soared, again forcing his pain into the periphery. He stretched his hand across the floor until he found one of the daggers spread around him. Gripping the hilt firmly, he rolled over and upward and threw himself at Armin, who had just risen to his feet. Perian pinned him to the window. The mage dodged to the side, and Perian's knife sliced over his upper arm instead of going into his heart.

Armin's eyes bulged black and a darkness swirled about his head. His snarl was terrifying. Perian held his breath, waiting for Armin's death strike. But the mage just hissed at him and flicked an invisible force that knocked Perian backward. As before, it penetrated his skin, searing every nerve ending.

Almost blinded by pain, Perian fell to one knee and looked up, wondering if he was capable of going for the mage again. In that moment his eyes caught movement beyond the room. He saw something in the near distance, something Armin had not – a white line growing exponentially within the frame of the window.

Before Perian could so much as blink to be sure he wasn't hallucinating, an almonos crashed through the glass and dove straight at Armin. Perian rolled across the floor, out of the way of the fighting, laughing inwardly at the look on his enemy's face.

Despite his shock, Armin scarcely faltered in his step. He flung the bird aside to crash awkwardly against the wall. The rest of the group, about ten huge white birds, had already shot through the glass on their leader's tail and fanned out along the other side of the table, changing shape into Aronaye's elite Almonos Guards before their feet even touched the floor. Magic flew from their hands the instant they changed, forming a powerful joint force aimed directly at the mage.

Armin instantly put up a shield to protect himself, but the combined power of the Almonos Guards forced him back toward the door. Magic flickered about the room, a dazzle of coloured lights that set fire to the tapestries and burned the carpets. Armin staggered under the force of the assault, yet unbelievably remained strong, shouting and roaring in his frustration.

Perian's arms and legs twitched and shook from the intensity of Armin's assault. Lightning still travelled in streaks through his muscles and his heart pumped much too fast. He lay curled amidst the battle, hoping he would not be killed in the crossfire. Lono lay motionless still, wedged against a table leg, but Grison, he could see, was beginning to stir. His lids flickered open and his eyes fell drowsily on Perian. They cleared rapidly as he remembered where he was. The sorcerer stood unsteadily and leant heavily upon the table.

Suddenly a shriek rose above the hiss and thud of magic and the continued banging on the door. Two Almonos Guards went down under a strike that crackled noisily from one to the next. Grison pushed forward to fill the gap, feebly at first but gaining strength as he moved.

Another of the Almonos Guards dropped to the floor, his head bouncing off the hearth. Perian wondered how long Armin could hold out – perhaps long enough to eliminate his foe one by one. His eyes fell on the leading almonos, who still lay stunned against the wall, limbs moving slowly. Perian's heart almost stopped, then beat faster than he thought his chest could take. Elian! His brother was alive. Not a prisoner after all. Hot tears of relief ran down his cheeks as Elian finally raised his head.

When he saw Perian looking at him, he smiled weakly, then frowned in concentration. Moving very slowly, he eased a hand toward one of Valamer's thrown knives. He had the weapon in his grasp when a knife from the other side of the room flew over the table and through Armin's shield. It lodged in his shoulder, though Perian thought it had been aimed at the mage's heart. That it had penetrated the shield at all was hopeful. The monster was finally weakening.

The Almonos Guard pushed to take advantage, as did Elian. He firmed his grip about the handle of the knife and threw it at Armin's chest. Like the first, it skidded on the shield, but lodged in the upper part of the arm already injured by Perian. Armin wasn't dead, but his use of magic was severely hampered; he fell to one knee and his retaliation ceased almost immediately, all his strength needed to maintain his shield and ward off the attack.

One of the Almonos Guards, who Perian recognised as Theo, gave a signal, and a purple light emanated from the remaining guards and circled about the mage – a holding light, Perian assumed. The instant it was cast, Grison glanced at Perian to ensure he was conscious, then turned to check on Valamer, whose eyes were fixed on Armin. He looked pleased with himself.

Theo looked from Valamer to Grison, and then briefly at Lono, who was still unconscious. 'Which of you is Grison?' He glanced around the room at his men, quickly taking in who was moving, who wasn't and who was possibly dead.

Grison turned a pale and weary face toward Theo. 'I am.'

Perian followed Grison with his eyes, the only movement that didn't hurt. The Almonos Guards were concentrating on Armin and the light that bound him and his shield, and by its looping movement, even the shield was beginning to waver as his blood dripped upon the floor.

Perian followed their gaze back to Armin. He studied the look on his face and the stance of his body – and grew cold. Armin slumped slightly, holding his wounded arm close to his side with the other, but this was not a look of defeat. Perian could clearly see him gathering his strength for the right moment.

Armin carefully moved his eyes to look at Perian directly, and Perian heard a click he could not immediately identify. Armin's lips twitched into a slight smile, and suddenly Perian understood what he had heard. Armin had withdrawn the wards placed on the door and released the lock. Now all he had to do was wait for the men in the corridor to break through.

Smoke from the smouldering tapestries began to sting Perian's eyes. He blinked vigorously to clear them, hoping the guards could see what Armin was about. He tried to speak, but the smoke stopped up his throat. He pushed himself up onto his haunches and waved a trembling arm to get someone's attention. No one was looking at him. All eyes were on Armin.

Suddenly the doors burst open with a great splintering of wood and a clutch of men pushed through, immediately crashing into

Armin's shield. They froze in the holding light. The Almonos Guards reflexively shifted the beam away from the men to release them. Armin looked triumphant. For the briefest of moments, only two beams held him, at the front, and in that moment he moved, leaping aside and away from the warriors with unexpected energy. A sweep of his good arm sent a streak of fire around the room. The Farans fell back, batting at their burning clothes, and Grison threw himself onto the carpet to smother the flames that had caught his sleeve.

Armin leapt up onto the table with the agility of a young man and strode across its surface, throwing himself out of the broken window before the chaos had subsided enough to stop him. Just as he disappeared below the sill, Perian heard him shout: 'This is not over, Perian. I will return for you!'

Clutching a blistering left hand to his chest, Valamer shouted orders to the Darna warriors to catch Armin and kill him without hesitation. They rushed from the room with two of the Almonos Guards following, calling out that they would need sorcerers to stop him.

Perian flopped back to sit on the floor, his back against a table leg, too weak to stand. Acrid smoke from the burning carpets and clothing filled his lungs and he coughed weakly. He could no longer see through his stinging eyes, his world becoming indistinct. He could hear Valamer's voice close by, filled with fear, but the words were not for him; they were for Lono, still lying unconscious. In a vague way, Perian found this strange. Lono was his slave, not Valamer's, but there was too much going on to think about it. There was nothing he should be doing. It was over – for the moment.

He sat lonely and isolated amidst the comings and goings, feet shuffling past his outstretched legs. Further away, men shouted in the corridor and the courtyard, and Valamer bellowed for a healer. But Perian wasn't afraid in the way he had been before, when he had been left immobilised on the floor of the entertainment hall after Elian and Jolint and Cerister had used him as a conduit for their magic. Eventually he would be noticed and assisted. In the meantime, he could indulge in a bit of self-pity.

Someone opened the other windows, releasing the roiling smoke that pressed at the glass, and a gust of wind blew in, cooling Perian's heated body and gathering smoke at the corners of the room. A fire flared up the far wall but was quickly doused with a carafe of water. It crackled and hissed and sent a nasty stink across the room, making Perian's nose run.

Finally, Elian knelt by his side. 'Perian, are you all right? What has he done to you?'

Perian's body still shook and needles pricked his extremities with a regular beat. His ears itched and his dry throat began to spasm so that he could hardly breathe, and the tickle in his nose grew worse again to the point of pain. He sneezed so unexpectedly and violently that his body lifted off the floor.

That he remained upright and his spasms were gradually decreasing he found encouraging: life was returning to his muscles, and he would live to wreak vengeance on the murderous Armin. Another day, though. Another year, even. In truth, he never wanted to meet the man again, and knowing that he would sent renewed tremors through him.

Elian eased Perian into a chair with the aid of a passing slave. 'How can I help you, my Zameel?' the slave asked once Perian was seated and his elbow propped, shuddering, on the table to support him.

Perian shook his head carefully.

'He is unhurt, thank you,' Elian said. 'Please continue on your way.'

'Jolint?' Perian squeezed out.

Elian cocked his head to one side. 'Safe. I left her heading through the northern woods toward a deserted cottage I found.'

'Was Radia with her?'

'No. The Shanessa and her youngest, Bardol.'

Perian shook his head slowly, but more confidently now. 'That could be a problem Valamer will have to deal with. But in the future.'

'They've left Jolint powerless in silver wristlets,' Elian continued. 'She'll need someone like Radia or Grison to get them off for her.' He plucked a piece of fluff unnecessarily from Perian's robe. 'Thank you for the warning, at the pie shop. Your timing was a bit tight, though. I only just had time to pull up my hood and slip out the back.' He looked down, away from Perian. 'I'd met her in Silaven; she's training to be one of the Almonos Guards. But I watched her from further up the street and she was searching for me. She had no good reason to be there, but without your warning I would not have questioned her presence too hard.'

Perian put a shaking hand on Elian's arm. He could tell Elian was not telling him everything and thought that he and this Felfar had probably known each other better than he was admitting. Lovers, even. 'I'm sorry,' he said. He'd think later about whether to tell Elian what would have happened had he not received his warning.

He turned his attention to what was happening in the rest of the room. Valamer had finally let someone salve and wrap his hand

and was issuing orders to the constant stream of warriors, healers and slaves, all the while watching the slaves carefully lift a groaning Lono onto a stretcher. The look of tenderness on Valamer's face surprised Perian, but he was distracted before he could analyse his half-brother's reaction.

Another slave was putting the final touches to a bandage on Grison's forearm; he sat with Theo, whose left foot was strapped where he had trodden on a patch of burning carpet, and the other Farans were in a group near the hearth, being treated for minor wounds. One was more seriously injured, but it didn't look life-threatening, and already he was beginning to rally and attempt to stand.

By the time the bustling had stilled and Perian and Elian were alone with Valamer, Grison and the Almonos Guards, he felt completely normal again. He moved his arms about and swung his legs back and forth with no sign of residual pricking or trembling.

'Will you stay as my guests for a while?' Perian heard Valamer say to Theo. 'I would be honoured if you would attend my coronation.'

Theo smiled. He was a little broader in the face than most Farans, but still very handsome in the way Farans were.

'Thank you, Zameel Valamer, but we were instructed to return immediately. Mage Armin will seek to punish those who have upset his plans, and we must be with our people should he look our way.'

'You must inform me if we can help in any way. I will send my best men to your aid.'

'Thank you. Now we must go – via the courtyard this time!'

His laugh brought a smile to Valamer's face. 'Of course.'

Theo and his men bowed to Perian as they filed out. Elian followed them, and Perian hoped he was merely going to say goodbye, but once they had vanished through the door, Valamer turned to Grison, who was next to him at the end of the table. 'Grison, go with them as my representative – an official farewell. I wish to speak with my brother alone.'

Grison appeared surprised. He hesitated, glancing from Perian to Valamer.

'I won't kill him. Now do as I ask, before our rescuers fly off with no proper farewell.'

26

Valamer poured wine for himself and Perian from a decanter within arm's reach. While the healers had been patching up the injured and warriors had been trudging back and forth taking orders, the slaves had tidied the room, replacing the tumbled and broken glasses and decanters upon the table, sweeping away the shards of shattered window and cabinet glass. Holding his glass in his good hand, Valamer eased himself back in his chair and, closing his eyes, dropped his head back onto its velvet neck-rest for a moment.

'Grison gave me a brief outline of your history, Tanais, but if you could indulge me, I would like to hear it from you too.' He opened his eyes again and glanced at Perian, waiting for his compliance. 'He said you were reborn to our father with full memory of your previous existence, but I don't believe in life after death. So convince me he told the truth.'

This was a signal regarding where he should start, and a push to be fully open, Perian thought.

'It is true,' he said, sipping his wine. The liquid slid pleasantly down his parched throat. 'I was born a triplet, the son of the Leader of a Faran tribe. Elian was one of my brothers then, and it was that father, our Faran father, who sent the Almonos Guards to us today.' He glanced at Valamer, who had closed his eyes again. 'Risenor – our third brother – and I were born seers, Elian a shapeshifter. We were questioned by the Magi when just little, though I don't remember this and nor does Elian. Who can tell what Risenor remembers – he was badly hurt when the head of another tribe attacked our enclave and kidnapped Elian and me. His injuries, and watching our mother die, left him deranged. Elian is the only one of us who is close to what we all should have been.

'Elian and I grew up under guard, never allowed to leave our wagon without an escort and taught nothing but lies, knowing only what Gisela – the woman who abducted us – wanted us to know. Neither of us even remembered our origins or what she had done to our mother and our brother. She used us and some other children she had stolen to gain power over the other tribes; she would force me into trances to see her way ahead, and one day, when she pushed me to the point of madness, I told her the Darna would take and rule Rashinder.

'That's when everything changed. She was determined to have Rashinder – for the Farans, she said, but in truth only for herself. She killed me, and I was reborn as planned to our father. I was meant to become Zamir so that Gisela could rule through me. Elian and our two friends were put into hibernation underground by Mage Armin so that their spirits could keep me company – and keep me to my task – until I released them from the spell. Gisela abandoned us when Grison sent me away with my mother's slave, fearing the demands of the priests.'

Valamer opened his eyes and stared at Perian. Grison clearly hadn't told him that bit. Perian put his glass down and slowly opened his shirt to display the wings upon his chest, then pulled the material together again at the look of shock upon Valamer's face.

'When Shimester ran his magic through my seer's star it fixed the tattoo in place. I will be marked with it for life.'

Valamer whistled through his teeth and gulped his wine. 'Please continue.'

'After our escape on the day of your invasion, I rode with Radia to ask Lord Fimian for help. He was indebted to our father and no help at all. So Radia and I separated, and I found Elian's hibernation chamber and released the wards that bound him and my other friends. Then Elian and I were abducted by the Almonos Guard and my first father locked me in a cell until I remembered my past. My visions continued and the Magi encouraged me, via Elian, to follow them, which I did.'

Valamer opened his eyes again and turned a fierce eye on Perian. 'Why? What was their motive, Tanais?'

Perian shook his head. 'From my visions and what I can put together myself, it was to open a view into the future for the Zamir – to prevent Queen Ishra from invading and taking Rashinder for herself. Ishra controls every aspect of her people's lives – they are all slaves and in fear of both spy and priestess. Our father let his people run amok by comparison.' Perian ignored Valamer's snort of suspicion and pursued the thought. 'Shanahan Leren was weak, and his lords were discontented with his lack of action and his brothers' demands, as were the people. Queen Ishra was already preparing to invade. How else do you think she could have mustered such an army so quickly? When you beat her to it, she saw the opening she had waited for. She assumed the kingdom was in chaos and your army was divided. She either knew or guessed that King Arnden would take his chance at Darna, and she took her chance here.'

'She would have succeeded had you not warned Father of her treachery.'

A silence fell between them. Finally, Valamer stirred.

'So, the purpose of the Magi was to prevent Ishra's conquest of Rashinder? Am I right?'

'I believe so. In part at least. Risenor and I must have predicted Ishra's successful invasion of Rashinder back when we were children, and that prompted the Magi to withdraw to the deserts and let fate do as it would, intervening as necessary. I believe they see Mage Armin as an instrument of fate – one they had to contain in the end, by getting my Faran father to send his elite guards.' Perian looked down at his hand, which shook slightly upon the table. 'But the threat isn't contained. Not for me.'

'I heard what he said, Tanais, but he won't have you. I won't let him.'

'But you said —'

'I know what I said,' Valamer interrupted. 'I was angry. In any case, you had just accused me of killing my brothers. Why did you do that?'

'It was what you said to me the first time we met. *I am next in line, and if the old man dies, I'll have your head on a spike.* Then Erely got me to scry a ring and I watched Soas die. What conclusion would you have come to, especially when you discovered that all the Zamir's male heirs had been dying off mysteriously? I just hadn't thought it out logically at that point. And I didn't like you.' Perian wasn't sure that he liked Valamer even now. But things were changing. He'd leave it open for the time being.

'And Erely really asked you to check on Soas? Lono said you were interested in their relationship. Now I see why.'

Lono, the slave with a double life. Valamer spoke of Lono as one would a friend. Perian stared at his half-brother, trying to put the pieces together. At least Lono had not betrayed him completely;

Valamer had not known about his tattoo.

He turned his mind back to Valamer's question. 'Yes. She wasn't surprised, but she was very upset. She may have had a sense that something was wrong, or perhaps word had reached her via another source.'

Valamer turned his glass about in his hands, watching the liquid within swirl about. 'Soas was Erely's favourite nephew. She will have taken it hard, I think.' He glanced up at Perian. 'He was kind, but firm – he would have made a good Zamir.' With a sudden movement, he put his glass loudly on the table and rubbed his eyes as though to extinguish his memories. 'I will be crowned Zamir in the morning, Tanais. You will stand at my side and fulfil your destiny.'

Perian tensed. He was tired of being ordered about, his life at the call of another. He wanted the freedom he had had for so many years, to do as he pleased and make his own choices.

Valamer caught the movement and inclined his head at Perian with a softening half-smile. 'I could force you, of course, but I won't. It is your choice. Neither of us has been free to choose for himself in this life – both prisoners of our birth. But together we could find our own freedoms within the confines of our duty. I have always longed to do what you did – wander the countryside without recognition or responsibility – but it was never my lot, and tomorrow it will only get worse. I would value your seer's insights to ease my way. But these insights must come willingly on your part for me to trust them. I must know that you are with me rather than against me.'

Now that Valamer had asked rather than ordered or assumed, Perian found, to his surprise, that it wasn't a difficult choice after all. What else would he do with his life and his seer's gift? Aronaye didn't need him, and he had never been really accepted by the Felfar, being so Darna in appearance. And the thought of helping Valamer reshape his empire had a certain appeal. If Valamer spoke the truth, he could always change his mind.

He looked down at his hands, which had stopped shaking. He would never be safe from Armin, but he would feel safer under Valamer's protection. He might even enjoy it. Unlike Valamer, he didn't relish the idea of going back to singing for his food again. There had been so little of it most of the time. And he quite liked the luxury his position provided. In time he might even be able to persuade Valamer to end slavery. That would certainly be worth staying for.

'I'll do it,' he said suddenly. 'I may as well have you bully me about as anyone else.'

Valamer laughed. 'You'll keep your old rooms, unless you prefer others. I'll send a slave to attend you. One with soft hands who hasn't been sent to the mines to punish me.'

So, he had been given Lono as his personal slave to torment Valamer; for some misdemeanour, or perhaps the Zamir had just disapproved of their closeness. Perian didn't rejoice at his father's death, but his and Valamer's lives would most certainly be easier without him.

When Elian arrived, Perian was soaking in his bath under the watchful eye of his new slave, Hector, a bear of a man with thick hairy arms. Elian stood in the doorframe and raised his eyebrows at Lono's replacement.

'When you're finished, I'll be in our usual place.'

Perian groaned and flicked water at his brother as he turned to go.

When he wandered back into his bedroom, Elian was bent over the fireplace, picking out bits of twig. Perian pulled his bathrobe tightly about him and flopped into his red chair. 'What are you doing? Surely Valamer hasn't sent you to clean the grate.'

Elian put the twigs to one side in a neat pile and pulled a chair closer to Perian. He swung one leg over the other and smiled happily. Perian waved a hand toward Elian's head, where a red patch extended from his hairline across his temple and cheek.

'That'll turn into a nasty bruise. You'll probably get a black eye. Does it still hurt?'

'Yes, but not much. Do you feel better?'

'I ache all over, but apart from that I'm well, considering. What are the sticks for?'

'I popped into Valamer's chambers to see Lono on the way back. He's well enough now that he's conscious, other than a headache, and tucked up in silk luxury looking very smug. He demanded that I pay my debt, so I'm to visit again with my twigs and dice when the coronation chaos is over.' He was silent for a while, rubbing his palm with his thumb. 'He said he saw himself walk through the door, and that you skewered his double with a knife before anyone else could register what was happening. Only a very skilled shapeshifter could replicate another human so convincingly.'

'I wouldn't have known it was a shapeshifter myself if I hadn't just seen Lono kneeling at Valamer's feet. I was closer than the others and saw the mage behind him. Lono would never have let him in against orders.' He glanced down at his own hands, clutched together in his lap. 'I am used to shapeshifters; the others aren't. But you're right, he was very convincing.'

'To copy Lono so well, this shapeshifter must have been in the palace for some time. We should search for anyone who's missing, whose place he might have taken. Although that may be difficult with all the fighting that's been going on.'

'What worries me is how many more shapeshifters Armin may have hidden within the palace, or even amongst the troops now facing Ishra.'

'Such skill is rare, as far as I know.'

'Well, he had at least two. The monkey that killed Soas is still at large, though that one wasn't copying a human, of course – given the time it would have taken to get here, this one was a different person. How will I ever be able to tell if I am looking at a duplicate or the real thing?'

'You probably can't, but you have me, and I can.'

Perian caught a whiff of ale upon Elian's breath. 'You've been drinking with the men,' he said. 'What news do they have?'

'Ishra has retreated, almost back over the border. Evidently Lord Fimian's men finally arrived at just the right time to make the difference. That unpleasant man will be a hero now, and we'll probably have to be nice to him at court. His sorcerer rode with the troops, too, which would have helped. Oh, and they found Radia at Ishra's old encampment on this side of the Silver River. She'd chained him to a tree and left him to die with a note pinned to his chest. The men didn't know what it said, though, and there was no mention of the Shanahan's brothers or his sons.'

'I hope that sorcerer is nicer to Radia than she was the last time they met.'

'I thought I might check on him, just for Jolint's sake,' Elian said.

But Perian was distracted. He had become aware that the sounds of cleaning up had been replaced by the movement of feet in the vestibule. He twisted his head back and forth, but couldn't see Hector.

Elian repeated his intention to check on Radia.

'No, don't do that. Saphrax doesn't know you and nor do any of the warriors, and even if you took a letter from Valamer, you could be killed by a disgruntled follower of the Sky God once they realised you were a man, and a Faran at that. Ishra has probably had him neutralised, as she did Jolint. They will bring him back for information. He is too valuable to kill or sell at a slave market on the way home.'

Perian put up his hand as Elian began to reply; slightly raised voices had begun to drift beneath the closed door, making it difficult to hear what was being said. An angry voice rose above Hector's softer tones.

'… leave, I say!' the other shouted. 'Zameel Valamer has ordered me to take your place and guard Zameel Tanais. Another slave will come shortly to see to his other needs.'

This was followed by the distinctive sound of something hard striking flesh. Perian and Elian stood at the same time, but Perian had only enough time to take a step toward the door before it opened with a bang. The warrior looked startled, but probably less so than Perian himself. He bowed quickly. Perian could see Hector pushing himself up from the floor behind him. Blood ran from his head.

'How dare you assault my slave!' Perian shouted at the man. He took another step forward.

The warrior put a fist to his chest. 'Forgive me, my Zameel, but he is no longer to serve you. Zameel Valamer has sent me in his stead.' The warrior took a step toward Perian, eyeing Elian nervously.

With a suddenness that made Perian flinch, Elian projected the warrior backward onto Hector with a flick of his hand. 'Shifter.'

Elian rushed forward, shifting into a wolf as he ran. He landed on the shapeshifter's chest just as Hector had managed to pull himself free and was beginning to rise to his feet. The warrior lay motionless, pinned beneath the weight of such a large wolf and the fear of Elian's teeth.

Perian's gaze caught on a slight outward movement of the shifter's arm. He didn't need to see the man's hand to know that it held a knife.

He pounced on the warrior's arm before he could plunge the weapon into Elian's back. Hector leant forward and drove his own knife into the warrior's shoulder. He shrieked and stiffened as Hector pulled his weapon free until he placed it on the man's neck. Only then did his appearance rapidly change to blond and beardless: a Faran.

Elian changed back and shouted for the guards, who were further down the corridor. Perian wondered briefly why they were so far away as the three of them crowded into the vestibule and watched as Elian studied them for a moment to ensure that there wasn't an army of shifters outside his door. Perian thought the attacker had most likely sent them away 'by order of Zameel Valamer'. It took just a second for them to assess the situation, and two guards dragged the bleeding Faran into the hall. Perian heard him groan as they dragged him down the stairs.

'Get a healer up here for Hector, and get someone to inform Zameel Valamer of what has happened. I am safe with Hector and Elian for the moment,' Perian said to one of the guards as he was about to dash down the hall. 'Who was he impersonating?'

'Commander Doran. Zameel Valamer's personal guard.'

No wonder they had obeyed his orders without question. 'Get someone to organise a search party for Doran, too. Hopefully, he still lives.'

Elian sat forward and put a hand on Perian's tight, white knuckles. 'What will you do now, Perian? Will you stay? Lono says that Valamer wishes it, but he thought you might need a little persuading.'

'I wish I could say that I did, but I don't. Where else would I go? Not to Silaven – that would just draw Armin to them. I cannot leave the palace and wander as I once did, and nor do I want to. Armin would be on me in less than a day. Well, perhaps a little more – he might need to get over his injuries first! But I chose this path. What is the point of being a seer if you don't use what you see?'

'Don't look so worried, Perian. I have no intention of returning to Silaven either. You and I have never been apart, and I have no desire to change that.'

The tightness constricting Perian's ribs suddenly eased and he took in a lungful of air. He took Elian's hand between his. 'But you were so happy there! You would have a position in Silaven and be amongst your own in the Almonos Guards. I saw how you led them tonight. I would not wish you to sacrifice such happiness to spend your life guarding me.'

'It won't be a sacrifice, you idiot. Yes, I'd have a position there, but it would be a difficult one. My presence would make Patria's situation unstable. According to tradition, I'm the rightful heir to the leadership, being the eldest child – as is Risenor, of course – but I have no desire for such responsibility, and Risenor is too deranged. Patria has been trained to replace Aronaye, and she will be very good at it.

I've already agreed to restrict my presence to the occasional visit and not contest her position.'

'And what if I had decided to return and live my life out there?'

'You wouldn't have. You were awkward and out of place in Silaven and you couldn't wait to get away.'

Perian laughed out loud. Elian was right. He was too tall, too big, the wrong colouring …

He thought of Valamer and the discussion they'd had in the Council Room. Valamer's reign would bring in a new era. He would enjoy being part of that, helping his half-brother to steer the two empires toward stability and peace. He had a position and a purpose, and it seemed to him that he might just fit in here; be happy even.

Acknowledgements

Many people, too many to name here, have contributed in small and sometimes big ways to the creation of this book. I thank you all.

My particular thanks to:

Peter Crocker, for years of listening, the odd bit of reading, valuable comments, and for the cover design.

Jennifer O'Donnell and Jennifer McGregor for their comments and encouragement, their belief in me and patient listening to my groans of frustration.

Nicole Rain Sellers for her support and valued criticism.

Claire Bradshaw, my marvellous editor, who pulled the whole thing into shape.

Graham Davidson of Rack and Rune for his invaluable help and putting it all together.

Kathleen Wiggins, Gaby Klika for their valued observations.

www.ingramcontent.com/pod-product-compliance
Lightning Source LLC
Chambersburg PA
CBHW032155190726
48290CB00005BC/1579